ALWAYS THE BOYFRIEND

ALLISON SPEKA

Author's Note

This is an **open door romance**. I always say light on the spice, heavy on the banter, because my favorite thing to write is flirty dialogue and tension between my two characters. However, there are **TWO open door intimate scenes** and **swearing** in this book.

This is a light-hearted romantic comedy, but there are some heavier subjects dealt with such as grieving a loved one.

Happy reading!

Always the Boyfriend

ONE

Hazel

Luck had never been kind to me.

My entire life had been littered with unfortunate circumstances, so it only made sense trouble would continue to plague me.

One moment, I was sky high, buzzing with excitement and possibilities. The next, I was being blackmailed.

Freaking *blackmailed*.

Okay, maybe the issue this time wasn't bad luck as much as it was an ill-advised, indiscreet post to my social media, but still. This situation was shit no matter which direction I looked at it from. Letting my handful of followers know about my newfound wealth might not have been my brightest idea to date, but hey, it wasn't every day someone won the lottery.

Certainly not someone like me.

Like I said, luck had never had much interest in me. It had taken one look at my birth certificate—Hazel Marigold Jacobs, born to Amanda Marie Jacobs in Southfield, Michigan on August 13th, the line for Father left blank—and said, "This girl is *not* for me." Maybe it was the whole 'born on Friday the 13th' thing. According to Gran, my mother used to say my birthday was cosmic favor, or something like that, but that could have just been an alcohol-induced haze talking.

I leaned over to the passenger side of my ancient sedan and pried open the glove box, searching for a napkin to wipe up the black mascara tears tracking down my cheeks. I wasn't typically above crying at work, but even I knew I looked like a complete and total mess. It had been less than twenty-four hours since I'd received the cursed text message, and I'd basically spent the entire night sobbing into my pillow.

Today would have been the perfect day to call in sick, but I couldn't afford to cancel any clients. Not if my modest lottery winnings were about to go toward paying off some sick asshole who got off on kidnapping cats and tormenting women who had absolutely nothing going for them.

My chest heaved again, but I swallowed the panic, wiped my face with the napkin, and dragged myself out of my car.

The strip mall was straight out of the nineties and had no character. I'd tried not to let that affect me when I'd first found the listing for an open stylist chair in the salon there. The ripped sign above the door that read *Hair Today Gone Tomorrow* had a weird energy about it. I'd urged the owner to let me fix it—and possibly rename the place while I was at it—but she wouldn't hear of it, despite my best efforts to convince her the name sounded like we were selling some sort of hair growth supplement.

The interior offered slightly more appeal than the exterior. Modern, cream-colored chairs added a touch of newness. The perpetually polished tile floor and the wall-to-wall mirrors made the space seem bigger. Sad little Halloween decorations still hung from the ceiling—crinkled bats and orange streamers.

"What happened?" Ruby's voice pierced through the small shop the moment I stepped across the threshold.

"Nothing," I said, my voice cracking as I walked over to my station and set my stuffed tote bag onto my styling chair.

Ruby rushed over to me, her blonde hair bouncing in

perfect waves and her blue eyes shining with concern. I wanted to run. She was lovely—radiant, really—and the last thing I needed was her perfection hovering next to my ogre-like self. I believed in self-love, I truly did. In theory. But I also knew, without a shred of doubt, that I was a spectacularly hideous crier.

"It's Vermont," I choked out.

Natalie, another stylist—a sweet, shy girl with mousey brown hair and bangs—gasped. "What's wrong with Vermont?"

"Enough." Miranda, the owner, gave me one harsh look before running a hand through her wispy white hair and jerking a finger to the back of the salon. She was *not* the warm and fuzzy type. "If you're going to have a breakdown, do it in the back. My first client is due any minute."

Jackson, the last of the other stylists at the tiny salon, snapped his gaze up from the front computer where he'd been zoning out. "Breakdown? Where?" His brown eyes met mine and I swore he looked hungry for gossip. Typical Jackson. He hadn't even clocked the mess I was when I walked in, but the second someone hinted at drama, he was all ears.

Ruby and Natalie hurried me to the back room, with Jackson hot on our tail. They guided me into one of the worn break room chairs before crowding around. The room was barely big enough to have a quick snack—definitely not the ideal spot for a mental breakdown. But I'd been kidding myself when I'd thought I could keep it together for the whole day.

"What happened?" Ruby demanded again.

"Don't spare a single detail," Jackson added before Natalie elbowed him in the ribs.

"Someone kidnapped Vermont," I said through a hiccup.

Ruby's eyebrows shot up, and she and Natalie exchanged a look before returning their gazes to assess me.

"Isn't that your cat?" Jackson asked. Honestly, I was surprised he even remembered I had a cat, let alone its name.

"Um, someone kidnapped your cat?" Natalie asked.

"Yes," I said through a sniffle.

"Are you sure he didn't run away? I told you not to let him outside." Ruby's words were incredibly unhelpful. I'd already been beating myself up enough about this.

"I only let him out in the courtyard for a minute," I insisted. "He was always whining at the door, acting all miserable. I was going to get him a leash, but…but…" I choked on another sob.

I had inherited Vermont, the orange tabby with lazy eyes and a sweet disposition, only thirty-seven days ago. The same day my grandmother passed away, leaving him an orphan. Leaving us both orphans, really. Could you be considered an orphan at twenty-five if the only person who ever took care of you was gone?

"I thought you didn't like the cat?" Jackson asked, pursing his lips.

"I never said that, and besides, that isn't the point!" I exclaimed. "He was hers. And we were just starting to bond."

Which was mostly true. He'd rubbed his head against my leg the other day, and I'd finally discovered a brand of dry food he didn't hate.

Gran had always loved cats, but I'd spent most of my childhood begging for a dog. Since we could never agree, we'd compromised, with a fish who, unfortunately, hadn't made it that long. It wasn't until I'd finally moved out of her house and in with my ex that she had taken the plunge and adopted Vermont. Almost immediately, like she'd been waiting for the chance. He had become her pride and joy.

Now, he was all I had left of her. Sure, we'd started out as unwilling roommates, but over the past few weeks, we'd managed to forge some kind of understanding. I was just starting to like having the little guy around. He was a comfort, something I desperately needed.

"He must have wandered off," Ruby continued. "He's not

familiar with the area. You got him microchipped, right? Did you call the local vets and shelters? We can help you…"

Her voice trailed off when she noticed me frantically shaking my head.

"He's been stolen." My phone shook as I pulled up the text that made me want to puke.

Natalie reached for my phone, but Jackson snatched it first, his brows drawing together in confusion as he read the message. Natalie and Ruby leaned in, squinting to read over his shoulder. Their eyes flicked from the screen to me, then back to the screen again.

"That's…" Ruby started.

"Absolutely unhinged," Jackson finished.

The message in question included a picture of Vermont—unharmed, thank the universe. He was curled up on some nondescript hardwood floor that looked like every other hardwood floor I'd ever seen. He looked content, rolled onto his back in search of pets. I could take comfort in that, at least. But the text that accompanied the picture made my blood boil and my soul crumple all at once.

> Unknown Number: I've taken your cat. He will remain unharmed so long as you follow my instructions. DO NOT tell anyone about this. DO NOT try and negotiate. In exchange for his return, you will pay me the sum of $40,000. I will choose the time and the place for the exchange. COME ALONE. You will only get the cat back after I've received a check for the total amount. If you fail to follow these instructions, I will be keeping him for myself, and you will never see him again.

"I got the text last night," I started. "I know I shouldn't let him out in the courtyard, but his meows sounded so sad. And he loves the grass. I never leave him unsupervised, but some jerk left a huge pile of dog crap right on the sidewalk. I swear

I was only in my apartment for maybe two minutes grabbing a plastic bag. I should have never left him."

Natalie shook a tissue box in front of my face.

I grabbed one and blew my nose before continuing. "When I came back out, he was gone. I didn't panic at first, but when I found his collar with his GPS tracker on it, I went into full-blown hysterics. I searched the neighborhood for at least two hours before I got the text."

I was still kicking myself for leaving him unattended.

"What kind of sicko would steal a cat?" Ruby's lips parted and lines creased her forehead.

"I thought everything was finally going my way," I wailed, using the now-drenched tissue to blot my eyes.

"I can't believe someone would kidnap a cat!" Natalie exclaimed. "What is wrong with people? You have to go to the police."

"I already filed a report," I said. I had been hysterical at the station last night, begging them to help and pulling up every picture of Vermont I had. The officers on duty had been less than sympathetic. "I don't think they're going to be much help."

"Of course not," Ruby huffed. "They never are. If they won't take a woman seriously when she's being stalked, they aren't going to do anything for a cat."

"Do you think it's someone from your apartment complex?" Jackson asked.

I shrugged helplessly. "I thought maybe, but I've only lived there six months. It's not like anyone there would know I've just become a prime candidate for extortion."

"Maybe they don't even know you won the lottery," Ruby offered. "It could just be some crazy coincidence."

I snorted. "They *have* to know. No one living in that apartment complex would have a spare forty thousand lying around."

"Shit, this sucks." Natalie gnawed at her bottom lip before

taking my phone from Jackson, bringing it two inches away from her face, and zooming in on the picture.

"It's that story you posted about winning," Jackson said. "I found out you won that way. Even before you brought the champagne into the salon and popped the bottle."

"It has to be the post." I groaned in my misery. My own, self-inflicted, stupid misery.

I'd left the hall after my grandma's funeral service, still in all-black, and walked straight to the nearest gas station. It was pouring rain, fitting for such a dismal day. I'd purchased exactly $100 worth of lottery tickets.

Not because I could afford it, or because I had been feeling particularly lucky. I bought them because it had been *our* thing. When I was growing up, any time I got a mediocre grade, my grandmother took me to buy a scratch-off. Someone was mean to me at school? Lottery ticket. I didn't make the high school soccer team? Lottery ticket.

She used to say it was like tempting fate. If enough was going badly in your life, your fortune was bound to take a turn eventually. It sounded almost spiritual when she put it that way, but as I'd grown older, I'd realized the woman just loved a good gamble. But still. It was *our* thing. Our ritual for bad days.

I had been convinced there was some truth to her madness, because of the night Dustin Turner stood me up for the big eighth-grade dance. Gran and I had driven to a gas station and bought slushies and one singular lottery ticket. Sitting in the passenger seat of her car, still in my sparkly navy dress, I'd scratched it off with a dirty quarter. My eyes had bulged when I'd looked at it, not believing it could be true. $750. The big winner. Gran took the ticket from my hands, put on her pink reading glasses, and let out a loud, "Whoop!"

We'd rolled the windows down, laughing and squealing with excitement, and driven ourselves straight to the nearest steakhouse for a nice dinner.

That was one of my shiniest memories of her. She'd still

dyed her hair back then. I could still picture it, fire engine red, as she sat across the booth from me. We'd ordered appetizers, drinks, and dessert with our meal. That was a big deal, considering that on the rare occasion we did dine out, it was entrées, water, and absolutely no extras.

It had felt like second nature to go get a handful of tickets on the day I said goodbye to her. It's what we would have done together, had she still been around.

I'd never much believed in religion, or God, or any of that. But something much bigger and all-encompassing had been present as I scratched off the last ticket. My grandmother must have made some type of deal with the devil, because that was the only logical explanation for that ticket winding up in my hands that night.

I'd done a double and triple take, only to be met with the same conclusion. I had won the jackpot. Sixty-freaking-grand.

Before I could evaluate how much that would change my entire life, I had driven straight to the nearest fancy restaurant, ordered the most expensive item on the menu, and lifted a glass, closing my eyes and pretending like she was there with me.

It sure felt like she had been.

And yes, like the world's biggest idiot to ever exist, I posted about it the next day. Because who wouldn't? Winning the lottery on the day of your beloved grandmother's funeral? That was a 'chicken soup for the soul' story if I'd ever heard one. How could I not share something that fantastical?

But it had bitten me right in the ass.

"It has to be someone you know," Natalie said.

Ruby nodded. "Exactly. They had your address, knew about Vermont, and clearly follow you online."

"Well, it wasn't me," Jackson said.

I scowled at him. "I never thought it was."

"Just saying." He held up his hands. "I know I said I was jealous when you won, but not in a weird, stalkery kind of way."

Miranda threw open the door to the room, shooting us all glares. She was a good boss, stern but understanding. Fair. Although her expression always frightened me just a little bit. "Jackson, get out here now. Your client is waiting."

"Oh shit, sorry." He hurried to the door, pausing just long enough to glance back and catch my eye. "Keep me updated."

Now it was just me, Ruby, and Natalie. They paced the microscopic room, getting progressively more heated.

"At least whoever has him isn't threatening to harm him," Natalie said.

"I guess." My voice came out as a whisper. As awful as the whole situation was, my heart softened watching Natalie and Ruby panic on my behalf. I'd only started at the salon a few months ago. I hadn't quite crossed the coworker-to-friend line with anyone yet, but it felt like I might be getting close.

"How long did they give you?" Natalie questioned at the same time Ruby asked, "Have you responded?"

"That was the only message," I said, taking my phone back from Natalie. "I've been freaking out too much to respond. But I can't even collect my winnings for a few more weeks, because apparently prizes over ten thousand need time to process, or some crap."

"Tell them that," Natalie said.

Ruby nodded in agreement. "Yeah, that will buy you some time to figure this out."

A pit formed in my stomach. The more time it took to figure out who was behind this, the more time Vermont would be stuck who-knew-where. This whole ordeal was becoming more hopeless by the second.

"I thought my life was finally turning around." The familiar burning of tears stung the back of my eyelids.

Natalie and Ruby stopped pacing, their expressions shifting from anger to sympathy. They knew what that kind of money meant to me. Honestly, it would mean a lot to anyone, but for someone like me, barely scraping together rent each month, drowning in credit card debt with no end in sight—

that kind of money was life-changing. I could finally start climbing out of the hole I'd been stuck in my entire life.

I tipped forward in the chair, my head collapsing into my hands as I rocked back and forth.

"I don't even know where to start," I said.

A moment of silence passed. The uncomfortable kind where everyone knew and acknowledged you were royally fucked. Sure, they were sad for you, but also immensely grateful the issue wasn't theirs to deal with.

Finally, Ruby gasped and grabbed my shoulder. "I know!"

"What?" I sounded desperately hopeful, but I didn't care. I *was* desperately hopeful.

"My brother," she said. "He's obsessed with true crime. He's in this whole online sleuth forum, where all they do is try to collect clues and solve mysteries."

My hope wavered a bit.

"I don't know," I said, not wanting to insult Ruby or her brother, whom I'd never even met. But I was not exactly brimming with confidence in the ability of some wannabe-internet-vigilante to untangle my complicated mess.

"No, seriously," she continued, pulling out her phone and typing. After a minute, she shoved it in front of my face. A news article displayed on the screen. "He and a group of his friends just solved a cold case last year. A missing person a few towns over. See?"

I scanned the headline. "Man arrested thanks to multiple tips from internet sleuths." I barely had time to skim the details before Ruby pulled her phone away and tucked it back in her pocket.

"He's good at this stuff, I promise," she insisted.

"It's worth a shot, Hazel," Natalie said. "What have you got to lose?"

"Nothing," I whispered, my tears threatening to spill as I realized the truth of that statement. My life had always been an old wooden rollercoaster, twisting and jerking aggressively in every direction. For a moment, I'd had a glimpse of what a smooth ride might be like. But now it seemed I was destined to stay on the same rickety track I'd always been on.

"I'll talk to him," Ruby said when I remained silent. "He'll want to help. He lives for this kind of stuff."

My resolve shattered. If her brother was generous enough to consider helping me with this, who was I to turn him away? Even if it felt like the longest shot in the world, I still had to try and get Vermont back.

For Gran.

My chest hollowed just thinking about her.

"You're sure?" I asked Ruby. "I have nothing to offer him. I mean, I guess I could pay him if I don't end up having to give all this money away."

The thought made me sick. But not quite as sick as the idea of never seeing Vermont again. My worst fear was that whoever this lunatic was would take my money *and* never give me my cat back.

Ruby shook her head. "I doubt Reid would accept anything. Let me talk to him."

Even though her eyes shone with determination, I couldn't force any hope to seep into my own veins. But I agreed. This could be the only chance I had.

I hoped my grandmother was still making good on that deal with the devil, or whatever magic she'd conjured to turn my luck around in the first place. Because at this point, all I could hope for was divine intervention.

TWO

Reid

Armchair_Detective: *Did you look at the timestamp on that photograph?*
WhiteKnight31: *Yeah, it's from the day prior and it doesn't look altered IMO. I'm thinking this isn't our guy.*
Armchair_Detective: *Good to rule him out, though. Everyone is always obsessed with the idea the boyfriend did it.*
WhiteKnight31: *Because it's always the boyfriend.*
ReidingRainbow: *Not always. We can't sequester ourselves into those narrow-minded stereotypes.*
WhiteKnight31: *Leave it to Reid to be the logical one. Whatever. It looks like the photo evidence backs you up this time.*
Armchair_Detective: *He could have still hired someone to take her.*
ReidingRainbow: *That seems farfetched. 10 years ago, this guy crashed his car trying to do donuts in an abandoned Kmart parking lot. (ATT: mugshot picture) You really think he masterminded this whole plan, so brilliantly that the police haven't figured anything out all these years later?*
Armchair_Detective: *Fine, you have a point. Let's move onto other theories. Like the fact that he claimed she was cheating on him and the police never looked further into that.*
ReidingRainbow: *Exactly. They thought they had their guy (kind*

of like you're trying to do now) so they didn't investigate anything he had to say.

"Reid?"

The faint sound of my name barely filtered through the giant noise-cancelling headphones engulfing my ears.

"Reid?"

Louder this time. I shot off a quick *"got to run"* to my group. I pulled off my headphones and nestled them around my neck before spinning around in my office chair.

My sister stood there, arms folded, leaning against the wooden door frame.

"Ruby." Exasperation seeped into my voice. I hated being snuck up on. "I told you, that key is for emergencies only."

She rolled her eyes and dangled her fuzzy, hot-pink, rabbit-foot keychain in front of her. "And I'd leave it for emergencies if you ever answered your phone. I texted you that I was here and called you, like, three times."

"Oh." Frowning, I pulled out my phone to see that she had, in fact, called. "My bad. I got caught up in something."

"I'm used to it." She pushed off the doorframe of my office and disappeared down my hallway.

My stiff back protested as I stood. The hours I'd spent holed up in the office, hunched over my computer, had taken their toll.

"Are you almost ready?" Ruby called from somewhere in my house.

"Just let me grab a sweater," I called back, veering to the right out of my office and walking the short distance to my bedroom at the end of the hall. It was late October, and I knew I'd regret leaving the house in just my t-shirt. After I'd thrown on my favorite gray crewneck, I assessed myself in the mirror, then patted down my short golden-brown hair that was sticking up haphazardly from wearing headphones all day.

Ruby said something else that was muffled by the hallway and multiple square feet between us.

"What?" I asked, padding out of my bedroom and down the hall that led to my very open-concept living, kitchen, and dining room. The high ceilings were what had sold me on the place when I'd first walked into this townhouse. For someone who spent most of his days in a dark room in front of a computer, I appreciated the haven of sunlight.

"I said, what do I need to grab?" My sister was parked in front of my fridge, door open. She assessed its contents, carefully arranged by category. "You know your refrigerator looks like a serial killer's, right?"

"Are serial killers the only people allowed to be organized?" I asked, walking behind her and pointing to the top shelf. "That container."

"No, but there is a certain obsessiveness to not having a single item out of place. It's food, Reid. It doesn't have to be this compulsively arranged." Ruby plucked out the covered glass bowl and closed the door with her hip.

"What is it?" she asked, peeling the lid open.

"Mediterranean orzo salad."

She sighed. "Why must you always be so impressive?"

"It took five minutes," I said with just a touch of defensiveness. Ruby saw me as the type of person who constantly put too much effort into things. Organizing a room so that it was just so. Color-coding my closet. Learning the science behind baking a soufflé. These traits apparently meant I lacked a certain…cool-guy essence. It didn't matter that being organized came naturally to me. It didn't matter that I *enjoyed* doing these things.

"It makes me look bad. All I'm contributing are the warm two liters of soda in my trunk."

"So, the usual," I said, which was met with a swift elbow to the side.

"Hey, I baked cookies literally last week."

"Cookies that bore a striking resemblance to the ones found in the bakery section of Meijer."

Her mouth dropped open in mock horror. "How dare you hurl that accusation at me."

My lips strained, tugging upward as the two of us headed outside. The small, shared garden space right off my front door was always meticulously kept. When I moved into this place a few months ago, one of the first things I had done was apply to be on the HOA board. Not long after I joined the board, I'd hired a new landscaper, someone who shared my obsession with perfection. Someone with an eye for detail, as if a Home and Garden magazine crew might show up at any moment to photograph our modest little complex.

Ruby and I climbed into her red SUV—relatively clean, but still too cluttered for my liking. Last year, I'd passive-aggressively gotten her a car wash subscription for her birthday. She'd snorted with laughter and said it felt more like a gift for me than for her. Between all the family gatherings and trips we took together, I was in Ruby's car a lot. She always insisted on driving, so was it so wrong that I wanted her car to be just a touch cleaner?

"Haven't had a chance to get to the car wash lately?" I asked, pointing to the streaks on the windshield.

Ruby barked out a laugh before throwing the car into reverse and pulling out of my short driveway.

"I'm never going there, just to spite you."

She cranked the volume up and started singing along to a new pop song that I wasn't familiar with. I settled into my seat and enjoyed the colors that painted the evening sky. It was rare to see such a colorful sunset this season; gray clouds typically blanketed Michigan's skies on fall days.

The drive to my parents' house was short, barely long enough to queue up two songs. The whole family lived within a ten-mile radius of each other. We were one of those obnoxiously close families, the kind that got together for weekly dinners, occasionally took group vacations, and actually enjoyed each other's company.

We pulled up to the quaint craftsman I'd grown up in. It wasn't enormous for a family of five, but the best memories of my life had happened behind the currently red door. That door must have been covered in hundreds of layers of paint by this point. My mom loved switching it up for the season, her moods, special occasions—whatever, really. For her, painting that door was like hanging a new photograph.

Ruby led the way up the front steps, and we walked through the door, which was never locked. The smell of onions and butter hit me immediately. Stepping inside felt like a warm hug compared to the slight chill in the air outside.

"We're here!" Ruby called, stepping out of her shoes and leaving them amongst the scattered pile that had a permanent place by the front door.

A guy about as tall as me, with dark features and a beaming smile, strode into the entryway before scooping my sister into a hug and planting a kiss right on top of her head.

"Gross," Ruby muttered, shoving him away. Her practiced look of disgust wasn't fooling anyone. Her crush on my best friend had been evident to pretty much the entire family— everyone except West—since he'd moved in with us our senior year of high school.

"Hey, man," I said, slapping him on the back. While not related by blood, West had been an addition to this family ever since we'd bonded over our shared hatred of playing soccer in middle school. One time, we'd even snuck home from practice to play video games in his parents' basement. Then, when we were seventeen and his family had to move to Australia for his father's job, my parents hadn't even hesitated before offering to take him in.

Now he was one of us. And he would never consider missing a Mitchell weekly dinner.

Ruby stared at the back of his head, then met my eyes—

just for a second—before quickly looking away. I wasn't the macho, overprotective-big-brother type. Ruby and West were adults. Her obvious crush on him didn't faze me. Not in the slightest.

What did bother me was the inevitability of it all. West had no idea how Ruby felt, and even if he did, he wouldn't feel the same. He'd let her down gently. He was good at that. Too good, if you asked me. Women liked him. Always had.

Me? Not so much. West had tried his best to be my wingman throughout high school and college, but I'd tanked every opportunity he set up. Then, I'd gotten into a long-term relationship, which had led to marriage—and unfortunately, recently, divorce. Now West was determined to once again be my wingman, despite the fact that I seemed to possess a natural talent for being entirely forgettable to most women.

"How did I beat you here?" West asked.

"We would have been here fifteen minutes ago, if *someone* had answered their phone in a timely fashion."

I shrugged. "I got caught up."

"With the sleuths," West confirmed. My entire family was well aware of my hobby. I didn't care. I wasn't ashamed of it. Besides, it would be hard to hide after we'd received national recognition for breaking a cold case last year. We'd started a blog and everything. Aside from working remotely in IT—something I didn't particularly love, but which paid well and didn't ask too much of me—and spending time with my family, internet sleuthing was basically the only activity I took part in. Despite my mother's relentless attempts at getting me into pickleball.

"We've hit a bit of a dead end on the case we're working now," I said.

"They're cold for a reason," Ruby said. "I wish you wouldn't spend so much time on them."

I didn't bother arguing with her. Almost everyone in my family had said that to me at one point or another. I didn't understand why they couldn't just accept it; if I joined an adult rec league and started swinging a bat at a ball a few times a week, would that somehow be a more legitimate hobby?

"Ugh, finally. I'm starving." My youngest sister, Regan, waltzed into the room and snatched the large container from my hands before lifting the lid and sniffing the contents. She'd moved home last summer after graduating college. Apparently it wasn't exactly a walk in the park to land a stable job that paid well enough to afford an apartment with a liberal arts degree.

"Mediterranean orzo salad," I said.

Regan and Ruby shared a look as we all moved like one unit from the front entryway, through the swinging door, into the large eat-in kitchen.

My parents' house was the opposite of an open concept. It was more of a how-many-rooms-can-we-stuff-into-1400-square-feet concept. Despite the modest size, we'd each had our own bedrooms growing up—likely what had allowed my parents to stay sane raising three kids.

The kitchen hadn't been updated in a couple of decades. It still had the same worn, white appliances and yellow daisy backsplash my dad had installed when I was just a toddler. There was something comforting about the way my parents liked to keep everything the same. Every corner of this place held memories.

The kitchen also held the familiar sight of my dad perched on the kitchen island, the table already set behind him, and my mom sautéing something mouthwateringly delicious on the stove. It was a scene I had witnessed more times than I could count.

"Almost ready," my mom said from the stove, leaning backward to receive a quick hug from Ruby and me. Her genes were strong. Ruby and Regan were the spitting image of our mother—dark blonde, with stick-straight hair and large almond eyes. I, on the other hand, could have passed for my dad's twin had I suddenly had access to a time machine and found myself back in 1992. We even had the same cropped haircut and black-rimmed glasses. My ex used to beg me to try contacts, but they dried out my eyes.

Like a well-rehearsed dance, we all joined my dad, crowding around the island, waiting until my mom finished cooking to make our plates.

"Have some candy while you wait." Mom pointed to a giant plastic bowl filled with individually wrapped chocolates.

"Before dinner?" Ruby asked, but grabbed one all the same.

"I bought too many bags."

"You *always* buy too many," I said, not taking one for myself. Every year it was the same. She acted like our street was about to become the number-one target destination for every trick-or-treater within a forty-mile radius. Next week, when they'd inevitably get a dozen kids max, she'd be stuck with pounds of Halloween candy that lasted until Christmas.

"What's new at work?" Dad asked West, before West launched into an update. They were both in sales and always had a lot to discuss.

I had never been social enough to consider that path. Behind the screen of a computer was where I functioned best. I had always been the most introverted in the family, and I didn't see anything wrong with that. My family, on the other hand, was always trying to meddle and said I needed to "get out there more"—whatever the hell that was supposed to mean. I got out enough. And I had friends. West and I saw each other all the time, and just because I only spoke to the guys from my sleuthing group online, didn't mean they weren't real.

Ruby retrieved mismatched glasses from one of the upper cabinets and placed them on the kitchen island before bending down to get the ice bucket we always used. Even though it was an extra step to get the ice from the fridge, put it in the bucket, and then add it to our glasses, it was something we always did. As kids, we loved the idea; it reminded us of staying in a hotel. Even a couple of decades later, we'd never lost the habit.

Ice clinked in our glasses, and diet soda fizzed.

Mom announced that dinner was ready, and instantly the kitchen sprang to life—a flurry of plates being passed around, bodies weaving near the stove, and a chorus of lively chatter as we eagerly served ourselves.

I had barely pulled my chair up to the kitchen table when Ruby squeezed in next to me and said, "Before I forget, I have a proposition for you."

I pulled my napkin from underneath my fork and placed it on my lap. "What sort of proposition?"

"Okay, see, this is going to sound strange, but I really need you to take it seriously."

My interest had officially been piqued. While everyone around us started digging into their plates, I leaned back and folded my arms, waiting for Ruby to reveal whatever it was she needed help with.

"Of course I'll take it seriously," I said.

She chewed her bottom lip before sighing. "It's my coworker, Hazel. She's a super-sweet girl, but she's been going through a hard time, and she just had something awful happen to her."

"What happened?" Mom's concerned voice rang out from across the table. Now everyone had stopped talking, eyes glued to me and Ruby.

"It's her cat."

My eyebrows shot up. "Her cat?"

"Yes," Ruby said. "He's been stolen."

My face scrunched into a mixture of disbelief and confusion before I could force my expression to remain neutral.

"How does she know it isn't lost?" West asked, voicing the first question that had gone through my own mind.

"Because she got a message from the person who stole

him," Ruby said, frowning. "It really is awful. I know we've never been much of a pet family, but I can't imagine someone stooping so low as to steal a cat."

"She got a message? Saying what?" I asked, shoveling up some rice and meat with my fork and stuffing it in my mouth.

"That she basically has to pay the person a shit-ton of money, or she'll never see Vermont again."

"The state?" Regan and my mom asked in unison.

"The cat," Ruby said.

"Cute name," Dad said, reaching over me to scoop some of the pasta salad I'd made onto his plate.

"So someone is holding her cat for ransom." Now I understood why Ruby had asked me to take it seriously. The entire situation sounded completely far-fetched, and helping random girls with lost cats wasn't exactly my area of expertise.

"Exactly." Ruby shook her head, tears already welling in her eyes. She'd always been a bit of an empath, deeply attuned to everyone else's emotions.

"Hey, don't worry about it. I'm sure the cat will turn up," West said, patting her on the shoulder. He'd always been easily affectionate with her. Did he have any idea how that affected her? Part of me felt like I should warn him, as my best friend. But the family loyalty I had toward Ruby held strong. The last thing I wanted was to cause her any embarrassment or discomfort. It was best if West stayed blissfully unaware.

"I don't know. It all seems kind of sinister." Ruby sniffled. "Will you please help her, Reid? I already told her you would."

My shoulders tensed and I dropped my fork. "Why would you do that?"

"Because you're a good person and you love a mystery." She batted her eyelashes innocently at me.

Damn. She knew me too well. I hated saying no to anyone who needed help, especially when it was someone close to me asking.

"More sleuthing?" Mom frowned, her expression contorting into one of clear disapproval. She could not wrap her head around the hobby at all, despite not being able to tear her eyes away from the TV any time I threw on a true crime documentary. "What Reid really needs is a date."

"Mom!" I dragged a hand along my jaw, anxiety simmering inside me. I *hated* dating. In fact, the only thing that I hated more than going on awkward dates with strangers, was discussing the concept with my family.

"I'm serious," she continued, either oblivious to my discomfort or content to ignore it. Likely the latter. "I know the divorce with Meghan was tough on you, but it's time to get back out there. You're always on a computer, and you don't need another excuse to lock yourself away in your office."

"Don't be so hard on him," Dad chimed in at the same time I said, "I *like* always being on a computer."

Regan snorted a laugh before covering her mouth with her hand. Her job search was typically the popular topic of conversation at family dinners. She was probably tickled that I was the one being questioned today instead of her.

"You're a lovely man. A real catch," Mom continued. "Someone is going to snatch you up so fast. If you're going to be on a computer, at least join one of those dating websites. I bet if you started online dating, you'd only need to be on there one day before you found someone."

West laughed and I shot him a glare. He raised his hand in a silent apology before staring down at his plate.

"Mom, that's delusional. Finding your soulmate online is literally impossible, trust me, I've tried," said Regan. "But I did hear bookstores are the new hot spot to meet women. You'd like a bookish girl." She pointed her fork at me.

"I'm not going to a bookstore under the guise of picking up women. That's creepy as hell."

"Is this coworker with that cat situation the one you wanted to set him up with?" Mom asked Ruby, suddenly hopeful.

"That was Natalie," Ruby hissed. "And thanks a lot for

bringing that up. He's never going to fall for my subtle plans to introduce them now."

I rolled my eyes. It wouldn't have been the first time Ruby had invited me out while secretly trying to set me up with a friend. I'd told her on numerous occasions that I would greatly prefer she stayed out of my love life altogether. She never listened, though. I swore she and West had some sort of bet about being the first person to help me find someone since I became single.

"Thanks for the heads up," I said, lifting my glass and taking a sip.

Ruby sighed. "As if being set up with my cute, sweet friend would be so painful."

"Meghan was almost a year ago," West added, unhelpfully.

I shot him another glare letting him know I felt every bit of his betrayal. "We were married. It's not like I can move on just like that."

"It isn't healthy to wallow, honey," Mom said.

"I'm not wallowing." I sighed in defeat. So much for simply enjoying my meal.

"It's okay to still be hung up on her," Dad added.

"I'm not."

"Do you still follow her on social media?" Ruby asked hesitantly.

"*Ruby*," Regan scolded. "We agreed we wouldn't ask."

My heart slipped right into my stomach. They knew something. They'd been talking about me behind my back. We had a family chat, but occasionally, if something happened that we needed to talk about without one or two people, side chats would be formed. They grew like bacteria. Birthdays, surprises, maybe one person was in a particularly sour mood. We pretty much had a side chat going for each scenario. "Family minus Ruby." "Family without Regan." "Just the siblings." The investigator in me should have clocked that all those chats had been suspiciously quiet this week, but I hadn't noticed. Now it was abundantly clear to me that they had been quiet because my family was discussing *me* somewhere off in the "Missing Reid" chat.

"What happened?" I asked.

They all looked at me guiltily, my dad all of a sudden completely engrossed in his dinner.

"Just tell me. Her social media isn't private. Even though I don't follow her, I'm just going to go look at her page as soon as this is over, so tell me what it is."

"A new boyfriend," Ruby blurted out.

"He looks like a thumb," Mom added.

Regan laughed before covering her mouth.

My chest tightened, but I forced my demeanor to remain calm. The news wasn't shocking, but that didn't make it any easier to swallow. I wasn't torn up about it like my family might have thought I'd be, but still. I preferred to pretend like my ex-wife didn't exist. Our divorce hadn't been bitter, per se, but the terms also hadn't been the best. It wasn't mutual, and she'd said some hurtful things at the end.

While I believed I was taking this time to focus on myself and take a break from dating, my family seemed to think that I was strung out, and unable to move on. They likely thought the news would break the delicate façade I was barely holding on to.

West clapped a hand on my shoulder. "She posted a few days ago. It's probably new."

"You're in on this too?" I asked, trying not to scowl.

He shrugged. "I got added to the *Missing Reid* group chat years ago."

"That's how you know we've truly accepted you," Ruby said, practically beaming up at him.

"Remind me to add you to *Family Minus Ruby*," I grunted.

She glared at me in response.

"Are you okay?" my mom asked, pouting.

"I'm fine, no thanks to you meddlers." I sighed. "Obviously, she would move on. She was looking for someone fun and outgoing, and she probably found that. Good for her. I truly don't care." Well, *almost* didn't care, but close enough. The news was really just a mild sting in the grand scheme of life. Nothing compared to the gut-punch that had accompanied the initial moment she'd told me she wanted out of our relatively short marriage.

"It would be nice if you could post something with a girl," Mom said.

"Yeah, really stick it to her," said Regan.

"Oh yeah, because nothing says, 'I moved on' like strategically posting in the hopes of bothering an ex."

My mom shrugged. "It could just be an added bonus."

"Can we talk about literally anything else?" I asked, picking up my fork and taking a bite, hoping to signal to the table that this line of conversation was officially over.

My family exchanged glances, and for a few seconds, the only sound filling the small, tiled room was the soft clinking of silverware against plates.

"So about my friend with the cat," Ruby said carefully after a minute.

I groaned, letting my head fall back. "I meant, let's talk about anything that *doesn't* have to do with me."

"Please Reid," she begged, clasping her hands and shaking them in front of my face. "Please at least meet with her. She looks so lost and hopeless right now. It's sad."

"I've never solved a live case," I pointed out. My group's entire focus was looking into cold cases that the police had botched.

"This could be your first!" she exclaimed.

"Are you really going to say no to some poor girl with a stolen cat?" Regan asked.

I rolled my eyes. "Not you too."

"Come on, just meet with her. See if there's any potential for you to help."

I let out a small grumble but didn't bother protesting. Ruby unclasped her hands, a slow smirk spreading across her face. She knew I'd already given in. Honestly, she had known I was going to give in from the start. And while I had no idea if I could help this woman or her lost cat, it certainly wouldn't kill me to try.

After a few more seconds of silence, my mom asked, "Is this girl single?"

THREE

Hazel

—————

MY BRAKES SQUEALED IN PROTEST AS I CAME TO AN ABRUPT stop in the nearly empty parking lot. Neon lights from the diner were the only things cutting through the dim morning. The sun had technically risen, but it clearly had no plans to make an appearance today. Gray clouds hung low overhead, and a few miserably frigid raindrops had already started to fall.

I unbuckled my seat belt and leaned over to pick up the folder next to me.

"Shit," I muttered, as papers and photographs spilled out and onto the floor of my passenger seat. My side dug into the center console as I stretched out my fingertips to collect them before stuffing the papers back inside.

I didn't bother to grab an umbrella as I dashed through the rain toward the front door.

The bells overhead jingled sharply as I stepped inside the nearly deserted diner. A pair of rough-looking men who might've been truck drivers occupied a booth in the far corner, their heavy jackets still damp from the storm. At a table near the center, a man in his fifties sat alone, a newspaper stretched wide in his hands as he sipped slowly from a steaming cup of coffee.

Finally, my eyes landed on him.

Reid was exactly as Ruby had described: serious-looking, with a long face, strong jaw, and glasses perched on a straight nose. His hair was cropped to perfection, meticulous, with not even a strand out of place. He was dressed casually in a long-sleeve t-shirt that looked like it might have been ironed.

He lifted a hesitant hand, offering me a wave as I bull-dozed in his direction, falling into the booth opposite him, nearly dropping my folder again in the process.

Warmth reflected in his golden eyes. I'd noticed it the moment I entered his vicinity.

I held out my hand. "Hazel Jacobs."

"Uh, Reid Mitchell." He gave my hand a shake. A quick surge of electricity—a small spark—passed between us. Or at least it had in my imagination. "Are you always so formal with your introductions?"

I shrugged. "Is a last name formal?"

He opened his mouth as if to answer before pausing to think a second. "I would say so, yes."

"I would argue it's more informative than formal."

He scrunched his face before it distorted into a smile. "Okay…"

"Thank you so much for meeting me," I said, changing the subject. "Ruby mentioned you might be able to help, and I'm beyond desperate at this point. Seriously, thank you so much for even taking the time. I know you must be busy."

A waitress stopped by, interrupting my rambling. "Coffee?" she asked.

"Please." I flipped over my chipped ceramic mug and gave her a grateful smile, the smell of the dark liquid already perking up my senses. I dumped in two creams before taking a sip.

When she was gone, Reid leaned forward, the booth making an unflattering squishing noise in the process.

"Look, I'm not sure what Ruby said—"

"She said that you were a bit of an investigator. That you and your friends have even solved a few cold cases."

"*One* cold case," he corrected.

"That's one more than anyone else I know," I said, my heart skittering a little faster. His whole demeanor screamed of someone who was trying to let me down easy. I knew that look. It had happened to me enough times.

"One cold case with thousands of online clues that just hadn't been put together in the right order yet," he continued. "Honestly, it was more luck than anything. We were able to track down camera footage the police never bothered to look into before."

"Ruby said it's your hobby—looking into mysteries and stuff."

"It is, but I'm essentially an armchair detective who loves true crime podcasts and spending way too many hours on forums." His words were careful. He seemed like the kind of person who did everything with care.

"Please, Reid. I-I'm not sure what else to do." This felt less like a conversation and more like an interview I was failing. But even with the hesitation rolling off him, sympathy still shone in his eyes. His entire face was soft with it.

"I've never dealt with a catnapping before."

Despite my misery over the situation, a clipped laugh escaped my lips. "Neither have I. I'd be willing to bet that most sane people have never had to deal with a catnapping in their entire lives."

His lip quirked up. "Fair point."

"But it's the unfortunate card I've been dealt," I said, sliding my coffee to the end of the table by the window to present my folder. "Here, let me just show you all the facts and then you can decide if you can help me or not. This person is obviously an amateur, I bet they left tons of clues and mistakes behind—*shit*." I stopped mid-sentence as the folder tumbled off the table, knocked loose by my over-eager slide.

I bent forward to collect the papers that had scattered across the floor. Reid got out from the booth and crouched down, grabbing the ones that had drifted too far out of reach. He held up a particularly cute shot of Vermont, staring at it as he righted himself.

"Why did you bring a folder?" he asked, studying the papers I'd brought—a mix of pictures as well as a print-out of the text thread with the assailant. Yes, I was choosing to call them an assailant. They were, after all, assailing my life.

"Oh, I don't know. It felt very private investigator."

He handed me back the papers, and I spread them out on the table between us.

"Did you go to a store specifically to buy it?" he asked.

"I mean…yes." Maybe I should feel silly that I had, in fact, gone to the dollar store the night prior with the intention of purchasing this folder—and the candy that had practically fallen into my basket. But the trip had given me a purpose in an otherwise out-of-control period in my life. Errands didn't always have to be necessary to be useful; like buying a candle just for the vibes, or stopping at a library to see the new releases.

"Why didn't you get one with pockets? This is for a filing cabinet." Damn. Ruby wasn't kidding when she said Reid had an attention for detail.

"This one looked the most official," I said.

The embarrassment that sat lightly on my chest lifted a little when I saw the corner of his mouth twitch up.

"You're right, it does look official. But I have to tell you, it's called internet sleuthing for a reason. Most everything is done online nowadays."

"I know, I know. I'm aware of the current century. I just wanted to bring anything that could be helpful."

"This is the cat?" Reid asked, holding up another picture, one of Vermont splayed out on my grandmother's lap. I'd felt a pang of guilt when I realized that almost every picture I had of Vermont was either taken by Gran or sent to me by her. But in my defense, I'd only gotten him a few weeks ago.

"Vermont," I confirmed, shoving another picture in his direction.

"Why Vermont?"

"I don't know? It's cute? My Grandma loved Ben & Jerry's? Does a pet's name have to be that deep?"

He chuckled. "I like it."

"He's honestly an overly friendly cat—like, literally loves everyone—so I'm not even surprised he just waltzed up to some stranger."

Reid nodded and picked up another picture. "This your grandma?" he asked.

"Yep." I froze, hoping there wouldn't be any follow-up questions. Not because I hated talking about her. The opposite, in fact. I just didn't want to start crying in front of a virtual stranger at seven a.m. in some random diner.

"And here are the texts." I handed him the printout of the exchange.

He took the paper in his long fingers. He lifted his glasses up to scan the thread, a line creasing his forehead as he read. I could tell the moment he absorbed it because his eyebrows shot up.

"Forty thousand dollars? Holy shit."

"I know."

"Can't you just tell them you don't have that? Why did you say you'd need thirty days?" he asked, poking my response to the threatening message.

"Because that's how long the lottery winnings will take to process."

Now his eyebrows dropped and drew together as he analyzed my words.

I groaned and slid down in the booth. "Trust me, I know this sounds like the most ridiculous far-fetched situation imaginable, but unfortunately it's my life right now." I drew in a breath and soldiered on. "I won the lottery, and now I'm being blackmailed."

"Blackmailed," he repeated looking from me back to the message.

"Yes."

"It sounds more like extortion to me."

A scoff escaped my lips as I lifted my wrist to circle it in the air. "I don't really see the need to get hung up on semantics. Either way, I'm screwed!"

Reid's expression softened. "So the lottery, huh?" he asked, disbelief dancing in his tone.

"Yes, I won it."

He looked at me like my head wasn't screwed on straight.

"Not, like, billions or millions or anything like that. I mean, I wish, right? But still a lot of money. Well, a lot for me. Tens of thousands. More than I could ever dream of winning."

"Okayyy," he said slowly, looking from me to the text thread and back to me, trying to process it all.

"So someone stole my cat, and now I have to pay up or I'll never see him again."

Reid opened his mouth to say something, closed it, squinted his eyes, and then took a small sip of coffee. I could practically see the calculations happening behind his glasses.

"I think I'm following," he finally said. "But how did someone know to extort you?"

"Well, I posted about it—"

"You posted that you won?"

"Yes, just a quick story."

"On social media?" Judgement flickered in his stare.

I sighed. "Yep."

"What did the post say, exactly?"

I winced, and pulled out my phone, scrolling for a minute before finding the post and showing him. He brought the phone to his face, pulling down his glasses and assessing it.

He let out a small laugh of disbelief. "You put the exact amount you won and everything."

"I know," I said.

"This is simply way too much information."

"I know."

"Keeping it to yourself is, like, the first rule of winning the lottery."

I sighed and repeated, "I know."

"You're just asking for something like this to happen."

"Can we stop victim blaming for a second?" I snapped.

"Sorry, this is just nuts," he said, readjusting his glasses and handing my phone back.

"I'm aware." Was the point of this meeting to make me feel worse about myself than I already did? Because if that was the case, Reid was doing a bang-up job.

"Why not contact the police?" he asked.

"They were no help," I said. "The police station was the first place I went. They let me file a report, but they gave me a look ten times worse than the one you're giving me right now when I explained everything."

Reid immediately closed his mouth and adjusted his face, so it once again read as serious rather than amused.

"Besides," I continued. "It's not like they have a track record of taking upset women seriously. I believe the word 'hysterical' was tossed around while I was there."

"Fair point," he said, which was at least a little bit reassuring. "I've looked into enough cold cases to realize you can't always trust a detective to investigate something thoroughly. Especially if there's no vested interest."

"So, do you think you can help?" I asked, doing my best to blink my lashes at him in what I hoped was a charming way. It wasn't like I thought I could win him over with flirting. I wasn't the kind of girl guys tripped over themselves for. But Reid was a softy, Ruby had said as much. And the quiet way he looked at me, taking in everything I was dealing with, only confirmed it.

He sighed in defeat, gathering all the papers I'd brought and stuffing them back into the folder. "I can try," he said.

I let out a squeal and he jumped back in the booth, jerking his head around to see if I'd captured anyone's attention. The old man was still reading, and the burly trucker-looking men were deep in conversation. The waitress, however, shot us a wink before going back to filling the sugar containers.

"I said *try*," he continued. "Like I said, this is different from anything I've looked into before. But I can at least see if I can help you come up with a theory."

"Where do we start?" I pulled out a small notebook from my tote and a pen before clicking it and poised myself to start writing.

Reid clocked my preparedness and smiled before lifting his eyes to the ceiling.

"Okay, first things first. We need to compile a suspect list."

"Got it," I said, writing "Suspect List" in big loopy letters at the top of the page.

Reid took his glasses off and held them while pinching the bridge of his nose. "Even though the social media post is unfortunate, I suppose we can narrow the search down to people who know you. Your phone number wouldn't be hard to get online if they knew your full name, but my gut says it's likely someone who had it already."

"Okay, okay," I said, writing everything down furiously.

"And I suppose we could narrow it down further to someone who knows where you live. There's always the chance it was some obsessive stalker, but this whole thing reeks of opportunity. Ruby said Vermont was snatched from your courtyard while you went inside for a second, right?"

"Right," I confirmed.

"So they might not have even come to take him. Maybe they came to talk to you, try to guilt you into giving them money, or even something totally unrelated, saw Vermont, and took the opportunity."

The way Reid analyzed the situation was already giving

me more hope than I'd had in days. He was treating it like a problem or a puzzle, and we just needed to collect the right pieces. I know he'd specifically said not to, but my hopes were already up.

"I guess we can probably narrow it down to people who know your address. How long have you lived there?" he asked.

I dropped my pen, cringing. "Um, not long."

Reid clocked my fallen face and leaned in. "What?" he demanded.

"Um, well. I might have made another post."

His head tipped back, and I watched his Adam's apple bob as he let out a loud groan. "Another social media post?" he asked.

I shifted uncomfortably. "I wanted to show off my new apartment."

"And I suppose you what? Posted the outside of the building?"

"Worse." I sank further into my seat, and he sat up straighter, eyes narrowing. I *really* needed to rethink my social media usage in the future.

"What? You didn't put the address in the caption or something?"

"I might have tagged the apartment complex," I said, dropping my eyes as I played with the edge of my notebook paper.

"*Hazel,*" he scolded, his voice sharp. "You need to be more careful. Do you know the kind of twisted people who are running rampant out there? You need to protect your privacy."

"I know," I said.

He shook his head, disappointment etched across his face. Funny, we'd just met, and I was already letting him down. It usually took me weeks to reach this point with a person.

"Maybe you should delete your social media."

I held up my phone. "Already deactivated it."

"Good, because clearly you can't be trusted." His tone had turned teasing, and I slowly met his gaze.

"Well, despite the problem your social media has gotten you into, it'll also be a clue. Whoever did this probably follows you—or *did* follow you." He brushed his chin before taking another sip of coffee. "Anyone that you might have pissed off recently? Enough to steal a cat?" he asked like the idea was preposterous. But the sad truth was that I already had a list going in my head.

"I can really only think of one person."

"Go ahead." He folded his arms across his chest and settled into his seat.

"He's my old boss, who isn't particularly fond of me for reasons I'd rather not get into."

Reid raised his eyebrows and cocked his head. "What did you do?"

"Why do you automatically assume I did something?"

"Did you?"

I shrugged and gave him a sheepish smile. "He started it?" I offered.

He shook his head and let out a laugh. "Well, before we get into the gory details, maybe you should try to negotiate," he said.

My arms froze at the suggestion. "The message said not to."

"That's what they always say, but they expect it. I bet if you offered them, like, a few thousand, they'd leave you alone."

"But—but I need that money," I said, something rough clenching around my chest. "And it's not like there's any guarantee they'll give Vermont back."

He shrugged, still thinking it over. "You'd still come into a good chunk of money. Of course there are never guarantees, but there isn't a guarantee we'll figure this out, either."

"You want to give up before we even start?" I asked, the hope dying inside me.

"What? No." He scrambled to sit straight up, eyes wide when he realized I was gathering my things in a hurry and stuffing them into my bag. Tears stung the back of my eyes and I needed to get out of that diner before Reid saw them fall.

"It's okay," I stammered, swallowing hard. "I know this whole thing is batshit crazy. You have no obligation to help me. I'll see…I'll try to figure something out." I set down some cash on the table and scootched out of the booth—something that unfortunately could not be done with any shred of dignity.

"Hazel, I didn't mean I wouldn't try to help you. I'm sorry."

He slid out of his side of the booth, standing almost a head taller than me. I forced my gaze up and plastered on the most convincing smile I could muster. (Spoiler alert, it likely wasn't that convincing.)

"It was nice meeting you, Reid Mitchell."

I held out my hand but when he didn't immediately shake it, I grabbed it from his side and awkwardly pumped once before shooting toward the doorway.

I was in my car, engine turned on, and sobbing on the highway before Reid even had a chance to blink.

He was a nice guy, but he didn't want to help me. Not really. And despite enjoying investigating, he didn't believe he *could* help me. I could see it in his eyes when he mentioned negotiating. Like it was my only real chance.

Whatever the case, that meeting had just cemented what I already knew deep down.

This whole thing—much like my life—was utterly hopeless.

FOUR

Reid

THE MEETING THE PRIOR MORNING WITH HAZEL RAN ON A
loop in my mind. The minute she'd rushed out of that diner,
I'd told myself it was for the best. The likelihood that I could
help her was slim. It was better we part ways early on than to
get her hopes up only to fail her.

But then my brain repainted the memory of her crumpled
face over and over again, and guilt seeped in. If she was so
willing to meet with her coworker's brother, how likely was it
that she had anyone else to turn to right now?

I didn't even know her, but I hated the thought of her
dealing with this all by herself. Ruby wasn't the only empath in
the family.

An alert pinged from the group chat with my sleuthing
crew.

Then another.

This was my usual routine: wake up early, knock out work,
then spend the afternoon chatting with them, digging through
clues, watching crime docs—whatever.

WhiteKnight31 was actually Scott, a single guy in his mid-
forties with an anime obsession who lived out in Seattle.
Armchair_Detective was Eddie, around my age and living just

over the state border in Ohio, with a wife and a baby on the way. We'd actually met up once, given our reasonably close proximity.

I'd kind of fallen into the group after my divorce. I'd always been into cold cases and mysteries, and suddenly I had a lot more free time, so I started spending that time on cold case forums. Eventually, I got into regular conversations with two guys who had been deep into a semi-local case—a woman who had gone missing walking to her car from the gym. Middle of the day. Broad daylight. It was absurd that, in this day and age, no one had figured out what happened.

After weeks of obsessing over details, even visiting the scene myself, we actually dug up something that led the police to the guy: her ex-husband. The one who *should've* been suspect number one, but had somehow slipped by with a garbage alibi.

Still, solving one case didn't make us pros. It was more dumb luck than the start of some groundbreaking internet detective squad. Which was why I kept telling myself that there was no way I'd be any help to Hazel.

WhiteKnight31: *And you just told her no!?*
ReidingRainbow: *I didn't tell her no. I just offered her a solution that might be easier.*
Armchair_Detective: *"Oh, your situation sounds hopeless, better just pay up and cross your fingers you get your cat back."*
ReidingRainbow: *It didn't go exactly like that…*
WhiteKnight31: *Help the poor girl save her cat, you monster.*
ReidingRainbow: *Alright, no name calling.*
Armchair_Detective: *We can help you. I'm insulted you didn't even ask for our help.*
WhiteKnight31: *Yeah, wtf Reid.*
Armchair_Detective: *This could be a blog post if we solve it! Changed names and facts obviously.*
WhiteKnight31: *You're right, people love a pet redemption story.*
Armchair_Detective: *Just think of John Wick.*

WhiteKnight31: *I prefer not to.*
ReidingRainbow: *Potential blog content isn't a good reason to do something.*
WhiteKnight31: *No, saving the cat is reason enough you dingbat. What is wrong with you?*
ReidingRainbow: *I never said no! She walked out.*
WhiteKnight31: *After you were being unhelpful.*
Armchair_Detective: *Doesn't she work with your sister? Doesn't seem like she'd be hard to track down if you really wanted to.*

A RANDOM WEEKDAY AFTERNOON WAS A GOOD A DAY AS ANY TO get a haircut.

At least that's what I told myself as I pulled into the parking lot of my sister's salon. I certainly didn't have an ulterior motive for being there—like, let's say, talking to a certain coworker of hers.

After thinking on it for a full twenty-four hours, I officially couldn't get Hazel out of my mind. Maybe it was the part of me who always wanted to be helpful, but I couldn't leave it alone.

The salon had seen better days. The paint had peeled off the cement façade, leaving it weathered and tired. The lines in the parking lot had completely vanished, with no traces left to even suggest where a space might've been. The owners of the building didn't do much to keep up the appearance, but I knew Ruby loved this place. I slammed the car door and bent down to adjust my glasses in the side mirror before straightening up. Shoulders squared, I walked straight into the salon. A bell rang above me to signal my entry.

The white-haired owner—a woman who always scared me a little—sat at the front desk.

"Appointment?" she asked.

"Um, I'm here to see—"

"Hey bro," Ruby interrupted with a bright smile, spinning in her salon chair at the front.

The owner immediately looked away from me and back to the computer.

"Hey," I said, nodding in her direction, my eyes scanning the entirety of the small space.

I must have been in at some point when Hazel was working, but haircuts for me were almost clinical. Get in, get out. It wasn't like I took the time to take in the space, let alone notice who was there and what they looked like.

Now I found her impossible *not* to notice, and not because she was the only stylist in the small space aside from Ruby. Her round face had this perpetually friendly look about it. Her long brown hair was pulled back into the messiest of buns. She talked animatedly with her hands, multitasking between grand gestures and brushing bleach over a woman's blonde hair. I willed her to look up at me, but she was too engrossed in her conversation.

"Were you here to get a haircut, or are you here to ogle Hazel?" Ruby teased.

I jerked my gaze away and walked over to her chair. "I wanted to ask her how it's going. With her cat and all."

She shrugged. "Oh, y'know. About exactly zero progress. She's stopped crying at work, which is a plus."

Guilt ensnared my chest and pulled tightly.

Ruby tapped her chin, squinting at me. Before I could take a seat in her chair, she spun it away from me. "Actually, if you want to talk to her, maybe you could let her take this appointment? I've got a client coming in fifteen, and her client is about to sit under a dryer for thirty minutes."

"What?" I must have looked horrified. "No way. Fifteen minutes is plenty for my hair and I'll just talk to her when you're done—"

"Hazel!" she called while I shot figurative daggers at her with my eyes.

Hazel and her client both looked toward the front of the

room. "Yeah?" she called back, giving me a small wave when she noticed me, her eyes wide like saucers.

"Mind cutting Reid's hair for me? I'm kind of swamped today."

"That's really alright," I tried to say, but Hazel was already nodding.

Shit. How had I not predicted Ruby would pull something like this?

"That's fine. Let me just put her under the dryer," Hazel said.

Five minutes later, I was in the back of the salon, sitting in Hazel's chair.

My foot bounced restlessly against the floor. It had been years since anyone besides Ruby had touched my hair. My haircut had been the same for twenty years, and I liked it just the way it was. I wasn't big on change. I tensed as Hazel gently lifted the hair at the crown of my head, inspecting it.

"Just a little off the top and clean up the neck, please."

"You sure?" she asked. I couldn't help but notice the two Band-Aids on her left hand. Was she in the practice of nicking herself during haircuts?

"I'm sure."

"If you kept the length on top and faded it into the back it would look really nice."

"I like it short," I said.

She frowned in response, still examining my hair. "It's fun to experiment," she tried again.

"Not for me." I blew out a breath and tried to remain calm as she plugged in her clippers and they came buzzing to life.

When she touched the back of my neck, she asked, "Any Halloween plans?" at the same time I said, "So about the other day."

We made eye contact in the mirror and she let out a nervous chuckle.

"I'm not a big Halloween guy," I said, answering her question. "I'll probably just stay home. If I'm feeling really festive, maybe I'll put on a scary movie." That was an understatement. I *hated* dressing up. West would most likely try to convince me to go out, but I was confident I could dodge his efforts.

"I'm not big on Halloween either," Hazel said. She continued to work on my hair in silence for a few moments before speaking again. "I'm sorry I ran out on you the other day."

I let out a breath. "I wanted to talk to you about that."

She shook her head. "Look, it was silly of me to think you could help. I've pretty much accepted my fate."

"Actually—"

"As soon as I get my winnings, I'll send them off and hope for the best."

"I was thinking—"

"It'll be a blow, but worth it if I can get Vermont back. I still don't trust this sicko, obviously, but what other choice do I have—"

"Hazel," I said, this time with more force. She paused mid-sentence, her lips slightly parted. She shut off the buzzer and I resisted the urge to touch the back of my neck to ensure she'd taken off the proper length.

"What?" she asked.

"I've been thinking about your…predicament some more, and I want to help."

"Y-you do?"

The fact that she was prepared to part with her entire winnings to save her cat made me even more sure I was making the right decision. She deserved to have someone on her side. Someone who would at least make an attempt to help her.

"I do. And I'm sorry for saying you should negotiate. You're right, I didn't even try to help you at first. I acted exactly like all the detectives in all of the cold cases that keep me up at night by just brushing you off and looking for the simplest solution."

"You're serious?" I could see hope blooming in her eyes. Damn, she was expressive.

"I am. Again, I'm not sure if I'll be able to help, but at the end of the day, what we're dealing with is an amateur, not some criminal mastermind. I think we at least have a shot."

Hazel squealed so loudly I jumped back in my chair.

"Oh my God, I could cry. Thank you, Reid."

"Hazel." Miranda gave her a warning glare from the front of the salon.

"Sorry," Hazel called.

A guy with sharp eyebrows and spiky hair emerged from the back room. "What's going on?" he asked, hovering near Hazel.

"Reid is going to help me find Vermont."

The guy held his hand over his heart and looked to the ceiling before gazing directly into my eyes. "Good. Hazel could use a break."

"Um, no problem." I shifted in my seat, the weight of their attention pressing down on me. "Maybe we could meet at the diner again to get started."

"Let's just get started right now," Hazel said turning the clippers back on. "Even though I'd basically given up hope, I thought a lot about what you told me. Think of the suspects. And I really think there's only one obvious choice—"

"Maybe you want to concentrate," I offered, pointing at my hair where she'd started buzzing again.

"Oh, I'm fine. I could do this in my sleep," she said.

I white-knuckled the arms of the chair and forced myself to trust the process. This was her job, after all. She wasn't about to shave an accidental bald spot into the back of my head.

Right?

"Alright then, who's the obvious choice?" I asked.

"My old boss," she said with a wince. "We didn't…well we didn't exactly part on the best of terms."

I furrowed my brows at her vague explanation, but I decided not to push it. "And you really think he has it out for you?" As someone who had worked remotely for years and had never had more than a cordial relationship with a manager, I found the idea hard to fathom.

She nodded, looking sheepish. "Well, *'have it out for'* is such a strong phrase. Let's just say we didn't have the greatest of relationships."

"I think it's Clinton for sure," the other stylist said. He was now sitting in the chair next to the one I was in, spinning toward us. "I'm Jackson, by the way."

"Reid," I said, with a small wave. "And why do you think it's your old boss?" I asked.

Hazel frowned, picking up her scissors and pulling my hair up. "It's silly—"

"He thinks you owe him money," Jackson said.

"Why would you owe your old boss money?"

Hazel huffed. "It's not like I stole from him, or something. Jackson is making it seem more dramatic than it was. He had unfair pricing tactics, and I organized a protest with some of the other stylists."

"It was a full-on strike. Went viral and everything," Jackson said.

I gave Hazel a look in the mirror.

"Well, that's certainly a good place to start," I said.

She averted her eyes. "And he stopped by the salon about a month ago, demanding I take down a few negative reviews I left."

"What?" I sat up straight. "Hazel, that's serious."

"He's harmless…I mean, I thought he was harmless."

"Showing up at your place of work is threatening," I said.

She chewed her lip. "He *is* kind of a dick."

"Like I said, suspect number one," Jackson said as if he was now in on this with the two of us. "What's the plan?"

I cringed when Hazel brought the clippers near my ear. Forcing my shoulders to relax, I let out a breath. "To start, I'd try to cyberstalk him and—"

"I know where he works," Hazel interrupted. "It's still the same salon."

Unease flickered in my chest. "But we can't just go there."

"A stakeout!" Jackson exclaimed.

"That's where investigations end, not start," I said.

"But if there's any evidence it's him, we could be done so quickly," Hazel pointed out.

"Or get caught so quickly," I argued, already regretting stepping into this salon today. What the hell had I gotten myself into? At this point, my inability to say no—or let people down—was seriously starting to annoy me.

"It *has* to be him. He definitely hates my guts. I can't think of anyone else." She chewed on her lip.

She looked chaotically adorable like that, bottom lip snagged under her teeth, eyes staring into the mirror at mine, but also staring right through. She was clearly already thinking ten steps ahead.

"Then we'll look into it," I said, attempting to reel her in. "There are other things we can do before just showing up at the guy's place of work."

"We can be discreet," she argued.

I let out a frustrated breath. "I'm absolutely not doing a stakeout."

FIVE

Reid

"Remind me again how this isn't a stakeout?"

"It's a casual drive by," Hazel said, pushing off her car and waving at me.

A few days ago, when she gave me her address at the salon and said she'd drive, I'd almost told her there was no way in hell I'd be tagging along. But then she'd looked at me, with those glassy, wide, helpless eyes, and I'd caved. This whole thing was so far outside my comfort zone it was ridiculous, but I'd said yes anyway.

It wasn't that I *couldn't* say no—though, sure, I usually didn't—it was that I didn't *want* to. We'd just met, and yet I felt compelled to help her. She seemed so defeated, like she didn't have much left. I couldn't stand the idea of being one more letdown.

"And what information are we going to glean?" I asked, approaching her ancient-looking sedan. Seriously, this thing could have been in a museum.

"I don't know? A brazenly guilty expression? A stray orange cat hair on his black shirt? We'll know it when we see it." She gave me a small smile and handed me one of the coffees teetering inside the holder in her hands. "It's a vanilla lavender soy latte. Hopefully that's okay. It was the special at the café down the street."

I tried not to turn my nose up at the strange sounding drink. "Interesting," I said, taking the cup from her.

Despite this being one of the strangest mornings of my life —meeting a girl I hardly knew, sipping a coffee I'd never usually try, about to drive to her old place of work to spy on her boss in search of clues for a kidnapped cat—I felt kind of…excited. Or maybe it was anxiety. I once read that the two felt almost identical, and I hadn't been able to unlearn that since. That fluttery, flippy sensation deep in your gut? It showed up for both. The main difference was that anxiety usually only preluded the unknown.

"Your hair looks great, by the way," Hazel said, opening her driver's side door and waving for me to get in.

"Thanks. It's grown on me." Not even a lie, either. At first, I'd had to bite my tongue when I realized she hadn't taken enough length off the top. I'd forced myself to be polite and leave, figuring I could always go back to Ruby to fix it at a time when Hazel wasn't there. But after looking in the mirror for a day, I had to accept that Hazel had been right. The shape *did* suit my face better.

The passenger side door handle stuck when I tried to open it.

"You have to yank a little," Hazel said, her voice muffled by the car window.

I pulled harder on the handle, but the door still didn't budge.

"Okay, you have to yank a lot. Really put your shoulder into it."

I braced one hand on the frame of the door and yanked— hard. It opened, almost whacking the glasses clean off my face. I jerked backward and shot her an accusatory glare.

"I've been meaning to get that fixed." The way she said it made me feel like she had absolutely zero intention of getting that fixed.

I started to slide into the seat but froze.

Her car was a disaster. Not just slightly messy—a full-blown catastrophe. If I thought Ruby was cluttered, Hazel was on a whole different level. Clothes were scattered across nearly every seat, an open CD case lay on the floor, and random papers were strewn everywhere like a tiny tornado had blown through.

"Sorry, it's a little messy." Hazel piled up the sweatshirt and receipts from the passenger seat and dumped them into the back.

It was almost physically painful to get into her car. My entire being rejected clutter, and it seemed, from my very limited knowledge of her, that Hazel's entire being *was* clutter.

"It's fine." I urged my voice not to go up an octave. As soon as I closed the door, the claustrophobia hit me right in the face. My fingers searched for the button to roll down the window.

"Oh, you have to roll it down, like actually roll it." Hazel held out her hand and made a turning motion with her fist before pointing to the door.

"Got it," I said, before urgently cranking the window down. She gave me a funny look, likely because it was only forty degrees outside, but I hoped she didn't ask me to put it back up. My skin was blazing hot, as it typically was any time I found myself in an uncomfortable or new social situation, and the icy air was the only thing keeping me sane.

"Thanks again for coming with me," she said, throwing the car into reverse. It made a loud creaking noise as she peeled out of the parking spot.

"Are you sure you don't want me to drive?"

"Nah, this is easier. I know where we're going."

"My phone—like many this day and age—has GPS," I said, wishing I had forced her to consider this alternate plan before I became a hostage in her passenger seat. Nothing about Hazel screamed 'safe and responsible driver.'

"Seriously, don't worry about it. Drink your latte and

relax. You're the one doing me a favor, I'm not going to force you to drive me around, too."

I didn't say it out loud, but letting me drive in this situation would actually *be* the favor. Although, I might have thought better of this plan halfway there and forced us to turn around. I had tried to tell Hazel that the best plan for getting her cat back was to come up with a few carefully thought-out hypotheses and then look for proof. The pool of suspects couldn't be huge. But we'd have to be cautious. Clearly, someone deranged enough to steal a cat wasn't in a great state of mind.

"Remind me again why you're so sure it's your old boss," I said, taking a tentative sip of my latte. It was shockingly delicious. I took another drawn-out sip.

"I kind of orchestrated a coup." She winced as the car rolled to a stop at a red light. The streets were empty, given the early hour. Hazel had mentioned her old boss, Clinton, always got to work at least an hour before the salon opened.

"A coup," I repeated. "As in a revolution? How does one do that at a hair salon?"

"He's a dick, Reid. You don't understand." Her tone grew more defensive. "He has this bullshit pay structure that I seriously doubt is even legal. He hires us under the guise that the salon itself is well known and going to bring in all this clientele, and then we'll work on commission. So if I brought in more clients one week, I'd get paid a bonus. It's bullshit, because we still had to find all our own clients and most of us were barely making minimum wage while Clinton was taking the majority of the earnings."

"That does sound shitty," I said.

"I was working there for a few months when I'd had it. I started talking to some of the other girls, and we were all fed up. I said we could go on a strike and post about it on social media."

"So you made a video on your social media dragging him?"

She licked her lips and glanced at me before returning her eyes to the road. "It's a tiny bit worse than that."

I slammed my foot against the floorboard instinctively as Hazel came a little too close to the truck in front of us.

"What did you do?"

"Well, I had access to the salon's social media."

"You didn't."

"I did. I posted from the main account, detailing how much he was screwing over the stylists. And it may have gone a teensy bit viral."

I balked at her, kind of horrified, but also kind of impressed.

"It wasn't crazy viral, but local-viral. His salon got bombarded with one-star reviews and he was livid. Said I ruined his business and fired me on the spot."

A laugh escaped me. Hazel certainly wasn't a pushover, that was for sure.

"So potentially a candidate for a severe grudge, but do you really think he'd blackmail you?"

"After I posted that I won the lottery—"

I shot her a disapproving glare.

"I know, I know, but you can't keep holding that against me. It's done. Anyway, he responded to my post, saying I should pay him back for everything I caused him to lose, or something like that. I took a screenshot if you want to see, but then I blocked him."

"So it's not outside the realm of possibility."

"Right," she said.

The car made another dying sound as if wheezing its last breath when she pulled into a parking lot. The salon was housed in a sleek white building at the far end of the plaza.

Hazel pulled into a spot, the brakes squealing when she stopped.

"Real discreet," I muttered. "This isn't exactly ideal for a stakeout, you know." I pointed to her car, easily the loudest vehicle I'd ever ridden in. It practically announced its arrival a block ahead.

"If I don't have to pay this psycho all of my winnings to get my cat back, maybe I can buy a new one."

"You should buy a new one regardless. This one can't be safe."

She smiled playfully. "I'm sorry, but are we or are we not here in one piece?"

"I think the bumper might have fallen off at the last light."

She rolled her eyes before unbuckling her seat belt and popping open the center console. I averted my gaze, figuring it best for my mental health to avoid seeing the unkempt state of that compartment.

I surveyed our surroundings. We had driven about fifteen minutes to get here. It was arguably a better part of town than the salon where Hazel and Ruby currently worked. Not that their salon was in a bad area, but this place was ritzy as hell. No potholes in the parking lot, fresh paint on every building, manicured planters, and not a flickering neon sign in sight. Rent here must cost a fortune. While her old boss sounded grimy for sure, my gut was telling me the person who was extorting Hazel would have a lot less to lose.

When I turned back to Hazel to relay this thought, I found her with binoculars pressed against her eyes as she leaned forward, looking through the windshield.

"What are you doing?" I asked, unable to keep the exasperation out of my voice.

She pulled the binoculars away and offered them to me. "Oh, sorry. You're right. You're the mystery solver. You should probably have these."

She said it earnestly, something I might've found endearingly ridiculous under different circumstances. But right now, I was on edge. There was pretty much a zero-percent chance we'd get out of this unnoticed. Not in Hazel's clunker of a car, and definitely not with her making it so painfully obvious we were snooping.

I placed a hand on the binoculars and lowered them. "No, I mean why did you bring them? Anyone walking by would probably call the police and say there are some stalking creeps in the parking lot."

"There's no one here."

"Yet," I pointed out.

"Fine." She folded her arms across her chest and leaned back into the seat. "We probably have at least ten or twenty minutes before he shows up."

"And when he does, we will stay very far away, observe from a distance, and then get the hell out of here," I said, still in disbelief she had convinced me to join this wild goose chase. In all of my time internet sleuthing, we rarely did anything that couldn't be done from behind a screen. While this was kind of exhilarating, it mostly made me feel nauseous.

"Right, of course." Hazel reached for the binoculars that were now on the console between us, but I swatted her hand away.

"And *no* binoculars."

"How am I supposed to discern a guilty expression or a stray piece of cat hair from this distance?" she huffed.

"You'll have to judge it by the rhythm of his walk."

"Why did we even come here if we're not going to properly investigate?"

I threw my arms up. "I didn't want to come here in the first place. In fact, I believe I insisted we didn't. I told you we should be building a case—writing down facts and seeing what we can figure out from the original message."

"Well, you're here now, aren't you?"

"Because—" My voice fell away.

Because you were insistent.

Because I couldn't say no.

Because, maybe, a small part of me is having more fun with you this morning than I've had in recent memory.

"Let's just get this over with so we can move on," I said instead. Her large amber eyes settled on me. Even when I looked away to examine the parking lot, I could still feel them on me.

"What got you into investigations in the first place?" she asked.

That all-too-familiar wave of self-consciousness washed over me. "I'm not sure. I guess I've always been a little bit addicted to true crime. Especially cold cases. I found them infuriating. How justice could go unserved like that."

My ex, Meghan, used to hate when I talked about this stuff. I believe her exact descriptors were "cringey and embarrassing." Didn't exactly do a whole lot for the old ego.

"And you decided you wanted to solve them?" Hazel asked. For a second, it was easy to forget the absurdity of where we were, and I faded into her question. I thought I caught a flicker of genuine interest beneath it, something more than just politeness.

"I was pretty active in some local online forums. I got talking to a few other users regularly. Honestly, we never thought we'd actually find something that could lead to a real-life arrest or anything like that."

"But you did, right?" Hazel confirmed.

My chest puffed out. Did she seem impressed?

"We did, yeah. We found the camera footage that cracked open a lead suspect's alibi. We sent it to the police, and they were able to make the arrest from there."

"Wow, that's impressive."

"It felt good," I admitted, prouder of that accomplishment than anything else I'd done.

"And you stay in touch with those people? The ones you solved it with."

I nodded. "They're my friends. We actually…we have a blog together."

Hazel's eyes went wide. "Seriously? That's so cool. What's it called? I want to read it." She was already pulling out her phone, poised to search. I was so used to cringing away when I shared that fact, but she wasn't making fun of me at all. She was a sweet girl. Maybe a bit of a hot mess, but warm and friendly, and unafraid to be herself. I decided I liked her. Maybe we could even be friends.

That theory was about to be tested.

A car pulled into the lot and Hazel sat straight up. "That's him. That's Clinton."

The car came to a stop in an empty space in front of the white building and a middle-aged man with long blond hair got out and slammed the door shut. He was a small guy and very…well-groomed looking. Nothing about his all-white, perfectly pressed outfit read as seedy catnapper to me.

"You should send a text to that number," I said. "We can see if he checks his phone…"

Before I could even finish my sentence, Hazel threw her shoulder into her door and pushed it open.

"What are you doing?!" I whisper-yelled, my heart already pounding in my throat.

But it was too late. Hazel was already outside the car and barreling toward Clinton with a fire in her eyes.

SIX

Hazel

"Clinton!" I shouted. His stupid smug face came into focus as I stalked toward him. It was like the sight of him had possessed me. Some alien entity had taken over my body, recklessly propelling me straight toward this man.

In the back of my brain, my processors vaguely alerted me that Reid was calling my name urgently from the car, but I couldn't be stopped. Every emotion that had been brewing within me—frustration, grief, anger, despair, you name it— had finally erupted to the surface. I needed to let it out on someone.

Now.

Clinton jerked his gaze toward me and squinted for a moment, as if trying to place me. Recognition flared in his eyes seconds before his mouth twisted into a scowl.

"I told you to stay the hell away from my salon," he yelled, in that semi-composed, throaty way people did when they didn't want to cause a scene.

"What are you doing?" Reid hissed. He had crossed the distance quickly and was now directly at my back.

"I had every right to post that video and you know it," I said, stopping only when I was a foot in front of my former boss. "You're a shit boss and you've built your empire on the backs of stylists you've taken advantage of."

Clinton barked out a bitter laugh and tossed his head back. "You are so fucking dramatic. Jesus, Hazel. Grow up. It's called business for a reason. Everything I did was above board, and part of a very clear contract that *you* signed."

My hands shook and tears of frustration pooled in the corners of my eyes. "Did you take him?" I asked.

"Hazel! Let's get out of here." Reid tugged on my arm, but my feet stayed planted, refusing to budge.

A puzzled look twisted across Clinton's face. "What? Take who?"

"My cat!"

"What the hell are you talking about?" he sneered and shook his head.

My vision of him was obstructed by a gray sweater. Reid had placed himself between us.

"Alright, we really need to go," he said, dipping his head to force me to make eye contact with him. I jerked my body to the side, peering around Reid to level my gaze at Clinton. He looked about as fed up as humanly possible, but I couldn't give two shits.

"Tell me the truth!" I demanded, scanning his features for any possible crack that would tell me he knew something—anything.

"You're literally *insane*," Clinton said, putting extra emphasis on the word. He backed away from me, toward the front of his gaudy salon, a place I was genuinely thrilled never to have to set foot in again. "If you come back here, I'm calling the police, and I will get a restraining order."

"That isn't necessary!" Reid said at the same time I spat out, "Sue me!"

"Seriously, get the hell out of here!" Clinton yelled, fiddling with his keys. He dropped them then dipped down to grab them in a flustered hurry.

"Is everything alright here?" A soft voice asked. The older

woman who owned the flower shop next door had poked her head out her front door.

"Everything's fine." Reid's voice cracked. He gripped my biceps and walked forward, practically dragging me along. "Hazel, move now. We need to go."

A few tears slipped down my cheeks, and I brushed them away with my sleeve before spinning on my heel and letting Reid herd me back to my car at the far end of the lot. I didn't leave without one last, "Fuck you, Clinton," throwing him a quick middle finger in the process.

Reid covered my raised hand with his and pulled it down. "*Stop it*," he scolded, guiding me to my passenger side door before stuffing me inside. He jogged around to the driver's side and put my keys—the ones that I had carelessly left behind when I'd stalked off—into the ignition. He placed a hand behind my headrest, looked behind him, and peeled out of the parking lot.

"Holy shit, Hazel! That was *not* a stakeout."

My breathing quickened as my mind finally caught up with my actions. I stared out the window as we whizzed away. Clinton had his head out the front door of his salon, raising a fist in the air like some cartoon villain. Then, Reid slammed on the gas and left the plaza in the rearview mirror.

I sank down into my seat, letting a few more tears fall freely before sniffing. I'd lost it. I wasn't usually that impulsive, but all my building emotions had finally broken free. My ex used to call me a loose cannon—mostly because I couldn't stay quiet when someone cut in line or mistreated a customer service worker. But I wasn't exactly known for picking fights. Not like what just happened back there.

That was it. I was cooked.

Reid wasn't going to help me anymore. Why would he believe this was out of character? I wasn't exactly stable. He probably thought my outburst was a run-of-the-mill morning for me. I chanced a look at him. His face was flushed, eyes locked on the road, and his breathing still came in sharp, audible bursts.

Without Reid, I was screwed. I could probably rule out Clinton as a suspect, since he genuinely hadn't seemed to know what the hell I was talking about, but I still wasn't any closer to solving this miserable mystery.

"Something came over me when I saw his stupid face," I said, attempting to defend my inexcusable actions.

But something really had. I hadn't been expecting it. Aside from this whole debacle, there was bad blood between Clinton and me. He'd fired me at a time in my life when I really couldn't afford to be fired. Granted, I'd deserved it, but I *had* tried talking to him first. I'd pointed out how he was being deceptive and underpaying his workers. He'd been smug and dismissive in response and that had pissed me off. So maybe I'd acted on instinct. And maybe my instinct was frequently irresponsible. I was still a human being. I deserved better than to be discarded like a piece of garbage.

"Are you okay?" Reid asked.

The softness in his tone surprised me and I lifted my gaze to meet his. He adjusted his glasses, glancing erratically from the road back to me.

"I'm fine," I said, unable to hide my surprise that he seemed to genuinely care.

He let out a ragged breath. "That was so dangerous. You can't just confront someone like that, especially someone you think might have it out for you."

Was he scolding me right now? Was he actually concerned for my safety? Despite my utter despondence, something brighter cracked through my chest.

"I don't think Clinton is the most dangerous guy around. I doubt he would do anything that could get his white pants dirty."

"I'm serious," Reid said, but then a snort of a laugh escaped him. "He *was* impeccably groomed."

"I've never seen him any other way. I wish I'd reached out and at least messed up his hair."

"He probably would have you arrested for assault."

"He'd probably *believe* it was assault, too," I said.

Reid was fully laughing now. "That guy looked ridiculous. But also, I think we can cross him off our suspect list. No way was that guy bending over to pick up a cat in someone's courtyard."

"You're probably right. I doubt he'd even be caught dead in my part of town," I said with a sigh, before perking up in my seat. "Wait. Did you say we?"

Reid scratched his chin absentmindedly. "What? Uh, yeah. We can cross him off the list."

"So, you're not done with me? You still want to help?"

He looked so focused. Hands at ten and two, shoulders squared, eyes unwavering on the empty road in front of us.

"Well, yeah." We came to a stop at the next red light, and he turned in his seat. "But I'm not doing that again, that's for sure. We're doing it my way next time."

I winced. "Understood."

"It might seem slow or frustrating to someone who likes to take action, but trust me, okay?"

"I do trust you," I said, somehow believing it. One of my flaws was trusting too easily. It had landed me in trouble before—phony friendships, deadbeat exes, even the occasional internet scam. But with Reid, I had a good feeling. Being around him felt…steady. His presence was calming in a way I hadn't experienced in a long time. Not since that last dinner with my grandmother, when we had curled up on her sofa to watch a movie afterward.

The memory slammed into me and my smile faded.

We rode the rest of the way to my building in silence.

The drive back had given me plenty of time to stew about my outburst, and the embarrassment had finally hit. Based on my behavior, one could assume I didn't give a shit what people thought about me. And they would be correct…mostly. But

Reid was so together. So buttoned-up. I wanted him to have at least an ounce of respect for me.

Reid turned off the ignition and tossed me the keys before we unbuckled and got out of the car.

"Uh, sorry about all this. The whole morning, really," I said, as we stood outside my front gate.

He nodded before tilting his head toward my gated courtyard. "This the scene of the crime?" he asked, then stepped toward the gate and slid his fingers through the wrought iron bars, peering into the small space.

"That would be it," I said, joining him. "Vermont loved being outside. And I felt so bad that he had to be taken in by a surrogate mother that I wanted him to be happy. He'd dart for the door every time I opened it. I have a small private balcony, and I wanted to make him a cute little caged-in area, but…"

"Hey, you might still be able to do that. Don't give up hope yet." He gave my arm a gentle squeeze, like grounding me came naturally. Butterflies stirred in my stomach at the touch, but I did my best to play it cool.

"What's next?" I asked.

His jaw clenched as he squinted through his glasses, taking in the full stretch of the front of my apartment complex. There wasn't much to see. It was a two-story, twelve-unit, U-shaped building surrounding a small grassy courtyard. The place was old, and owned by one of those sleazy new property management companies that had snapped up nearly every apartment in the area, cutting corners and charging rent like they were running a luxury hotel.

"Next, we do things my way."

"Do tell. What is your way?" I asked.

He gave me a little smirk. "*That's* my way." He pointed to the far-right portion of the roof that hung over the gate. Mounted there was a small black camera I had never noticed before.

Positioned to face the courtyard.

SEVEN

Hazel

THE INTERNET WAS ROTTING OUR BRAINS. WASN'T THAT WHAT the experts said? After what must have been at least three hours straight of mindlessly scrolling on my phone, I was starting to believe it. Every new and mildly interesting post was like a small hit of dopamine—exciting, and incredibly short-lived. It wasn't until I finally snapped out of my internet haze that I realized just how numb and depressed I felt.

I pulled up the recent photo I'd received of Vermont.

It had been Reid's idea to ask the number for a "proof of life" picture. He thought the person might slip up and send something incriminating.

This new pic was just of Vermont, though, splayed out on a generic gray rug, belly up. He looked content. Too content, honestly. I was grateful he was safe, but where the hell did he get off looking so goddamn comfortable? Didn't he know I was sick out of my mind with worry? He could at least have the decency to look contrite.

Without taking my eyes off my phone, I got off my couch and moved to the kitchen to grab a cookie from the plastic container on top of my microwave. It was almost eleven, but I hadn't had breakfast yet. My only clients were later this afternoon, so I was taking the opportunity to waste away on my couch.

I leaned against the kitchen counter and swiped out of the picture of Vermont to open the list Reid had asked me to work on. He'd provided me with all the usernames that had viewed my post about winning the lottery. He'd also sent me the picture I'd posted and asked if it had been worth it.

My heart clenched looking down at my smiling face, holding up the ticket and a drink. Happy, but still puffy from crying at Gran's funeral. Beyond the happiness, I saw the relief in my eyes. Relief that I'd finally be able to break free from the debt caused by the expensive assisted-living facility my grandma had been in. I'd been working since I was fourteen years old, but never anything steady. Never enough. Most days it felt like nothing I did would ever be enough.

The names on the list swirled in front of my eyes. The brain fog was heavy today. The only person who seemed like a possibility to me other than my former boss was, unfortunately, Paul. My ex-boyfriend.

I hated the idea of it, though. We'd been together for years. Lived together, too. He had basically been my only friend when I'd moved out here. Sure, he was *kind of* an ass. We had broken up, after all. But there had been some good times, too.

I'd been the dumper in the situation, and he hadn't been thrilled with me. It was a regular thing for him to show up at my apartment unannounced, usually with an angry plea to try and win me back. He hadn't done that in months, mind you, but the mere fact that he had done so in the past made him the only major suspect.

There were plenty of other names on the list who weren't my biggest fans. I wasn't exactly familiar with the word 'popularity.' I'd always been a little odd—'unique,' as Gran always said—and had only one notable friend, Zoe, for my entire childhood and into my twenties. But as unpopular as I was, most of these people lived hours away, on the other side of the state. I'd grown up closer to Detroit, on the east side of Michigan, and had only moved out to the west side a few years ago. I doubted anyone would go through the trouble of tracking me down all the way over here.

My phone vibrated.

> Reid: Your property manager finally got back to me. Says they don't give out footage, but we're working on it.

> Hazel: Trying to charm them?

> Reid: I'm doing my best.

Life had been kicking me around lately, and exhaustion chased me. Loneliness wrapped around me like a weighted vest. But every time Reid texted, that feeling eased. The fact that he was still talking to me after I had gone full Hazel-mode during that misguided stakeout meant a lot to me.

Like I said, Friendships had never come easily for me, and whatever I had going with Reid was nice—comforting even. I felt an itch to keep him close, even though I wasn't quite sure how.

I'd heard it said that people come into your life for a reason, a season, or a lifetime, and I'd found that to be pretty true. I'd had plenty of casual friendships: people I bonded with because we worked the same shift, or people I hung out with because they were dating someone I knew. Most of those connections had faded out once the context changed. That part never surprised me.

The part that felt harder was finding the "lifetime" kind of connection. The kind that would stick even when things got messy, inconvenient, or quiet. I was still learning how to find that. Or maybe how to *be* that.

My absentee mother could be to blame. Getting rejected right from the start by the one person who was supposed to love you unconditionally had to leave a mark, right? Thankfully, Gran had stepped in and done her best to fill all the cracks.

Was it that people always filtered in and out of my life because I was unlovable? Or was it a self-fulfilling prophecy?

The truth was, from the moment I met someone, I expected them to leave.

A COUPLE OF HOURS LATER, MY BRAIN SUFFICIENTLY corroded, I closed the door to my modest apartment to head to the salon.

"Sweetie, how are you doing?" Mrs. Edenbury from across the hall stood at her door, poised to turn the key in the lock.

My face softened when I saw her. "I'm hanging in there. Thanks for asking."

"You're welcome to borrow one of my babies if you're missing your own and need a friendly face."

She had been the first person I'd told about Vermont's kidnapping. She had been in the hall when I was rushing around and sobbing like a mad woman. She'd comforted me and sat me down in my apartment before making me a cup of tea.

Mrs. Edenbury was somewhere north of seventy, with hair that had been dyed blonde so many times, I wasn't sure it could grow out gray if it wanted to. And she was, funnily enough, a huge cat person. She had given me treats and toys when I'd first brought Vermont home, after I'd told her he was my late grandmother's and I had no idea how to take care of a cat. Mrs. Edenbury might have reminded me of Gran, except she didn't swear like a sailor, and I doubted she had ever begged anyone to allow her to start chain smoking again.

"Thank you. That's sweet. I might take you up on that." I probably wouldn't, though. Her apartment gave me the creeps. I'd only been inside once and that was enough for me. She had life-sized dolls perched on the couch. Nowadays, when she wanted to have tea, I always suggested she come to my place instead.

"Do you need help carrying your groceries in?"

Her smile faded. "Oh, no. That's alright dear. You get to where you're headed. I've got these."

"You sure?" I reached for a bag, but she pulled away.

"Yes, I'm sure. You go on. I'll stop by for tea sometime soon." With that, she slipped into her apartment and closed the door behind her.

Zipping up my coat, I stepped outside.

I zoned out during the short drive to the salon and all throughout my first appointment. It was just a touch-up job and this particular client was a talker. All I had to do was nod and ask a few follow-up questions, and she could keep the conversation going for hours.

I enjoyed my work. Gran had let me dye her hair from a young age, and I'd had fun with it. I liked the challenge when someone brought me in a picture to recreate, as long as their expectations were reasonable. I loved the social aspect and being somewhat in charge of my own schedule. Working with different types of people kept me on my toes, and renting my own chair at Miranda's salon was kind of like running my own small business. I posted on social media, got my own clients, managed my own bookings. Way better than working for that asshat, Clinton.

I cringed just thinking about him. Hopefully I'd never see the guy again. My outburst was just as embarrassing as it had been cathartic.

"What's eating you?" Jackson asked. His client had just vacated his chair and now he was sweeping up the surrounding area.

"Nothing. I'm fine," I said, which was true. Objectively I *was* fine. Not great. Not good. Not amazing. Not terrible. Fine. I was making it through.

"Ruby's brother not bringing any optimism to your current predicament?" he asked in a low voice. He jerked his gaze to where Ruby was at the front, laughing while concentrating on trimming a client's bangs.

I rolled my eyes. He was such a gossip.

"Reid is great," I said. "He's the only thing giving me an iota of hope about the crappy situation. But it's *still* a crappy situation. I thought I'd be booking myself a little vacation by now to celebrate my turn of events. Now I might be catless and penniless."

"Well, you're not really a cat person anyway."

I gawked at him. "I'm a Vermont person. I can't believe you'd say that to me. He was my grandmother's."

"I know, I know." Jackson waved off my obvious offense. "I'm just saying, were you really going to take care of a cat for the rest of its life? They can live to, like, twenty."

"Good. That'll be twenty years longer than anyone else has stayed in my life," I mumbled, turning away from Jackson. I liked him, I really did. But no one would ever accuse him of being too empathetic.

"Don't go feeling sorry for yourself." Jackson came around to my station and guided me to my chair. He placed his hands on my shoulders and forced me to sit. He started pulling up pieces of my long brown hair and examining them. "Have you ever thought about a different color? Or bangs?"

"Uh, what are you doing?" Natalie scurried over from across the aisle, eyes wide. "Hazel, now might not be a good time for a change."

"Don't look so worried," Jackson said, grabbing a spray bottle off his station.

"I'm just saying. A time of great stress is not the best time to be making hair decisions." Natalie bit her full lip and looked back and forth between the two of us.

"Some would argue it's actually the best time. Besides, Hazel has really let herself go this past month. She's looking shaggy."

"Thanks." My voice came out dry. Even in my stupor, I still found the energy to be insulted. I didn't think my hair was *that* bad. Sure, it could use a trim, but so what if I had been neglecting my appearance ever-so-slightly? I did have other things going on.

"May I?" Jackson asked, holding up his scissors.

I sighed, relenting. "Just a trim. Nothing drastic."

Natalie was sweet, trying to make sure I didn't make some giant hair mistake right now, like cutting a pixie on my too-round face. But I didn't care. Who the hell was I trying to impress? I hadn't been on a date in ages, and I seriously doubted anyone would be asking me out any time soon. Besides, it was just hair. It'd grow back.

"You're sure?" Natalie looked horrified as Jackson sprayed my hair down with water.

I shrugged. "I could use a change."

Natalie sighed. "Famous last words."

EIGHT

Reid

WhiteKnight31: *No luck on tracing the phone number. Looks like they're using one of those free-number services.*
ReidingRainbow: *I figured as much. Whoever it is, Hazel probably already has their real number saved.*
Armchair_Detective: *Too bad that old boss didn't pan out. I think you should write about the stakeout for the blog.*
WhiteKnight31: *Agreed.*
ReidingRainbow: *No way in hell.*
Armchair_Detective: *I'd pay money to see Reid confronting a random man in a strip mall parking lot at eight in the morning.*
ReidingRainbow: *That is absolutely not what happened.*
Armchair_Detective: *That's how I'm choosing to picture it.*
ReidingRainbow: *Moving on. I had Hazel reach out to the police officer who took her report to see if they could help her get access to the footage, but they just gave her a generic, "We'll look into it."*
Armchair_Detective: *Damn cops. Why can't they take a stolen pet seriously?*
ReidingRainbow: *I don't know, but I'll figure out a way to get that footage one way or another. Meanwhile, we should move on to looking at other suspects.*
WhiteKnight31: *Like the boyfriend.*

Armchair_Detective: *It's always the boyfriend.*
ReidingRainbow: *EX-boyfriend*
Armchair_Detective: *Do I sense a little hostility in that "EX"?*
WhiteKnight31: *You were quick to correct that one.*
Armchair_Detective: *Does someone have a crush?*
ReidingRainbow: *I'm simply correcting a fact. This is an investigation, after all.*

A LOUD CLANG FROM SOMEWHERE IN MY HOUSE HAD ME ripping off my headphones. I bolted out of my chair and jogged into the hallway, my racing heart slowing as soon as I spotted my sister, Regan. She walked over to my sofa holding a bag of chips, not looking guilty in the slightest.

"Sorry. I knocked a pan over trying to get to these." She shook the bag. "You really shouldn't keep your snacks in such a high cabinet."

"It's not high up for me," I pointed out. "You know, the person who actually lives here? That key is for emergencies." I might as well be a broken record at this point.

"It *was* an emergency. Mom and Dad are driving me nuts." She flung herself across my sofa and picked up the TV remote.

"Shouldn't you be job hunting or something?" I asked. I was seriously considering changing my locks and *not* giving an extra key to every single one of my family members this time around. Clearly, I was too generous in assuming they could handle a few simple boundaries.

Regan groaned. "Ugh, not you too. I filled out some applications this morning. It's not like the job market for a liberal arts major with zero work experience is super-hot right now."

"Can you keep it down at least? I'm busy."

"It's past six. I know you're not working."

I moved into the kitchen and pulled open the fridge before nabbing a soda water. "It's not with work."

"Ohh, right." She snapped her fingers. "This is about the catnapping."

Hearing her call it that made something simmer inside me. It made it sound like a joke, which it absolutely was not to Hazel. It was her life, and she was really struggling right now.

"It's not funny," I said, resigning myself to the fact that I probably wasn't going to convince Regan to go anywhere. I settled into the leather armchair positioned perpendicular to the couch.

"I didn't say it was." She held up her hands defensively. Regan was the least serious one in the family. A 'free spirit,' as my mom always called her. She lacked a strong sense of responsibility and loved to try new things. Living at our parents' house probably stifled her, but it wasn't my fault she hadn't made a concrete plan. We'd all warned her not to just skate by in college, and to spend more time focusing on her future.

My front door rattled before swinging open. Ruby and West sauntered through like they also lived here.

"Excuse me. Did I know you two were coming?" There wasn't any bite to my words. While I wished my family could at least shoot me a warning text, I liked how close we all were. I'd take an unexpected visit over not seeing my sisters at all, any day. They'd recently started stopping by a lot more. I knew why. It was one hundred percent due to my divorce.

"Regan said she was here," Ruby said unapologetically.

West shrugged. "And Ruby texted me to head over."

"Glad someone thought to give me the heads up," I said, but no one acknowledged me. Instead, West splayed out on my couch, propping his feet up on the matching ottoman.

"I was hoping you'd want to grab dinner," he said.

"I'm down." I had a bad habit of tuning out my body whenever I got caught up in something online, and I hadn't even noticed I was hungry until West mentioned food. Now my stomach growled like it had been starving for hours.

"Same," Regan said.

"Only if you pay for yourself," Ruby warned, lingering behind the couch.

Regan pouted and draped her head over the back of the seat. "Can't you take pity on your poor, broke, unemployed sister?"

"That worked when you were a college student, but not anymore," Ruby said.

West laughed. "Nice try, kid."

"Mexican?" I asked, standing and brushing the wrinkles out of my pants.

Ruby rolled her eyes. "You always pick that place."

"It's delicious and it's down the street." I didn't mention that I'd just gotten lunch from there the other day. I had my favorite spots, and I liked knowing exactly what to expect when I went out to eat. Trying somewhere new was a risk.

"Fine with me," West said.

"Let me just tell the guys I have to run. Regan interrupted me."

"Are you working on Hazel's thing?" Ruby asked, eyes shining with interest. "She seemed kind of down at work yesterday. I wanted to ask, but I was slammed with clients."

My chest tightened.

She seemed down? I hated that.

We obviously weren't any closer to figuring this out, but I thought she was at least a little bit more optimistic. She came across that way over text, anyway.

"Any leads?" West asked.

I chewed on the inside of my lip, biting back a laugh just thinking about the stakeout. "Um, not really. She thought it might be her old boss but…it didn't pan out."

"Shoot. And there's no one else you can look into?" Ruby asked.

"Unfortunately, not yet." Which was killing me. We'd just started, and I definitely wasn't an expert in these matters, but I still thought I'd have more ideas by now. It was definitely an amateur; the perpetrator couldn't be that slick. They must have left clues, and made mistakes.

"There's a camera pointing to her courtyard. I was hoping to get access to the videos, but so far, no luck."

"Does she have a doorman?" Regan asked.

"It's not that kind of apartment complex." But as I said it, I realized that there actually had to be a leasing office somewhere on the property. I'd noticed the call button when I'd buzzed Hazel's unit the other day. Maybe they wouldn't be able to help, but getting in front of a real person was usually better than dealing with a call center.

I shot a text to Hazel.

> Reid: I have an idea.

"Come on, put your phone away and let's go," West said, clapping my shoulder. I shot off another message to the mobile version of the sleuthing group chat before silencing my ringer.

Ruby and Regan piled into their respective cars, and I slid into the passenger side of West's. If they were going to ambush me, the least one of them could do was give me a ride.

"How are you doing?" he asked before we even pulled out of the driveway.

"I'm fine." My senses tingled, alerting me that something about his question was off.

"You haven't been snooping on social media? Meghan's been posting stuff with that new guy non-stop, and you haven't even mentioned it since we brought it up at the last dinner."

Honestly, I'd completely forgotten about that. Seeing my ex-wife with her new boyfriend should have at least warranted a mild crash-out, but helping Hazel was the only thing preoccupying me lately. While I was doing better—I really was—it still sucked to see Meghan move on before I did. Especially since she'd been the one to end it. Maybe, deep down, I'd known we weren't right for each other. But when she'd pulled up a chair that random Wednesday night and told me we needed to talk, I hadn't expected it. I'd go as far as to say that she'd blindsided me. She'd said she wanted more. That I couldn't change, and she had no desire to try and push me any longer. She wanted excitement, and I just wasn't the guy who could give it to her.

"I haven't looked," I said.

West shot me a quick glance, eyebrows raised. "Seriously? You weren't curious? I thought for sure you'd go on a stalking spree the moment you found out. Ruby had to force me not to drive to your house that night to try and talk you off a ledge."

I slid back in my seat. West had been around for the entirety of mine and Meghan's relationship. He knew how in love I'd been, and he'd seen how far I'd fallen when she'd told me she wanted out. But that was nearly a year ago. I'd moved on. Just because I hadn't met someone new, didn't mean I couldn't be over her.

"I appreciate the sentiment, but I really don't care."

It was clear from his silence that he didn't believe me. No one in my family did, even if it was the truth. Now that I was out of that relationship, I could see how draining it had been. It wasn't like we fought a lot, but we were never on the same page. Never wanted to do the same things. It was dumb stuff, like, she'd want a night out while I just wanted to cook together and watch a movie. Or she'd want to ditch my family's annual trip to Florida so she could go to Italy instead. Being with Meghan had left me constantly doubting myself, feeling like who I was just wasn't enough. Honestly, being alone had been freeing.

I didn't need some rebound. I needed to finally accept myself, after years of feeling like I wasn't amounting to much as a husband.

"I'm here if you need me, man," West said.

"I know." And I did. Because he'd always been there for me. I knew without a doubt that West always had my back.

At the restaurant, Ruby and Regan were already waiting for us at a table. The four of us spent the entire dinner having lively conversation. Part of me was present, enjoying myself and laughing along.

Another part of me was somewhere else entirely.

It wasn't until West dropped me back at home that I realized I'd been consciously stopping myself from checking my phone all night, resisting the urge to see if Hazel had texted me back.

NINE

Hazel

"Your hair," Reid said, as I pulled down the handle on
the front gate and stepped aside so that he could slip by.

"What do you think?" I asked, fluffing out my midnight-
blue choppy layers. Jackson, it turned out, did not believe in
subtle change. Thankfully, he hadn't lopped it all off. He had,
however, insisted on curtain bangs that hung in my eyes unless
properly styled, which annoyed me to no end. Overall,
though, I appreciated the change. It was nice to look in the
mirror and see a different reflection. My old one had been
growing duller each time I caught sight of her.

"It suits you," Reid said, taking me in from behind his
black-rimmed glasses. His thick gray peacoat looked so warm
I wanted to tuck right into it. The weather channel had
threatened snow, but right now it was just dark, dreary, and
cold.

"Why are you in a t-shirt?" he asked, sizing up the rest of
me after the distraction of my new hair wore off.

"Because I live literally right there." I pointed to my
entrance. When I saw his car pull up, I'd rushed out in
nothing but an old band t-shirt and leggings. Honestly, he was
lucky I was wearing pants. They were usually the first thing to

go anytime I was alone inside the confines of my small apartment.

"You're going to freeze to death." He placed a hand between my shoulder blades and guided me back to my door.

"The office is that way." I pointed behind me.

"And we'll go once you're properly dressed." He waited for me to open the glass-paned wood door that led to my hallway.

"Bossy," I mumbled, slipping the key into the lock and shoving open the door. It was warped and didn't quite fit into its frame anymore, so I had to really shove it every time.

"It's this one," I said, pointing to the first door on the right. I hadn't bothered locking it, so I nudged it open with one hand and waited for him to go in first. When he didn't, I looked up to find him staring down at me with raised eyebrows.

"Unlocked?" he questioned.

"I was right outside."

He gave his head a small shake and placed a hand on his forehead. "Are you serious right now?"

I sighed and went inside first. "What? It's a safe area."

"Except for the whole stalker-slash-cat-thief situation."

"Right. Except that." I winked and shot him a smile that he didn't reciprocate.

Reid was inside now, standing on my crocheted doormat, scanning my apartment with a slow, deliberate sweep of his head.

"This is the place," I said, when he remained silent.

"This is…wow," was all he said.

I grabbed a sweatshirt that I had abandoned on my yellowy-orangey velvet sofa earlier and pulled it on. "Too eclectic for you?" I guessed.

"It's very…you."

I chose to take that as a compliment, even though Reid didn't know me all that well—and even though it probably wasn't a compliment. What did he know about me, aside from the fact that my life was a mess? That didn't exactly scream "great interior design taste." But whatever. He was right. This place *was* me.

Reid couldn't take his eyes off the massive grandfather clock that separated my kitchen and living room. Technically, it was placed in the middle of what should be an open floor-plan, but I liked it there.

"This has no hands," he pointed out.

I shrugged. "It came that way."

He balked. "But...it's a clock...with no hands. What purpose does it serve?"

"Um, it looks cool?" I offered. "And who uses a clock to tell time anyway?"

His eyebrows shot up. "Plenty of people."

I waved him off. "I inherited a lot of stuff when my grandma moved into assisted living," I explained.

"I can see that." His attention was now trained on a large antique mirror propped up next to the fireplace. I tried to take in the place from his perspective. Knickknacks invaded every inch, taking over any empty space like they'd won a battle. But I liked it that way. It was cozy. Most of all, it reminded me of her and the house I'd grown up in. Maybe some people rejected memories when they lost loved ones, got rid of things instead of hanging onto them because thinking about what was lost was too painful. Not me. The present was what was painful. These reminded me of when times were better. Not necessarily simpler—we'd always been struggling with money, or something or other—but more...full. Gran really knew how to fill up a life.

"You ready?" I asked, once I pulled the sweatshirt over my head. "I'm eighty-two percent sure the office is only occupied until noon."

He took one look at me and said, "Coat."

My eyes rolled to the ceiling, but I walked over and pulled open my front closet, grabbing my puffy blue jacket with one hand and holding the rest of the over-stuffed contents in one place with my other. I pulled hard and the puffer jacket broke free from the cluster.

I slipped it on. "Happy?"

"Thrilled," he deadpanned. "Now, what's the plan? Do you know who works in there?" Reid followed me out of my apartment and into the courtyard—after insisting I lock up, of course.

"I think it rotates, but it's usually this older guy. I've had to pick up a package or two from there before." When we reached the entrance to the small office, I stood on my tiptoes to peer into the window. Reid stole a glance too, before taking me by the arm and pulling me a step away.

"Okay, gameplan." He rubbed his hands together. My brain couldn't help but pause on how adorably into-this he looked. "I'm thinking we lead with the fact that your cat was stolen by a nonresident. Tell them that we've filed a police report and everything. They don't need to know that the police have been zero help. Hopefully, if they think we've got law enforcement involved, they'll give us the footage without asking any follow-up questions or waiting for a formal request." There was a distinct twinkle in his eye. For someone who had resisted the stakeout so hard, he was absolutely eating this up.

"You love this," I said, biting back a smile.

Reid's lips parted before he cleared his throat. "What? Uh, no. I don't know. I guess. I'm used to doing this kind of thing from behind an e-mail address."

"Not as thrilling?" I asked.

"I mean, my heart *is* racing a little."

"As much as the other morning?"

His jaw tensed. "No more stakeouts, Hazel. This is just a simple request, nothing fancy. If we act like it's no big deal and we're expecting him to hand the footage over with zero argument, maybe he'll comply."

"So, nonchalant. Got it."

"Can you do nonchalant?" he asked, eyebrows raised.

"Yes, thank you very much. I was just a little heated the other day."

He smirked down at me and shook his head. A rush of something crept into my chest. He didn't make me feel ashamed for my outburst, not even for a second. While his disapproval was evident, he'd done nothing except make a joke or two. And despite having every reason to be embarrassed, he wasn't. He was still here. Invested. Acting like he cared.

Appreciation overwhelmed me. "Thanks for doing this," I said.

His eyes widened. "Uh, no problem. I want to help."

And I believed him. Which might not seem like a big deal, but in that moment, it felt important.

"You ready?" I asked.

"Let's do it."

I led the way, pushing open the door, Reid right on my tail. The office was only big enough to fit a desk and a rickety wooden bookshelf that looked like it had been assembled without anyone reading the directions in full. A few packages lay forgotten in the corner. A man sat behind the computer, lounging back in his chair, scrolling on his phone. I'd seen him a few times before. He was maybe fifty, with salt and pepper hair. He jerked up when he noticed us and set his phone face down on the desk.

"Hi," I said sweetly, putting on my best charming smile like I was suiting up for battle. "We just had a quick question."

Reid nudged me in the back. *Right, don't ask. Tell.*

"Um, I mean, we just need something. It shouldn't take long."

"What can I help you with?" he asked.

"See, I actually had something of mine stolen recently. From the shared courtyard," I started.

"And we're in the middle of a police investigation," Reid continued. "Her cat was taken from right out front. Thankfully, we noticed you have cameras set up that record the exact place the crime took place."

The man's forehead scrunched as he tipped back in his chair to look out the window. "Stolen? How do you know the cat didn't run away?" he asked.

Man, I was really getting tired of that question.

"Hazel here has received some threatening messages from the person who stole him." Reid placed an arm around my shoulder. I tried to ignore the zing that went through my entire body.

He frowned. "Shoot, I'm sorry about that. I hadn't heard."

"Right—" I squinted to read the name plate on the desk. "Mason. It's awful," I said. "But we need to get the footage from last Thursday morning, around seven a.m."

Eagerness seeped into my voice, I couldn't help it. Mason's wide eyes narrowed slowly as he looked between Reid and me.

"And you said there's a police investigation?" he asked.

"Yep," Reid said.

"Then why aren't they here asking for the footage themselves?"

"They said it would be easier if I came in to ask. But they'd be happy to come down if you need them to." Shit. Did I sound too hopeful? Was he buying this?

Mason eyed us for a second longer before letting out a long sigh, then gave a small shake of his head. I went completely still.

"We really aren't supposed to give that footage out. I could get in trouble with the boss," he said.

"There must be a process for a police investigation. We can give you the report number." Reid had his calm, pleasant voice on. He looked respectable in his glasses and peacoat, the kind of guy you could trust. A stark contrast to me in my ancient puffer jacket with down feathers poking out sporadically, and messy hair I'd forgotten to run a brush through this morning.

"Ah, I'm sorry, man. I'd like to help, but I think the police have to be here in person, or maybe have a warrant or something? I'm not sure. I really can't get written up again."

"It's less than an hour of footage," Reid pressed. "Please. Someone came onto the property and stole something. This is bigger than just one resident."

"My hands are tied." Mason seemed genuinely sorry about the whole thing, but he also wasn't budging.

Pressure had started to build behind my eyes, and I made the split-second decision to lean into it. I let out an exaggerated gasp and flung up my hands to cover my face.

"Hazel?" Reid's voice was thick with alarm.

"It's just s-so hopeless." I inflated the crack in my voice and willed tears to squeeze out of my eyes.

"Oh, honey." Mason's concerned voice came through now.

I forced out another sob. "Vermont is my best friend. He's everything to me." Okay, that was laying it on a little thick, but I did want my fucking cat back. "I thought the cameras would finally get us an answer. We're losing time. It's almost been a week since he was taken."

Mason went silent and I split my fingers, chancing a look at him. He stared at the computer in front of him. He looked uncomfortable—stiff, yet somehow at the same time, ready to bolt. A woman in tears tended to have that effect on men.

"One second," he finally said. Relief coursed through me as he typed a few keys and moved the mouse.

My eyes shot up to Reid's and he narrowed his as if to say, "Play it cool."

"Thank you so much," I whispered, wiping away a tear that had fallen.

It was quiet except for the sound of the keyboard, for what felt like forever. I was suddenly conscious of my whole body and how stiff my muscles were from standing in this musty office. I rocked back and forth on my heels, willing this interaction to be over soon. A small ball of anxiety had formed in my stomach at the thought of seeing what went down that day. Who hated me enough to do this?

"Ah shit," Mason said.

My heart sunk straight to the floor.

"What?" Reid asked, an edge to his tone.

Mason ran a hand over his face and looked up at us apologetically. "It looks like the recordings are only saved for seventy-two hours, and then the drive overwrites itself. The footage isn't here anymore."

"Are you sure?" Reid asked, looking like he was itching to walk behind the desk, shove Mason away from the computer, and check for himself.

"That's what it says."

"Thanks for trying." My words barely made it out.

Disappointment choked me. We were *so* close. I'd thought we'd finally have something solid to take to the police. With real evidence, maybe they'd step up and do something. Or if not, maybe I'd have to confront the person myself. Either way, I thought we'd walk out of here with answers.

"It's okay, Hazel." Gentle hands rubbed my shoulders. I looked up into Reid's warm honey eyes. Or were they almost green? The color seemed to change by the day. "We'll still figure this out."

I appreciated his optimism, but it would take some time before even a spark of it found its way back to me.

"Wait, did you say Hazel?" Mason asked.

"I'm Hazel. Why?"

He shifted in his office chair and rifled through a small stack of papers. "These came to the office, since they didn't have an apartment number." He handed me two envelopes.

I said thanks, and he gave his condolences about my cat, before Reid and I went back outside, our heads hung low. The snow had finally started, soft flakes coming down in scattered increments. Nothing collected on the ground yet. This weather was the perfect excuse to crawl under a blanket and grieve this new loss. Maybe I could get snacks delivered.

Would that be sad? Certainly not financially responsible, but going to the store right now sounded exhausting.

The paper sliced into my index finger as I opened the first letter. "Ouch," I muttered, sucking the drop of blood that formed from the paper cut.

"Careful," Reid said.

"Nothing new." I held up my other hand, currently the home of two Band-Aids from cuts I'd given myself at work. When I returned my attention to the letter, my frown deepened. I tore open the second to find a similar message.

"Crap," I said.

Reid gave me a puzzled look, and I handed him the letters. He adjusted his glasses before scanning them quickly.

"*Don't forget about the money. I know where you live.*" His jaw tensed as his eyes met mine again. "Hazel, these are threats."

"Weak ones," I said. "Whoever this is already has my cat. I don't know why they felt the need to go all Zodiac-killer on me."

He looked at me with clear exasperation. "This is serious."

I shrugged, completely detached from it all.

"If they wanted to hurt me, they would have. This is about one thing. Money. Money that won't even be deposited into my account for a couple more weeks. There's no way whoever did all this is planning to, like, stalk and kill me or something. They probably just watched one to many cheesy thriller movies."

Reid shook his head frantically. "You can't predict what someone like this would do. Clearly they're desperate."

I waved off Reid's concern. I had two clients later today, and if I crawled underneath my covers now, I could squeeze in a good sulk and maybe half a movie before I had to drag myself to the salon.

"It's fine," I said. "So what's next? I've been working on the suspect list like you told me to."

"I really don't like how casual you're being about this," Reid continued, ignoring my question and following me.

"This person is lurking around, watching you, threatening you. I don't like it."

Two lines formed between his brows. I had to admit, his distress was sweet.

"I mean, I'm not a fan of it either, but it is what it is. Too bad the note is typed, or maybe we could have gotten a handwriting expert on the case."

"I don't exactly have one of those on retainer," he said dryly, dragging a hand along his face and looking up. "You shouldn't stay here."

I shrugged. "Well, this is where I live, and I can't exactly afford a hotel room if I have to hand over all of my winnings at the end of this, so…"

"You could stay with me," he offered. "I have an extra bedroom—"

Aa snort escaped me before he could even finish the proposal.

"I'm good, Reid. I appreciate your concern, but no."

He still followed me up the steps instead of making the turn toward the gate that would have led him to his parked car.

"What about another friend you could stay with?" he asked.

"Not really on that level with anyone out here," I said, which was the sad truth. My closest friend was still Zoe, from back where I grew up, and I'd hardly spoken to her in weeks. She didn't even know what was going on with Vermont. I should probably text her.

"I'm being serious. You shouldn't be here alone. Do you know how many cold cases I've looked into where a woman was abducted right from her home, or worse?"

He paused, licking his lips and shaking his head.

Maybe I was being naïve, but the threats truly felt baseless. If this person wanted my money—which I didn't even have yet—why would they come after me now?

"I really think this is just a scare tactic. Don't let it get to you."

He crossed his arms and tilted his head. "I'm not comfortable with you staying here alone."

"Sorry, but I don't have another option." He opened his mouth to protest, but I interrupted. "I'm not going to your house. That would be weird." My stomach flipped just thinking about it. Maybe weird was the wrong word.

"Please, consider it."

"I'm good." Truthfully, I found his offer quite sweet, but I was a creature of comfort. The last thing I wanted to do was pack up my stuff and go to this virtual stranger's house. No matter how cute he looked in his black beanie.

"Hazel." His arms flung up in the air. "I can't in good conscience let you stay here by yourself."

His protective insistence melted my heart a little, but I stayed strong.

"And I'm not going anywhere, so where does that leave us?" I asked.

A single snowflake settled on the frame of his glasses as he closed his eyes in defeat.

TEN

Reid

———

"Slumber party!" Hazel said, as she yanked open her
door with a beaming smile.

When I'd packed my overnight bag, I could hardly believe
what I was about to do. In fact, I'd almost convinced myself I
wouldn't. This was going too far—*way* above and beyond the
call of duty.

After I'd finished work, I'd tried to log on and help the
guys write our next blog post—one about a woman who had
gone missing in Michigan back in the nineties—but those
damn threatening notes kept flashing through my mind.

The thought of her being there alone churned my gut. I
didn't like it. Especially when we hadn't gotten the security
footage and were no closer to deciphering this mystery. And
maybe it had been my imagination, but I swore I detected a
hint of relief in Hazel's voice when I'd called to insist on
spending the night. I'd expected some resistance, but she
almost seemed excited about the prospect of some company.

"I just ordered Chinese, get in here!" she exclaimed, stepping aside so that I could come in and set down my tan
leather duffle.

Hazel's space overwhelmed me the same way it had when I'd been there earlier.

At first, I'd been in shock.

Every inch of space was covered. How was that even possible? There were pictures of various sizes on every wall. I realized now that I could get a closer look that her walls were painted green. Why even bother? Rugs overlapped each other on the ground. Two coffee tables—yes, two—were wedged up right next to each other, so that you could barely step around them to get to the basically neon-orange couch that looked straight out of the sixties.

This place was my nightmare. I itched to bring in bins and help her donate ninety percent of this stuff. I bit my tongue, though. That would be rude. A completely out-of-line suggestion.

"Did you bring your own pillow?" she asked with a laugh.

"It's got just the right neck support," I said. I would have brought my entire bed if I could. My routine was sacred to me. My bed, my things, my space; they put me at ease. The last woman I'd casually dated got frustrated with me because I didn't spend enough time at her house. I could never get a good night's sleep away. Tonight was about to be rough. The couch looked visibly lumpy, and I'd surely be breathing in an unhealthy amount of dust bunnies.

When I'd made the offer, I hadn't really been thinking about myself. All I could focus on was not wanting Hazel to be alone. I wouldn't have been able to forgive myself if something happened to her. But now that I was here, settling into my discomfort, I realized that this was in no way a long-term solution. I hadn't thought about much beyond tonight, but me crashing on her couch for the foreseeable future was *not* going to happen.

Hazel took my duffel and pillow and set them on the floor next to the couch. When I picked up the pillow and set it on top of my duffel, she gave me a strange look.

"Want anything to drink?" she asked, stepping into her

cramped kitchen, a room that dripped top to bottom with cheap laminate and vinyl. "I've got soda or water."

"Water is fine." I edged into the living room, worried something might spring out at me at any moment. Honestly, if it weren't for the threatening messages, I wouldn't have been surprised to find Vermont just hiding amongst the clutter.

She came back in holding two glasses and set them both on one of the coffee tables—all these knickknacks and not a coaster in sight—before sitting back on the couch and pulling out her laptop.

"This is so fun," she said. "I feel like we're about to do some sort of sting operation. Should we work on the case while you're here? What's the plan?"

Despite my discomfort, I couldn't help but smile at her enthusiasm. One of the first things I'd noticed when I'd first met Hazel was the lack of light in her eyes. Since that day at the diner, it had flickered on and off. But now, tonight, she was vibrant and full of life. She'd been dealt a rough hand, and seeing her eyes light up like that made me want to do whatever I could to help her get that spark back.

I pushed aside my unease about the apartment and my looming lack of sleep and sank in next to her on the couch. It was surprisingly not as uncomfortable as it appeared.

"To start, I think we should ask your neighbors."

"I already asked Mrs. Edenbury, and she said she didn't see anything."

"What about the rest of the complex?"

She shrugged. "I haven't met anyone else. I tried knocking on a few doors after it happened, but no one answered. Probably thought I was trying to sell them a magazine subscription or something stupid."

I took my phone out and pulled up an application before entering her zip code.

"I'll make a post on the Neighborhood app. Say your cat was stolen, add a picture, and see if anyone has information."

She nodded. "Okay, yeah. Worth a shot."

I fired off a quick description of the situation (leaving out the extortion part, obviously) and attached a picture of Vermont Hazel had sent me before publishing the post.

"There, we'll see if we get any information."

"Now what?" she asked, shifting in her seat. The loose sweater she wore slipped off her shoulder. I made a conscious effort to keep my eyes off the soft, newly-exposed skin.

"Now, I think it's past time we look into suspect number one," I said.

Her forehead crinkled. "We already ruled out Clinton."

"I meant your ex."

"Why is he suspect number one?" she asked.

"Because it's always the boyfriend," I said, parroting the tagline of many of my group members. We had even thought about using that as the name of our blog, but had worried it might be too insensitive.

Hazel groaned and flopped back into the couch. She wore baggy sweatpants while I was still in jeans. I had overanalyzed what to wear over here, like the dork that I was. While this was miles away from any sort of romantic endeavor, it was still a long time since I'd spent the night at a woman's house. I hadn't wanted to look like a slob. But seeing how comfortable Hazel was made me realize how ridiculously overdressed I was.

"I can't reach out to him," Hazel said. "He has me blocked on everything."

"Which is sketchy," I continued, pulling my own laptop from my backpack and placing it on my lap. "He was following you the day you posted your lottery story. Speaking of which—" I opened up a document that contained a short list of names. "Do you recognize any of these other usernames? I used the login info that you gave me and put this together. They are all people who followed you that day but have since unfollowed you. I figured there could be something fishy about that."

Hazel's eyes scanned the names. "I mean, those two are

just randoms from high school." She gasped when she noticed the third name. "Kiara unfollowed me? That bitch!"

"Does that mean something to you?" My voice went up an octave. Maybe we were on to something.

Hazel still glared at the list. "Just that she's fake and she sucks. I can't believe she'd do that. She always used to have the decency to at least pretend to be civil."

"Who is she?" I demanded, pulling up her profile, which thankfully wasn't private. She had ash-blonde hair and a pouty pose in nearly every picture.

"We went to high school together. She's close with my childhood best friend, Zoe." Hazel leaned over me and pointed to a picture. I could smell the citrus shampoo she must use. "There, that one is Zoe."

"But you two aren't friends?" I guessed.

Hazel snorted. "No. She's always been mean to me. Zoe and I went to middle school together, but Kiara showed up in high school. She's a classic mean girl, but Zoe could never see it. Either that, or she just only directed that energy at me." Hazel let out a defeated sigh. "She just moved to this side of the state, and Zoe keeps asking if the two of us are going to hang out. I didn't want to, but I invited Kiara over for a trashy movie night a few weeks ago. She said she was coming and everything, then just didn't show up. She hates me."

"So she knows where you live."

Hazel met my eyes and shook her head. "You think Kiara could have stolen Vermont? No way. She might be mean, but she isn't sadistic."

"We can't rule anyone out. She's in the area, doesn't like you, and for whatever reason, unfollowed you right after you posted about winning the lottery." I held up a finger each time I made a point. Hazel reached over and put her hand around my fingers, forcing them closed.

"I get what you're saying, but I'm telling you. There's no way. That girl does not think about me enough to do something like this. I barely register as a person to her." She frowned. "I hate to say it, but I guess we probably should start with Paul."

My blood heated at the name. "Paul? Is that the ex?"

"The one and only," she said with a drawn-out sigh.

"Didn't end on great terms?" I asked, doing my best to keep the curiosity out of my voice. It was strictly for the investigation. I had no personal interest in her romantic history.

"Not really." She grimaced and sipped her water before setting it back down. "He did *not* want to break up. But we fought, like, all the time. I'm still annoyed with myself that it took me so long to end it."

"And you think he could do this?"

She looked at the wall for a moment before nodding. "I mean, maybe? We only broke up six months ago. I actually moved out here with him a couple of years ago, from metro Detroit. We went to high school together but didn't start dating until we were twenty-two."

I pulled up his profile on my phone. Once again, it wasn't private. Did anyone care about security in this day and age?

"I can see what you saw in him." I flashed her my phone, which had one of his hundreds of shirtless gym pictures pulled up.

"Oh, God." She giggled and covered her face. "Don't judge me. In my defense, we did have fun together."

I scrolled down and pulled up another picture of him, a friend who had a very similar meathead demeanor, and Hazel —all smiling at the camera. I looked at the date. Three months ago.

"I thought you broke up six months ago?" I asked, cringing at the next picture of a flexed bicep, veins bulging. There was no way this guy was natural. He looked like a walking advertisement for steroids. Hazel had really dated this guy? I mean, I hadn't spent too much time considering her ex-boyfriend, but this wasn't what I had been expecting. Maybe a class clown type. Someone goofy, who didn't take life too seriously. Not *this* guy.

Her lip curled up. "Again, don't judge me. A clean break is hard after being with someone for so long. Paul invited me to his friend Callum's house party, and I was bored and alone on a Saturday night."

I made a mental note to invite Hazel along on any future weekend plans, even though my own social roster was virtually blank.

"Why'd you break up?" I asked.

She sat forward, tugging the throw pillow from behind her back and placing it in her lap. "He was a touch on the manipulative side, although I didn't realize it for a while, and *very* codependent. As someone who spent a lot of time alone or being ignored by guys all through high school, it was kind of nice, at first." Her admission made my heart sink. I couldn't imagine ignoring someone like Hazel. She was larger than life.

"Anyway, the honeymoon period was short-lived, but it was my first serious relationship. I didn't know any better. When we started to fight constantly, I thought it was just normal growing pains." She sucked in a breath before continuing. "When Gran got sick a couple of years ago, she wanted to come out here, be closer to Lake Michigan. She always liked how rural it was. We found her a nice assisted-living place—way out of budget, but I made do. Paul came with me, I didn't even have to ask him to. And despite all our fighting, it was nice to have his support. My grandma is—" The word caught in her throat, and I fought the urge to reach out and touch her arm. "*Was* my only family. It had always been just the two of us. Paul made me feel less lonely. But he hated when I went out without him, or tried to make friends, so my world was basically only him."

That made my blood simmer. I loathed guys like that. A classic emotional manipulator. I had read about enough of them while doing my little armchair investigations. Hazel didn't deserve that. She walked through life in a way I'd never be confident enough to do. To think about someone trying to rein her in made me physically ill.

My throat burned with follow-up questions. Was high school hard for her? What had she and Paul fought about? What was her grandma like? Why was she Hazel's only family? But none of those were related to the investigation at hand. I could see the hurt etched on Hazel's face, so I propelled forward instead.

"And Paul knows where you live now?" I asked.

She nodded. "He's been here before, too. Used to show up drunk every so often and throw shit at my window to get my attention."

My spine stiffened. "What? Hazel, are you serious?"

She rolled her eyes as if my concern was over the top. "He hasn't shown up in months, okay?"

I let out a sigh. "Okay, but I still hate that. You definitely can't be here by yourself."

She waved off my very valid point. "Like I said, this was months ago. When we first broke up. I haven't seen him since the night of that party you found a picture of." She chewed on her lip. "Aside from my grandma's funeral, that is. I reached out to him. I felt guilty not inviting him, since he'd always been so good to her." She shook her head. "It was a mistake. He tried to use my grief and vulnerability against me. Made a pathetic attempt to try and get me to go home with him. I got mad and told him to leave. He blocked me after that. I should never have invited him, I know that. But I-I really didn't want to be alone that day." The last words came out in a choked whisper.

My heart plummeted to the ground. "Were you alone?"

She offered me an encouraging smile that didn't bring me much comfort. "Some of her friends came. Back from Detroit, and from the nursing home. An old neighbor was there, too. I hadn't really told anyone else, though."

"What about your friend. Zoe?"

"She was out of town when it happened." Her voice was quiet. I hardly recognized it. This time I didn't resist the urge to reach out and squeeze her shoulder.

"You were close to your grandma, then?" I asked after a minute. It seemed like a stupidly obvious question. Vermont had been her grandmother's, and she was clearly distraught about losing him. I barely knew my grandparents myself, so it was hard for me to picture. My dad's parents had passed away when I was still young, and my mom's lived in Arizona. They sent cards with checks every birthday, and had last visited half a decade ago. Nice people, but not family-oriented. Likely why my mom had always been desperate for a close family of her own.

"She raised me," Hazel said, further spearing my chest. "My mom…she was never in the picture. Not really."

Shit. I felt like an ass for taking this long to ask her more about herself.

"And your dad?" I asked.

"Not even sure who he is." She shrugged like that was fine. Like that answer had no effect on her. I ached to ask her more, but the way she brushed off the question made me feel like I had no right to. Like I had to earn that piece of her.

A loud buzzing from the door saved us both from the silence and Hazel sprang to her feet. She stepped over a book that lay face down on the carpet and pressed a button before yanking open her front door. After a few seconds, a teenage boy materialized and handed her a plastic bag that looked like it must weigh close to twenty pounds. She passed him some cash before shutting the door with her foot and holding up the bounty. "Hope you're hungry."

She set the food down on one of the coffee tables and started taking out each box.

"Want me to get plates?" I offered, poised to stand.

"Don't worry about it." She tossed me chopsticks.

"An army couldn't finish all this food," I said, eyeing everything.

"I like leftovers," she said. "Help yourself. There's sesame tofu, Mongolian beef, orange chicken, fried rice—I basically got one of everything, because I didn't know what you liked."

"Looks good," I said, taking one of the containers and eyeing it. I desperately longed for an actual plate to scoop my portion onto. Were we really about to dive into the same boxes with our utensils? Seemed oddly intimate. Part of me wanted to ask if she had a clean bill of health, but I stuffed the question down deep inside. Ruby and Regan were always telling me I was too uptight. I *could* eat Chinese food out of a shared carton, damnit.

I could.

Hazel took a couple of big bites of fried rice before handing me the box. "Rice?" she asked.

I forced myself not to wince. "I'm good with this," I said, clutching the beef close to my chest. Maybe she wouldn't call me out if I only ate from the one container.

"What's the plan for Paul?" she asked, continuing to migrate from box to box as she sat cross-legged on the floor, back pressed against the bottom of the couch.

I chewed my last bite and swallowed before setting down the beef. "Are you familiar with catfishing?"

"Um, considering it's the twenty-first century and I don't live under a rock, duh," she said.

This time when Hazel offered me the box that contained the orange chicken she'd just had a bite of, I took it.

"That's the plan. We catfish him."

She clapped her hands. "Like we get to make a fake profile? How fun! I call picking the pictures."

I chuckled at her eagerness. "It's a lot more complicated than that. You need to have followers, build a presence. A random account with nothing to it looks suspicious."

"Um, spoiler alert, Reid. Paul isn't the smartest person in *any* room. We do not have to put in that much effort."

Her throwing that dig at her ex made my chest swell. "Even still. Better not to raise any eyebrows." I set down the box and wiped my hand on a brown napkin that had come in the bag. I took my phone and opened a profile before handing Hazel the phone. She squinted her eyes and scrolled.

"AngelineRox? Who is this?"

"The girl that's about to slide into Paul's DMs."

"This profile is fake? It looks real. There are so many pictures."

"We've used it before. We actually made a few fake accounts for this exact purpose."

"Who's the girl?" she asked.

"Somone in the group's cousin. We got permission to use her likeness. And this account is perfect because she has a few pictures with cats."

Hazel eyed me, clearly not following. "So…"

"So, we message Paul. Try to be all flirty. If he takes the bait, we can work in that we have a cat and see if he says anything. If he's as dumb as you say he is, maybe he'll cave and use a picture of Vermont."

Her eyes widened. "Shit, that's kind of genius. Paul would completely fall for something like that. The only problem is that there is, like, a seventy-five-percent chance we get an unsolicited dick pick."

That made me snort. "Don't worry, I'll field any incoming messages."

"You shouldn't have to subject yourself to that. Unfortunately for me, I've already seen it numerous times, so it won't be as scarring."

My jaw ticked. Obviously she had seen her ex-boyfriend naked, but I didn't like hearing her talk about it.

I took my phone back and hit the "follow" button for Paul's account. Then I popped over to an app I had for generic stock images and picked a random one of a cat sitting on a sofa that looked like the one from some of her other pictures. I added it to the AngelineRox profile stories, then went back to Paul's profile and hit "message."

"Alright. What should our opening line be?" I asked.

"Tell him he looks unreal in his last gym selfie. He eats that shit up." Hazel rolled her eyes as I typed out the message and sent it. I added a wink emoji for full effect.

"Nice touch," she said with a smile. "Now what?"

"Now we wait and hope he answers." Before closing out of the app, I went back to her friend-of-a-friend's profile. Kiara. "You sure there's nothing here? I think we at least need to look into this girl."

Hazel bit her lip. Self-consciousness practically glimmered in her eyes. "I guess I can broach the subject of hanging out again. Or potentially use Zoe as a buffer." She said it like the idea was the most painful thing she could think of. "If we were in the same room, maybe I could get a read on her."

"Good." I looked at her expectantly while she shoved a crab rangoon into her mouth, a crumb falling onto her sweater.

"Time is of the essence," I pushed.

She looked to the ceiling before wiping her hand on her pants and firing off a quick message on her phone. "There, sent her a text. Don't hold your breath, though. Even if she isn't the culprit, the chances of her responding to me are still low."

"Worth a shot," I said. "We can think of something else if she doesn't end up answering."

And then what?

I was in over my head here. My ideas were limited. I loved combing through details of an old case, obsessing over theories and doing internet sleuthing. But when the stakes were live? When there was hardly anything available to go on? This wasn't what I was used to at all. I probably should have done a better job of setting Hazel's expectations. I couldn't stand the idea of letting her down.

"I've got my friends working on it, too," I said, wanting to offer her something else. "Obviously we don't have much to go on, but if they think of anything they'll let me know."

"This is your crime fighting group?" she clarified. "The one you do the blog with?"

"Those are the ones," I said, cringing at how lame "crime fighting group" sounded.

"How does one get involved with something like that?" Hazel asked.

"One spends about fifty hours too many on a cold case thread and gets on a first name basis with other commenters."

"That's fun," she said, without even a hint of sarcasm. "Good idea for meeting people."

I straightened up. "Will you tell my family that? They just think I'm pathetic for spending so much time online."

"Any time you spend doing something you love with people you like isn't wasted. Besides, you're even helping people. It's honorable."

My chest warmed at her words. It was exactly how I felt.

Hazel picked up the remote and switched on the TV. "Down for a movie? I could use a break from thinking about all this stuff."

"Whatever you want." I scootched over on the couch so she could join me.

She pressed play on an old romcom I'd seen at least a dozen times. It was one of Ruby and Regan's favorites.

"Is this okay?" she asked. "Paul used to hate this movie."

I waved off her comment. "I have two sisters. I can probably quote this movie better than you can."

That got a smile out of her—a real one, genuine and unguarded. Since the day I'd met Hazel, I'd sensed that the truest parts of her were buried beneath a quiet sadness. She still shone through; her spirit wasn't something that could be easily extinguished. But there was always a part of her that held back, like she was moving through the world slightly numb.

"You seem close with your family. Ruby talks about you all a lot," she said while the opening credits played.

"We're kind of obnoxiously close," I said. "No boundaries, or personal space."

"That sounds nice."

I chuckled. "Nice, suffocating, some days it's hard to tell the difference."

She laughed. "They sound sweet."

"I guess. They've just been extra in my business lately. They worry about me." My eyes met hers before drifting away. It would be easier to put this fact out there, get it over with. "I-I got divorced last year and I think they think I'm struggling to move on or something."

"Oh," she said casually, but I could see the subtle shift in her expression. Mentally calculating my age. I was only twenty-nine, and some people were surprised I already carried the title of divorcé. "Are you? Struggling to move on, I mean."

"We were together since college, it's a long story," I explained, hoping to wrap this up quickly. "Well, I guess, not really. Long relationship, short marriage. Probably should have realized we had issues before walking down the aisle. Whatever. Despite what my family thinks, I really am over it."

She nodded, her lips parting but no sound coming out. She probably wanted to ask about the details. What happened? What was she like? I didn't really like to talk about it. I worried it didn't paint me in the best light, since, after all, she had dumped me. For whatever reason, I didn't want Hazel to think I was damaged goods.

"You don't have any siblings, right?" I asked, shifting the focus back to her. Guilt seeped in for continuing to prod into her personal life without really sharing much of mine.

"Just me and Gran," she said matter-of-factly. I wanted more. I wanted to know about her dynamic. She'd mentioned a few times that her grandmother was her only family, but never why.

She eyed me, and as if reading my mind, said, "You're curious about my parents."

"I didn't say that," I said quickly.

"You didn't have to." She sat up straighter, tucking her legs underneath her. "It's alright, everyone is always curious. My mom was a bit of an alcoholic—I think, at least. I practically had to drag details out of Gran. She ended up getting pregnant with me a few months before she turned thirty, with no idea who the father was. She was still living with my grandma at the time. Gran had always been there for her, tried to support her, but when I came around, things changed. At least, that's what she always told me. Suddenly there was a new baby in her life, and she couldn't make as many excuses for her daughter anymore. They had no money, and once I came along, there was even less. My grandma was determined to break the cycle. She wanted better for me. I guess my mom liked partying more than the idea of being a parent. She left me with Gran when I was just a baby."

"We don't have to talk about this," I said, feeling awful I'd even asked. I had no idea Hazel had been through all that. Her story made me want to tuck her into my side and keep her safe.

"No, it's okay." A ghost of a smile haunted her face. "It's nice to talk about her. Maybe not so much the other stuff, but it's been weeks since someone has asked me anything about Gran."

I felt a little stab in my chest then. The pain was all over her face. She wasn't just dealing with losing a pet or being extorted. She was dealing with the loss of the most important person in her life.

"So your mom was never in the picture?" I asked hesitantly.

"No. She died when I was only three. I don't really know all the details. Something with a car accident. Gran never wanted to talk about it. We never talked about her much at all."

"Shit, Hazel. I had no idea." I sat up, eyes locked on hers. "I can't even imagine."

Even though she was looking at me, she had a far-off look in her eyes and I wished I could reach out and hold her.

"It's strange...sometimes I wonder if I remember my mother at all. I have this hazy memory of her coming by one time and taking me to get a donut. I think it was winter. I was all bundled up and excited because we never got treats like that. But at this point, it's hard to remember if it's real or if it's just something Gran had mentioned to me once."

"That must be hard. To never know your mom." This time I did reach out and squeeze her arm. I had to do something. I felt like a heel for not having anything insightful to say about the situation, but I had nothing to offer her. No wise words. I'd grown up in a stable household, overflowing with love. Any words of empathy out of me would sound fake.

"It was harder when I was younger. Gran always did her best to make it feel like we were a complete family, but the stigma stuck to me. People would whisper about it at school. I was the girl being raised by my grandma, as if that was something to be ashamed of."

We sat in silence for a minute, the movie playing forgotten in the background.

"Your grandma sounds like an amazing woman," I finally said.

She smiled. "Oh, she was. She was kind of a tough woman, but she had a good heart. She'd spend all Friday night out at a poker game, then knit me a sweater the next morning."

"A true woman of the world."

She laughed melodically. "Exactly."

"Are you…are you okay?" I asked. What a stupid question. Of course she wasn't okay. I wanted to hit myself.

Her eyes narrowed as she looked from the TV back to me. "With how I grew up, or…?"

"Without your grandma," I clarified. "When you mentioned she passed, I hadn't realized how close you two were."

She nodded, eyes glassy. "I'm doing better now. She'd been sick for a while, so theoretically I should have been preparing myself for it. She smoked and drank my entire life. She was never the picture of health. But she was still so vibrant. The day before it happened, I was at her place having lunch. We had plans for that weekend…" Her voice trailed off, causing my chest to squeeze tightly. Fuck, I wanted to hug her.

"Preparing for something hard usually doesn't make it hurt less when it happens," I said.

Hazel gave me a small smile. "The part that was the hardest was just how mundane it all was. A few sympathetic frowns from the nurses, and then it was straight to filling out some paperwork. People get old, they pass away. Once you reach a certain age, no one even asks why. It's just life. But for me, it was like losing everything.

"Anyway, that's why Vermont is so important to me. Obviously I love him, and I'd want him back regardless, but he was really her baby. She got him from the rescue a few years ago and he was her companion. By her side right until the end." She nearly choked on the last word, that far-off look back in her eyes. "Which is why I need him back, under any circumstances. Ideally, not by paying for him, though. That money might not seem like a lot to you—"

"It's a lot of money," I said gently. I did okay for myself now, but I grew up securely lower-middle class. My parents stretched each paycheck as best as they could. I understood what money could mean for someone.

"It is. I'm…" she bit her lip. "I'm not in a great place right now. I have so much credit card debt, and—"

That snapped me out of my trance. "Hazel," I scolded. "How could you let yourself rack up credit card debt? That's the biggest scam there is."

"I know, I know. But it wasn't like I did it on purpose. It wasn't like I woke up one day and thought, you know what, I'll go on a shopping spree and charge it all to the Visa. I wasn't in a good place, Reid. My grandma's assisted living home was more than I could afford, but I wasn't about to ask her to move. Her comfort was the most important thing. And it's just my luck that as soon as the luckiest thing in the world happened to me, the unluckiest thing would too."

"I get it," I said, still mentally reeling about the credit card debt, but biting my tongue. If she'd needed to do it, she'd needed to do it. Who the hell was I to judge? All I could do now was help her.

I could tell Hazel had had enough of the heavy talk, as she nestled back into the couch.

We managed to refocus on the movie, for about two minutes. Then Hazel went off about how ridiculously the main character was acting, and just like that, we were back to chatting.

We stuck to lighthearted stuff this time. We talked right through the rest of the film as we finished off an absurd amount of Chinese food. Joking about how unbelievable it was that the heroine gave the first guy a chance. Laughing at the terrible wigs. I even quoted a few of my favorite lines.

Eventually, Hazel's breathing deepened, and a weight shifted onto my shoulder. She'd fallen asleep with her legs curled up at her side, leaning into me.

It was incredibly uncomfortable, yet I had absolutely no desire to move. My eyelids drooped with heaviness. I took off my glasses and set them on a coffee table, allowing myself to slowly drift off as the familiar movie played in the background. Hazel was cuddled into my side, warm and close, and I let sleep start to pull me under.

ELEVEN

Hazel

REID HAD TO BE GONE. THERE WAS NO WAY HE'D STUCK around after last night.

I'd overshared, my apartment was a disaster, and to top it off, I'd fallen asleep on the couch, practically draped across his personal space. But when I opened my bedroom door, there he was, bent over in the kitchen, rummaging through cabinets like he belonged there.

"Oh, good morning. Where are your mugs?" he asked when he caught sight of me.

I flattened my hair, currently thrown half-up into a loose bun, my bangs squished flat against the sides of my forehead. He looked perfect, already changed and somehow polished despite the early hour.

"In there." I pointed to the large black buffet underneath the window in the kitchen. Reid slid open one of the doors, then his eyebrows shot up and he looked over at me.

"No person would ever need to own this many mugs." He picked up one at the front. It had a worn mountain range on it, with the words "Rise and Shine" along the bottom.

"We used to collect them," I said, taking the hot pink mug he handed me before he closed the cabinet.

"Did you also collect *everything* else?" he asked, gesturing to my apartment, basically bursting at the seams.

I just shrugged. "She loved a thrift store. I don't want to get rid of any of it."

His entire expression softened at that.

"I made coffee." He pulled out the carafe, which was also basically an antique. I think my grandma bought it in the eighties, and somehow, it still worked. She always swore they used to build appliances better—sturdier and made to last. Unlike now, when every company just slapped together some cheap plastic and hoped you'd have to buy another one every other year.

"Do you need milk or anything?" he asked.

"I think I have some hazelnut creamer in the fridge."

Reid filled up my mug and opened my refrigerator. He visibly cringed when he took in the sparse contents—half an onion on one shelf, and a door full of condiments.

He found the white bottle and set it on the counter. I added a splash before bringing my mug to my lips and taking an appreciative sip. The ordinariness of it all brought on a rush of nostalgia. Gran and I used to sit down with a cup of coffee together most mornings until I moved out at twenty-two. Even after that, we would meet for breakfast pretty frequently. Bad diner coffee was her favorite. "The burnter the better," she'd always say.

"Look who responded." Reid held out his phone. My heart hammered in my chest as I grabbed it.

The catfish profile. I'd almost forgotten.

"What did he say?" I asked, even as I scanned the messages between Paul and the fake account.

Paul: *"Hey babe, glad you like what you see."*

Barf.

AngelineRox: *blushing emoji. "Do you like what you see?"*

I looked up and raised an eyebrow at Reid. "You wrote this?"

His eyes narrowed. "Don't judge me. I've had practice."

That made me laugh as I continued to scan through the messages. Just a short, flirty convo. Nothing of substance, but also no damning evidence against him. The last text was a picture of the girl cuddled up with a cat to which he just said "Cutie" in response.

"He didn't take the bait," I said with a frown.

"Yet," Reid added. "Let's give it a couple days."

"Would this be a bad time to point out that I know his address?" I handed his phone back and Reid tipped his head back and groaned.

"No more stakeouts, Hazel."

I held up my hands. "Not a stakeout. Just a quick peep through a window, you know, see if we see anything."

"And get caught trespassing."

I shrugged. "It's an apartment building in a busy area. We could just be walking by. Plus we follow him on socials now." I pointed to his phone. "That man cannot go to the gym without telling the world about it, trust me. We could sneak over the next time we know he's gone and just have a quick snoop."

Reid chewed his lip as if considering it.

"Maybe," he finally relented. "But only as a last resort."

"Yes!" I pumped the fist not holding my coffee. Some splashed onto the floor anyway, and I swiped my sock-covered foot over it to clean it up. When I met Reid's eyes again, his chin had dipped as he looked at me over the frames of his glasses, the judgement clear in his gaze.

"What? Like I'm going to break out a mop for a spill that tiny?"

He said nothing in return, but I could see the disapproval written all over his face. I didn't mind, though. There was something about the non-subtle way that he judged me that made me feel weirdly not judged at all. Accepted, almost.

We squeezed around the small table tucked against the kitchen wall, cradling our coffee cups as we tossed around more ideas, trying to piece together a plan for what to do next.

Reid was very against anything that involved illegal trespassing. *Boring.* I couldn't say that I agreed, but I had to admit it hadn't gone well for us the first time.

He was hung up on finding more suspects, but I had tried to explain to him that my world wasn't all that big. Sure, I overshared on social media, but I really didn't think I had droves of people willing to track me down, steal my cat, and go through with this elaborate blackmailing scheme.

"Shit! It's almost eight," I said, when I caught a glimpse of the stove. You could barely read the numbers because the light on the clock was so dim. "I've got to go. My first client is in thirty minutes."

He balked at me. "Thirty minutes? You should already be there."

I rolled my eyes. "But then I'd miss out on my morning with you."

Reid bit back a smile. "I have to get home and log into work."

"What do you do, again?" I asked as he started collecting his stuff and I made my way back to the bedroom.

"IT for a bank," he said.

I laughed, as I partially closed my bedroom door so I could take off my pajamas and throw on an all-black outfit. "You couldn't make that sound drier if you tried," I called out.

"It's remote, pays well, and is incredibly flexible. Plus, I like it. It's basically just solving tech issues all day."

I ran a brush through my hair and put on exactly one coat of mascara before returning to the living room.

"Sounds like the perfect job for you," I said.

He shrugged. "It kind of is."

He already had his duffel shrugged onto his shoulder.

"So," he started.

"So," I said.

"You planning on staying here tonight?"

I laughed. "I *do* live here."

He rubbed his face with both hands, sliding his hands underneath his glasses. "You really can't go to a friend's? Or anywhere else?"

I thought about my very limited social roster. Jackson was cool, but also kind of…a lot. Plus we worked together. Sharing a space could be awkward. What if I pissed him off, and then we still had to see each other every day? The same went for Natalie and Ruby. Our friendships were still new, hovering in that awkward space between coworker and acquaintance.

"I *should* offer to stay another night," Reid continued. "And I don't want to be difficult, but it's really hard for me to be away from home and break up my routine. I hardly got any sleep last night."

That stirred a mix of guilt and irritation in me. "I didn't ask you to stay here. I promise you, I'll be fine."

I walked to my front door and Reid trailed behind me. This topic had run its course. His attempt at chivalry was sweet, and even though I'd kind of enjoyed our sleepover, I was a grown woman. I didn't need him. I'd be fine staying here by myself.

"I also won't get any sleep if I know you're here alone," he said with a sigh.

"Can't help you there, champ." I held open the door as he shuffled past me.

I closed it behind him and locked the door right as Mrs. Edenbury was about to walk into her own apartment.

"Morning," I said cheerily. She looked a little surprised to see us, jumping before carefully closing the door she'd just unlocked, keeping her back to it.

"Morning, sweetie. How are you doing?" She eyed Reid up and down with raised eyebrows.

"I'm hanging in there," I said.

"And who's this young man?"

"Reid," he said, holding out his—quite large—hand. I hadn't realized the size until it engulfed hers.

"I like your sweater," Reid said to her, noting the black crewneck with a variety of kittens embroidered across the chest.

"Oh, this old thing. Thank you." She smiled, looking down at it.

"We should really do tea sometime this week," I said.

"Only if we do it at your place, mine is a mess," she replied.

"Sounds good."

"And before I forget…" Her words trailed off as she rummaged around in her red leather bag. "This got delivered to my mailbox by mistake." She handed me a letter with no return address.

Reid and I shared a look. It was the same envelope as the notes from yesterday. It had to be another letter from the blackmailer.

Great.

"Thanks for this," I said, holding it up. "I'll see you later."

She nodded and waved goodbye before slipping into her apartment.

Reid opened the door to outside and held it open for me. I ducked under his arm, my body brushing against his as I stepped outside.

When we were at our cars, mine parked behind his on the street, he whirled around, glancing toward the building and then back at me.

"Well, that was suspicious as hell," he said.

My mind snapped to high alert, but Reid's words blurred. I had zero clue what he was talking about. "What was suspicious?"

"Are you serious?" he looked flabbergasted. "That neighbor of yours."

"Mrs. Edenbury?"

"Ms. Cat Lady herself? Yes! And she lives right across

from you. Talk about opportunity. What does that letter say that she just handed you? Bet it's something threatening."

"You're reaching, dude. She's frail. Plus, the sweetest person alive."

"Does she know you won the lottery?"

I paused. She had been one of the first people I'd told. I'd run into her the next morning, and she'd asked me about my grandmother's funeral. I'd told her about the winning lottery ticket, and she'd rejoiced with me.

"So what if she does? That doesn't prove anything."

I opened the envelope to reveal exactly what we thought we'd find. A typed note that said, *you only have two more weeks.* Reid arched an eyebrow and gave me an "I told you so" look.

"This proves nothing." I stuffed the note into my bag. "In fact, it's further proof of her innocence. Why would she just hand it to me? That's so obvious. If it was really her, she'd keep putting them at the front office, or mail them, or something. And she obviously knows my apartment number."

"Is she really all there?"

I bit my lip. She *was* quite forgetful. There was that time a couple months ago, where I'd run to the grocery store to grab her some sugar. When I'd knocked on her door to deliver it, she'd forgotten she'd even asked me.

Could someone like that even pull off stealing a cat?

"It wasn't her," I insisted.

He held up his hand, raising a finger with each point. "She has means. If she has all these cats, it's not like taking care of one more would be that hard. Opportunity. She would have been right here when you ran inside that day, making Vermont an easy grab for her. And she has motive, if she knew you won the lottery…" he trailed off.

"She might not even need the money. I don't know her situation."

"I mean, she lives here. She can't be loaded."

"Hey!" I exclaimed, swatting him in the chest with the note I still held. "*I* live here."

"What, no offense." He held up his hands. "I'm just saying, clearly she isn't rolling in disposable income."

I couldn't be upset with him for stating the obvious. This apartment complex was one of the cheapest in the area, complete with small units, chipped paint, outdated appliances—the works.

My eyes swept back to the building. "You really think it could be her?"

"I think we'd be crazy not to look into it." His tone was gentle. As much as I still found the idea incredibly unlikely, I relented. It couldn't hurt to look into every possibility.

"Alright," I said with a sigh, hating the idea that the only person in my building who'd shown me kindness could be the culprit. "You're the sleuth. We can look into her. Any idea where to start?"

"I'll think of something." He walked around to his car and opened the driver's side door before sliding into his seat in one smooth motion. He rolled the window down and added, "Whatever you do, don't break into her apartment without me."

A smile crept onto my face. "You have no faith in me," I called out as he drove away.

TWELVE

Hazel

Jackson greeted me with a loud groan and a tsking sound. "You have to *style* it, Hazel."

I tried to push past him but he was already falling into step with me, taking his round brush and attempting to fluff out my bangs.

"I told you when you were cutting it that I would never style it."

"I thought maybe you'd have some self-respect and change your mind once you saw my masterpiece. Have you no decency? You're a stylist, for crying out loud. No one will want to work with you if you show up a hot mess."

Natalie stepped away from her station, grabbed Jackson's wrist and yanked it away from my mane. Then she pulled me away from his onslaught, toward the back of the salon.

"Ignore Jackson, he's in a mood this morning," she said.

"When is he not in a mood?" I muttered, flipping my bangs back out of my eyes.

"You all would be a lot more productive at your own stations," Miranda called from the front, shooting us a disapproving glance. She hated when we lingered, our conversation increasing in volume as we got more animated. But she also never did anything about it. Not really.

"How are you?" Natalie whispered, appeasing Miranda by taking half a step backward toward her own station. I set down my bag and checked the time. My client was a few minutes late, but she'd texted to say that'd be the case.

"I'm fine. Getting by."

She jutted out her bottom lip. "Any updates?"

Jackson caught up to us, making a move to stick his brush back in my hair, but I jerked away.

"Not really," I said, giving him a warning glare. "But we're working on a few suspects."

"No word on how the little guy is doing?" Jackson asked, finally dropping his hands and leaving my hair alone.

"Nope." I'd asked for another proof of life picture this morning but hadn't received a response yet.

"What a monster," Jackson said, as he plugged in a curling iron.

I shot him a warning look. "Don't even think about coming near me with that thing. My client will be here any second."

"All the more reason to look presentable."

I rolled my eyes, but a few seconds later when the tool heated up, I let him curl my front pieces. Resisting him was futile at this point.

Once my first client came in, it was easy to tune out the noise in my head for an hour while I worked on her cut. It felt good to get lost in the art of getting someone's hair just right. An added bonus was that this client in particular was a talker. All I had to do was nod, lend a sympathetic ear, and ask her, "What's new," and she filled the silence with ease. It was refreshing to hear about someone else's troubles and pretend like my own didn't exist for a little while.

Most of my clients were loyal ones. They'd followed me even though I'd been at three different salons in the past two years. Some might say that the changes made me look flighty or unprofessional, but my clients still sought me out every time. I chose to take that as a sign I did a halfway decent job. And hopefully this salon stuck. Even though I'd only been here a few months, something about it made me want to stay. I was comfortable here. I could be myself.

After three clients back to back, I plopped down in my chair and took a sip of the beverage Jackson had picked up for me earlier. I winced. Matcha? I'd told him a dozen times it wasn't my cup of tea—literally—but he maintained I just hadn't had a good one yet. I braced myself for the second sip, but it wasn't that bad. Was that vanilla syrup?

"Hey, Hazel," a soft voice drifted behind me.

I turned to find Ruby standing there, shifting back and forth in her bright white tennis shoes.

"Oh, hey." I smiled at her. "I didn't think you were coming in today."

"I had a last-minute request this afternoon." She chewed on her lip, and I stared at her, waiting for her to say something. It wasn't like Ruby to be so quiet.

"Did you need something?" I asked.

Jackson, stopped talking, the highlight brush in his right hand poised above his client's hair. He didn't need to glance in our direction for me to know he was eavesdropping.

Ruby tipped her head back and groaned. "See, I told him this would be forced and awkward."

My shoulders tensed. "What would be forced and awkward?"

"Me, bringing this up." She let out a huff. "It's Reid. He asked me to talk to you," she said.

Now my whole body stiffened. Reid asked Ruby to talk to me? "This isn't about the apartment thing, is it?" I asked, already knowing it likely was.

She nodded and winced. "He wanted me to tell you that he truly isn't a creep, and that his town house is huge. His guest bedroom is basically like a hotel. It wouldn't be weird at all—I swear, this is all him making me tell you this. I'm not trying to pressure you into staying there."

The part about him *not* being a creep made me smile. As if I needed Ruby's seal of approval to know that. The way we'd spent last night watching romcoms and eating takeout—without him making even the slightest move—was all the proof I needed. I already trusted Reid more than any other man in my life right now. Not a challenging feat to accomplish, but still.

"I told him I'm fine. I can't believe he bugged you to talk to me."

She twisted a long lock of blonde hair between her fingers. It was hard not to be caught off guard by how pretty Ruby was. She certainly wasn't ever on the receiving end of any of Jackson's lectures about *looking presentable.*

"He told me about the letters," she admitted.

"What letters?" Jackson asked. His client, a woman somewhere north of fifty, peered out from behind her layers of hair. *Great.* Guess I was in charge of entertainment at the salon today.

"Threatening ones," Ruby continued, completely comfortable airing my business for everyone to hear. "From the guy who's blackmailing Hazel. They've been sending them to her apartment."

"Or woman," I muttered, although I had a hard time believing there was any weight to Reid's theories that Kiara or Mrs. Edenbury could be suspects. "But again, this person has been so sloppy, there's no way I'm in actual danger."

"Reid said he even stopped by the police station this morning to see if the letters would add anything to your case. They added it to the report, but they said without substantial proof of a credible threat, they couldn't do anything."

My jaw dropped. "He went to the police?"

She shrugged. "I think he feels a little helpless. He loves a mystery, and he loves helping, but he doesn't love that this one isn't the easiest to crack. Also, he hates the idea that you could be in danger."

Ugh, Reid. Why did he have to be so freaking sweet?

"I'm fine. And it's not really his fault we aren't making much progress. There's basically nothing to go on."

"You can stay with me," Jackson offered.

"Um…that's nice of you," I said after a pause, racking my brain for how to turn him down politely.

"It's only a studio, and I'm not giving up the right to have guys over, but the couch is yours if you want it."

"Oh wow, that's generous," I said gnawing on my lip. I would absolutely *not* be crashing on Jackson's couch.

"You really shouldn't stay at your house if you've got a stalker," his client chimed in. "A girlfriend of mine had the same thing happen—threatening letters, the sicko even sent flowers. She brushed it off too, until one day he finally broke in."

Jackson gasped. "What happened?"

"Thankfully she beat him off with an old lacrosse stick, but it could have been bad. Even after the break-in, she had a hard time getting a restraining order."

My heart sank as she continued to regale us with the details. Was I being too nonchalant about this? Was I the dumb bitch in a horror movie who got picked off first? I didn't want to be the woman everyone was screaming at to take a threat more seriously.

"Okay, that settles that. Hazel couldn't fight off anyone with anything," Jackson said with a frown. "There's no way you can stay there by yourself."

I opened my mouth to protest but snapped it shut when three sets of determined—and slightly judgmental—eyes stared back at me.

I'd never even taken so much as a self-defense class. Unless I could pin an intruder underneath my massive grandfather clock, or assault him with glass figurines, I was pretty much screwed.

I sighed in defeat.

Reid was right.

"You have no idea how happy I am that you changed your mind." Reid stood in his doorway, his hair messy and damp from a recent shower. A loose black t-shirt and sweatpants hung off his tall frame. He looked comfortable in a way I hadn't seen him before.

"Ruby is right behind me," I added.

At the end of the day, when I'd weighed my options, Reid's guest bedroom sounded a hell of a lot better than Jackson's couch. Once I'd made the decision to take him up on his offer, Ruby had suggested she come by tonight too, just to make things more comfortable. I appreciated the sentiment, but stepping into Reid's house wasn't nearly as unsettling as I'd expected it to be. There was a sense of ease between us, a kind of quiet solace I didn't usually find so quickly with people. Plus, I liked spending time with Reid. A lot.

"This all you brought?" he asked, eyeing my backpack.

"My bigger suitcase is in the car. I was hoping you could grab it for me." I blinked up at him.

"On it," he said, rushing down his steps, not even bothering to throw on shoes.

I lingered by the door, trying to peek down the hallway to get an idea of the place. He must have really thought my apartment was a shithole if he lived *here*. There was more square footage in his front entryway than I had in my entire living room.

"Come in, come in," he said, dragging my rolling suitcase behind him.

I stepped inside and he closed the door.

"This is the place." He led me down the long hallway, where there wasn't so much as a loose shoe on the ground. Damn, this guy was tidy.

The high ceilings in the main living area contained skylights that would drench the place with natural light once the sun rose in the morning. His furniture all looked brand new. Pristine, and very…gray. My head was on a swivel, looking at it all. His kitchen was all harsh lines and granite, with not a spot to be found.

"It's very nice…neutral," I said, then wanted to kick myself.

He chuckled. "It's not quite as homey as your place, but I like it."

"Homey is generous." We exchanged smiles, but anxiety radiated off both of us. Last night had felt temporary, plus we had been in my space. My terms. Now, I'd told him I'd stay here until the situation was resolved. That could be anywhere from tomorrow, to two weeks from now.

"It's a great house, Reid," I added, feeling rude for not complimenting it yet.

"Thanks. I was kind of in a bind after the divorce. Our house sold in just one weekend on the market, and I needed to find something quick."

"You got lucky, then. This place is perfect." I kept my tone casual. Blasé. As if I hadn't even thought about the fact that last night he'd mentioned he was divorced.

In reality, I was *dying* to ask him more. Mostly, what his ex was like. As far as I could tell, Reid was a goddamn catch. How had she let him go? But I knew how much breakups sucked. I hated rehashing stuff about Paul; I could only imagine that being married just made things even messier. So I forced myself to let it go. Reid would share more if he wanted to.

"Your room is down this way." He pointed to the hall off the dining room. "And mine is back through the other hallway." He jerked a finger toward the hallway off the living room on the opposite side of the large room. "Just like I said, plenty of space."

Heat pricked the back of my neck as I thought about the

proximity of his bedroom to mine. It didn't seem like a whole lot of space to me. Not when I was noticing the little vein bulging every time he flexed his forearm.

"Thanks again, Reid." *Shit.* Did my voice sound breathy? "If this gets to be too much, you can totally ask me to leave."

"It's fine." He rolled my suitcase to the guest room, and I followed close behind. "I never even use this room. I probably won't even realize you're here."

He switched on the lights, and the room came into view. It looked *exactly* like a hotel. And not one of those charming boutique ones with funky decorations; nope, this one was straight out of a giant-hotel-chain decorating handbook. White sheets, white duvet, black headboard, matching side tables, and a dresser. Exactly one piece of artwork hung above the bed, one which looked like it had been purchased at one of those big-box home goods stores. The space had zero soul, but I smiled nonetheless.

"This is perfect."

"I never got around to painting." He said it like that had been his intent. As if every other room I'd seen on my brief walk around his house wasn't stark white.

"I think this place suits you," I said.

He raised an eyebrow. "Because you think I'm boring?"

That made me laugh. "I didn't say that. Why? Are you calling your own place boring?"

He shrugged. "I don't know. I never really thought about it before, but after seeing yours, it probably seems like I just moved in."

"I think you like simplicity. This place is exactly what I expected." I took my suitcase from him and set it down on the bench at the end of the bed.

"The drawers are empty if you want to unpack," he said.

"Don't worry. I promise I won't tornado my stuff all over the room."

He eyed me from behind his glasses. "Hazel, I want you to be comfortable here. If that means a few pieces of clothing lying on the ground, then I'm alright with that. I won't even come in here. This is your space."

"Just for a little while," I added.

"Still. I need you to be comfortable. I hate the idea of you feeling like you need to walk on eggshells around here. Seriously, whatever you need to feel at home, do it."

"And you promise not to organize a passive-aggressive chore list and stick it to the fridge?" I joked.

He thought for a moment before smiling. "I can't promise that."

I couldn't help but notice he must have forgotten to shave today. A trace of stubble shadowed his chin; barely a five o'clock shadow. Maybe staying over at my place had thrown off his routine. I hadn't known Reid long, but so far he had never been anything other than perfectly put together and clean shaven. I liked this almost imperceptible crack in his polish.

"Alright," he said, clapping his hands together. "I'll let you get settled in before Ruby gets here with the food."

Then he was gone, closing the door softly behind him.

I fell back onto the bed, letting the plush comforter embrace me. Even though he said he never came in this room, it smelled like him. Reid struck me as the kind of guy who would buy the same scent for everything—candles, soap, air freshener. I liked it, though. Leather and spice. Subtle and soft, but it still lingered everywhere.

I picked up a pillow and breathed in the scent. Yep. Reid was definitely the kind of person who purchased room spray. Whatever the hell that was.

My suitcase begged to stay in its open state so that I could rifle through it any time I needed something—and make a progressively bigger mess as the days went on. But I wanted to be a good house guest, which was why I pulled open a dresser drawer and started to unpack my clothes.

I wasn't the unpacking type on trips, so it felt strange just dumping my stuff into a foreign dresser. Admittedly, I hadn't had many opportunities to pack and unpack lately. Or ever. When would I find the time or money to travel? The last trip I'd been on was up north for a night, to a casino. There was a show Gran had wanted to see, so we'd left Paul behind and gone, just us two. We'd splurged on the cheapest hotel room they had, drank too many margaritas, and spent too much money at the slot machines. We'd had a blast.

It was the last trip I'd taken with her.

I hadn't realized it would be the last at the time.

My hands folded, and bunched, and refolded the same sweater before I stuffed it in the drawer. I was torn between chasing down the memory to savor it or running away.

Instead, I forced my thoughts to stay on the present moment. Specifically, how surprisingly *not weird* this was. Being at Reid's. A place like this should, theoretically, leave me feeling suffocated, like I couldn't breathe without wrinkling the duvet or breaking something. But Reid, and even his house, had a calming energy. I liked being here—around him. And despite my earlier confidence that everything was going to be fine, I was actually happy not to be alone right now.

It wasn't even about the safety aspect. It was lonely in that apartment. I'd moved there after breaking up with Paul, and it was the only place I'd lived by myself. Despite packing the space from floor to ceiling in an effort to feel something, it remained stubbornly void of life—like all the energy had quietly slipped out while I wasn't looking.

Which was strange.

Because here I was, settling into the blandest guest bedroom I'd ever seen at the home of a guy I hardly knew.

And yet…for the first time in a long while, I didn't feel quite so empty.

"Pizza is here."

Ruby held up two brown boxes like an offering. Reid had already produced three matching plates from a cabinet.

"Wow, fancy," I said, taking one.

"I suppose you usually just eat out of the box," he said before taking the boxes from Ruby and setting them on his impossibly clean stone island.

"Sometimes, I grab a piece of paper towel."

His grin widened. He produced a roll of paper towels from underneath the sink and handed them to me. "Make yourself at home."

"I'm so glad you're here, Hazel," Ruby said, not waiting for us before grabbing a slice of pepperoni pizza and setting it on her plate. She dabbed at the pizza grease with a paper towel. "You shouldn't be in that apartment right now. Reid is always going on about some cold case, and it's disgusting what people are capable of. It's better to be safe than sorry."

"I am not *always* going on about some cold case," Reid muttered.

"Always," Ruby insisted. "Even when we beg him not to."

I chuckled. It was fun seeing Reid and Ruby interact. They had that sibling energy I'd only seen on sitcoms.

"I do feel safer," I said. I swore Reid's cheeks flushed when I glanced over at him.

Ruby gave me a warm smile and said, "Good."

I liked Ruby. She'd always been sweet, and had made an effort to include me as soon as I started at the salon. I think we were right on the verge of becoming real friends when Gran died. That kind of hit pause on everything. Grieving was awful, but it was also…awkward. Everyone at the salon had been kind and thoughtful, but there was something strange about mourning in front of people who barely knew me. Their sympathy came by the bucketfuls, but no one knew her —or me—enough to make a difference. They pitied me from a safe distance instead of crying next to me.

Funny. I already felt closer to Reid than I did to her. Sure, we'd had a sleepover to solidify our blossoming, friend-adjacent relationship, but I was still surprised by it. The two of us had so little in common.

"Are you all table people?" I asked, tilting my head in the direction of the giant wooden dining table.

"Reid is." Ruby rolled her eyes and led the way to the table.

"Sorry I don't believe the couch was meant to be eaten on," he said.

I pulled out a chair and plopped down as Reid moved the pizza boxes to the center. A splotch of steam still smudged his glasses from when he'd opened the box. I resisted the urge to reach out with my sleeve and wipe it away. He beat me to it anyway, pulling them off and wiping them on his shirt.

"You probably had a heart attack yesterday when we ate straight from the takeout cartons on my couch," I said.

Ruby laughed. "No way! Do you have photographic evidence?"

Reid shrugged. "I didn't mind."

"Did you share cartons and everything?" she asked.

I nodded.

She tilted her head, glancing between the two of us. "Reid *never* shares food. When we were kids, he used to build a napkin wall around his plate because he was sick of us asking if we could try whatever he got. It became a running joke to attempt to get him to share."

"Can we change the subject, please?" he asked, visibly unamused by his sister's story.

Ruby chuckled and shook her head. "Hazel, don't let his rules fool you. We always ate on the couch growing up. The table-only-thing is an adult development."

Reid shook his head. "Not *always*."

"At *least* every Friday."

"Only because Mom worked late and Dad was in charge of dinner," he said.

"And he'd order take-out, and we'd watch a movie on the couch. Those memories aren't fond ones for you?"

There wasn't much behind my smile as I observed their back and forth. As an only child, I'd never had that kind of familiarity with anyone. Watching close friends or siblings interact always made me feel like I was missing out on something, like there was this big life experience I'd never get to know simply because I'd been born alone.

"Hazel can eat on the couch if she wants to." The sound of my name interrupted my thoughts.

"I'm alright. I wouldn't dare disrupt your household."

"See?" Ruby held out a hand. "She thinks you're rigid."

Reid let out a long sigh. "I am not rigid."

Ruby and I exchanged a look.

"I'm not," he said again.

"I didn't say that," I offered, although I had to bite the inside of my cheek to keep from smirking. Reid was the definition of rigid. He was sweet and kind, which is why he was putting up with me for as long as he already had, but he was still stiff. Inflexible. He had a robot vacuum, countertops so shiny you could see your reflection in them, and not a single thing in his house was out of place.

We had a few more slices of pizza before Ruby leaned toward me, concern dancing in her eyes. "So how are you really doing?" she asked.

"Oh, y'know, been better." The lightness in my voice was forced. "I just wish this could all be over. And it's so hard not to blame myself."

"You can't blame yourself for some twisted person trying to take advantage of you," Reid said, a determined set to his jaw.

I smiled gratefully at him. "But it *was* me who posted way too much information on social media. I should never have done that."

"It sucks we have to be vigilant with our privacy, but that doesn't make this your fault. Crimes will always be the fault of the person stalking, or harassing, or taking advantage. You're a victim, Hazel. And you're allowed to feel frustrated and upset.

But not at yourself." His words were unexpected, but I appreciated them nonetheless. I smiled when he caught my eye.

"Yeah, we're all guilty of oversharing. You can't beat yourself up about that," Ruby added.

I groaned. "It's hard not to. If it weren't for my own stupid post, I'd be cuddled up with my cat on my couch, online shopping for something nice to buy myself once my check cleared."

"Well, after you paid off your debt," Reid interjected.

I rolled my eyes. "Yes, Reid. After I paid off all my debt. Geez, can't I buy something fun in my own fantasy?"

Ruby laughed. "If you're trying to prove to us that you aren't rigid, a snide comment about financial responsibility isn't helping your case."

We ate the rest of the pizza and conversation flowed. They asked about where I grew up, how I liked this side of the state. Ruby and I talked about our career choices. Apparently, she wanted to switch to doing more weddings and events. A good friend of hers was a makeup artist and had a side gig. She asked if I'd ever want to join them for some larger events, and I agreed without hesitation.

Eventually we moved to the couch. Ruby said she'd stay for one episode of some home renovation show before leaving, but three episodes later, she and Reid were both asleep on the couch. I was still awake, curled up into the corner, a fleece blanket surrounding me. Bed sounded amazing, but I couldn't quite motivate myself to stand up, brush my teeth, and do the whole pre-bedtime ordeal. Not just yet.

The couch was perfectly smooshed around my body and my eyelids sagged as I watched yet another subway tile backsplash get installed. It occurred to me that this was the most relaxed I'd been in a while. The knot of anxiety that had been wound up inside me for weeks had loosened a little. It wasn't gone completely, not by a long shot, but I found that for once, I could take a deep breath.

I looked at Reid, watching as he breathed softly, his glasses falling down his nose. He was so damned likable. He had no reason to be so kind to me, to offer his home when he hardly knew me. To help me tackle what was beginning to seem like an impossible mystery.

My life was a mess—*I* was a mess—and he was still taking the time to put some pieces back in place.

As if sensing my eyes on him, he stirred. He blinked a few times before focusing on me. I didn't bother looking away. He smiled and shifted, getting up and stretching before draping a blanket over Ruby's sleeping form.

I got up too, walking heavily toward the hallway that led to my room.

"Do you need anything?" Reid whispered.

"I'm good."

"You sure?"

I smiled sleepily. "I'm sure."

"Alright. If you change your mind, you know where to find me." He pointed behind him, toward his room.

"Night, Reid."

"Night, Hazel."

THIRTEEN

Hazel

"And you're just playing house with the guy?" Zoe asked, sipping her smoothie on the other end of the video call. She had giant sunglasses on, despite the partially cloudy Michigan weather. She always claimed her blue eyes were extra sensitive. From the looks of it, she was parked in her car, probably right outside the smoothie place, heaters blasting to counteract the cold beverage.

We hadn't caught up in ages, and I'd just filled her in on all of the miserable details of my life lately. Zoe had oohed and ahhed in all the right places and expressed proper outrage over Vermont and the thief. But even with that whole ordeal, she was hung up on one detail in particular. Which didn't surprise me in the least.

"What does he look like? Do you have a picture?" she asked.

"I don't have a picture."

"What're his socials?" The video paused as she exited out of the call to pull up an app.

"He doesn't have any," I said.

"Red flag. Who doesn't have social media?"

"He's private."

"That's what they all say."

I rolled my eyes at my friend. Zoe had always seemed larger than life to me. She marched to the beat of her own drummer, but somehow, it was a beat everyone else wanted to follow. I didn't mind living in her shadow, not really. It had gotten me through high school, and those shaky, formative years after. She hadn't gone to college either, and though we never lived together, I'd spent more late nights at her place than my own. We only really started to drift apart once I started dating Paul. And even though Paul and I were long over, Zoe and I had never quite found our way back. She had plenty of other friends to fall back on, after all; friends I'd never clicked with.

"Reid is a good one, I promise."

"Hazel, I totally believe you, but I'm gonna need a picture of the guy you're shacking up with, like, immediately."

Even with the sunglasses on, I could visualize the glint in her eyes.

I minimized the video chat to pull up a browser. I searched his full name. Reid Mitchell. A ton of results. I searched again, this time with our location, but there was nothing. Not even an article about that cold case he and his group solved. It didn't surprise me that he wouldn't have wanted to be mentioned by name.

"I just googled him. There's nothing," I said, bringing the call with Zoe back up. "I'll try to sneak one when he gets home."

Reid had left the townhouse around five, right as I was getting back from work, to help his dad with something at his house. Cleaning a dryer vent? Something with a radiator? I'd zoned out when he explained it to me. It was certainly something I had never done, and I could promise Gran had never done, in our old house.

But so far, living at his house was going pretty smoothly.

This morning, I'd had that initial moment of waking up in a new place and momentarily forgetting where I was, but other than that, it had been pretty normal. When I'd stumbled into the kitchen, Reid had already been sitting at the dining table, drinking coffee and scrolling his phone.

I pulled a mug out of the cabinet and poured myself a cup.

"Oh, there's milk in the fridge if you want."

I held up the cup. "I'm good with black."

Then he'd given me a strange look when I grabbed a cold slice of leftover pizza and plopped down next to him.

"Pizza for breakfast?" he'd asked, like that wasn't a perfectly valid thing to do.

But then he'd smiled, and I forced him to have one too. He'd insisted he didn't like cold pizza and I'd promptly told him that was impossible. I'd said it was basically like a pastry. He ate the slice. Maybe just to appease me, but it was the best breakfast I'd had in a while.

Zoe slurped loudly, drawing my attention back to the call at hand. "Have you guys hooked up?"

"No!" I was getting a little fed up with this line of questioning.

"Really?" She lifted her shades, eyes searching mine through the phone screen.

"Really! We met last week."

"So? That's a perfectly reasonable amount of time to know someone before having sex. Hell, I've waited a lot less."

"We're friends," I said, surprised to find I actually believed the words.

"And friends don't sleep together?" Zoe asked.

"You're impossible. You don't even know what he looks like."

"I can tell from your red cheeks that he isn't hideous."

That just made me flush even more. It was true, Reid was far from hideous. In fact, seeing him waltz about his house in sweatpants last night and this morning had just fanned the flame of my growing attraction.

"He's cute," I admitted.

"Knew it." She smiled triumphantly, settling back into her seat. "So how are you doing otherwise? I mean, you know, with everything."

The question caught me off guard. I loved Zoe, but deep conversations weren't really her thing. She was more the queen of distraction. She'd get your mind off something, not pick it apart.

"I'm doing okay. Better now." A part of me should probably analyze why I'd only started to feel better since meeting Reid, but I didn't want to delve too much into it.

"Seems like you could use a night out," she said. And there it was. That was the Zoe I knew.

"You know I hate bars," I said. Which was true. They were loud, too crowded, and the floors were always suspiciously sticky.

"I'm coming into town next weekend to visit Kiara. We're going out for my birthday."

I sucked in my lips to try to hide my surprise. She'd already made plans to visit? She hadn't even mentioned it to me. In the few years since I'd moved, she hadn't visited me *once*. Granted, I used to live with Paul, and he wasn't her favorite, but still. We'd met halfway between our places a couple of times, and I'd spent a few weekends at her house, but that was it.

"Sounds fun." I forced my tone into one of indifference.

She laughed, clearly missing my shift in mood. "You don't have to lie. You just have to come out with us. I insist."

"Alright." My voice sounded strange. Fake to my own ears.

We caught up for a while longer, mostly talking about her failed online date the night before. Then we ended the call.

My inferiority complex was flaring up, big-time. Zoe had been my only constant friend throughout the years, but to her, I was just one of many. She collected people like some people collected handbags. Her visit to Kiara just confirmed what I always knew, deep down. They were closer. I hated how much that stung. Especially since I'd tried so hard to get it right. I showed up. I was fun. I hung out when she needed company, played wing woman when she needed backup. But clearly, something about me didn't stick. I never quite fit. I was always a little too much, or not quite enough. Easy to overlook, even when I was trying my hardest to be seen.

"Hazel, you home?" A voice echoed from the front entry. I sat up straight on the couch, pulling my feet off it. Which was ridiculous. Reid wouldn't care if my socks were on his couch. Nevertheless, I wanted to appear to be the perfect house guest.

"In here," I called.

Reid rounded the corner, cheeks red from the cold outside, talking a mile a minute. "The post we made on the Neighborhood app. Remember? About Vermont? Someone replied. They said they found an orange cat two blocks away from your house the other day and dropped it at the animal shelter."

"Is there a picture?" I asked, springing up.

"No, and it might be nothing, but we have to at least check it out."

THE ORANGE CAT STARED UP AT US AS IT BARED ITS FANGS, giving me what could only be described as a crotchety hiss. He looked almost like an old man: long whiskers, slightly gray eyebrows, and lazy eyes that were simultaneously annoyed and tired.

Certainly not the familiar, friendly face I was hoping for.

"That's not Vermont." I frowned, looking at him longer, willing him to somehow transform into the cat I remembered so vividly.

"Damn." Reid shot me an apologetic look.

The concrete hallway was lined with plastic windows, putting the cats that were there on display like some sad zoo. The smell of litter and disinfectant sat heavy in my nostrils. I hadn't really expected it to be that easy, but during the drive over, a small, stupid part of me had let the fantasy play out. Maybe this would be it. Maybe Vermont would be here. I'd walk out with him, the money would land in my account in a couple of weeks, I'd pay off my debt, stash the rest in savings, maybe even buy myself something nice for once.

But life didn't work like that. Not mine, anyway.

"It was worth a try," Reid said. He put a hand on my shoulder and gave it a small squeeze. The comfort of his gesture was quickly swallowed by the flip my stomach did at his touch.

I slumped against the glass, taking in the other cats lounging about the room.

"Would you like to go in and meet them?" A worker in a blue apron asked as she walked past us.

"I'm okay," I said at the same time Reid said, "Sure."

I raised my eyebrows, looking at him.

"Oh, uh. I mean, not if it's too painful or something like that." Reid cleared his throat and shifted from foot to foot, stuffing his hands into the pocket of his dark blue hoodie.

"Are you trying to do a side quest and adopt a cat right now?" I asked.

"No, I, uh. I mean, we're already here." He shrugged. "I just like cats."

I turned back to the worker who still had a smile plastered to her face.

"I guess we would like to go in."

She reached past me and unlocked the door. "Just ring the bell when you're done and someone will be in to help you."

She ushered us into a room filled with cat towers and wide windows facing the street. Now, it wasn't only the cats on display for every passerby—so were we.

The orange cat, Mr. Hissy, immediately retreated to the back corner of the room and glared at us for having the audacity to infiltrate his space. A gray kitten approached first, unfazed as he rubbed against Reid's shoe before falling over and playfully pawing at his shoelaces.

"Hi there," Reid cooed, dropping to his knees to pet the little guy.

"Huh," I said as I watched him grow more and more infatuated with the kitten.

"What?" Reid asked, not willing to take his eyes off the purring bundle of fluff to look up at me.

"All this time I thought you were helping me out of the goodness of your heart, but really, you're a secret cat person."

He stroked the kitten's back before it flopped over again. "I mean, they're cute," he said. "I always wanted a pet growing up, but my parents were very anti-pet. They let me have a fish once, but even then complained it was too much work. And it didn't fill the void, anyway. You can't cuddle a fish."

"Way inferior," I agreed. "But they are pretty low maintenance."

"Spoken like someone who has no idea about the proper protocol for tank care."

I grimaced. "This is probably a bad time to tell you that Gran and I had a fish once. We kept it in an old vodka bottle."

His gaze met mine, eyes narrowed.

"Emptied and cleaned out, obviously," I added.

"I'm going to pretend I didn't hear that."

I chuckled, dropping to my knees to pet the brown cat that had joined our impromptu meet-and-greet. "In our defense, we had no clue what we were doing. And Gran had no idea how to use Google."

"You could have asked the pet store worker you got it from," he said, not willing to give me an inch of grace.

"Oh, the sixteen-year-old making minimum wage who was probably high while on the job? Great idea. We should have thought of that."

The smile that lingered on Reid's face as he gazed at the kitten—soft, genuine, a little crooked—made my heart completely melt. This guy really was a big softie.

"Why don't you have a cat if you love them so much?" I

asked, the brown cat now aggressively purring as he pressed his head against my ankles. My heart ached that he was here, until I saw the small "On Hold" tag around his neck. *Phew.* I could not handle adopting another cat right now.

Reid's smile faltered. "I always wanted to. But my ex was resistant to the idea."

"Allergic?" I asked.

"Just not a cat person," he said. "Or a pet person, really. She always used to cross the street anytime we passed someone walking their dog."

"A sin," I said.

He chuckled. "She wasn't the warmest and fuzziest of people."

"Why didn't you get one after?" I meant 'after the divorce,' but didn't quite get the words out. I still had a hard time wrapping my head around the fact that he'd been married before. Had already had this whole other life he thought would be forever. It wasn't like I didn't have a past; I had lived with Paul for nearly two years. But marriage had *never* crossed my mind. We were young and had bickered constantly toward the end. I think I felt a strange sense of loyalty toward him for wanting to be with me. For picking me. I realized how absurd that was, now. Someone wanting me was the bare minimum. Below the bare minimum, even.

"I thought about getting one when I got my own place, but I never did. I think I always saw it as a step I wanted to take in a relationship. You move in together, adopt a pet, get married, have kids. You know. Not that life is some inflexible checklist of things I need to tick off," he added hurriedly. "I just thought it sounded nice. Going with someone to adopt your pet together…that probably sounds dumb." He shot me a self-deprecating smile. I forced my arms to remain at my sides, because that look made me want to wrap him up in a hug.

"That doesn't sound dumb at all, Reid." My heart ached for him. I wanted to ask more about the divorce, but I didn't want to pry. Was he over her? He said it was over a year ago, but how long had they been together? He must have really loved her to get married. Suddenly flashes of Reid in a tux waiting at the end of the aisle infiltrated my mind.

"You should get one now," I said.

He shot his gaze toward me, then back at the two kittens now swarming his shoes. "I'm not ready."

I laughed. "What do you mean? Like, you don't have the stuff? We can pick it up."

"I haven't done the proper research." He frowned. "I-I don't like to be unprepared for things."

"I've noticed." I bit back a smile.

There were no guarantees that two people were meant to be. Marriages that started out with so much love and the best of intentions ended every day. It wasn't like one half of each divorced couple was a monster. But I couldn't help but feel that Reid's ex had fumbled the ball big time. As I watched him scoop a kitten up in his arms and stroke it under its chin, laughing when it latched onto his t-shirt, I knew for sure that he was something special. He had a good heart.

Gran had always told me to watch out for that. She said you could fix a lot of things, or even learn to look past them, but genuineness was something engrained in a person.

And Reid had genuineness in spades.

FOURTEEN

Reid

____

Armchair_Detective: _Who's updating the blog post today?_
WhiteKnight31: _I did it last week._
ReidingRainbow: _I can do it._
WhiteKnight31: _Shouldn't you be busy solving that cat cold case?_
Armchair_Detective: _Wouldn't it be considered a live case? It's active._
WhiteKnight31: _Right, whatever. Either way, you should be busy._
ReidingRainbow: _Kind of hitting a bit of a dead end. The ex seems like a solid suspect, but he hasn't taken the fake-profile bait._
Armchair_Detective: _I've said it before and I'll say it again, it's always the boyfriend._
WhiteKnight31: _Did you tell him you were a cat person?_
Armchair_Detective: _Maybe your flirting could use some work._
WhiteKnight31: _Yeah, are you a professional at flirting with socio-pathic men?_
ReidingRainbow: _I've had my practice._
Armchair_Detective: _Any other suspects?_
ReidingRainbow: _Her neighbor is kind of fishy. Strange older lady. Already has a ton of cats. Hazel doesn't want to believe it, but I think the circumstances are too perfect._

Armchair_Detective: *How old we talking? Does it seem like she'd be able to figure out a burner phone number?*
ReidingRainbow: *I'm not sure, but regardless, we can't rule her out as a suspect.*

"Come on, add two more twenty-pounders." West picked up two plates and placed them at the ends of the weight bar while I scowled at him.

"I'm already lifting past my goal," I argued, but he slipped the plates on anyway. He always ignored my protests, insisted I didn't push myself enough. Which, fair, I probably didn't.

Going to the gym had been one of our shared routines since our college days. It had started out as more of West's thing, but he'd dragged me along enough times that eventually, I'd started to enjoy it too. It felt good to move my body, to lift something heavy. The dopamine effect wasn't a myth.

This gym was massive; I'd nearly gotten lost just walking in. When I told West we should switch things up, he'd given me a strange look. Our usual gym was a small, locally owned one. We knew the owners by name and the place was always spotless and easy to get a bench at. This place was the complete opposite—huge, industrial, packed with people trying to cram in a post-work workout. One of those chains that were everywhere. Decidedly not our scene. But they were offering a free trial, and I just so happened to know—thanks to some persistent location-tagging—that this was where a certain ex-boyfriend of Hazel's liked to work out.

The idea that I would come here to spy on her ex was ridiculous. So ridiculous, I hadn't even admitted it to Hazel. Because seriously—what could I possibly learn from watching him work out? Unless he was bragging about his catnapping skills to the person blending smoothies at the front desk, I highly doubted I was going to gain any real insight. Still, I was stuck. We weren't getting any closer to solving the case and I didn't want to let her down. Plus, after spending a little too long stalking Paul's profile, and seeing one too many old pictures of him and Hazel together, an obsessive curiosity had started digging its claws into my brain.

This was the guy. The guy Hazel had lived with. The one she claimed had been kind of an ass, but also marginally helpful when her grandma's health had deteriorated. Was her type really gym rats with thick necks and bulking shoulders? If so, then what did she think of me? I wasn't scrawny. I had muscles. But I was built lean, no matter how many protein shakes West had tried to shove down my throat over the years.

"Dude, let's go. I'll spot you," West said.

I gave up trying to get him to remove the extra weights and laid down on the bench. The ceiling lights blurred above me as I gripped the bar and lifted it off the rack with a grunt. My glasses were set on a towel by my water bottle nearby.

I pulled the bar to my chest and lifted it with ease three times before West let out a whistle.

"See? I told you. You always undersell yourself. You get hung up on your goal weight and you don't even try to do more."

I did two more sets, slower each time, before I managed to get the bar back on the rack and sit up.

"I just did more, didn't I?" I grabbed my water bottle and took a large sip while I wiped the sheen off my forehead. I scanned the surrounding area.

West shot me a disapproving look. "Only because I'm here."

"And you're always here."

"Whatever. You're impossible, man." He shook his head and leaned against the rack as we took a small break to let our muscles reset.

I hadn't realized how much I'd needed this session to blow off some steam. Hazel had been staying at my place for two days now, and while I'd call the experience mostly positive, there was this low, unspoken tension hanging in the air. I was surprisingly at ease around her, and she was clearly making an effort to be tidy, even though it didn't come naturally to her. But still. Something felt…off. Just out of reach.

I kept telling myself it was her situation—the one I was supposed to be helping her fix. Maybe the guilt of not having any answers yet was settling in. Maybe I felt like I was failing her.

Deep down, I knew that wasn't it.

The tension wasn't constant. It only showed up when she was close, when we talked, when we made contact. Like the other day, when I was grabbing a bowl from the kitchen cabinet and she'd reached past me for a glass of water. She laid a hand on my waist, just to keep me from backing into her. But the way my entire body locked up at that single touch?

Yeah. Hard to pretend that didn't mean something.

And it was also hard to pretend that my heart wasn't racing a little as I scanned the gym for a face I'd only cyber-stalked up until this point. He had to be here. He was *always* here.

"How's the new house guest?" West asked, reading my mind as per usual.

"She's good," I said, knowing full well that Ruby had probably already filled him in on all the details. I knew they talked a lot. In fact, I was positive everything had made it back to my entire family by now. That was their way. Gossip spread faster than a cough during flu season.

"Just good?"

I shrugged and took another sip of water. West was always the talker in our friendship. Which I supposed I was grateful for. If it weren't for him, I'd likely have way more of a shell surrounding me.

"Seems like you're fishing for something," I said.

He frowned at me. "Yes, I'm fishing. For something fucking interesting. You have a single, attractive girl living in your guest room and you have nothing to say about it?"

"How did you know she's attractive?"

He smirked. "I didn't, but you just confirmed it."

I squeezed my eyes shut. "She's got a lot on her mind. We're just cohabitating," I said.

A slight lie. We'd had some solid conversations. While I might have expected us to retreat to our own corners of the house every evening, that hadn't been the case. After we got back from the animal shelter last night, she'd lingered in the kitchen while I made dinner. She'd said she didn't want any, but I made way too much on purpose, insisting she take some. Then we'd watched another movie—rather, we'd talked through another movie. For someone who liked my space so much, I was surprised to find that I also genuinely liked having Hazel around.

"And you haven't made a move?" West asked.

I looked to the ceiling for patience. "She's grieving. Her grandmother passed away a month ago, she had her cat stolen, and she has money problems. The last thing she wants is for me to *make a move*." I said the last words in a mocking tone. This line of questioning from West was something I'd expected. Ever since my divorce, he'd been hounding me to meet someone new. If they had it their way, West and my sisters would be managing my dating life, and I'd be going on blind dates five times a week to increase my odds.

But that wasn't me.

"There's no flirtatious vibe there? Absolutely nothing?" West asked.

I hesitated—just for a split second—but that was all it took.

"I knew it!" West clapped me on the shoulder, his brown eyes brightening with excitement. "You like her."

I shoved his hand away. "I *do* like her, just not in the way you're thinking. She's a nice girl. I want to help her. Maybe we could be friends. But she's a mess, West."

My pulse pounded as those words spilled out of my mouth. Guilt swarmed me. Hazel *was* a bit of a mess. It was part of her charm. But saying the words out loud like that, to West who didn't even know her, felt like an act of betrayal.

West frowned at my answer. "You're never going to find someone who likes color coding as much as you do, Reid."

"Did I even say that was high on my list of criteria?"

He sighed. "You didn't have to. It's written all over the way you refuse to bend for anyone."

"I have a stranger living in my house right now. Is that not bending?"

The corner of his mouth tugged up. "It *is* bending. Which is exactly why I know this girl is more than nothing to you."

"Jesus…"

I let my words trail off as I snatched my glasses from where they rested on the floor. I wiped them off on my t-shirt and put them on. I could make out West well enough without them, but he somehow looked even smugger in twenty-twenty.

I gave the gym another cursory scan now that I could see more clearly. The bar benches had filled up since we'd arrived, but I didn't see the person I was searching for. I watched absentmindedly as the guy next to me lifted nearly twice what I was doing. His biceps flexed as he struggled with the weight and a flash of irritation coursed through me as I noticed he didn't have a spotter. Some people were so irresponsible, and…

"*Shit*," I hissed, tearing my gaze away.

"What?" West looked up from his phone where he'd been typing a message.

I jerked my head backward, toward the guy. "That's the guy," I whispered.

West glanced at him and then back at me. "You're going to have to give me more details than that."

"Hazel's ex," I whispered. I'd already filled him in on the catfishing plan.

West looked again and snorted softly. "That guy? He's a total meathead."

"Shh."

He scrunched his forehead. "Relax. He has no idea who we are."

West was right. Even though I had examined every nook and cranny of his social media and online presence, Paul had no idea who the hell I was. He would likely be deeply disturbed if he knew I was the mind behind the girl who had slid into his DMs.

West's eyes went wide. "Wait, is that why you wanted to try out this stupid gym? To run into him?"

"Shhh." I gave him a warning glare before picking up my phone and sneaking a quick picture before shooting it to Hazel. I knew she was at work, so I wasn't expecting her to answer right away, but a response came in immediately.

Hazel: Omg! That's Paul.

Hazel: Feel free to not help him when that weight inevitably gets stuck on his chest. I've heard being crushed to death by your own ego is a brutal way to go.

Her words made me smile as I shot back a quick reply and stuffed my phone back into my pocket.

"You going to say something?" West asked, not bothering to be subtle in his stare at Paul.

"What? Why would I say something?" I asked, appalled at the idea.

"Isn't that why you dragged us here in the first place? Investigate your top suspect?"

"No," I said, although hadn't I done that? Because if I wasn't here to investigate Paul as a suspect, why the hell was I so curious about Hazel's ex? The thought made me cringe.

"You should get a read on the guy," West said.

"'Cat thief' isn't exactly something easily readable." I squinted at Paul, taking the chance to size him up while he was distracted. He looked...very into himself. His shirt was cut so low it was practically a vest, leaving half his chest and one entire arm on full display.

My chest heated. I *wanted* to judge the hell out of him. Really, I did. But if I was being honest? What I actually felt was…jealousy, maybe? Was that what this was? A tiny, embarrassing flicker of envy? Maybe West was right. Maybe I *did* need to get out more if a girl showing me just an inkling of friendship was enough to trigger this kind of insecure, high-school-level spiral.

West leaned against the weight rack. "You need to take a profiling class or something."

"My profiling senses are already telling me that could be the guy. I don't need to speak to him to get a better idea."

To my horror—but not to my surprise—West ignored me and called out, "Hey man, nice set."

Two benches over, Paul put his bar back on the rack, his entire body beet red from the effort.

"Thanks," he grunted.

"*Stop*," I whispered. What was it with people and being so eager to confront suspects? First Hazel and her old boss, and now this? I mean, I knew it was technically my fault we were running into Paul in the first place, but I at least had the instinct to lay low. Sometimes I wished my online friends were here in real life, because I could guarantee both of them would be a hell of a lot subtler.

West continued to ignore me and smiled at Paul. "What was that, like three hundred?"

"Three fifteen," Paul said, still barely acknowledging us before putting his headphones back in.

"Friendly guy," West whispered before taking my spot on the bench.

"Was that necessary?" I asked, shooting daggers at my friend.

West laid down and gripped the bar. "I think you can take him."

"His biceps are the size of my head," I said, unenthused.

West smiled up at me. "You've got at least half a foot on him. And you're no slouch. We just need to work on your confrontation skills."

"Everyone around me is confrontational enough," I muttered, spotting him as he lifted the bar off the bench.

My eyes kept wandering back to Paul. Another guy had joined him. Shorter, slightly less meaty. Caleb, maybe? I recognized him from an old, blurry picture with Hazel and Paul. Man, I could not picture her hanging out with these guys. What had Hazel seen in him? She'd really dated him for years? Lived with him? I couldn't wrap my mind around it. Hazel was all warmth and chaos, bubbly, eccentric, impossible to ignore. And this guy? He gave off the vibe of a damp dishrag. Okay, maybe that was harsh. But come on. There was no way this guy could hold an actual conversation, right?

The more I thought about them together, the worse that small knot of jealousy in my chest became. My knuckles went white around the bar as I stepped in to help West rack the weight, letting the strain ground me.

As much as I didn't want West to be right, he was. There *wasn't* nothing between Hazel and me. In fact, there was most definitely something. At least on my end. Was that inappropriate? I was letting her stay in my house to avoid some creep, and here I was developing a crush on her. But I couldn't lie to myself. She had been taking up a lot of space in my mind lately, and it wasn't because of the cat case. It was because of her. She was unlike anyone I'd ever met. On paper, I shouldn't be able to stand her. She represented everything I thought I didn't like. Messy, unorganized, flighty, unpredictable, financially irresponsible.

And yet…

There she was.

The girl who was stronger than she appeared.

The girl I'd stayed up with multiple nights in a row, quoting cheesy movies.

The girl I wanted to protect and shelter, to rescue from the shitty position she was currently in.

The girl I was excited to get back home to.

FIFTEEN

Hazel

"You sure you don't want to crash at my place?" Jackson asked.

I had to tear my gaze away from the picture Reid had texted me. The fact that he was at the gym with my ex *right now* made my skin physically crawl. Would he say something to Paul? Would Paul say something to him? I mean, either scenario seemed highly unlikely. Paul had no idea who Reid was, and Reid wasn't the type to engage in small talk with a suspect. Still. I didn't like it.

"I appreciate the offer, but I'm okay." I bit my thumbnail, waiting for Reid to text me back.

My last client of the day hadn't arrived yet. The Greek salad I had picked up from the diner next door sat forgotten on my lap.

"But it sounds fun," Jackson pouted, organizing his heat styling tools. "I've always wanted a roommate."

"Then get one. But I'm not moving into your tiny-ass studio."

"It's cozy," he argued.

"And my apartment-less-ness is temporary. I'll be home soon enough."

With or without Vermont.

Queasiness roiled in my gut at the thought.

I had made the mistake of allowing optimism to work its way into my mind recently. I blamed Reid. He had this way about him that made me feel like everything would work out. Just being around the guy had been a pretty solid distraction as of late, but any time I stopped to think about my situation for even a second, dread descended. Because in reality, we weren't any closer to finding answers.

I looked back at the message Reid had sent me. A picture of my ex in his natural habitat—the gym.

Could Paul really have done this to me? Part of me had slowly become convinced. Who else could it possibly be? But at the same time, I still found it hard to believe that he could stoop to such a level. Our breakup had pissed him off, though. I couldn't deny that. Before he'd cut off contact, he used to alternate between being angry at me and begging me to take him back. His drunk dialing had been relentless, begging me to come to his apartment and talk things through.

If it was him, he hadn't cracked yet, and we were running out of time. He'd said nothing about a cat to the fake profile Reid was using to message him. I knew where Paul lived, and it might be time to convince Reid to take a slightly more aggressive action.

"Do you have an extra comb?" Ruby asked. She stood above me, right behind Jackson.

I set the salad on my counter—my appetite was long gone, anyway—and pulled out a fresh comb from my drawer. "Here you go," I said, handing it to her.

"Thanks." She smiled and leaned to the side, jutting one hip out. "How have the past few days been?"

She didn't have to be specific to make her line of questioning clear. She wasn't asking how work had been, or about the state of my mental health (fragile, for anyone wondering). Nope. She was asking how it was staying with Reid.

"Oh, okay, I guess. I feel bad for invading his space, but

he's seriously been so nice about it. Thank you for having such a kind brother," I said, as if she had somehow had a hand in making him that way.

She laughed. "He's always been like this. Saint Reid, we used to call him. Always been our parents' favorite—although they try and deny it. He's sweet and responsible, and easy to have in your life."

Easy to have in your life.

That described Reid perfectly. Ever since I met him, I'd wanted him around. He made everything lighter.

Unfortunately, no one would ever use the words *easy to have in your life* to describe me. I was the opposite of easy. Challenging, my Gran used to say. Paul too, for that matter.

Heat rose to my cheeks. Was I weighing Reid down?

Of course I was, who the hell was I kidding. And he was far too nice to say anything about it. Was he counting down the minutes until our time together was over? What did I really bring to the table, aside from a laundry list of problems to solve?

"I think he's having fun with you," Ruby continued, oblivious to my spiraling. "It's all he talks about lately. Or doesn't talk about, I should say. You can always tell how happy Reid is by how much he ignores the family chats. If he's ever too quick to respond in those, you know he's having a rough time."

"You think he's having…fun?" I hated the hope rising in my voice. But I needed a little reassurance that I wasn't the menace I thought I was.

"For sure. Hey, you should come by for family dinner this Friday."

"I couldn't intrude." The thought of meeting the rest of Reid's family made my heart hammer violently against my chest.

"Can I come?" Jackson asked.

Ruby ignored him and stayed focused on me. "I'm serious.

It'd be fun. Plus, our whole family has heard about you by this point. They'd be really excited to meet you."

I bit my tongue to keep from asking what, exactly, they'd heard. There was no way it could be all that flattering.

"Maybe," I offered, fully planning on coming up with an excuse to bail later. I wasn't about to crash Reid's family dinner when he hadn't even invited me himself. Not after I had already infiltrated every nook and cranny of the rest of his life.

Ruby gave me one last, seemingly genuine, smile and went back to her station and client.

"What, you don't like them or something?" Jackson asked, once she was back at the front of the salon.

"Jackson," I scolded, jerking my head in the direction of his client who sat in the chair, eyes covered by bangs.

"Oh, don't stop gossiping on my account," she said. "I've been seeing Jackson for years. I'm used to it."

Jackson pursed his lips and tilted his head giving me a "see" look.

I sighed and shook my head. "I like Ruby and Reid," I insisted, snatching my salad back and forcing a bite into my mouth. I glanced at the time, realizing I only had fifteen minutes until my next appointment. "But I don't want to be any more of a burden then I already am. I know when people are being nice to me because they feel sorry for me. I appreciate the gesture, but I'm not going to take advantage."

Jackson raised his eyebrows and pulled away from his client to fold his arms across his chest. "Taking someone up on an earnestly offered dinner invitation is not taking advantage, Hazel."

I just shrugged in response.

He could think what he wanted, but I had years of evidence to back me up. Sleepovers where Zoe was the main invite and I was the obligatory plus-one. Coworkers who included me in plans just because the whole salon was going. People didn't really *like* me. That was just my reality. I'd gotten used to the look people got when a conversation with me stretched on too long, like a light slowly dimming behind their eyes.

When I'd started dating Paul, it had been easy to pull back even more. I stopped even making an effort with other people. Aside from Gran, I'd let him be the center of my life. I realized later there was a name for that. Codependency. I had liked not being alone more than I liked him.

"So, how is it living with the guy?" Jackson asked when he realized I had stopped talking and was instead inhaling my salad.

When I glanced at him through the mirror that ran across the entire side of the salon, he and his client were both staring back at me.

"It's fine, but I'm just ready for this nightmare to be over."

Jackson dipped his chin and narrowed his eyes. "That's the dullest answer you could have given me. Fine? You're living with Ruby's hot brother, and you haven't made a single move?"

My cheeks burned. "You think Reid is hot?"

"Oh yeah," he looked down at his client. "He's got this whole tall, adorable, nerdy thing going on. And that jawline? Hard to ignore. Right, Hazel?"

"I guess."

I more than guessed. Reid's attractiveness had smacked me right in the face the moment I met him, and now it constantly prodded at me—*tortured* me. And after spending the past week with him, his personality had sent me into full-blown crush mode. He was just so freaking *nice*. And genuine. And seemingly looking out for my best interests.

Jackson snorted. "Whatever. Maybe he's not your type. You seem like someone who would go for a bad boy, or someone a bit more reckless."

"I think I've had more than my fair share of those," I muttered. "Can we stop talking about this twenty feet away from the guy in question's *sister*?"

I jerked my head in Ruby's direction.

Jackson twisted his face into one of annoyance. "She can't even hear us."

"I'd prefer not to take that chance."

He sighed dramatically before going back to sectioning off his client's hair. Finally they fell back into conversation about her ex-husband, and I was able to effectively tune them out, grateful the attention was off me.

I didn't care that Jackson had called it on the nose. I wasn't about to go through the embarrassment of admitting out loud that I liked Reid. Especially since there was no realm in any universe where he would ever go for someone like me. After seeing his house, and how he lived, I was more certain than ever that he thought I was a complete and total hot mess. He was all organization and routine. I was all spontaneity and chaos.

And yet…

Why did I feel so accepted around him? Was he just that patient? Or was I reading too much into basic human kindness? Maybe *everyone* felt like this after talking to Reid. Ruby did say their family used to call him "Saint Reid," after all. For all I knew, I was just one more lost soul mistaking calm energy for connection.

My next appointment walked in before I could spiral further. Her red-box-dye hair was twisted into a lopsided bun, and tear tracks were still fresh on her cheeks.

"Oh, honey." I sighed and guided her into my chair, already switching gears.

***

REID'S HOUSE SMELLED AMAZING. I SLIPPED OFF MY SHOES AND tucked them neatly into the cabinet by the door, resisting the urge to leave them kicked off in the middle of the floor like I usually did. No way was I messing up his perfectly tidy vibe. I would be a good house guest if it killed me.

"How was your day?" Reid asked when I strolled into the main living area. The scent of onions and butter wafted through the air. I breathed it in as I collapsed on one of the stools surrounding the island.

"Long. My last client came in with a hair emergency and it took me two hours to fix."

His eyebrows shot up. "Two hours? I think I'd lose my mind if I had to sit still for that long."

"We threw on that trashy reality show, *Tough Love*, and talked through it the whole time. It was kind of fun."

I pulled out my phone to show him the before and after pictures. She'd left with healthier hair than she'd come in with. It was now a soft, chestnut brown that fit her features a lot better than the harsh red. I was proud of that.

Reid squinted at it, the glare reflecting in his glasses. "That's incredible. Her hair looked about ready to fall off in the before shot."

"Don't bleach your hair at home," I said, setting my phone face down.

He turned his back to me to shake the pan. "Why do I feel like you don't follow your own advice?"

"Hairdressers abide by a different set of rules," I said, thinking fondly of the time I had tried to do a rainbow underlayer at home for Pride month. "Can I help with anything?"

"Nope, almost done. Hope you're hungry, because I made way too much pasta. Apparently, I can either cook for one person or a dozen, there is no in-between."

I smiled. "That's alright. I'll happily eat for at least three. Can I send you some money for groceries, or—"

"It's fine. Don't worry about it," he cut me off.

I had tried to broach the subject of money with Reid twice before now. He was letting me stay in his house rent free, he was helping me out of the goodness of his heart, and now he was feeding me. I owed him. Big time. Even though he said I didn't, I refused to be someone who took advantage of someone's good nature. I'd think of a way to make it up to him, somehow.

"Do you cook much?" he asked.

"Does boxed mac and cheese count?"

He poured the onions into a larger pot and stirred its contents. "Hazel," he scolded. "You should know how to cook."

It should have concerned me how much I loved when he used that slightly stern tone with me.

"I've dabbled here and there, but usually everything I make turns out meh. No one ever taught me. Gran was never much of a talent in the kitchen either. Her idea of a home-cooked meal was a pot of hamburger helper or jarred alfredo sauce."

And what I wouldn't give to taste one of her store-bought-homecooked meals again. They were the definition of comfort food for me.

Reid scanned my face before setting down the spatula on a rubber mat. "I could teach you. If you wanted, that is. I'm not saying I'm a gourmet chef or anything, but I like to cook."

Ugh, see? *So* freaking nice. This guy was literally irre-sistible. "That could be fun," I said. Reid shot me a shy smile and something warm settled into my gut and made itself at home.

Reid continued to cook while I went to get the plates down from his perfectly organized cabinets. The big, thick ones were just out of my reach, so without thinking, I hiked up my knee to rest on the counter and hoisted myself up a few inches to grab them before jumping down again.

"Hazel!" Reid barked, behind me in an instant.

"Shit," I scrambled backward, nearly dropping the plates. "I'm sorry." Crap, had I grossed him out by putting my knee on the counter, or something? I hadn't even thought twice about it. It was my go-to maneuver for reaching into high cabinets.

"Careful," he said, pinching the bridge of his nose. "Ask me to get them next time, or we can get you a stool."

"Oh, um…" My voice trailed off. Was he…worried about my safety? I wasn't sure what to say to that, so I settled on, "Alright."

We ate our steaming bowls of garlicky penne at the table, a habit I realized I quite liked. Maybe it was Reid's company, but there was something cozy about sitting down at a table for a meal. It made it easier to focus on each other, to actually talk without distractions.

He set a piece of bread onto my plate as we started effortlessly rehashing the details of our days, trading little stories and observations. It felt ordinary in the most special way possible.

"I can't believe you saw Paul at the gym," I said after we were both onto our second servings. I had been delaying bringing this up. First, because I was slightly worried Reid would judge me for dating someone who looked and acted like Paul. And second, because I knew he was absolutely going to hate the idea I was about to propose.

I swear I saw his jaw tense. "No offense, Hazel, but that guy seems like a jerk."

A laugh escaped me. "No offense taken. He kind of is."

With the food cleared from both of our plates, I got up, grabbed Reid's, and carried them over to the dishwasher.

"So, I have an idea." My words were cautious.

Reid being too observant for his own good, immediately narrowed his eyes.

"What?" There was more apprehension in that word than I would have thought possible.

"Just hear me out," I said while grabbing the pan and putting the leftovers into a glass container he'd gotten out earlier.

He lifted his glasses, pinching the bridge of his nose. "I already don't like the sound of this."

I carried on anyway. "Paul is at the gym *constantly*; you saw it yourself. And since he isn't taking the bait with our fake catfish profile, maybe it's time we took a more hands-on approach."

"No."

"I know where he lives. It's not far from here. We can just wait until he posts a gym selfie, rush on over, and peek through a window. See if we see anything."

"No."

"He lives alone, last I checked. He also lives on the first floor. It would be so easy just to take a quick look." I batted my eyelashes innocently, as if I didn't know how opposed Reid would be to this idea.

Reid let out a sigh that must have completely emptied the air from his lungs. To my surprise, he sat there in silence for a moment, his eyes zoning out as if he were mulling over the risks.

"Please?" I pushed, sensing his wavering resolve. "We're getting down to the wire here."

His eyes met mine. "You just want to peek through the window?" he clarified.

"That's it, I swear." I crossed my heart. "No confrontations will be had. He won't even be there."

He rubbed his chin. When his shoulders sagged in defeat, I knew I had him. A small squeal escaped me as I clapped.

"You're a little too excited about this for my liking," he said.

"I'm only excited at the thought of actually finding Vermont and putting this whole thing to bed."

Which was true. Mostly. I *did* want this to be over, and I wanted Gran's cat—*my* cat—back, more than anything. But I'd be lying if I said I didn't get a small thrill from investigating with Reid. There was something exciting about the idea that an answer could be waiting around any corner. Sure, it was crushing when we hit dead ends, but Reid had this way of keeping my hope alive. Like we were getting closer, even when we weren't.

"I'll think about it," he said.

But I was pretty sure I already had him.

SIXTEEN

Reid

Operation WAIT-UNTIL-PAUL-IS-AT-THE-GYM-AND-LOOK-through-his-window was at a bit of a standstill. Hazel had proposed the idea two nights ago and, of course, Paul had decided to take his first break from the gym in what felt like years. I had only been following the guy since the catfish profile, but every day since he'd been sliding into the fake profile's DMs with a gym selfie of himself flexing. Now? Radio silence. Nothing. It was almost as if he knew.

Hazel was getting increasingly impatient, but there was nothing we could do except wait for our moment to strike. I still wasn't keen on the idea, but a quick glimpse into a window while the suspect wasn't home seemed like a relatively low risk for what could be a big payoff.

"What about this one?" Hazel asked, holding up a painting that looked like a first grader might have created it.

My nose involuntarily scrunched in disapproval. "What about not?"

"You can't reject everything I suggest." She put the painting back before grabbing a lava lamp and sticking it into the cart without waiting for the okay from me.

When I raised an eyebrow at her, she shrugged. "What?

It's portable. I can take it with me if it doesn't grow on you, but I promise you it will."

"You have no room in your apartment for a lava lamp," I said.

"Oh, Reid. There's always room." She winked before scampering ahead to look at a vase.

It was kind of addictive watching Hazel navigate the aisles of the thrift store. She clearly felt at home here.

Her hair tumbled down the back of the oversized gray cardigan she wore. I tried not to stare. Was it weird that I liked her hair so much? The midnight blue had faded a little since she'd first dyed it. Now it was lighter and fit her skin tone perfectly. Her waves were always messy. Wild. Yet somehow, they looked intentional.

She glanced behind her and gave me a puzzled smile when she saw me staring. My cheeks flushed with warmth as I jerked my eyes away.

"What about this?" I asked, pointing to the first thing that caught my eye on the shelf next to me.

She frowned. "A hardboiled-egg maker?"

"Um…yes." My voice cracked as I realized what I was pointing to. The ceramic finish on the old appliance was chipped, and the thing probably hadn't worked in years.

Hazel laughed and shook her head. "I think even I draw a line at that," she said, before turning and continuing to peruse the aisle.

Fucking great. Now she was associating me with hard-boiled eggs, arguably the least attractive breakfast food. In what world was that better than me just owning up to the fact that I had been staring at her?

One wheel of the cart kept dragging as I followed her down the crammed aisle. It was my first time in a thrift store; used items weren't exactly my jam. Thrifting was good for the environment, but I couldn't bring myself to forget about the lives the things had before. Who sat on that couch? Did anyone ever clean that? Was that mystery stain *really* going to come out if I took it home?

For someone who preferred things new and spotless, I had a hard time getting on board with this. Hazel, however, had no such hangups. This Saturday morning, while we sat at the table drinking our coffees, I had mentioned maybe getting a few things to make the guest room more welcoming, and she had practically jumped at the chance. I had envisioned us going to a department store, but she had dragged us here instead.

I would have gone anywhere with her, honestly.

I was just grateful she wanted to spend time with me outside the obligation of the investigation. Last night, when I had been on my way out the door for family dinner, something tugged in my chest at the sight of Hazel curled up on the couch alone. I'd asked if she had plans and she said her only intentions were to eat popcorn and binge reality TV. I'd told her popcorn wasn't a real dinner and she'd shrugged me off. An invitation to my parents' house almost slipped through my lips before I caught it at the last second. Was I really ready to subject her to my family? There would be assumptions if I brought a girl home. Assumptions I wasn't sure I was ready to face.

Hazel came to a halt, forcing me to stop the cart. "What about this?" She held up a basket that had been spray painted within an inch of its life.

"I swear you're picking the ugliest stuff on purpose."

She gave me a sly smile. "Actually, Gran and I used to wander thrift stores on the weekends and sometimes we *would* pick the ugliest paintings on purpose. We figured they needed a home and if we didn't get them, no one else would. It was like we were rescuing them."

"That explains your apartment," I said.

She laughed and shoved my shoulder. "Hey!"

The lava lamp now sat in the cart along with a portrait of dogs sitting around a table mimicking the last supper, an old cuckoo clock that surely didn't work, and a photograph of a city neither of us could place. I wasn't exactly sure what type of aesthetic she was going for with this random assortment of items, but then again, that was kind of Hazel. Random and all over the place. When I thought of the décor in that way, it made me like it a little more.

"What about these plates?" she grabbed a set that were rimmed with yellow and had a picture of a barn in the center.

"I have plates."

"You have exactly six plates."

"Why would I need more than that?"

"You have to constantly run the dishwasher. And what if you have people over?"

The pack I'd purchased had come with six of every plate, bowl, and utensil. Six was enough if my family ever came over to eat, which they rarely did. We were always at my parents' house.

"I haven't run into an issue yet."

She let out a drawn-out sigh and put the dishes back.

"Your cabinets are virtually empty, Reid. You should fill them. And maybe one day you *will* have people over."

"I don't really like to entertain." My house was always clean, and I preferred to keep it that way. The last time my family had come for a dinner and game night, the place had been destroyed. Okay, maybe *destroyed* was exaggerating, but I'd still had to spend the entire next day tidying up. "It's hard for me to relax and enjoy myself while my space is actively getting messed up."

I held my breath when she picked up a teacup in the shape of a snowman and slowly blew it out when she put it back on the shelf.

"Sorry you're stuck hosting. It must be driving you nuts watching me mess up your space," she said, her playful tone almost completely covering up the self-consciousness I could see in her eyes.

"You're not messing anything up," I said, before adding. "I like having you around."

She smiled. "I'm trying *incredibly* hard. You have no idea the restraint it takes to not leave so much as a sweatshirt lying around your living room."

"I can imagine. I've seen your place, remember?"

She kept moving down the aisle. "My place must be your nightmare."

"It wasn't so bad," I surprised myself by saying. When I'd first stepped inside her apartment, I'd wanted to bolt. But in hindsight, I could see the charm. Hazel had me loosening up more than I thought possible. If my family could see the items in my cart right now, they'd be convinced I'd lost my mind.

Hazel picked up a butter dish shaped like a potato. "Okay, but you're getting this. No arguments."

She put it in the cart and, before she moved on, I took a step back and grabbed the plates she'd liked. I set them carefully in the cart.

She met my eye and grinned.

"We can use these tonight to eat the dinner you make us," I said.

Her smile turned into a frown. I'd promised to teach her how to cook tonight and for some reason, she was adorably nervous about it.

"What if I accidentally poison you?" she asked.

"Considering I'll be with you when you buy the ingredients, I highly doubt that will happen."

"You never know. I wouldn't doubt my ineptitude if I were you."

We continued strolling until Hazel stopped at two large, Victorian-looking dolls.

"Please don't get those," I begged. "They look haunted."

She giggled. "I can't stand dolls. I hate being stared at. They remind me of my neighbor's place. Her apartment gives me the creeps. Dolls everywhere."

"Mrs. Edenbury? We really need to look into her more," I said.

"I'm telling you, there's no way."

"But we have to look into every possibility. It's not like we're flush with suspects. We can't put all our eggs into Paul's basket," I said gently.

She gazed up at me with her big, round eyes before nodding. "I guess you're right."

"And what about that friend. Kiara, was it? The one who lives here and supposedly doesn't like you. Did she ever text you back?"

"No, but…" Hazel's face fell, and I regretted bringing her up.

"What?" I asked.

"My friend Zoe wants me to go out for her birthday this Wednesday. Kiara and some other girls from high school will be there, too."

"That's perfect," I said, but retracted my excitement when I noticed her crestfallen face. "Or, maybe not?"

She sighed. "It's fine. Those girls just always have a way of making me a little insecure."

The lost look in her eyes pained me. I regretted even bringing it up. I wanted the smiling Hazel from a few minutes ago back. "Zoe is your friend, right?" I asked, trying not to push too hard.

"Right," she said.

"Then you should go. We can tick Kiara off our list, and you can have fun with your friends. You could use a night out."

She nodded. "You're right. I'll go. I don't want to disappoint Zoe."

I wanted to pull her to me and give her a hug. Instead, we wandered into the next aisle in silence, her shoulders slightly slumped. Hoping to lift her mood, I grabbed a painting of a rooster that was both disturbingly lifelike and terrifyingly animated at the same time.

"What about this one?" I asked.

She glanced up, her sad demeanor cracking as soon as she saw it. "That's perfect," she said through a laugh.

The spell was broken. Her smile was back.

At the checkout line, I tried to pay for her selections, but Hazel insisted. Thankfully, it wasn't too expensive, or I would have fought her harder. If I was being honest, her financial situation had me far more stressed out than I should be. And knowing that if I failed to locate Vermont she'd be sending all of her newfound lotto wealth to some psychopath made me even more concerned. I hated to sound heartless, but if I had any say in the matter, I might have suggested she pay off her debts and let the cat live out the rest of its days in its new home. But I knew exactly the kind of look Hazel would give me if I said that out loud. And the last thing I wanted was for her to think less of me.

Still, knowing she had all that credit card debt made my stomach sink. I hated the idea of her struggling for money all these years.

We carried our "treasures," as Hazel called them, out to the car and loaded them into the trunk. With that mission complete, I drove us to the grocery store, landing us a parking spot right up front.

"You know you passed three other stores on your way here, right?" she asked, as we got out of the car and walked to the entrance.

"This is my grocery store," I said. It was farther away, but I liked this one. It was the cleanest in the area and the best stocked.

She let out a soft laugh. "Of course it is."

Something about grocery shopping in the fall hit different. There were poinsettias and wreaths on display outside, advertisements for holiday deals everywhere you turned, extra cookies in the baked goods section. Grocery shopping had always been one of my favorite errands.

I grabbed the cart and pushed it to the produce section, Hazel by my side.

"What should we make?" she asked, eyeing a bag of peppers. "Oh, what about Indian! I saw a recipe on the Food Network the other day that looked amazing."

I chuckled. "Indian? I think that's a bit ambitious for your first meal."

"That's why it'll be fun to try."

"It's taco night," I said matter-of-factly. I always had tacos on Saturday. It was the perfect meal to make too much of and use as leftovers for lunch over the following days.

Hazel's lips parted in that cute way they always did when I said something incomprehensible to her. "Seriously? You have a pre-planned menu."

I shrugged. "I mean, not for every single day, but sometimes it's nice to have a line-up of dinners."

"It's also nice to try something new."

I bagged a head of lettuce and set it in the cart. "You cooking is the new part of the evening. We don't need to add anything extra."

Hazel bit back her smile. Her eyes twinkled as she readied her next argument.

"Reid?" A new voice called my name.

Hazel's confused eyes met mine for a brief second before we both turned.

Recognition slammed into my brain a second before I saw her.

"Meghan," I breathed. My ex-wife stood before us, looking obnoxiously good in her athleisure wear. Her blonde hair was pulled back into an impossibly tight ponytail. She stood next to a guy just a few inches taller than her. He was thin and obviously older, by the faint wrinkles lining his eyes. I didn't have to ask to know that this was her new boyfriend.

"I can't believe it's you." Her eyes flashed with a hint of panic at first, but she covered it quickly. I probably only caught it this time because I'd seen that exact look a million times—usually aimed at my family. The classic *ugh, I really don't want to talk to you right now, but I have to pretend to be polite* expression.

"You know I come here," I said, irritated. This had always been *my* favorite store. She used to complain the prices were too high and pushed us to shop somewhere else. But now, apparently she'd had a change of heart. I wondered if it had to do with the guy by her side.

"This is the only place you can get good organic stuff, right babe?" the boyfriend said. Yep, there it was.

"Right," she said, shooting me a nervous glance.

As far as divorces go, ours hadn't been the worst. The marriage had been short, the legalities amicable. And by no means did I hate her or wish anything negative to befall her. With that said, I'd still have preferred never to see her again. She'd said some hurtful things at the end. Things I hadn't forgotten.

Meghan looked at my cart, any nerves transforming into a smug smile as she spotted the lettuce and avocado I'd already picked out.

"Taco night? Wow, some things really never change," she said.

A hand squeezed my bicep.

"Actually, we're trying Indian fusion tonight. Something new," Hazel said in a bright voice.

Meghan's gaze shifted to her as if just noticing her for the first time.

"Really?" she said, jutting out her lip. "That doesn't sound like Reid." Even though her gaze didn't visibly drift, I could tell she was sizing Hazel up.

Hazel was only a few years younger than Meghan, but she had that effortless, youthful glow about her, her hair flowing free, cheeks dewy, wrapped in one of the oversized sweaters she practically lived in—she looked relaxed, unbothered, and completely herself.

My eyes met Hazel's and I hoped they conveyed my

appreciation. She had covered for me. I didn't want Meghan to believe she knew me as well as she thought she did. I wanted her to know the things she'd said about me during the breakup weren't true.

Even though she'd been right. I *was* uptight and stiff.

And I was attempting to force taco night, yet again.

"Huh," Hazel said, brow furrowed. "That's interesting. It was his idea—always trying something new, this one. You should see some of the stuff he just picked out at the thrift store. It's going to be fun giving his house a little makeover."

I bit my lip trying not to laugh. I wanted to hug Hazel right then. She had a way of taking a moment that should've felt small and heavy, and flipping it on its head. One second, I was bracing myself for the awkward tension of running into my ex for the first time since we'd swapped the last of our stuff. The next, I was simply standing in a grocery store, grabbing ingredients with Hazel, excited about teaching her how to cook. I didn't give a fuck who else was there.

And just like that, I realized what moving on really felt like.

It felt like *this*.

Like not caring.

Meghan's mouth hung open for a second before she snapped it shut. "T-thrift store?" she whispered in confusion, the words barely audible.

Then we were all just standing there, both with our carts, not quite sure how to extricate ourselves from this painful social interaction.

"Man, it's good to meet you," the boyfriend said, huge smile glued to his face. "I'll break the uncomfortable tension in the room. Always weird to run into exes. I'm Bernard, by the way." He gave a small wave.

Hazel laughed. "I'm Hazel." The way Hazel said it clearly implied that she and I were more than friends—and I didn't bother correcting her. Not because I wanted Meghan to feel jealous—she wouldn't, and I wouldn't want her to—and not because her surprised expression gave me any kind of petty satisfaction. It didn't. I honestly didn't care about any of that.

What *did* catch me off guard was how good the idea felt of introducing Hazel as something more. Before I could stop it, a fantasy had started playing out in my mind. One where running to the grocery store together was a typical weekend activity.

Meghan laughed and rocked back and forth on her heels. It was strange seeing her in such a normal place. Somewhere I ran errands. We'd been in this same aisle together many times before, except in that alternate timeline, we were pushing the same cart in a comfortable silence. It was hard to remember that version of myself. The one who thought I'd soon be starting a family of my own. Who thought I'd settled into my routine life. Back before Meghan had changed the rules of the game.

"Well," Meghan finally said, lips tight. "It was good to see you."

"You too," I said, and that was that.

We parted ways.

Except we were both shopping in the same goddamn grocery store, so the rest of the trip involved Hazel and me awkwardly bumping into them in nearly every freaking aisle we went down.

"Kill me," I muttered after we'd picked out the rest of our produce and spotted them ten feet away at the butcher.

"I'd say we should give up and abandon the cart, but we can't let them know they're getting to us," Hazel said through the smile pasted on her face. Out of nowhere, she burst into a loud fit of laughter, pointing at a random sale sign for a salmon fillet.

I jerked back. "What was that for?"

"Laugh," she hissed. "We need to make it look like we're having fun." She tossed the ground turkey into the cart.

I chuckled, shaking my head at her ridiculousness. "I *am*

having fun. With you." I added the last part in case it wasn't obvious. Hazel was the only thing making today enjoyable.

Maybe it was my imagination, but I swore I saw hint of pink spreading across her cheeks.

When we got to the spice aisle, Hazel tossed in curry powder.

I raised my eyebrows but before I could protest, she said, "Nope. You're trying something new, Reid, whether you like it or not."

I kind of realized I *did* like it. Not necessarily trying something new, but *her* making me try something new.

We hastily moved to the other side of the store and finished our shopping as quickly as possible. The entire thing felt like a bad concept for a game show—we'd only win the prize if we grabbed our items and got out of each aisle before spotting my ex again.

Back in the car, after we wrapped up, Hazel turned to me and smiled. "Kind of crazy that we ran into your ex a few days after you ran into mine."

I nearly choked on my own spit. I hadn't expected her to bring him up.

"Uh, yeah. This town is too small," I said, instead of admitting the truth—that I had tracked her ex down because of some sort of morbid curiosity. I think I'd die of humiliation if Hazel sniffed out my jealousy.

"I can't believe you talked me into changing the dinner plans to Indian taco night," I said, throwing the car into drive and hoping she'd accept my change of subject.

She clapped her hands and rubbed them together. "You're in for a treat, Reid. They're going to be delicious."

SEVENTEEN

Hazel

"THESE ARE...GOOD?" REID'S COMMENT SOUNDED A LOT
more like a question than a statement.

I chewed, suffering through another bite of the concoction. "They aren't terrible."

He smirked. "Exactly what you were going for, right?"

"The flavor profile with the texture of tacos is...kind of
weird," I admitted, forcing myself to swallow without triggering my gag reflex.

It turned out there was a reason there weren't any
recipes online for Indian tacos. I set down my failed attempt
at fusion and offered Reid an apologetic smile. He had been
so supportive throughout the entire cooking process, despite
a few side-eyes any time I added a new seasoning to
the mix.

"At least my chopping was on point," I said.

The moment I'd started attacking the vegetables with a
knife, Reid had panicked and stepped in right away. He gently
repositioned my fingers, showing me how to hold them so I
didn't accidentally slice one off, then hovered nearby, ready to
intervene at the first sign of danger.

Reid laughed at that and graciously finished the taco on

his plate. "These are the best-cut vegetables I've ever had. You should really start a food truck or something."

"I'm thinking about it."

We smiled across the table from each other.

"Has it ever occurred to you," he started while grabbing my abandoned plate. "That you aren't a bad cook, you're just a bit too experimental?"

"If I don't experiment, how will I come up with the next great recipe?"

"Is that the goal?" he asked, forehead scrunched as he placed the dishes in the sink.

"What else would the goal be?" I took my napkin and wiped off the crumbs that lingered on the table. Try as I might, I could never keep a clean place setting while eating.

"I think the goal is to prepare and eat a delicious meal."

"Bor-ing." I emphasized the two syllables.

Today with Reid had been exactly what I needed to take my mind off everything. Bringing him to the thrift store felt like leading an alien on their first excursion to Earth. He'd seemed both terrified and intrigued. Okay, mostly terrified, but it had still been fun. And my heart got all warm and fuzzy that he let me pick out whatever I wanted, even though he must have thought the finds were horrid.

Even running into his ex at the store hadn't been enough to ruin the day. At first, I'd been disconcerted. She was *stunning* —like, catalog-model pretty. That was Reid's ex-wife? I didn't stand a chance in comparison. But then I saw the way he tensed up the moment he spotted her. I'd stepped in instinctively, standing up for him, shifting the mood, doing whatever I could to ease the awkwardness.

And I could tell he appreciated it. There was this unspoken sense that we were on the same team. For the first time in a long time, I felt like I was *in* something with someone —not circling around the edges, not tagging along, but actually inside it. Together.

"So, how are you feeling about the big run-in?" I asked

cautiously. Reid hadn't said anything about Meghan and the boyfriend since we got home. He didn't seem overly affected, but I also couldn't imagine Reid crashing out. Holding in emotion seemed more his move.

Reid sighed and leaned against the kitchen island. "It was fine. Honestly, better than I would have thought. It was good that you were there."

"Really?" My heart pounded at the admission.

"Yeah, I was more relaxed. And you making a joke out of the thing really broke the tension. Thanks for that."

"No problem." I chewed my lip, dying to ask him more. "You said the divorce was a while ago, right?"

"Just over a year."

"And you were together for…"

"Since senior year of college, so six-ish years."

"Holy shit, that's a long time," I blurted out before smacking my hand to my mouth. *Damnit Hazel. Play it cool.*

But he just shrugged, as if he didn't care. "I mean, I thought it was going to be much longer before she told me otherwise," he joked, a smile reaching his eyes.

I studied him, searching for even an inkling that he wasn't okay. It had to be hard, thinking you'd spend your whole life with someone, only to have it end. Especially since it didn't sound like it had been his decision.

"And you haven't moved on since her?" I asked, shifting the topic of conversation back to him.

Our gaze broke like a trance as he started scrubbing the dishes in the sink. "I mean, I've dated a little, but it isn't exactly a priority for me."

"You don't want another relationship?" I wondered if he'd ever consider getting married again, but I didn't ask. I wasn't sure if it was because it felt inappropriate, or because I was afraid the answer would be no. Even though there was nothing even close to official between us, I still didn't want his answer to be no. Not at all.

"I mean, I'm fine with the idea of moving on, I just want

it to happen naturally. I'm happy on my own. I've got a life, and I'd rather be by myself than change just to fit someone else's standards."

"And she tried to change you? Your ex?"

"Kind of. She always wanted me to try new things, branch out. Maybe it's a character flaw of mine that I didn't want to, but I liked my life. I was happy."

I turned around completely in my chair, leaning my chin against the back as I watched him. "But she wasn't?" I asked.

He shrugged. "I guess not. Maybe it was just incompatibility at the end of the day, and no one's fault, but it still stung that I wasn't enough for her."

Reid was so sweet—soft, kind, wouldn't hurt a fly. The idea of someone hurting *him* made my stomach twist.

After a second, I let out a breath. "I know what you mean. My ex was always trying to change me. Said I should dress cuter, or be quieter, or clean more." I stuck out my tongue, pretending to gag. "Eventually, I'd had enough. I couldn't sit through his constant criticisms when, at the end of the day, what was he even bringing to the table? It was like he wanted me to take care of him, but I could barely take care of myself."

"Hazel." Reid's voice was soft, gentle. "You take care of yourself just fine."

"I think my current predicament would argue otherwise," I joked half-heartedly.

"Your current predicament isn't your fault."

"You keep saying that, but if I had just been more responsible—"

"No, it's not your fault," he insisted, sharper this time. "I mean, I wouldn't hate it if you were a touch more responsible. Like, maybe don't post your whereabouts and your exact financial situation for people to take advantage of, and whatnot."

My lip turned up in amusement. "I'll have to give that a try going forward."

"And for the record, your ex sounds like a complete idiot."

"For the record, so does yours."

He snorted. "She's really not."

"If she let you go, she definitely can't be that smart."

His eyes locked onto mine through the lenses of his glasses, piercing and unreadable. The tension between us heightened, but I couldn't stop myself. The words had slipped out before I could pull them back. Maybe this whole crush I'd been quietly nursing was misguided, completely one-sided. Maybe I was reading too much into every glance, every soft moment we shared. But something was there. It crackled just beneath the surface, waiting to break through.

It couldn't all be in my head…could it?

"Did she break your heart?" The question tumbled out before I could snatch it back.

He looked away from me and squinted out the large window. The sun had already set, the sky just getting to the point where it was almost completely dark, but you could still make out the outlines of trees. I thought for sure I'd over-stepped, but when he met my eyes again, his expression was soft and warm.

"It's funny, you're the first person to ask me that. I think my family just assumed I was a blubbering mess after it happened. They checked in on me daily, forced me to go on all these activities. At the time, I'd found their overbearingness pretty annoying. I had just gotten friendlier with the guys in the internet sleuthing forum, and I was having way more fun going over cold cases to distract myself. My family thought it was a cry for help."

"So you *weren't* heartbroken?" The glimmer of hope in my voice made me cringe.

"You know, not really, I guess. It hurt, that's for sure. I felt blindsided by the whole thing. She said…she said, she fell out of love with me. That she could picture our whole life together already, because in twenty years we'd be doing the exact same things we were doing now. She wanted something new. Something different."

"Ouch." I winced, hating the thought of anyone saying that to Reid. I regretted not being ruder to Meghan at the store. I should've hit her with some passive-aggressive line about how "comfortable" her outfit looked, or something equally petty.

"Yeah, it sucked at the time. Made me question everything—who I was, the way I lived my life."

"I hoped you told her stability isn't so bad," I said softly. "Some people crave it more than anything."

Shit. Why had I said that? Now he was looking at me with a heavy gaze. The air in the room was even thicker than it had been before.

"Is that…something you crave?" he asked, tripping a little over the words.

Our eyes lingered on each other's for a breath too long. "Yeah. It really is."

I pulled my feet up, tucking them underneath myself. He pushed himself away from the sink, and stepped toward the table, leaning against it. He hovered just feet away from me.

"Hazel…" He licked his lips but didn't seem like he knew quite what to say. I was used to that. Used to people pitying me because my childhood story didn't fit into the stereotypical happy one.

"I didn't mean I haven't had any stability," I added.

His eyes flickered to mine, not leaving this time. I felt pinned underneath his gaze.

"Really, though," I said, rambling. "Gran was always there for me the best she could be. I was happy growing up. I just—I guess, sometimes I wanted more."

Guilt consumed me saying those words out loud. As if Gran hadn't sacrificed so much to give me the childhood I'd had. A tear slipped down my cheek.

"Hey," Reid said gently. My breath caught in my throat when he stepped closer, reaching out to brush it away. "You can be grateful for everything she gave you and grieve what you never had at the same time."

I sniffled and pulled the sleeves of my sweater over my hands. How could a guy who'd just met me nail my emotions so effortlessly? That was exactly what it felt like. My whole life, I'd always had certain things in the back of my mind, things I'd felt I was missing. Parents. A close extended family. A white-picket-fence house in a nice suburb. A ton of close friends. I loved Gran so much, but I couldn't completely forget what I lacked.

Then, she was gone.

"Now that she's gone, I regret ever thinking she wasn't enough," I whispered.

Reid crouched down, wrapping me against him. I inhaled his scent, clutching the fabric of his sweater lightly as I let myself get lost in how good he felt. He pulled away too soon. I swiped at my eyes and forced a smile.

"Sorry, I don't know what's gotten into me."

"Don't apologize for having feelings, Hazel. Not ever," he said, still kneeling before me. "And I might not have known your gran, but if the way you speak about her is any indication, you two had a special relationship. I don't think she doubted for one second how much you loved her."

"I know…you're right."

I gave him a shaky smile, knowing deep down his words were the truth. Gran and I had spoken every day. We had a bond that I'd never get with anyone else. I'd miss her the rest of my life, but I could never let myself doubt that she knew how much I cared.

Reid held my gaze for a breath longer before clearing his throat. He leaned back on his heels before stretching to a standing position.

"So, uh, did you want to go hang those decorations?" His gaze shifted to the paper bags from the thrift store we'd abandoned on the floor next to his couch.

I laughed, wiping the last remaining tear from my cheek.

"You're actually going to let me put those things up in your pristine guest room?"

Reid scratched the back of his neck. "Sure," he said, but the way he chewed on the inside of his cheek told me he was still reeling with uncertainty.

"I figured you were being polite and would just donate them right back," I teased, hoisting myself off the chair.

He chuckled "Maybe it's past time I let some chaos into my life."

I tried my best not to beam. "I think chaos arrived the moment you agreed to meet me in that diner."

"And I'm so glad I did."

My voice caught in my throat. I forced my expression into something neutral, willing myself not to let his words sink too deep.

"Um, let's do it," I said, grabbing one of the larger bags that held some of the paintings while he grabbed the lava lamp that I was basically in love with. How I had made it twenty-five years without owning a single lava lamp was beyond me.

Once in the bedroom, I pointed to random spots around the room while Reid held up one of the pictures, waiting for my approval. Once I gave the okay, he pulled a hammer and a nail from a toolbox I hadn't even seen him grab. I blinked. Wow—an actual hole in the wall instead of a sticky hook? *Noted.* This man was committing.

"Is there a method to your madness? Because the spots you're choosing are random and not correlated in the slightest."

"What did you expect? For me to map it all out like a blueprint?"

"Isn't that the hack for gallery walls? I remember Meghan spending hours planning one out with painter's tape at our old place."

"The best method for a gallery wall is to build it slowly, not all at once. You get pieces as they speak to you, and you hang them until they take over the wall, slowly expanding until they form one giant organism. That's what gives it character. You can't just go out, buy all the pieces at once, and hang them in some preplanned way. That sucks the soul right out of the project."

Reid squinted as he held up a nail to the wall and tapped the hammer lightly a few times. "I think that's exactly what we did at our old house. She even ordered all the prints from the same website."

I clutched my chest and staggered backward. "Ouch, that hurts."

Reid laughed.

"It's a good thing I'm here now," I continued. "I'll liven this place up if it kills me."

After Reid hung the few pictures we'd purchased, he held up the lava lamp. "And what are we doing with this little number?"

I pointed to the bedside table. "Right here."

He hesitated. "This is not a practical bedside lamp."

"Why not?"

"It's too dim. You won't be able to read from it. You'll strain your eyes."

I had to bite down on my lip to keep from laughing. He looked so earnest. So deeply concerned for my eyesight.

"Reid, chill out. A lava lamp provides an excellent source of light."

He did not look like he believed me but went ahead and plugged in the lamp anyway. I turned off the overhead light and told him to switch the new one on. When he did, the room was immediately cast in a pinkish glow. The globs of whatever it was inside a lava lamp began to bubble and move around.

"It's perfect," I said, clapping my hands, and moving to stand next to him by the edge of the bed.

"It looks ridiculous," he said, craning his neck to take in all the additions.

He wasn't wrong. The walls were stark white, and the ceilings were incredibly high. The few pictures looked almost comically out of place.

I loved it instantly. "You have to start somewhere," I said.

"Hazel?" Reid asked.

"Yeah?" I looked up at him, suddenly aware of just how close he was. The space between us had all but disappeared, and the bed was right there, just a step away. The air was charged with something unspoken.

"Do yourself a favor and don't quit your day job, okay? I don't think you're cut out for a career in interior design."

"Excuse you, Mister Beige-and-White-Everything." I nudged him in the chest.

My heart stuttered as his gaze dropped—just briefly—to my mouth. Now my imagination was running completely out of control. I couldn't stop myself from imagining what it would be like if he leaned in a little closer, eyes locked on mine, then on my lips. What it would feel like if he finally closed the distance between us and…

Heat flooded my body. Wow. Say what you will about a lava lamp, but this lighting really set the mood.

Reid's gaze darkened ever so slightly. There was something there, behind his normally buttoned-up exterior. Or was that just wishful thinking on my part? Was I mistaking his kindness for something else entirely?

Then I saw it—a vein in his jaw standing out as he clenched it. That *definitely* wasn't my imagination. God, what I wouldn't give to be the kind of person who could simply stand up on their tiptoes and kiss him without overthinking it. I *needed* to know what his lips tasted like.

Was he a good kisser? Good in the bedroom?

It had admittedly been a while for me, so it wasn't shocking that merely being alone in a bedroom with Reid was enough to fire up my imagination. I'd had approximately three awkward first dates and one terrible second date since Paul and I had broken up. Only one of those dates had resulted in intimacy, and it was mediocre at best. I hadn't even come, and he'd barely said goodbye after he pulled out and hightailed it out of my apartment.

Being with Reid would be nothing like that. I knew it in my bones. He would be careful. Thoughtful. He was the type to make sure a partner was alright and take care of her afterward. He wouldn't rush.

The fantasy had every nerve in my body at attention. Shit. How long had I just been standing here staring at him? I'd be embarrassed, but he was right here with me. We were both drowning in the silence.

Before I could second-guess it, I leaned toward him.

That seemed to break whatever spell we were under. Reid blinked a few times and looked to the wall.

"Well, uh—I'd better get some sleep," he said, his voice far deeper than it had been a moment ago.

"Oh, yeah, same. I'm pretty tired." I was not tired in the slightest. It was only eight.

"Goodnight, Hazel." Instead of brushing past me, he put a hand on my shoulder and gave it a small squeeze."

"Night, Reid."

Then he was gone, the only evidence of our moment the intense tingling sensation raging on my shoulder from where he'd just touched it.

EIGHTEEN

Reid

"How the hell did you convince me to do this?" I grabbed Hazel's hand and gave it a tug so that she wouldn't walk too far ahead of me.

"We'll take a look and be out of here in five minutes," she said, offering me a smile that did absolutely nothing to reassure me.

We'd parked around the corner, and despite every ounce of good judgement I possessed, we were now slinking up the sidewalk toward Paul's apartment.

It was my fault for saying anything. I'd known it would lead us here. An hour ago, I'd been about to make dinner when my phone buzzed with a notification. The catfish account had received a message from Paul. He was at the gym, flexing a bicep. "Getting some sets in after work," he'd written.

I'd shown Hazel and she'd practically flown to her car without giving me the option to protest. I'd tried to convince her that we needed to think this through, but she wouldn't hear of it. She'd insisted we had to go right then, or we'd lose our opportunity. And since there was no way in hell I was about to let her go alone, here I was, trailing behind her.

"Which one is his?" I asked, my voice barely above a whisper.

"You don't have to talk so quietly. We're on a public sidewalk," she said at full volume.

"Shhh." I held a finger to my lips out of instinct.

She wrapped her coat around her and let out a laugh. "You're ridiculous. He's at the gym. He won't even know we're here."

We crept around the side of the building, staying close to the wall. At least I could be comforted by the fact that it was dark outside.

The apartment complex was one of those boxy new builds—glass, steel, sharp angles, and absolutely zero charm. It stood five stories tall, but apparently Paul's apartment was on the ground level. Assuming he'd left his blinds open, we'd have a clear view inside. Could we possibly be that lucky? Part of me hoped no, but it was about time something finally went our way. We needed answers.

In a minute, we could solve this mystery. In a minute, Hazel's life could turn into something a hell of a lot better than its current state. I wanted that for her. *Badly*. She had been dealt a shitty hand of cards. She deserved more. And we were getting down to the wire. There were fewer than ten days left until the winnings hit her bank account and she'd be forced to make a decision.

Unfortunately for us, the predator knew exactly when that money would arrive, because Hazel had been forthcoming about it. I knew I was beating a dead horse, but I still felt the need to give her another little lecture on privacy. She'd already given me access to her computer the other day and let me set up some more secure passwords.

The girl stressed me out.

Not in a way that weighed me down, but in a way that told me I cared a hell of a lot more than I probably should.

At this point, Hazel had not just entered my life, but settled right into the center of it. I couldn't ignore the stark fact that I had been happier since she'd come around. I'd been spending less time online, which I did feel bad about. I'd have to write a killer blog post for the guys next week to make up for my shortcomings.

In my defense, I had a lot on my mind. Time was of the essence, and failing Hazel was not an option I wanted to consider.

Hazel came to an abrupt halt. A small jolt surged through me—possibly excitement, likely panic—as she silently pointed to the next window and mouthed, "This is it."

We jerked our heads, looking up and down the dark street. Empty.

"Cover me," Hazel said, crouching down and bracing herself to hop into the ground-level patio.

"Absolutely the fuck not." I grabbed her arm and stopped her mid-pounce.

Lines creased her forehead like she was oblivious as to why I wouldn't want her to go down there first. "What? This is his unit."

I sighed. "Let me look. If he's in there, I don't want to risk him seeing you."

"He's at the gym."

I narrowed my eyes. "Hazel, stay here."

She stood up and crossed her arms. Her hair was tucked under a knit beanie that was borderline threadbare. Would it be weird if I bought her a new one?

Forcing any anxiety from my system, I hopped down onto the patio. It was just a three by seven slab of concrete with a sliding glass door. Paul hadn't done much to make the space homey. There was a dirty folding chair, and some crunched-up energy drink cans littering the floor. Classy guy.

The curtain had been pulled partially closed, but there was at least a foot-wide gap I could see through. The apartment looked exactly what you'd expect a guy like Paul's apartment to look like. Beat-up gray couch in the corner, clothes strewn about. A sad bachelor's pad. I squinted and scanned the place. It wasn't big. Thankfully, he'd left the light on so I could see most of the living room and kitchen area.

No sign of movement.

There was another, smaller window at the edge of the patio with the blinds wide open. I sidestepped over to it to peek through. It was his empty bedroom, devoid of anything except a sad looking gray comforter and a plywood dresser. A walk-in closet opened off the room, its door half-ajar. From this angle, I could see only part of the closet and a narrow glimpse of the bathroom beyond it.

Everything looked still. Empty.

"I don't see anything," I said.

"Let me look." A hand pressed against my arm, and I jumped.

"Hazel—what the hell? I told you to keep watch."

"Oops, I forgot." She blinked up at me, a coy smile on her lips. "Now let me see."

I sighed and shook my head, stepping aside to let her take a look for herself. I edged toward the corner of the patio, scanning the quiet residential street, but it was empty. No movement, no sign of anyone. Just stillness. It was the kind of cold November evening that chilled your bones. The kind that kept people indoors unless they had absolutely no choice.

"Hurry," I said as Hazel scanned the place.

She narrowed her eyes and pressed her face even closer to the glass. "Hey, look at this."

My heart jumped and I squeezed in next to her, stealing glances behind me every half a second to make sure the coast was still clear.

"What?" I asked, looking for a litter box, food, anything—but not spotting anything of interest.

"The floor." She pulled out her phone and the message thread we had examined a hundred times. The pictures of Vermont, the first taken on some sort of hardwood floor.

I looked at the picture and then back at the apartment. My heart sank.

"His have a wider panel and are basically gray. They look nothing like the picture," I said.

"I see that." The defeat in her voice made me want to take her home, wrap her into my arms, and never let her leave.

"I mean, I guess technically we can't see the entire bedroom," I said, knowing it was a weak point.

"It just looks so lifeless," she said. "I doubt Vermont would just be holed up back there." She tapped on the window a few times, as if the sound alone might draw him out. I caught her hand and gently pulled it away. Then I climbed back up to street level and reached down to help Hazel up after me.

"We need to get out of here. We've pushed our luck enough," I said, pulling her further down the sidewalk, away from the apartment.

"Okay." Her eyes were glossy. She looked crushed—heart-broken, even. The sight of her like this drove me mad with frustration. I needed to make her smile again. I wanted to fix this for her, more than anything. I wanted to see who she was without all the grief, the weight, and the sadness dragging her down. I wanted to set her free.

"Hey." I hooked a finger under her chin and pulled her gaze up to meet mine. "It's going to be okay."

"You can't promise that." She gave me a half-smile. "And with my luck, it probably won't be."

"Whatever happens, you'll get through this. You're stronger than you should have to be."

Silently, I begged for the wetness in her eyes to retreat. Seeing her cry again right now would gut me.

She sniffled before surprising me. She lunged forward and wrapped her arms around my middle, her head pressed against my chest. It took me a second to react, but when I did, I placed one arm around her waist, and the other around her shoulders so I could cradle the back of her head in my hand.

"I've got you. You'll get through this," I said into her hair. Because at least that I *could* promise her.

She laughed softly against me. "I don't know if I believe you, but for some reason, when you say it, I feel better."

"Good," I said.

We stood there, locked in an embrace for a few more seconds. I didn't want to be the first to step away. When she finally loosened her grip, I forced myself to let her.

"We'll figure this out. We're not giving up." I gave her hand a squeeze. "Whatever happens, I'm right here. We're in this together."

She offered me a small smile and looked at the ground before meeting my eyes again.

"Reid?"

"Yeah?"

"Please don't say that to me unless you mean it."

I'd be willing to bet that she had no idea just how much I meant it.

"Hazel? What the fuck?"

Hazel jerked away from me, eyes wide. My stomach sank as I turned, my eyes landing on Paul. He stood there, dressed ridiculously in shorts and a cut-off t-shirt despite it being twenty-five degrees outside. He blinked, slow and uncertain.

"Hey," she squeaked out, attempting to keep an even, nonchalant voice. I wanted to laugh at how not-casual this was.

At this moment, I was immensely grateful we'd taken at least a few strides away from his patio. Maybe we still looked suspicious, but at least we weren't caught aggressively red-handed.

Paul's little friend from the gym the other day was behind him, looking bored.

"What are you doing here? Are you here to see me?" Paul asked, eyebrows raised.

I tugged Hazel's arm to place her partially behind me. Maybe it was irrational, but I didn't care.

Paul eyed me, sizing me up. I silently prayed he wouldn't recognize me from the gym. Thankfully, he'd barely glanced my way that day, because zero recognition flashed in his dark eyes.

"Oh, um, no." Hazel licked her lips. I was mentally screaming at her to play it cool. I wasn't sure I could take a repeat of her getting in someone's face and yelling at them. Unlike her frilly ex-boss, these two looked like they'd fight dirty. I wanted no part of that.

"We were touring that apartment," I said quickly, pointing to another new build right across the street.

Paul and his friend turned their heads to follow my gesture.

"Do you live over here?" Hazel asked, finding her voice again. "I totally forgot. All of these new builds look the same."

I wanted to hug her for sounding so believable.

"You two?" Paul looked appalled. "You're with *this* guy? Are you serious?" He wasn't even bothering to hide the anger in his voice. I couldn't blame the guy. He and Hazel had broken up not too long ago, and here she was, allegedly apartment shopping with some other guy.

I must not be mentally okay, because that idea went straight to my head. When I slipped an arm around her shoulder, I tried to tell myself that I was playing a part, not being possessive.

"I know it's fast, but we basically already live together," she said. I nearly snorted at the not-quite-lie but I kept my face composed. To my immense satisfaction, she leaned into me. "But we've been talking about moving in together next year anyway. And there's been some theft in my building lately. We figured we might as well find somewhere more secure."

My heart pounded at her not-so-subtle mention of the theft, but Paul looked completely unfazed. Or, I guess I should say he seemed completely unfazed about *that*. He looked pissed. Real pissed. He shot me a withering look, not bothering with any pleasantries.

His friend, doucheface, snorted. "That's fast, don't you think, Hazel?"

She rolled her eyes. "Nice to see you again, Callum."

"Are you taking advantage of her?" Paul shocked me by asking, staring me up and down.

"Never," I said, glaring at the guy. Who the fuck did he think he was? *Me* taking advantage of her? I bit my tongue to keep from going off on him.

"We'd better go," Hazel said flatly.

Paul took a step forward, like he wanted to reach out and grab her to keep her there. I hoped he wouldn't, or I'd be the one physically escalating the situation this time, not Hazel.

"Hazel, your gran *just* died. Is this really the time to be jumping into a relationship?"

What a manipulative dick.

I bristled at his words, and Hazel tensed underneath my arm.

He must have noticed the shift in her, because his eyes did a quick calculation before he took a small step forward. "Can we talk some time? Please?"

I stifled the "No" that threatened to break free from my mouth. Even if I was supposed to be her fake boyfriend in this scenario, I still didn't want to come off like some controlling freak—the way Hazel had said Paul used to be.

"I don't think so," she said cooly. Suddenly I could breathe again.

"We've got to go." I squeezed her shoulder and spun us around.

"Let it go, man." I heard Paul's friend say. *Yeah, dude. Listen to your friend. Back off.*

Hazel and I quickened our pace, not stopping until we'd rounded the corner. The car was still a block ahead and to my surprise, she ran, sprinting for it.

Without thinking, I took off after her, boots pounding against the sidewalk, heart racing. When I reached her at the car, I froze, dreading seeing her face. Would it be crumpled? Sad? Would she be crying?

But when she faced me, she was laughing, hard, wheezing

in and out through her mouth. Despite my bewilderment, a grin broke out on my face.

"Are you okay?" I asked, unsure if the laughter was some kind of coping mechanism or if she had finally lost it under the pressure.

"I can't believe my stupid plan almost got us caught," she said, laughing harder. "You should really stop listening to me."

I snorted. "I really should."

Her laughter fizzled and she wiped away a stray tear that had escaped. "I think we've hit our quota for the year on running into exes."

"You can say that again," I said, climbing into the car.

Armchair_Detective: No luck at the boyfriends?

*ReidingRainbow: *Ex-boyfriend's. And no.*

WhiteKnight31: So sensitive about that word.

ReidingRainbow: No sign of the cat, and no evidence the pictures were taken there. In fact, almost seems certain that they weren't taken there.

WhiteKnight31: Bummer. I was holding out hope he'd be the one.

Armchair_Detective: I tried tracking down the number again, but still no luck. I can confirm it was created in Grand Rapids, but that doesn't exactly help us narrow down the list.

WhiteKnight31: Now what?

ReidingRainbow: The cat lady across the hall is still fishy.

WhiteKnight31: What about the friend who unfollowed her?

ReidingRainbow: Hazel doesn't think that's a possibility. But she's going out with those girls tomorrow night, so we'll see.

NINETEEN

Reid

———

"You look great," I said, as Hazel came out in what must have been at least her seventh outfit change of the evening.

"Is it too casual?" she asked, running her hands along her light-washed jeans. "It's too casual. I'm going to change."

I leapt up from the couch and raced after her to her room. I grabbed her hand, spinning her around to face me.

"Hey." Her hand was clammy beneath mine. I gave it a squeeze. "You just changed out of that black dress because it was too dressy. I think you're going in circles here."

She nodded, but her eyes were a million miles away. My chest tightened at the panic I saw there.

When I'd encouraged her to go out with her friends tonight to get a read on Kiara, I hadn't realized how much I was asking of her. I'd thought this would be the easiest lead to check out so far. But judging by how anxious she looked right now, I couldn't have been more mistaken. I wanted to ease her discomfort, but no matter what I said or how encouraging I tried to be, she still vibrated with nervous energy.

"I swear I always make the wrong call." She pulled at the tight top that hugged her frame. "Last time, I wore a dress, because the time before that, I'd worn jeans, and they dragged me to some fancy club. But that time? We ended up at a stupid pop-up carnival, whatever the hell that's supposed to be. I can never win."

"Can't you text them and ask?"

"Zoe isn't answering." She bit her lip, and I was about ten seconds away from telling her to call the whole thing off, throw on some sweats, and let me wrap her up in a blanket. Would she let me cuddle her? Was it weird that I was thinking that? Probably.

She pulled away from me to examine the contents of her closet. There were already so many discarded items on the bed that you could barely make out the color of the comforter.

"What about this." I snatched a black top she'd been wearing earlier and a pair of darker jeans. "This is safe. Could be casual, but it also wouldn't stand out if the others were more dressed up."

She eyed it before taking the pieces. "It's perfect. How did you do that?"

"Two sisters," I said with a smirk.

She tore off into the bathroom. I leaned against the wall, twiddling my thumbs and waiting while she changed. When she stepped out, I had to fight the urge to tell her exactly how beautiful she looked. The jeans hugged her curves like they were made for her, and that small sliver of exposed stomach was seriously testing my self-control. Her hair was wild and curled, and the smoky makeup around her eyes was different than the natural look she typically wore. I shifted, trying to ignore the sudden tightness in my jeans.

I cleared my throat. "You look good."

"You think?" She stood in front of the mirror, tugging at her top.

"Definitely." My voice sounded gruff. I cleared my throat.

She gave a final nod of resolution. "Okay, okay. I should just get in a cab before I change my mind again."

"And you're headed downtown, right?" I asked, following her out of her room. She'd told me the plan earlier that day, and I wanted to confirm. I felt better knowing where she'd be.

"Yep. We're doing dinner and then Zoe wants to check out that new cocktail bar. We'll probably just stay there all night."

"Tell me if you end up moving, okay?"

"Alright," she said pulling on boots and checking her phone again. I hoped she really would remember to text me. She seemed all over the place right now.

"Hey, wait," I said.

She turned, her expression frazzled.

I pulled her in for a hug, rubbing what I hoped was a soothing circle against her back. She was stiff for a second before melting into me. "Try to have fun, okay? Don't stress. Call me if you need anything."

She pulled away from me, and I forced myself to let her go.

"Thanks, Reid." She gazed up at me with the first genuine smile I'd seen out of her all evening.

It hit me then, watching her go. I kind of knew it, but I hadn't accepted it until now—just how completely gone I was for her.

My phone vibrated in my lap. I pulled it out and set it onto the table, but it wasn't Hazel, just my sleuthing group chat. I muted it.

It had been approximately three hours since I'd ushered Hazel into a rideshare and told her to have a good night. I hadn't stopped thinking about her from the moment the car left my line of sight. I'd never seen her so nervous. Had high school been tough for her? Were these girls bullies?

I kicked myself for not asking her more about the group dynamic, but it hadn't even occurred to me. I'd had a solid group of friends in high school. West was the only one I still talked to regularly, but every now and then, we'd all meet up and shoot the shit. It was easy. Chill. I'd taken that for granted, and just assumed Hazel had something similar.

But I couldn't shake the look she'd given me, like she was a guppy being set loose in a bowl full of piranhas. Like she was scared and trying to put on a brave face just for me.

I hated it.

"A phone? Seriously, Reid? Pay attention. We're never going to get through the game at this rate." Regan tried to take my phone, but I snatched it away.

My mom gave a disapproving tsk. "A phone while we're trying to learn a new game? You know better."

"Sorry." I stuffed it back into my pocket, but not before ensuring the ringer was turned to loud just in case Hazel tried to call me.

"It's your turn," my dad said.

I rolled the dice and moved my piece forward before passing the dice to West.

Game nights weren't a regular occurrence in our family.

Occasionally we'd squeeze one in after family night dinners, but a whole night dedicated just to playing? I couldn't handle that on a recurrent basis. Mom, Regan, and West were highly competitive, even going so far as to talk smack. We'd had to outlaw rummy in this house following an especially heated game that ended with Regan yelling at the table and storming off to her room. My dad and Ruby couldn't care less about games and usually had to be talked through the rules every turn, somehow forgetting them. Every. Single. Time. I didn't mind games in theory, but the stark difference in the dynamic usually had me zoning out. I could only sit through my mom and dad bickering about not knowing the correct strategy so many times. They sucked the fun out of it.

But tonight, Mom had begged us to come over to play a new game she'd bought, even bribed us with homemade cake. I couldn't say no, but I felt bad for not being more into it.

Usually, I at least made an attempt. But not tonight. Tonight, I was distracted.

West took his turn. My ringer went off again and I scrambled to check my phone, putting it away as soon as I saw it wasn't Hazel.

"Well, that's not distracting," Ruby muttered,

"I'm waiting on a text from someone," I said.

"A girl?" West demanded, eyes wide.

"A girl!" My mom gasped. I rolled my eyes. The dramatics in this family.

"It's not a girl. We'd know about it," Ruby said with confidence. As if I told my every secret to them. In reality, they were just nosy. Mention the tiniest thing to any one of them and all of a sudden, it was headline news. West had been my confidante until he started to be a little too loose with his lips. Especially where Ruby was concerned. The two talked more than they led on. Everyone knew the only vault in this family was me.

"I'm waiting to hear from Hazel," I said.

"Oh." Ruby gave a sigh of disappointment. Like me harboring a secret girlfriend might be the most interesting possible turn of events.

"You're still in the thick of that?" Mom asked.

"She's been living with him," Regan said.

"What?" Mom's eyes went wide as saucers, and I shot my sister an accusatory glare.

"It's nothing. The creep who took her cat is still out there, threatening her. She's just crashing in my guest bedroom until we can figure this out."

"Sure, she's staying in the *guest bedroom*." West waggled his eyebrows. I elbowed him in the ribs.

"How is this the first I'm hearing about this?" Mom demanded.

My dad rolled the dice, taking his turn—incorrectly—without looking up. "Let Reid be. You all are like vultures."

"Yes, vultures is a great analogy. Circling, desperate to

peck off the tiniest bit of gossip from my rotting carcass," I said with a drawn-out sigh. "Hazel is just a friend and I'm helping her out. Absolutely nothing is going on between us."

My mom frowned, refusing to take her eyes off me.

What I conveniently left out was just how badly I *wanted* there to be something between Hazel and me. But there was zero fucking chance I was sharing that with my family. If I told them how I felt before I told her, they'd somehow find a way to spill it to her first—even though more than half the people at this table hadn't even met her yet. Besides, could I really see myself with someone like Hazel? All over the place, unfiltered, a bit frenzied?

Yes. Yes, I could. It freaked me out just how much I could picture it.

"She isn't cute?" My mom raised an eyebrow while shoving the bowl of chips in my direction. I took it from her and shook my head.

"She's fine, but she's not for me. Believe it or not, I'm more than capable of having a woman as a friend."

The words sat sticky on my tongue. My mind immediately drifted to the other night in her bedroom, while we were hanging those awful paintings she'd picked out. I was ninety-percent sure I'd felt some sort of spark between us. The tension had been thick after that. I'd become aware of exactly how far her face was from mine. How all it would take would be the smallest dip of my head and I could find out what she tasted like.

I'd avoided her after that. Not outright, we still had dinner together and saw each other in the morning, but I'd spent more time holed up in my office, getting lost in true crime forums and writing extra blog posts.

"Wow. She's *fine?* You're a real charmer. That's exactly how every woman dreams of being described." Ruby shot me a disapproving look as she quoted my description back to me.

I groaned, dying for this conversation to be over. I had been the center of attention far too often at this dinner table lately. "I'm sure she'd say the same about me. Can you all stop reading so much into this and just play the game?"

Mom got a bit huffy after that. "I can't know what's going on in my own son's life?" she'd said. But thankfully for me, she'd finally noticed my dad had messed up his turn and started to lay into him about cheating. He just shook his head and sat back in defeat.

After we *finally* wrapped up the game, my parents and sisters drifted into the living room to argue over what movie to watch. West and I hung back in the kitchen, putting away the game pieces.

"So," he said, handing me the folded-up board so I could pack it in the box.

"What?"

"Hazel?" He raised his eyebrows, and it took everything in me not to toss my head back in irritation. I was already on edge because I hadn't heard from her yet, and everyone bringing her up constantly wasn't giving my mind a single second of peace.

How was her night going? Was she okay? Was she having fun?

"There's nothing to tell."

"Aw, come on man." He leaned against the counter, folding his arms. "I don't buy that for a second. We've been best friends for twenty years. I know your tells."

"My tells?"

"The little things that give it away when you like a girl."

"There are no tells."

"Inviting her into your space." He held up a finger. "Meghan had to bug you for a whole year to move in with her, and she was your long-term girlfriend."

"Circumstances are extenuating with Hazel. It's not like I thought it would be fun."

Admittedly, I hadn't minded having her in my space nearly as much as I thought I would. I wasn't about to admit it to

West, but I wasn't exactly looking forward to the day she'd have to leave.

"Two," West continued, unfazed. "You're checking your phone every five seconds to see if she's texted you. You're a notoriously bad texter. You get caught up in a book, or a project, or a conversation, and you forget to check your phone for hours. Now suddenly it's glued to your hand?"

I shoved the lid to the game back on the box. "Again, extenuating circumstances. She's out with her high school friends and one of them could be a suspect."

"Three, you've hardly talked about her and if someone brings her up, you change the subject."

"That isn't new—"

"Exactly," he interrupted, smile smug. "You *hate* talking about girls you're interested in. If you were truly just in this for the mystery of it all, you'd be begging to talk my ear off about it. You told me months ago that you wished the fam took more of an interest in your sleuthing hobby. You asked if we read the blog."

Shit.

He'd walked me right into this corner, one that, to be honest, I hadn't even thought about. But he wasn't wrong. Sleuthing was the one subject I didn't mind getting grilled about. I liked talking about new breaks in a case. I'd happily give anyone a rundown on new developments. But not with Hazel's. I told myself it was because it was too personal. I knew her. I was living it with her. I saw the pain and the hurt in her eyes every time we ran into a dead end. That had to be it.

It had nothing to do with any developing feelings.

"You're way off." I crossed my arms and leaned against the counter next to him. "I feel bad for her."

I winced as soon as I heard how that sounded. I *did* feel bad for her, but there was a hell of a lot more to it than that.

"Look," I continued. "She's literally a mess. I've never met someone who has their life together less than Hazel does. You should see her apartment."

West snorted. "She's living with you *and* she's messy? I'm shocked you haven't killed her yet. I barely survived one year as your roommate in college."

"She tries to be neat at my place," I said, my heart snagging a little. Organization didn't come naturally to Hazel, but I could tell she was making an effort. Every now and then, especially when she was in a rush, her stuff would end up scattered across the room—but she always tried to tidy it up afterward. Funny thing was, that should've pleased me. Normally, clutter drove me crazy. But with Hazel, it made me wonder if she wasn't totally comfortable in my space. I didn't like that thought.

"The point is, she and I are in no way compatible. I need someone more…"

"Polished," West finished, nodding in agreement, seemingly convinced. "Yeah, I guess you're right. I can't see you with someone so all over the place. If she really is that haphazard, I'm surprised you're even calling her a friend."

That made my blood boil, but I kept my cool. He was finally getting off my back. Exactly what I'd wanted.

"Sorry I keep bugging you, I just hate that Meghan moved on before you. You deserve someone who makes you happy."

I snorted. "Says the guy who hasn't had a serious girlfriend in almost a decade."

"It's different for me. I never wanted to settle down like you did."

"And I *was* settled down," I reminded him. "For years. If anything, I need a break from that. It's nice being on my own."

West gave me a look like he wanted to protest but must have thought better of it. "Whatever you want, man. It's your life. Just don't get too set in your own ways. You don't want to make it impossible for someone else to join the picture at some point."

Something stuck in my throat. Had I been too set in my ways? Too unwilling to change? I hadn't thought so, but Hazel barging into my life was making me second guess a lot of things. It couldn't be a coincidence that I'd been happier these couple of weeks with her than I had been in a while. Maybe I'd been mistaking complacency for contentment.

My phone dinged. I whipped it out of my back pocket and scanned the new text.

My heart dropped straight into my stomach.

Hazel: I need your help.

TWENTY

Hazel

I slipped my phone back into my bag and assessed myself in the mirror. Reid hadn't responded and it had been almost ten minutes. I had to go back out there, or they'd think something was wrong.

Or maybe they wouldn't even notice I'd left.

Tonight had been a terrible idea. I should've known better. The second I'd arrived at the restaurant, every insecurity I'd ever wrestled with came bubbling to the surface. I gave the host our reservation name, only to find out no one else had shown up yet. A few minutes later, Zoe had texted me to say they were pregaming at Kiara's and running late. I waited at the front, clinging to the hope they'd still come. But then she texted again: they were canceling dinner and just ordering pizza before heading straight to the bar. She apologized, a lot —but didn't extend an invite.

I'd strongly debated going home, but the thought of Reid asking me how it went had kept me from fleeing. So I left the restaurant, dragged myself to the cocktail bar we were all supposed to meet at, and sat there alone, eating soggy nachos and feeling every bit as pathetic as I looked.

When the girls finally arrived, the night hadn't gotten much better.

Thankfully, Zoe had walked in first—already plenty buzzed—and threw her arms around my neck. "It's so good to see you," she'd said, hanging on for a second longer than necessary.

I'd returned the hug from my oldest friend and pasted on a smile, trying my best to give the rest of the evening a fair shot. Kiara, Desiree, and Stephanie gave me short, one-armed hugs before we all went to the booth they'd reserved for Zoe's birthday.

Kiara, Desiree, and Stephanie had always been around in high school. Zoe and I had been thick as thieves, but after she got close with Kiara through field hockey, things were never quite the same. Kiara acted friendly to my face, but the second Zoe left the room, silence always fell between us. She'd find any excuse not to hang out one-on-one. Desiree and Stephanie had gradually glommed on over the next few years, but instead of us being a fivesome, it was more like they were a foursome, and Zoe and I were a completely separate twosome.

It hadn't exactly felt great, but it wasn't awful either. I got invited to things. I had a decent social life. But after high school, we all slowly drifted apart. Zoe was the only one I kept in touch with, other than the occasional shallow social media comment. And even my relationship with her had faded once I moved.

Kiara had been out here less than two months, and Zoe was already here for a birthday trip. I told myself maybe I wasn't pushy enough. Maybe I hadn't thrown out enough invitations, but deep down I felt stupid. Like even my closest friend didn't like me all that much.

And now here I was, hiding out in the bathroom while the rest of them did tequila shots at the table. A scene I knew all too well. I dabbed at my eyes, not letting the single tear that fell make it past my cheek.

Still no answer from Reid. I'd hoped he might fake a phone call and give me an excuse to bail early, but his silence pretty much said it all: time to suck it up and get back out there.

Maybe the weird vibes were my fault. Maybe I was just being antisocial.

Before shoving my phone in my bag, I shot off a quick text to Jackson. "We should grab drinks next week."

He might be overbearing and a total gossip, but his attempts at befriending me seemed genuine. I needed to make more of an effort. Here I was, wallowing in self-pity over being alone, when I was equally as guilty of actively running away from potential friendships.

The music hit me like a wall the second I stepped out of the bathroom—too loud, too bass-heavy, the kind that made it hard to think, let alone talk. The bar was packed, considering it wasn't a weekend, and the lights were dim except for the occasional flash of neon from the signs behind the counter. It was new and trendy and had a cover charge. Not a place I'd typically go, but it was Kiara's favorite, apparently.

I steered myself back toward our corner booth, threw on a practiced smile, and slipped into my seat like nothing was wrong.

"Hazel's back!" Zoe smiled drunkenly at me. She was several drinks deep and I doubted she'd make it much longer. She was at that point where she was on an energetic high, ready to take on the dance floor and bounce around for another hour before completely crashing out and demanding a burrito before falling asleep on the cab ride home. I knew her pattern well.

"You've got something on your shirt," Kiara said, giving me a smile that somehow looked more like a grimace.

"It's just water," I said, without looking down. I knew I'd accidentally splashed myself from the sink.

"Oh, good. Thought it was a stain. You've always been such a klutz." I bristled but ignored Kiara's snide comment. I caught the way she looked me over, her distaste obvious. The four of them were dressed in tiny, curve-hugging dresses with plunging necklines, practically a uniform. My outfit blended in just fine with the rest of the bar crowd, but apparently it didn't meet their standards. Whatever. I refused to let them shrink me.

"How's your new place?" I asked Kiara, hoping I sounded friendly and like I gave a shit.

"Really nice," she yelled over the music. "It costs, like, a fortune, but thankfully with the new promotion at work I can afford it. I seriously feel like royalty living there. You should see the pool, it's insane."

"Sounds great." My voice was tight. Kiara had always been the type to flash what she had. Just because I expected it, didn't make it any less grating.

"Where are you at nowadays? By the highway, right?" She spun the straw in her drink before bringing it to her lips.

"Yep." I took a long sip of my own drink.

This was fun.

"Well, I can let you know if something in my building opens up. The studios are more affordable, if you're interested."

"I'm good," I said. She and I both knew full well I couldn't afford a studio in her building. It didn't matter if it was half the price she paid, it was still way outside my budget.

"Oh my God, Hazel!" Desiree squealed, leaning over Stephanie to be heard over the DJ. "I almost forgot, didn't you, like, just win the lottery or something?"

"Yeah," Stephanie said. "I remember seeing your post. Shouldn't drinks be on you?"

Damn that post.

I gulped and forced myself to get it out.

"About that…Someone actually stole my grandma's cat a couple of weeks ago. I'm not sure who it was—" My gaze shifted to Kiara as I said this to gauge her reaction, but she looked bored, swirling her drink. "—but they're blackmailing me. They know about my winnings and are threatening to keep Vermont if I don't hand over the money as soon as it clears my account."

"Vermont?" Desiree questioned.

"The cat," I said.

Stephanie gasped. "That's horrible! Why didn't you tell us?"

Because I'm pathetic. Because it makes me feel more like a loser than I already did. Because I was stupid enough to believe my life was finally taking a turn for the better. I shrugged haplessly but didn't say anything.

Zoe tapped my nose. "Hazel has a hot detective working the case already."

Kiara narrowed her eyes. "A detective?"

"He isn't really a detective." I sighed, shaking my head. "It's just this guy I know. He's been helping me try to figure it out."

"Figure out a way into your pants," Zoe said, giggling and linking her arm through mine.

I gave a half-hearted scoff but couldn't stop my smile from forming. Zoe was always like this, and it was hard for me to stay annoyed at her.

"It's just all been a lot to handle," I said.

"Why would someone go through all that trouble for five hundred bucks?" Kiara asked.

"Try, like, fifty grand," Zoe said.

The way Kiara's eyes bulged at that news looked genuine. She hadn't known. She'd probably barely registered my post at all, let alone read the caption. Because that's how little she thought of me.

"Fifty thousand for you is insane, Hazel. Holy shit," she said.

I clocked the way she emphasized, "for you."

"Yep."

"And someone is trying to blackmail you for it?" Stephanie asked, sitting up.

"That's the unluckiest thing I've ever heard," Kiara said with a snort.

Zoe's leg pressed into mine as she reached around my shoulders to give me a squeeze. "Are you okay?" She looked at me, glassy-eyed.

"I'm okay." I gave her leg a squeeze in return. I realized those words were only true because of one person. If Reid wasn't around, I wasn't sure where I'd be. He had been keeping me sane, grounded, and mildly optimistic through all this.

"Well, forget the cat and keep the money." Kiara set her drink down and folded her arms across her chest. She twirled her long hair around one of her perfectly manicured fingers.

"She can't do that," Zoe said, eyes narrowed. "It was her gran's cat."

Kiara laughed. "So? My grandma has three cats, and I wouldn't know them from a stray one off the street."

My cheeks burned. She was *such* a bitch.

"And money is money," she continued. "It's not like they're threatening to hurt the cat, just keep it, right?"

"Kiara doesn't understand pets," Zoe offered, wincing at the harshness of her words. "She's allergic."

"Remember that time you were casually dating that guy and he never mentioned he had a cat? You woke up after the first time you had sex and couldn't breathe, so he had to drive you to urgent care." Desiree burst out laughing.

Kiara shuddered. "Don't remind me. I ghosted him after that."

The conversation moved on to chatter about Kiara's failed dating attempts, and any interest in my predicament fell to the wayside. It wasn't like I demanded to be the center of attention, but it still kind of stung.

Zoe swayed beside me, half-listening to the conversation. She glanced over when she caught my stare and smiled like she didn't have a care in the world, like she sensed my pain but only just barely.

This was my closest friend. She was the one I'd had my first sleepover with. The girl I'd choreographed cheesy dances with in my garage. The first person I called the night I lost my virginity in senior year.

But the distance between us had grown. We texted sometimes, talked even less, and lately, saw each other almost never. I didn't like her any less, but the closeness we'd once shared just…wasn't there anymore.

We'd been drifting for years, if I was being honest with myself. Maybe I was partially to blame, getting caught up in a relationship and all, but if I thought about it, hanging out with Zoe didn't make me feel good anymore. It was okay when it was just the two of us, but it was *never* just the two of us. She always dragged around a clique of people who never seemed to care for me much.

It was past time I found some friends who actually liked me. That was possible, right? I might have thought otherwise a couple of weeks ago. Until Reid.

"I think I'm going to call it a night," I announced, standing.

"What no! Don't go." Zoe grabbed my hand and tried to pull me back down, but I just patted it and gently extracted myself.

"Happy Birthday, Zoe. Get home safe, okay?" I hugged her and she loosely wrapped her arms around me.

"Stay," she pouted.

"It's getting late and I'm pretty tired."

"It's not even eleven," Kiara said, sounding bored.

I shrugged and offered them a small wave, eager to get out of there as quickly as possible. "Night."

Before I could turn away, I saw Kiara's eyes widen and look behind me. A presence hovered near me.

Hands grabbed onto my shoulders, and I let out a yelp of surprise, ready to put my nonexistent self-defense moves into action. But when I turned, I collided with a broad chest. I looked up to see a familiar face.

Reid.

My whole body sagged with relief. "What are you doing here?" I couldn't help the smile that tugged at my lips.

"Are you alright?" he demanded, eyes scanning my face.

"I'm fine. I was just leaving."

He blew out a breath and raked a hand through his hair. I realized he looked frazzled.

"This your detective?" Zoe asked with a smirk.

I nodded.

"See, hot," she said to the rest of the girls. I think it was her attempt at a whisper, but her voice still carried over the bar noise.

Reid's cheeks flushed as he jerked his gaze from me to the table of women.

I grabbed onto his arm and stood on my tiptoes to whisper in his ear. "Can we get out of here?"

"Yes," he said.

Without even a wave of acknowledgement, he pulled me away from the table. I didn't miss Kiara's surprise as she stared at Reid. A petty part of myself filed that in my "win" folder. Because Reid *was* hot, especially with this whole dark, smoldering look he had going on right now. The fact that he didn't even give Kiara the time of day pleased me more than it should.

The bar was packed nearly shoulder to shoulder as Reid guided me through. Bodies banged into mine even as he tried his best to shield me. When we finally made it to the front, away from the blasting music, he paused before the exit.

"Are you sure you're okay?" he asked, eyes scanning my face.

I nodded. "How did you find me?"

"You said this was the bar you were going to. What happened?" he asked, eyes still studying me.

"I'm fine, why—oh, shoot. The text. My bad. I was going to ask if you could call me with an excuse so I could leave early, but I ended up just growing a pair and excusing myself."

He let out a deep sigh of relief and removed his hand from my shoulders to run his fingers through his hair. "Shit, Hazel. You scared me. You need to add some more context."

"You didn't text me back," I said.

"I did." He pulled his phone from his pocket and waved it in my face. "Three times. Then I called you. Twice." The worry lines were still etched in his forehead.

I scrambled to pull my phone back out, but I had no new notifications. There was an SOS icon in the corner, though. "Shoot, sorry. I guess the service in here isn't great. The signal must have been going in and out when I sent that."

He lifted his gaze to the ceiling and shook his head. "Do me a favor? Next time, don't just text 'Need help.' Okay?"

"You got it," I said, warmth flooding my chest despite his frustration. He cared. He cared and he came. For me.

"Let's go home," he said. Those words had my entire nervous system on high alert. I knew he just meant 'home' in the logistical sense, but I liked the way it sounded coming from him.

Reid took me by the hand and ushered me outside.

Once the frosty evening air hit, I slipped on my jacket. Reid led us to his car, parked just down the street. The side-walks buzzed with a handful of people milling about, switching bars or in search of food after a night out.

"So how was it?" he asked, opening the passenger car door and letting me spill in first.

"Fine." My answer was clipped.

He circled around and slipped into the driver's seat. He gave me a once-over, his expression tightening. "You don't look fine. Was it Kiara? Did something happen?"

A defeated sigh escaped my lips. "No, not really. We can rule her out as a suspect, though. She clearly doesn't need any extra money and, apparently, she's deathly allergic to cats."

Reid grimaced. "I mean, she was a loose theory, but it's still good to check her off the list."

I nodded. Instead of starting the car, he continued to stare at me.

"Hazel, what's wrong. You're being quiet?"

A soft laugh escaped my lips. He was always so observant. "Are you trying to tell me I'm normally loud? Because I hate to break it to you, Reid, but you haven't seen the worst of me."

"What's the worst of you?"

"Well, for one, don't even think about dragging me to karaoke. I'll hog the machine all night. And post me up in front of a bad horror movie, and I promise you I'll talk through the entire thing. It doesn't even matter if we're in the theater."

"Something to look forward to."

"My commentary is unmatched."

He smiled, but it faded quickly. He was completely turned in his seat, assessing me. "Seriously, Hazel. Talk to me. Your shoulders are hunched, you can barely look at me. You seem...sad."

I briefly met his concerned gaze. "I guess I *am* a little sad. I don't really like hanging out with those girls."

"I thought they were your friends."

"Kind of. Not really." I blew out a breath. "Zoe was always my friend, and they were her friends. We hung out in high school and a bit after graduation, before I moved. But I never fit in. I thought Zoe and I were still good, but we've definitely been growing distant for a while. I think tonight I finally came to the realization that we aren't that close anymore. Kind of sucks, is all. It's okay, nothing has changed. Just my perception of our relationship."

Reid nodded, taking in my words. "You know that saying. People come into our lives for a reason, a season, or forever. Maybe your season is just coming to an end."

Tears formed in my eyes as soon as he said the words. That was *my* saying. How many times had Gran said those exact words to me?

Reid seemed to register my crumpled face and

backpedaled. "I'm sorry. Was that the wrong thing to say? Crap. I didn't want to make you feel worse."

"No it's f-fine." My voice shook. "It's just…every person that has ever come into my life has been for a reason or for a season. I've got no forevers. That was Gran, and now she's gone. I thought Zoe was a forever, but she's not. Or even if she is, she's a distant forever. Like maybe we'll always talk but we'll never be that close, y'know? Not 'sleepover, going on trips together, talk about everything and anything,' close."

Reid continued to study me.

"You'll find your forevers, Hazel."

"I appreciate the vote of confidence, but I've made it twenty-five years without much to show. Some people aren't that likable."

"You're likable," he said.

"And you're kind." A few tears fell but I was beyond the point of being embarrassed by them. If I trusted anyone to see me in my most vulnerable state, it was Reid.

"I'm not saying it to be kind." His finger and thumb brushed my chin. He gently pulled my face around so that I'd be forced to look at him. "I'm saying it because it's true. I've never met anyone like you, Hazel."

"Exactly the problem." I lifted my hands as if to say, 'see.'

"You wear your emotions on your sleeve. You go through life like every day is different. You don't take anything too seriously. You look for beauty where there is none, and you create adventures out of nothing. You don't have a way you take your coffee."

"Coffee?" He'd lost me.

Reid sighed. "I like to pick up on the little things, like how people take their coffee. I store the information away and use it to be thoughtful in the future. But you take it differently every time. Sometimes black, with sugar, without. You bought some weird nut creamer last time we were at the grocery store. Sometimes it's vanilla and sometimes it's hazelnut."

"So what? It's all delicious. Life's too short to drink my coffee the same way every day."

"*Exactly*." He pinched my chin lightly before dropping his hand. I missed his touch as soon as it was gone. "That's how you live life. Fuck routines; you make the ordinary into something new and exciting."

"It's coffee, Reid." I shook my head. "I'm not adventurous. I've never even been out of the country before."

"But you inject life into the ordinary. That takes a special person. Traveling and money can make anyone *seem* interesting. But you actually are."

We sat in the silence for a few moments as I let his words wash over me.

"Forget those so-called friends," he said, finally turning in his seat and putting the car into reverse. "Real friends don't make you question whether you're enough."

He pulled away, the lights of the small city blurring as I gazed out the windshield.

"Thank you," I said.

"Of course."

"Not just for coming to get me, and for the pep talk. For everything. For helping me when you didn't have to. For letting me stay at your place…for being a friend."

I spoke the last word cautiously, hoping I didn't cross some hypothetical boundary.

Reid smiled. "I got you."

The simple sentiment branded itself right onto my heart.

To lighten the mood, I turned the radio up as a throwback song came on. I sang along, loudly and badly, using it as some sort of cathartic release. Reid drove, not singing, but also not dropping his smile. A few miles away from his house, something caught my attention.

"Oh, can you stop here?" I pointed to the twenty-four-hour gas station.

"We have snacks at home." Again, with the "we" and the

"home." If this man didn't stop it right now, I'd end up falling in love with him.

Despite his disapproving words, Reid pulled into the empty parking lot without a fight.

"I'll be right back, you can stay in the car."

But he was already turning off the engine and climbing out.

"You don't have to come in," I said again, walking up to the brightly lit entrance and pushing the door open.

Reid rolled his eyes and grabbed the door, holding it while I stepped through and started browsing the aisles. "As if I would let you go into a gas station by yourself at midnight."

"My protector," I teased.

"Well, you clearly need one."

No snack called my name. Instead, I snagged a cup off the back wall and examined the slushy flavors before pouring myself a lemon-lime one.

"Really?"

"Are you telling me you don't like slushies?" I asked, licking the top of my lid where some had started to overflow.

"I did when I was ten."

"You're missing out."

"It's, like, thirty degrees outside."

"Good thing your car has a heater."

We meandered to the front of the store where one man lingered, paying for cigarettes. He patted his pockets and slid over one dollar at a time. After finally coming up with exact change, he stepped away and we moved to the front.

"Just this?" The young woman behind the glass divider asked, pointing to my drink.

"And a daily double," I said, scanning the selection of tickets behind her.

I could feel Reid's eyes on me, but I ignored him. When I tried to pull out my wallet to pay, Reid was too quick, already sliding a few bills across the counter.

Once we were back in his car, engine on, he let out a sigh.

"Hazel, I hate to be the bearer of bad news, but the odds of you winning the lottery twice are incomprehensible."

"Actually, the odds are the same as when I won the first time. I think that means I have an even better chance. I mean, who wins the lottery, right?" I smiled up at him, opening his center console to search for a quarter or something to reveal the ticket.

He laughed. "I can promise you, it doesn't work like that."

"This sucker right here is my best shot at the so-called American Dream."

He squinted and watched me as I scratched it off.

"Damn, not this time." I surveyed the losing numbers before giving a silent nod to Gran, wherever she was in the universe.

"I could have told you that before you even bought the ticket," he said, pulling the car into reverse and driving us back to his house.

We rode in silence for a bit, just the sound of the radio softly playing in the background. When we pulled into his driveway, I guzzled the last of my slushie.

"I'm freezing," I said, teeth chattering.

"You're ridiculous."

We spilled into his door, and I gratefully peeled off my heeled boots and coat. I'd never been more ready to get into PJs and get into bed.

"It's a waste of money, you know?" When I turned to look at Reid, he was standing there, rubbing the back of his neck. He looked pained, like he didn't want to say whatever it was he was about to say next.

"Look, I know it's none of my business, but gambling—playing the lottery—I know you won once, but it's still a hell of a way to burn through money. I-I just hope you're being careful."

My cheeks burned, either from embarrassment or because I was secretly pleased he cared enough to bring it up.

"I don't play that often," I said.

"Pulling over at midnight just to buy a ticket—"

"It was a thing with my grandma," I said, before he could lecture me further. "You'll probably think it's silly, but any time one of us had a hard day, we'd buy a lottery ticket. She always said it was the best time to try, because our luck was bound to take a turn."

Reid jerked his eyes up from the floor to study me.

"Oh," he finally said.

"The ticket I won with? I bought it the day of her funeral."

His eyebrows drew together. "Shit, Hazel. I'm sorry. I shouldn't be talking to you like you're an irresponsible kid or something."

I laughed, moving into his house and plopping myself down on his couch. "I mean, I *am* kind of irresponsible. Struggled with it my whole life."

"Seems like you had to do a lot on your own," he said. Instead of sitting at the end of the couch, he sat down half on my cushion, our knees bumping.

"Not really. Gran was always there for me."

"Parents," he said carefully. "Friends. Those are important life pillars too."

I pursed my lips, thinking about it. "There was always a hole. A small one," I admitted softly.

"It's okay to say that." Reid took my hands in his as I squeezed my eyes shut.

"Gran did everything for me. I owe her everything. She raised me when she didn't have to. She made all of these happy moments in my childhood when there shouldn't have been any."

"It's not being ungrateful to admit you missed out on things," he whispered.

"So many people have less."

"And so many people have more." He tilted his head down, dragging my gaze back to his. "That doesn't mean you have to suppress how you feel."

Another tear escaped the corner of my eye and I laughed, taking one of my hands from his and wiping it away.

"Stop making me get all sentimental."

Reid's face remained stoic. "I worry about you."

That snagged on my heart. Here I was, rapidly forming a kind of huge crush on the guy, and he *worried* about me? I mean, sweet in theory, but it wasn't exactly what a girl wanted to hear.

"You don't have to worry about me."

"Don't I?"

We stayed quiet for a moment, searching for something in the silence between us. Suddenly, every part of my body came alive. I was hyper aware of every microscopic skin cell in the hand still entwined with Reid's.

"I've always been alright," I whispered.

"What if I want you to be more than alright?"

"What does that even mean?"

"Exactly," he said. "You shouldn't have to wonder what 'more than alright' means. You should just know. You should be living it every day."

"You know what's funny?" I asked.

"What?"

"My grandma passing, this whole catnapping nightmare, I should be the worst I've ever been. In a lot of ways, I'm not doing great." He frowned, but I continued. "But anytime I'm with you, or even just knowing you're around…makes me feel…more than alright."

He sucked in a breath and continued to stare at me.

"I love being around you, Hazel. I'm not like you, I'm hardly ever lonely. In fact, I've always wanted *more* time alone. Between my overbearing family, a nosy best friend, and an ex-wife who hated my hobbies, I've hardly had any room to breathe."

"So much love you could drown in it," I joked softly.

"Exactly," he said. "And yet…yet you being in my space feels so fucking right. It kind of freaks me out, if I'm being honest. I want to help you solve your problems more than anything, but a little part of me isn't looking forward to it. Because that means you'll be gone."

My heart was now full-on pounding out of my chest.

"No more kitchen disasters," I said. "And you'll be able to take down my hideous paintings."

"Those hideous paintings aren't going anywhere. I might bolt them to the wall."

I laughed, shaking my head. I caught myself leaning in subconsciously. His stare completely trapped me. I couldn't look away if I wanted to. Was I losing it? Was he getting closer? Did he want to kiss me? Before I could wonder anymore, I didn't have to. Because Reid leaned in and closed the distance between us.

Soft. Careful. Gentle. Exactly what I'd expect from a kiss with Reid.

Except it was also somehow so much better.

He wrapped his free hand around my neck, brushing my jaw with his thumb as his lips pressed against mine, exploring. My hands fell to his waist, clutching the soft fabric of his t-shirt.

Ugh, he smelled good.

Was I seriously making out with Reid right now? On his couch? This is absolutely not where I'd thought the night would lead me.

I never thought I'd share the most vulnerable parts of me and have him willingly dive in for more.

A low rumble came from his throat as he pressed into me, our chests now touching. Heat pooled in my stomach. I wanted this, I wanted him. Without thinking, I moved my legs, which had been curled up underneath me, and shifted them onto his lap, setting one on either side of him. I nearly gasped as his hard length pressed into me through our layers of clothes. He wanted me. *Actually* wanted me. I mean, I thought the kiss and the way he was gripping the sides of my face to hold me in place were good indicators, but I could still hardly believe my luck.

I rocked into him, a nearly inaudible moan passing between our mouths.

"Hazel," he whispered against my lips, before letting his tongue slip past my defenses. Damn. Reid could really kiss. I mean *really* kiss. I could do this for hours.

My back arched and my hips pressed against him, but almost as soon as it started, he broke away from me.

"Is something wrong?" My words were shaky. I started to climb off him, but his grip tightened ever so slightly, silently asking me not to move yet.

"I-I'm sorry. I didn't mean to jump all over you like that," he said, adjusting his glasses, which had been pushed up.

I shot him a shy smile. "I didn't exactly mind."

He let out a breath of a laugh and shook his head, squeezing his eyes shut before opening them again. "No, I know that. I just…you were just being so vulnerable, I wanted to be there for you. Not take advantage of the situation."

"You didn't," I insisted.

His arms wrapped around me, and he pulled me in for the most all-encompassing hug I'd had in ages.

"I'm glad you're here," he whispered into my ear. "I don't want to scare you off."

"You aren't." He was doing the exact opposite of scaring me off, but I didn't say that.

"You had a hard night. I don't want to take advantage of anything."

My eyebrows drew together. "You aren't, Reid." This was probably the part where I was supposed to tell him I'd been thinking about kissing him for a lot longer than just this evening, but I decided to refrain.

What if this was his excuse to let me down gently? It sure as hell didn't feel that way, but my self-preservation mode kicked in all the same. If he wanted to kiss me, he would, right? Wasn't that, like, basic human instinct?

"You should probably get to bed," he said, giving me a final squeeze before I scrambled off of him and we both stood up.

"I have a few clients early in the morning," I offered pathetically, wanting to seem like going to bed was just as much my idea as it was his.

We stood, idling awkwardly near each other.

"Um, well. Goodnight," I said at the same time as he leaned in.

He pulled me in for another quick hug.

I let him hold on for a second longer, trying not to get lost in how good his arms felt around me.

TWENTY-ONE

Hazel

Two days.

Two freaking days and no word about the kiss. Everything was at a standstill lately and I hated it. Patience wasn't my thing. I'd always been the type to move fast. I dropped out of community college and enrolled in cosmetology school on a whim. I bought the first clunker car I found online that fit my budget. I *definitely* moved in with Paul too quickly. I wasn't one to overanalyze. I liked instant gratification, and I liked taking action.

So, two days with absolutely zero mention of the kiss we'd shared was driving me up the wall. I mean, technically it had only been a day and a half. It happened two nights ago, and it was only eleven a.m. right now, but it might as well have been an *eternity*.

Granted, Reid and I hadn't seen much of each other since. I'd had back-to-back clients yesterday and then he met up with a friend after work before getting online with his investigator group all evening. Apparently, my case had put them behind on a cold case they were blogging about, and they had a new break they wanted to discuss.

I wanted to ask him about it. It was interesting. I hadn't

mentioned it to him, but I'd started reading his blogs. They were good. Enticing. I knew from talking to him that their group split up the work. They'd take turns writing, editing, and posting. Each of their different styles shone through in the blog and made it a compelling read. I was dying to know what else they would uncover on some of these cases.

I poured myself a bowl of cereal and slurped up a spoonful.

"Shit," I muttered when a splash of milk dribbled out of my mouth and onto my sweater. I was already dressed for work in head-to-toe black. I was already running late as it was. I pulled out a piece of paper towel and dabbed at the damp spot.

"Oh, you're still here."

I froze.

Reid stood in the hallway that led from the open living area to his bedroom and office.

Shit, was it possible he looked better since the kiss? Ever since I'd cut his hair, he'd been letting it grow out. It was thick and slightly wavy. Honestly, it was a total crime that he used to buzz it all off. Some people would kill for that head of hair.

"I was just about to head out," I said at the same time he said, "Want any lunch?"

I cringed, looking down at my bowl of sugary cereal. It was the first thing I'd eaten all day. I hadn't meant to sleep in, but I'd stayed up way too late last night scrolling on my phone.

"I'm covered," I said, holding up my bowl.

His gaze was heavy with judgement as he took it in. "Nothing like a balanced meal."

"Exactly. Whole grains, dairy. I'm covered."

"Who needs protein and complex carbs."

"Exactly." I laughed, hating how nervous it sounded.

"You sure I can't make you lunch?" he asked again.

"Nope. I'm already late." I rinsed out my bowl and opened the dishwasher to slide it in. Reid was the kind of guy who had a *very specific* way of loading dishes, and I still hadn't figured it out. I just hoped the fact that I never left anything in the sink counted for something.

I walked toward the entry, throwing him an apologetic smile. "Dinner, maybe?"

He paused, leaning against the hallway. "I have dinner with my family tonight."

"Oh," I said, disappointment evident in my tone.

"You should come." He tossed it out there so casually I almost thought I'd misheard him.

"To dinner? With your family?" The invite shocked me.

"Why not?" he said. "You already know Ruby. And everyone else has been dying to meet you."

He wanted me to meet his family? Before we'd even discussed the other night? Was this a good sign? It had to be, right? "Um, I guess I could," was all I said.

"I really want you to come," he added.

I forced a smile and nodded. "Okay, then."

Reid's eyes twinkled. He must have realized how flustered I looked. "Okay, then," he parroted back my words.

And that was it.

His invitation rattled around in my brain the entire drive to the salon.

Everyone was dying to meet me? He really wanted me to come?

The words did not compute. The fact that Reid's family knew about me made me all sorts of self-conscious. I'd never cared much about what people thought of me, but with Reid…I really didn't want his family to dislike me. Would they think I was good enough for their son? Was I delusional for even having that thought? He'd mentioned nothing of the kiss since it happened, and for all I knew he had zero interest in doing it again.

But even without knowing how he felt, it still occupied every corner of my mind. The kiss was growing like an infection. Soon it would be the only thing I could think or talk about.

I pushed open the door to the salon and relief flooded through me that Ruby wasn't at her station. I wasn't sure I could handle the added pressure of acting nonchalant around her right now.

"Nice of you to join us," Jackson said, as I rushed to my chair and tied on my apron.

"I'm on time." Technically I was, but my client walked through the door not even a minute later.

"Morning, Denise."

I smiled brightly at the graying woman. She was just here for a trim. Her usual. She came to me once a month like clockwork and was one of the clients who'd moved to this salon with me after I'd left the last place. She said she'd never liked the energy there. She was sweet and kind. She'd given me a tissue and let me cry the week after Gran passed away.

"What's new, Denise?" Jackson asked, sitting in his chair and spinning toward us.

"I've got a speed dating event at the rec center tomorrow," she said coyly.

Jackson grinned. "Denise! You player. Hazel, get this woman looking her best."

"Obviously," I said, taking her over to the sink to give her a quick wash.

As my gloved hands worked through her short hair, my mind kept wandering to Reid's dinner invitation. Part of me was tempted to ask Jackson for advice. He was the closest thing I had to a friend, lately. I hadn't even heard from Zoe since her birthday. She'd said thanks for coming, and I'd told her to let me know if she wanted to do breakfast or lunch before she left. She never responded. It hurt, but having already had the realization that we just weren't that close anymore lessened the blow.

"What's got you all worked up?" Jackson asked when I walked Denise back to my chair. I pulled out a comb and concentrated, trimming the ends as little as I could. I knew from experience she preferred it just brushing her shoulders. Nothing even a centimeter shorter.

"Nothing," I said, snipping away at the dead ends.

He dipped his chin. "Are you serious? The lines between your eyebrows are so deep, I can practically see the stress headache forming."

"I'll tell you later," I said, eyeing my client in the mirror and narrowing my eyes at him.

Jackson crossed his legs and zipped his lips.

About twenty minutes later, Denise stepped out of my chair with a fresh blowout, running her fingers through her hair and smiling at her reflection. I gave her a quick wave as she left, then turned just in time to see Jackson standing up, eyeing me.

"Okay, spill," he demanded.

There really was no escaping him. One time, he'd mentioned not liking his last salon because everyone was so boring. Once I'd gotten to know him, I'd wondered if they were boring, or just desperately attempting to hold on to a personal boundary.

"You were really holding that in, huh?" I asked.

"You were absent-minded the entire appointment. Denise and I talked more than you two did."

I chewed my lip, debating where to start. He didn't even know about the kiss the other night.

"What's up?" Natalie bounced over, having just rung up her last client.

Crap. I was gaining an audience.

Miranda was the only person still working on someone's highlights. I half-expected her to demand we go to the back, but she was lost in her own conversation, even throwing her head back to laugh occasionally.

"Oh, um, it's nothing," I said instinctively. Natalie was sweet. Honestly one of the nicest people I'd ever met. Which is exactly why I didn't want to go full-force on her with all my drama.

"Tell us. Now." Jackson glared at me. Natalie leaned against his chair, eyes wide with anticipation.

"Is it about Vermont? Have you figured anything out?" she asked. See? Sweet. Sometimes I didn't even know if Jackson remembered my missing cat situation. He was a little self-absorbed like that. It was something I appreciated about him. Quick to gossip. Quick to forget. He was real.

"It's not about Vermont. Not really."

"It's about Reid," Jackson said, even though I hadn't confirmed that yet. Funny, he forgot about my actual issues, but when it came to any sort of possible relationship drama, he had the memory of an elephant.

"Ruby's brother," Natalie confirmed. I remembered a conversation I'd had with Ruby and Natalie weeks ago over lunch. Ruby had mentioned wanting to set up Reid and Natalie. That they'd be perfect for each other. Given her soft, quiet demeanor, I couldn't help but think Ruby was right. They would complement each other nicely. Unlike me.

"There's nothing to tell," I conceded.

Jackson squeezed his eyes shut and took in a dramatic breath. "Hazel, I swear if you don't tell me what's going on right now—"

"Okay, okay. Geez. Don't be dramatic."

The two of them stared at me expectantly.

"We kissed," I blurted it out. Jackson gasped and Natalie smiled. A genuine one. She probably didn't even remember Ruby's one-off comment. I only did because I couldn't help but notice Ruby'd said nothing about setting *me* up with someone.

"And?" Jackson pressed.

"And…that's it. It was the night before last. He rescued me after a shitty night out and we got to talking, and next thing I knew we were kissing."

"You kissed him, or he kissed you?" Jackson asked.

I tried to think back on it. Who had initiated it exactly? "Does it matter?"

"Yes," he said while Natalie shook her head, "No."

"I think it was him."

"And you like him?" Natalie asked.

"I don't know." I chewed on my lip, tasting the lie. After a brief moment, I tossed my head back in defeat. "Ugh, yes, I do."

Jackson clapped gleefully. "Does Ruby know?" he asked.

I shot him a glare. "No, and please don't tell her." The last thing I wanted her to think was that I was obsessed with her brother or something. Would she even want the two of us together? Be okay with it? Obviously we were adults, but I didn't want to step on any toes and make things awkward at work.

Natalie twirled her hair. "Have you talked to Reid about this kiss?"

"Not a word. He stopped the kiss and—"

"Wait. He stopped it?" Jackson's eyes went wide.

"Yes. We were getting a little…heated. And he stopped it."

Natalie and Jackson exchanged a look which didn't help my rising anxiety.

"What? He said he didn't want to rush things."

"Says every red-blooded American male," Jackson said.

"Reid isn't like that." But Jackson was bringing to light my worst fear. That Reid had been politely rejecting me.

"He invited me to his family dinner tonight," I added. "That means something, right?"

"It could." Jackson tilted his head from side to side, weighing my words. "Are you going to go?" he asked.

"I mean, yes? I was thinking about it."

"You should. They seem sweet, from what Ruby has said," Natalie added.

Ruby. Come to think of it, she had thrown me a casual invite the other day, too. Which pretty much confirmed there was at least *some* truth to the idea that his family actually wanted to meet me.

"You're going," Jackson decided, jaw set.

"Well, thank you for making the decision for me," I said dryly.

"What harm could it do?"

"I agree." Natalie nodded in support.

"And seeing how he acts around you in front of his family could be very telling."

"Like…" I looked between the two of them, grasping at straws.

Natalie tapped her chin. "Like if he's attentive. If he sticks near you the whole time."

"Yeah, it'll be obvious," Jackson assured me.

I wasn't certain about that. But I figured I was about to find out.

TWENTY-TWO

Reid

Armchair_Detective*: How is the suspect list dead in the water?*
WhiteKnight31*: I think we might need to go back through every
person.*
Armchair_Detective*: What about the old boss? In hindsight, he
certainly seemed to have the biggest beef with Hazel.*
WhiteKnight31*: And she monetarily affected him.*
ReidingRainbow*: He just seemed way too polished, if I'm being
honest. The type to bully on social media, sure, but to sneak into her
courtyard and steal a cat? I can't picture it.*
Armchair_Detective*: We can't rule anyone out. Same with the ex-
boyfriend.*
ReidingRainbow*: I don't know. Vermont was nowhere in sight,
plus his floors were different than the pictures.*
WhiteKnight31*: Ugh we have to be missing something! No way this
amateur can show us up.*
ReidingRainbow*: We're amateurs too.*
WhiteKnight31*: We solved a case.*
ReidingRainbow*: One with a ton of information that was clearly
botched by law enforcement.*
WhiteKnight31*: So? A solve is a solve. We've got to figure this
one out.*

ReidingRainbow*: I still want to look into the neighbor, I just haven't quite figured out how to do it yet. I was thinking Hazel and I could stop by her apartment and see if we see anything.*
Armchair_Detective*: Look at you, suggesting a stakeout.*
ReidingRainbow*: It's not a stakeout if Hazel lives there.*
WhiteKnight31*: How's she holding up? Every time my cat curls up in my lap, I think about how hard this must be for her.*
ReidingRainbow*: She's alright. Hanging in there. I feel bad I can't do more.*
WhiteKnight31*: Oh…I'm sure you could do more. ;)*
ReidingRainbow*: Enough.*
WhiteKnight31*: So sensitive on the Hazel topic.*
Armchair_Detective*: There's got to be something there.*
ReidingRainbow*: Drop it.*
WhiteKnight31*: He isn't denying it! That's basically an admission.*

I SHOOK MY HEAD, SMILING AS I PULLED OFF MY OVERSIZED headphones and closed out of the group chat.

They were right, there *was* something. But I wasn't about to air out my personal life for them to examine. Especially when I hadn't quite figured out what was going on yet. Hazel hadn't brought up the kiss from the other night, which kind of surprised me. I thought for sure I'd wake up to her confronting me in the kitchen—at least a note or something. But nothing. Everything had been very cordial since then. Borderline awkward.

Part of me worried she wasn't interested.

But the way her cheeks flushed every time I walked into a room seemed to tell a different story. Maybe inviting her to family dinner was rushing things, but I wanted them to meet her. I wanted to open the door wider and let her into more of my world.

As for the kiss…we'd figure that out. We could talk about it tonight, on the way home. I just hoped she didn't think I was some jerk for kissing her when she was vulnerable. That was never my intention.

In reality, I had thought about kissing Hazel quite a bit. I liked who I was around her. She made me looser, messier. I felt more carefree just having her around.

My family would say that I was notoriously picky when it came to women. When I'd first met Meghan, it had taken me months to decide we should be in a relationship. And since the divorce, I'd had a hard time committing to anything serious. It wasn't that I didn't want to have a relationship again, it was that I overanalyzed every woman I even considered bringing into my life. How would they fit? Would we mesh well together long term?

Then Hazel came barreling in, someone I would've sworn had no place in my world. But she'd slipped in somehow, effortlessly weaving herself into my days and taking up every spare thought I had. She made me want to throw out the rulebook I'd clung to for so long. Made me want to rewrite it with her in mind.

There was something about being with her that stirred up this strange kind of nostalgia. I didn't even know if that made sense. It was like the way you look back on a memory and romanticize it, glossing over any pain points. She did that—except not for my past, but my *present*. Even the mundane things—making dinner, folding laundry, just sitting together on the couch—felt electric when she was around. And lately, the thought of her leaving had started to settle in like an ache in my chest.

I rolled my chair back and stood up, stretching before leaving my office and heading into the living room. A quick glance at my stove clock told me Hazel should be home by now. I hadn't meant to keep track of her schedule; it was quite difficult, given the fact that she could schedule clients at any time of day. But I always made it a point to ask her what her day looked like, either in person or via text. I liked knowing.

A thump came from the other end of the hallway. I approached with caution, arriving at her closed door and giving it a soft knock.

"Hazel?" I called.

The door flung open, and there she stood. She wore sheer black tights underneath a soft cream sweater dress. Her hair was styled in careful waves, neater than she typically wore it.

"Is this okay?" she asked, clearly flustered. "I've changed like seven times since I got back. What's the vibe? Casual? Jeans?"

My heart damn near melted.

"You look perfect," I assured her, meaning every word. She looked beautiful. I wanted to tell her as much, but I bit my tongue, not wanting to overwhelm her any more than she already was.

"You sure?" she asked. "Are you wearing that? Because we don't look like we're going to the same event."

I chuckled, glancing down at my sweats. "I'm changing into jeans and a sweater. Mom likes when we look nice."

"You're positive this is okay?"

Her nerves buzzed like live wires. I wanted to reach out and pull her into me, to ground her somehow, but we weren't there yet and I didn't want to push it.

"Please don't be anxious. My family is nice. They like everyone and there's no pressure."

"I'm not anxious," she squeaked. "Why? Do I seem anxious? Oh—" She cut herself off and walked to her bedside table; lava lamp on, of course. She picked up a multicolored bouquet of flowers and presented it to me. "I got these for your mom. Do you think she'll like them?"

"She'll love them."

"You're sure—"

"Hazel." I reached out and took a hold of her arms, using my thumbs to rub firm circles into them. "They're lovely, *you're* lovely. It's going to be great."

Her body softened in front of my eyes, and I watched as her shoulders loosened.

"Thanks for that. It's not every day I meet the family of the guy who's helping me investigate a cat kidnapper."

It was obviously a joke, but hearing those words come out of her mouth still didn't sit right with me. It should've been "the family of the guy who likes me." Or better yet, "the family of the guy I like." But that was on me, partially. We hadn't cleared the air since the kiss. I had every intention of doing so tonight. First, though, we had to get through dinner.

"Come on, let's head out. It just started snowing and it's going to be a big storm. We don't want to get caught on the roads."

TWENTY-THREE

Hazel

Storm was an understatement. It was a freaking blizzard outside. Reid had to go ten under the speed limit as the wipers frantically worked overtime to keep the windshield clear.

His parents only lived about ten miles away, but we took a couple of back roads to avoid any cars sliding out on the main road. The drive was silent as I made sure not to say anything to distract Reid. It was the kind of storm where you could barely see a few feet in front of you.

When we finally pulled into his parents' driveway, we let out sighs of relief.

"Made it. Thanks to these snow tires."

"Seriously, that got bad fast." I pulled my coat tight around me as we jumped out of the car, racing for his front porch. Even in the apocalyptic snowstorm, I could see how idyllic this house was. It had a front porch where I was sure a rocking chair or something sat in the summer months, and shutters bordering each window. The whole place screamed cozy and inviting.

That vibe was amplified by about one hundred when Reid pulled open the door. Warmth and the smells of something delicious roasting in the oven wafted out to meet us.

"Reid, is that you?" A woman in her fifties with kind eyes walked down the hall and into the entryway. She wore a fuzzy sweater, and slippers poked out underneath her jeans. "Oh, and you finally brought Hazel."

The way she said *finally* made me smile. As if I wasn't some girl who had only been in her son's life for a matter of weeks.

"Hi, Mrs. Mitchell. It's so nice to meet you. Your house is beautiful." I handed her the flowers that I had managed to keep mostly protected from the pelting snow outside.

"Aren't you sweet," she said, pulling me in for a quick hug before giving Reid a kiss on the cheek. "Come in. Let me get these into some water."

I followed her through the short hallway. The doors to each room were propped open, and family pictures lined the halls. The floorboards creaked underneath the worn runner.

"This is where you grew up?" I asked Reid. It wasn't a huge house, but it was homey to the max.

"Yep."

"We've been here for thirty-five years, believe it or not. Bought the place right after we got married," Mrs. Mitchell said.

The kitchen was right out of the nineties in the best possible way. Reid's childhood home was so relaxed compared to the harsh white lines of his townhouse.

"Ah, is this Hazel?" An older man with a warm smile, who looked a bit more like Reid than Ruby, stepped into the kitchen and gave me an outstretched hand.

"Mr. Mitchell. Thank you for having me." My smile was natural, not forced, as they welcomed me into their home.

"Nice of you to finally show. We're starving." A girl trailed behind Reid's dad. She was tall, probably at least 5'9", and looked a lot like Ruby.

"And this is Regan. My younger sister."

"Hazel!" she exclaimed when she noticed me. "Yay, I'm so glad he brought you."

She wrapped her arms around me, and any tension I'd been holding onto disappeared. Reid wasn't kidding when he said his family was welcoming. This was way more than I had been expecting, and my guard fell away immediately.

"The roads are shit out there," Reid said. "Took us twice as long to get here."

Reid's mom pursed her lips and looked out the window. It was nearly black outside, but we could still see the outlines of trees getting whipped around in the storm.

"It's a lot worse than they said it was going to be," she said. "We've already got a few inches that are sticking, and with the freezing temperatures tonight, some of that will surely ice over."

"Where are Ruby and West?" Reid asked. I knew from talking to him that West was his best friend and always attended family dinners.

"They should have been here by now. I hope the roads didn't give them trouble." His mom's tone held a hint of concern, but before she could dwell on it, a phone rang. They all reached for theirs, but it was Regan who held hers up.

"It's Ruby," she said, answering the call. "Hey, where are you?"

I could hear a muffled voice on the other end. Regan nodded. "Okay, I'll tell them. Glad nothing worse happened. Stay inside and stay safe."

"What happened?" Mr. Mitchell demanded, his face tight with concern.

"They skidded into a ditch in their neighborhood. West was able to push them out, but they turned around and went back to his house after. Said the roads were too bad, and they were sliding everywhere."

"Thank goodness they're okay." Reid's mom clutched her heart before her expression transformed into a quizzical one. "Wait. Why were they together?"

Regan shrugged. "I mean, they only live like two streets away from each other."

"West probably offered to drive because of the storm, or something," Reid said. There was something in his eyes that looked like he was calculating, though. "I keep telling them both to get snow tires," he added.

"We can't all be Mr. Responsible," Regan said, with an exaggerated sigh that made me laugh.

She smirked and shot me a wink. Something told me Regan and I would get along just fine.

"Hazel, what can I get you to drink?" Mr. Mitchell asked.

"Oh, water is fine."

"I hope you like lasagna." Mrs. Mitchell pulled out a pan from the oven.

"It smells amazing."

A small squeeze of my forearm. Reid stayed by my side, shooting me a smile when I looked up.

The scene was impossibly picturesque, like something straight out of a movie. If I'd ever tried to imagine the perfect little family moment, this would be it. Everyone was pitching in to get dinner on the table, someone setting out plates and silverware, their laughter echoing as they swapped stories from the week.

It made my chest tighten, thinking of Gran. Our dinners had never looked quite this perfect, not in the glossy, magazine-cover kind of way. But the love? The sentiment? That was always there.

Conversation flowed easily as we all gathered around the table. They made answering question after question about myself seem friendly instead of like an interrogation.

"How do you like the salon? I know Ruby is really happy you're there."

"What made you want to be a hairstylist?

"Where did you grow up?"

None of the questions were about the extortion situation, my Gran, or Vermont, for which I was immensely grateful. It was nice to feel normal and not like a spectacle. They treated me like a girl Reid brought home to meet the family, not like his current charity case.

Which wasn't how I felt. Not really. But sometimes my intrusive thoughts got the better of me.

After we'd all had seconds—thirds if you were Reid—Regan started clearing the plates. I jumped up to help, but Reid's mom put a firm hand on my shoulder. "Hazel, you're a guest. You relax. Do you like mint chocolate chip cookies? I just baked some fresh."

Ugh, they really were perfect. I stayed seated while his mom brought over a heaping plate of cookies. My stomach was near-bursting but they looked way too soft and delicious not to have at least two.

"You can see why dinners are only weekly." Reid took one off the plate. "If we were here more often than that, I think my arteries would get blocked."

His mom waved off the comment. "You need food that sticks to your bones. You eat enough healthy stuff."

"Yeah, not everything needs to go into a macro tracker," Regan added.

I settled into my seat. They had welcomed me with open arms, and I couldn't be more grateful Reid had asked me to come tonight.

"Does your family get together often?" his mom asked me.

"Oh, uh, no, not really," I started.

"Mom." Reid glared at her.

"No, no, it's alright," I added hurriedly. "My gran was my only family, and she passed away last month."

"I'm so sorry." Reid's mom reached out and grabbed my hand, giving it a squeeze. "Reid mentioned that, but I didn't realize…Anyway, you're welcome here anytime."

"Thank you," I said. The weight behind my eyes loomed, like I might cry at any moment, but it wasn't so bad. Because this time it was a mixture of sadness and happiness.

"And we don't have to talk about it, of course, but I hate

what you're going through right now. I hope you're doing okay."

"People absolutely suck," Regan chimed in, shaking her head.

"We're here if you need anything," his dad said.

That was it. Now the tears were really in danger of spilling over.

"I appreciate that. Would you just excuse me one second. Where's the bathroom?" I stood up, the chair squeaking across the tiled floor.

"Down the hall to the left." Mr. Mitchell pointed behind him.

I rushed off down the hallway, rounded the corner, and enclosed myself in the tiny pink powder room. A few tears spilled out almost immediately and I tore off a piece of toilet paper to wipe them away.

A soft knock came at the door. I quickly blew my nose and wiped at my face. My eyes glistened and were a little red, but overall, I looked put together.

"Hazel? It's me. Open up." Reid's concern shone through even with his voice muffled.

I unlocked the pocket door and slid it open. His eyes widened when they saw me, before he pulled his glasses off and squeezed the bridge of his nose in frustration. "Shit. Are you okay? I should have warned them not to say anything."

"I'm fine," I said.

"You were crying."

"Barely," I whispered, wiping the last stray tear away.

"Then that's not okay," he said.

"It is, though. Your family is so sweet. I shouldn't have expected anything else, since they raised you after all, but still. I can't believe how welcoming they are. I'm tearing up because I can't remember the last time I felt so at home. The love is like, literally palpable here. I'm just happy to be a part of it, even if it's only for one night."

Reid let out a slow breath and gave a curt nod, like my

answer had satisfied him—at least enough to stop him from storming back into the kitchen to scold his family.

"You can come next week, too." Reid reached out and laced his fingers through mine. His thumb rubbed the back of my hand. "And the week after."

I laughed. "Watch it, or I might take you up on that offer."

"I hope you do." The corner of his lip lifted before it fell. His eyes searched mine before he leaned down and pressed a soft kiss to my lips. My chest nearly exploded.

When he pulled away, he lingered close, forehead pressed to mine.

"I've been thinking about doing that all day," he whispered. And just like that, a dam burst. Relief gushed through me. It hadn't just been me replaying our kiss a million times in my mind.

"Why did you wait?" I asked.

"I don't want you to think I'm taking advantage of you when you're all vulnerable. Especially since you're staying at my house."

A nervous laugh escaped me. "Reid?"

"Yeah?"

"Don't take this the wrong way, but *please* take advantage of me."

TWENTY-FOUR

Hazel

After dinner we retired to the living room to play a rowdy game of dominos. Well, rowdy if you were Regan and Mrs. Mitchell. They got way too into it, while Reid repeatedly apologized for their competitiveness.

Even though he acted like he didn't care, Reid won every time, to the point where I started accusing him of cheating. Regan was more than happy to join in on that accusation.

We laughed so hard my stomach ached.

His dad insisted I try his barrel-aged, something something—whiskey he'd imported. We all had tumblers with a thimble-full in them. The sip warmed my entire soul. I hardly drank, mostly because I knew what vices had done to my mother. But a sip of whiskey every once in a while was pleasant. Certainly on a night like tonight.

We were all lounging around the living room, chatting aimlessly, when Reid's mother pulled away the curtain to assess the weather outside.

"Okay, there is no way you two are driving anywhere tonight. I don't care how close Reid's house is."

"We'll be fine," Reid said, but as soon as he stood to look

out the window, he brought his hand to his face, rubbing it along his jaw. "Shit. It's a mess out there."

The snow was basically blowing sideways by the bucketful. The roads weren't even visible.

"It's not worth it," his dad said. "You can take your old room downstairs."

"I have sweats you can borrow, Hazel," Regan offered.

"That would be great." I wasn't at all eager to leave the comfort of this house. A little sleepover sounded nice.

Reid's mom pushed herself off the couch. "I'll go throw clean sheets on the bed. Regan, why don't you take Hazel to your room?"

Regan waved for me to follow her to the front of the house, where narrow wooden steps led to the second floor. More family pictures lined the staircase, and I stopped when I spotted what must have been Reid's senior portrait. He wore a buttoned-up white shirt and no trace of a smile.

"He looks so serious," I said with a laugh.

"That's Reid for you. He picked out that shirt himself. Mom asked him to go more casual, but he wouldn't budge."

I continued following her up the stairs. They let out at a short hallway with four identical doors.

Regan walked to the one on the end and opened it. It was small, with a twin bed and posters lining the wall. "Here's the room. Don't get jealous of the glamorous life I lead."

"I lived with my gran until I was twenty-two," I offered. "Honestly, I kind of wish I'd have lived with her longer, instead of shacking up with my ex."

"Yeah, it's not so bad. I moved out for college, so sometimes I miss my independence, but Mom and Dad are alright. Can't beat the savings of living at home."

"Exactly," I said.

Regan rifled through her top drawer before producing gray sweatpants and a maroon t-shirt. "These work?" she asked.

"Perfect."

"I'm sure my mom will supply a toothbrush and all that. She loves company, so you two being forced to spend the night is, like, her dream come true."

"Reid doesn't stay here much?"

"He does more now…now that he's single."

"Oh, got it." I didn't want to pry.

Thankfully, Regan didn't seem to like to stay quiet, because I didn't even have to push for her to share more on the subject.

"Meghan—his ex—was fine. She just wasn't very…warm. She didn't like to do stuff with the family. Her own parents lived across the country, and she only saw them for holidays. I hate to say that I was relieved when he got the divorce, but… it's like I got my brother back. He's here every week now and I can go over to his house whenever."

"She didn't let you come over?" The idea shocked me.

Regan shrugged. "Not really."

Family was important. I'd always been desperate for a big one, but the little one I did have, I cherished. And even Paul, for all his faults, had never denied me that. He was actually really great with Gran, albeit irresponsible. He'd drive her to the casino, they'd hit the slot machines until past midnight, and be excited about winning twenty dollars—even though they wouldn't tell me how much money they put in. Honestly, the way he had been with her was one of the main reasons I'd stayed with him as long as I had. The memory was welcome. It had become so easy to remember the bad that I'd forgotten there had been good parts to that relationship, too.

"That sucks. If I had a family like yours, I'd be over here all the time."

She laughed. "You're welcome to them."

"I appreciate your willingness to take in strays," I said with a self-deprecating laugh.

She eyed me. "You're more than a stray. Reid really likes you."

That caught me off guard. I wasn't sure how to respond.

"I-I don't know," I said. Even though I kind of did. Despite all of my insecurities, there was something undeniable there. The chemistry practically crackled. And now that he'd kissed me, it felt like we were both ready to face whatever was going on between us.

"He likes having you around. Which is a surprise, because he *hates* houseguests. He even told us explicitly not to stop by unannounced while you're staying with him, so you don't feel uncomfortable."

My face twisted into one of horror. "Oh no, please stop by." The last thing I wanted to be was the reason Reid spent less time with his family. "Seriously, any time. I would have been happy to meet you, or get out of your way, or whatever. Don't not come over on account of me."

She laughed. "Don't worry about it. He hates when we come over without warning, or at least he *says* he does. I'm not sure I buy it."

"You're family. You don't need an invitation."

A slow smile crept onto Regan's face. "Exactly. You get it. I knew I'd like you."

I stepped into the upstairs bathroom and changed into the sweats Regan had given me. Regan came out in her own flannel pajama bottoms, and we went back downstairs. Reid and his parents were all scattered around the living room.

"Hazel, would you think it's the most boring thing in the world if we all watched a movie together?" Reid's mom looked at me expectantly from where she sat on the sofa, curled up next to her husband, with a blanket across their laps.

"We can just go to bed," Reid added from the oversized armchair.

I smiled, taking it all in. "I'd love to watch a movie."

Regan pulled a pillow from the couch and dropped it on the floor, laying down and nestling into it. They'd turned on the electric fireplace, and flames danced around.

Reid shifted over on the chair and patted it. "There's enough room here."

It took everything in me to force the blush from spreading to my cheeks as I sat next to him. There was *hardly* room. Our entire thighs and hips pressed tightly against each other.

"Is this okay?" he whispered. "I can sit on the floor."

"It's fine." 'More than fine' would have been the appropriate answer. I leaned back into the chair so that our shoulders pressed together, too. He lifted the arm that was between us and rested it along the back of the chair. The movement made my head kind of naturally settle into the crook of his arm, and I didn't fight it.

His mom put on an old John Hughes movie. When I said this was one of my gran's and my favorites, Reid squeezed me tightly.

We made it about halfway through the movie, and to my delight, I learned that Reid's family loved talking through movies almost as much as I did. Well, his mom and Regan did. Reid and his dad kept trying to shush them. But once I joined in, quoting lines and pointing out the outrageously good outfits I wished I could still buy today, they finally gave up and let the commentary roll.

This was what feeling at home was like.

It had been a minute.

"Your bedroom is in the basement?" I asked, eyebrows raised. Reid hovered behind me in the doorway. The rest of the family had already said their goodnights and headed upstairs.

"Once Regan and Ruby were too old to want to share a room, our parents finished the basement so I could move down here. As a teenager, I wasn't about to complain. It was like having my own apartment."

We made our way down the carpeted stairs, and at the

bottom, I found a surprisingly cozy basement. Not a hint of dampness in the air, just a comforting, lived-in sensation. There was wall-to-wall beige carpet against blue walls and a worn leather sofa that sagged in one corner, facing an ancient TV that looked like it had been there forever.

"There used to be another bed down here. West stayed with us our senior year when his parents moved away."

He led me to a door off the main room. Inside was a small bedroom, just big enough for a full-size mattress, two end tables, and not much else. There was a dog-eared book sitting on one of the end tables. I picked it up. *IT Architecture for Dummies.*

"You spend a lot of nights here?" I asked.

"Not really. Other than holidays, there's no need to since we all live so close."

"It seemed like your mom was really excited to have you under the same roof."

He chuckled. "I guarantee my mom will make a ridiculous breakfast spread in the morning. Sorry in advance."

"There's nothing to be sorry for. I love your family."

His smile spread before he dropped his chin and rubbed the back of his neck. "The bathroom is just through there. My mom has spare toothbrushes in the drawer. Oh, and here." He handed me a small towel, rolled into a neat spiral.

Our fingers brushed as I took it. Sparks.

I ducked my head and rushed into the bathroom. I brushed my teeth with the new toothbrush before evaluating myself in the mirror. My bangs lay flat against my forehead. I tried to fluff them out, even though the basement was dark and Reid was already quite familiar with how I looked.

My heart pounded thinking of the one bed just beyond that door. One bed, and just one tiny full-sized mattress.

Would we both be sleeping there? He hadn't said as much, but he also hadn't said anything against it. Frankly, there was nothing I wanted more than to curl up next to Reid all night. It would be the ideal ending to an already perfect evening.

When I stepped back into the room, Reid had changed into old sweats with a hole in the thigh and a threadbare t-shirt. He nodded at me. "You can have the bed. I'll take the loveseat."

My heart dropped a little. "No way. You're too tall. I'll take the couch."

He rolled his eyes. "I'm not letting you sleep on the couch."

"I'm not letting *you* sleep on the couch."

He sighed and glanced from me to the bed. I chewed on the inside of my cheek, my heart hammering in my chest.

"We could both sleep here," I offered, voice shakier than I wanted it to be.

His gaze flew back to mine. "Are you sure?" Did I detect a hint of hope in his tone?

"Definitely. There's plenty of room." I padded to one side of the bed and moved the covers. There wasn't actually all that much room, but I had absolutely zero issue with pressing our bodies against each other tonight. It was chilly down here and I could hear the faint sound of the wind whistling outside through the egress window.

"If you're sure," he said. He moved to the other side with cautious steps, as though afraid that any sudden motion might scare me off.

We both got into bed, and I settled into the sheets.

Suddenly, I wasn't tired at all. I was the most wide-awake I'd ever been, as every molecule of my being sensed Reid barely an inch away.

"Hazel?" his voice was soft, right by my ear.

"Yeah?"

"I'm really glad you came tonight."

I bit back a smile as my stomach went all fluttery. "I'm really glad I came tonight, too."

He turned the dim bedside light off and darkness filled the room. I shifted so that I was facing the edge of the bed. Reid moved behind me, his arm bumping my back. It wasn't lost on me that if we were just *a little* closer, we'd be spooning.

Heat pooled inside me and my entire body tingled. I brushed my lips with my fingertips, thinking of the kiss earlier tonight.

Shit.

I wanted more. Badly.

Now the question was, did I have the balls to go for it?

What would be the worst thing that could happen? He'd reject me? That would suck, and might very well send me into a tailspin of sadness, seeing as Reid was the only thing lifting my mood lately…but was it enough to get me to stop?

I had never been great with self-preservation, which is why my body started to move of its own accord. I shifted back an inch, and then two inches, until finally my butt made contact with his groin and my back pressed into his chest.

There. I could just be looking for a cuddle. I could have just casually shifted my position. I could bail right out of this if he pulled away.

Reid's breath tickled my neck, and it sent a painfully good quiver down my entire spine. Almost imperceptibly, I moved my hips to rock against him. He inhaled sharply. When he didn't pull away, I took that as a positive sign and moved my hips again. Another sharp inhale.

"What are you doing?" he asked, his voice gruff and his clear desire ringing right through.

"What do you mean?" I whispered innocently, now full-on grinding my butt into him for good measure.

He let out a low grunt. "You're really testing my self-control here."

"What if I told you I wished your self-control would finally get lost for once?"

Reid was quiet for a moment before his hand roamed over my shoulder and down my arm, his fingertips slowly leaving a trail. I nearly gasped at the unexpected touch. My body flooded with anticipation as he brushed down my arm before landing his hand flat on my stomach.

He stilled for a moment, gauging my response. When I gave a little excited shimmy, he pulled my t-shirt up, and traced lazy circles around my abdomen, teasing at the waistband of my sweats.

Yep, that was all it took.

Pressure started to build. Every part of me screamed, begging to be touched. I rocked back into him again.

He groaned, his hot breath tickling my ear. That just set me off even more.

"You sure?" he asked. "We haven't even talked through anything."

I tilted my head so I could whisper back at him. "Please touch me or I'm going to go crazy."

He growled—*actually* growled. This version of Reid made me want to pass out with giddiness as his strong arm gripped me tighter. He nipped my ear before dipping his hand below my waistband. This time I did gasp as his fingers slipped below my panties and found my core.

"Shit, Hazel," he said when he felt how wet I was for him. I bucked against him, begging for him to touch me.

When he finally slipped a finger inside me, my back arched. I wanted to cry with relief.

"Reid," I moaned, likely too loudly considering we were in his family's house. "Shit," I said, covering my mouth with a pillow.

"It's okay," he whispered, slipping another finger inside me and making me clutch the blankets. "We're two floors away and this storm is raging. No one can hear anything."

I let out another soft moan as he pumped his fingers in and out of me. When his thumb found my clit, I jumped and let out a startlingly loud gasp. Hey, it had been a while since I'd been touched by anything other than my vibrator.

Reid grabbed my neck and angled my head toward him as he sat up. He leaned down, capturing my mouth with his. His fingers became more persistent, and now my moans were lost against his lips as he swallowed them.

"Don't stop," I said against his mouth, when his fingers hooked, hitting *right* where I needed them to. The pressure was absolutely delicious, and I could hardly believe it was Reid who was giving it to me right now.

I reached one arm back to wrap around his head, tangling my fingers in his hair and melding our mouths even closer together. I put my other hand over his, pressing down and letting the friction of his palm work its magic while his other fingers moved inside me.

God this felt good.

I had thought about this more times than I cared to admit, but I hadn't been sure it would happen.

His fingers pumped faster, in and out, and I stifled my groans against his mouth.

The pressure continued to build, and I forced myself to not cry out. But it felt so good. I rocked my hips against him, climbing until I finally reached my release.

Panting, I turned toward him. Before he said anything, he crushed his mouth against me, slowly and carefully moving his lips over mine.

When he was done, he pressed his forehead to mine and stared into my eyes. We could hardly make each other out in the dark bedroom. The whistling wind outside and our deep breathing were the only sounds.

Shyness came over me. I pulled the blanket up to cover the grin that was slowly creeping across my mouth. He let out a laugh and pulled the blanket back. I could just make out the shadows of his features in the dark room.

"Don't hide from me."

"I'm not," I replied, the smile now evident in my voice.

His gaze flickered over my face. He pushed my bangs away from my eyes. "Are you okay?"

I nearly choked on a laugh. "Are you serious? You just

gave me the best orgasm I've had in years, and you're asking if I'm okay?"

A grin transformed his face. I could make out the soft glow of his teeth. "The best, huh?"

"Don't let it go to your head."

We stared at each other for a minute, his eyes slowly coming into focus as mine got more used to the dark. Our bodies were still pressed together, and the need I'd felt moments ago was already returning. Would having sex with Reid be crazy right now? That would be too soon, right? But he'd just fingered me; that was already taking it way beyond friendly territory.

"What are you thinking about?" he asked softly, brushing my hair behind my ear.

"Whether it's too soon for us to have sex," I whispered.

He let out a strangled sound.

"What? Like you weren't thinking it," I said.

He chuckled and shook his head, resuming playing with my hair. "I've thought about it a few times. But we don't have to rush anything."

"It's been a while for me," I admitted, unafraid to lay all my cards on the table with Reid.

"For me too," he said.

I shifted, propping my head up on my hand. "Really? How long?"

He let out a groan. "Seriously? Does it really matter?"

"Yes. I want to know down to the very minute."

"You're nosy."

"Yes, I am."

He sighed before mirroring my posture, propping himself up on one hand as well. "It was after my divorce, if that's what you're wondering. I don't like casual sex. I dated one woman for a couple of months in the summer, and that was the last time. It didn't work out. She was looking for a commitment faster than I could give her one."

That kind of had my gut doing a flip. Was he ready for a

commitment now? *Was I?* This thing between Reid and me wasn't casual. We were friends first. We'd talked about so many things from my past; he knew me better than anyone at this point. Which, granted, wasn't that hard to do, but still.

"I don't like casual sex either," I said.

He ran his other hand up and down my arm. "Fair enough."

We continued to stare in silence, the mix of need and satisfaction still swirling in my body.

"Hazel," Reid whispered.

"Reid?"

"Just so you know, this isn't casual. For me, at least."

My heart pounded. Reid leaned in and kissed me on the forehead before moving to my mouth and pressing a soft kiss there, too. I let my head fall to his chest and he wrapped his arms around me.

"It's not casual for me either," I said as I drifted off to sleep in his arms.

I barely heard his, "I know."

I hadn't felt that safe in a long time.

TWENTY-FIVE

Reid

"YOU DIDN'T HAVE TO COME," HAZEL SAID, PUSHING OPEN THE gate to her apartment. It got stuck on a pile of snow, but she shoved it until we could squeeze into the courtyard.

"Like I was going to let you go alone."

After the lavish breakfast spread my mom presented us with at eight a.m., Hazel announced that she had some errands to run today. A normal person would have let her go by herself—told her to enjoy her day, and that I'd see her later.

If it had been a different snowy Saturday and Hazel wasn't in my life, I might find myself spending the day at my computer, lost in a chat about some cold case. But that didn't appeal to me as much today. She could have said her errand was to buy shampoo at the drugstore or wait in line at the DMV and I still would have wanted to tag along. But when she'd casually mentioned that her errand involved dropping by her apartment to grab a few things, there was no way in hell I was staying behind. Mostly because I didn't like her hanging around there alone, given everything, but I did have an ulterior motive.

The neighbor. Mrs. Edenbury.

At this point, she was still a shaky suspect on a dwindling list of options.

I had nothing to go on except for the fact that she could have easily committed the crime. It was painfully obvious at this stage that I was an amateur chasing an amateur. My group hadn't come up with any new theories either; we were a lot more used to working with evidence that someone else had already collected. Trying to piece everything together from scratch was hard as hell.

Hazel unlocked the door to her hallway and led us in. The entire time she fiddled with the lock on her apartment, I stared at Mrs. Edenbury's door. Was she there? Sleeping?

"She usually does something with her church group on weekends."

"Huh?" I jerked my gaze back to Hazel, who had her door propped open.

"She'll probably be leaving soon," she said, checking her phone.

"We should try to catch her." I slid in behind Hazel and let the door swing shut behind me.

She breezed through the cramped space to her bedroom.

"Did your stuff expand since we were last here?" I wedged myself past the giant clock and followed her.

"Ha. Ha. You're hilarious." Her tone implied I was anything but.

I propped myself in the doorway, watching her sift through dresser drawers. This was my first time seeing her bedroom. It matched the rest of her space perfectly, every wall covered in pictures, shelves, or knickknacks. Her curtains looked straight out of the seventies. An old landline phone sitting on her dresser didn't even appear to have a cord attached to it. The bed was ridiculously high, on an iron bedframe. Like, *ridiculously* high. It nearly came up to my hip.

"Do you have a stepstool for this thing?" I patted the handmade, multi-colored quilt on her bed.

"Nope," she said, before turning away from the dresser she

was rummaging through and launching herself at the bed. She had to use both arms to hoist herself up but then she was on, bouncing on the plush mattress.

"If you need a running start, the bed is too high," I said.

She laughed. "I disagree. It keeps me spry."

"You shouldn't have to do a track and field event every night before bed."

"That's part of the fun." She twisted her finger in a loose thread. "I begged for this bedframe for my sixteenth birthday. I thought it looked Parisian."

"Much like the rest of your décor," I said sarcastically, nodding toward the beat-up poster of a popular nineties boy band near my left shoulder.

"Eclectic, Reid. Learn the word. Love the word."

Smirking, I set my palms on her bed and hoisted myself up so that we were next to each other. My entire body immediately sank into the mattress.

"This is too soft."

"Too high. Too soft. Too much personality." Hazel laughed while mocking my voice. I pinched her side, and she let out a small squeal before bursting into laughter again.

"I'm serious," I said. "This can't be good for your back."

"I so appreciate your concern for my spinal health." She batted her eyelashes at me, and I moved my head to steal a kiss. It happened so suddenly, I didn't even question it. But when I pulled away, she blinked a few times, the blush apparent on her cheeks.

For a second, I doubted myself. Were we not at the level of stolen kisses yet? But when I saw her bite her lip to keep from smiling any wider, I knew she was feeling just as giddy about whatever was brewing between us as I was.

"Okay, let me get what I came here for." She hoisted herself toward the edge of the bed. It was almost comical how she had to slide off. Back at the dresser, she continued pulling clothes out of a drawer that was packed to the brim.

I slid off the bed and joined her, carefully watching her selections.

"I like that one," I said. She'd just pulled out a vintage-looking sweatshirt that said Key Ridge Ski Resort.

"Me too," she held it close to her. "It was Gran's. She went there a million years ago."

"Did you two go on many vacations?"

She stuffed the sweatshirt into a tote bag she'd taken off the back of her door, which was crammed with a variety of items hanging off hooks. "Not really. Unless you count the indoor water park in Ohio."

"Oh, that definitely counts. I love that place."

"We should go some time." Her eyes twinkled as she looked up at me. I loved that look. Hazel wasn't meant to be sad. Ever. She was meant to always have *this* look about her, the one with the bright eyes and the fizzy giggles.

She pulled out another one and I squinted to read the text.

"Haven High School Wrestling Championship?" I looked from the piece of clothing to her with raised eyebrows.

"It was Paul's," she admitted.

"And you still have it?"

"It's the perfect oversize fit. Plus, he took my favorite sweatshirt and loaned it to his friend, who claimed to have lost it." She rolled her eyes and put air quotes around *lost it*. "It was tie-dye and soft, and I miss it every day. So, it's only fair I have this."

Yeah, I didn't love that. Half-jokingly, I folded up Paul's sweatshirt and set it back in the top drawer.

"Hey." She laughed and tried to snatch it back.

"I don't think you need that one," I said, still trying to stuff it back into the drawer.

"But it's comfortable," she argued.

"I'll get you a new sweatshirt."

"But old ones are the best. They need to have that worn-in feel."

"You can have one of mine."

"Seriously?" She paused, considering it.

"Yes."

"Which one?"

"Any one you want."

"What if it's your favorite?" she asked, smirking up at me.

"I'd rather hand over every sweatshirt I've ever owned than see you walking around my living room in that."

She scrunched her nose and shook her head, not fighting me when I pressed the piece of clothing back into the drawer before sliding it closed.

"You're cute when you're jealous," she teased through a smile before grabbing a few more items.

I didn't bother correcting her. I *was* a little jealous. Not in that over-the-top, possessive way, but in the way where the only clothes I wanted to see Hazel in were my own. This was the honeymoon phase. The couldn't-get-enough-of-each-other stage. Every second felt like something to soak in, not waste thinking about her stupid ex. Immature? Probably. But I hadn't felt like this in a long time.

Movement outside the window caught my eye. An older lady slid into the driver's side of a car parked across the street. I could add the fact that this apartment had no secure parking garage to my list of grievances with the place. I did *not* want Hazel living here, even after all this was over.

"Is that…" I raced to the window. Hazel followed me, banging her hip on her bedframe in her haste.

"Shit," she muttered, rubbing her side. "What is it?"

"Mrs. Edenbury." I pointed.

Her eyes scanned until they landed on the car. "Yep, that's her car. Must be off to church."

"Hurry, let's see if we can catch her."

I was already halfway out of Hazel's apartment, moving fast, but by the time I'd flung open the door to the courtyard, it was too late. The white sedan had already pulled away from the curb, taillights glowing as it disappeared down the street. I had no chance of catching up.

Back in the hallway Hazel wore an amused expression.

"What exactly was your plan? Ask her outright if she has Vermont?"

I dragged a hand over my face, pulse racing. I didn't know what my plan had been exactly, but I was starting to get desperate.

"I don't know," I admitted.

She giggled. "You know you're turning into me, right? A week ago, I would have been the one chasing down a suspect."

"Yeah, yeah. Whatever." I placed a hand on the wall by her head, unapologetically gazing down at her. The way her bright eyes shone back at me made my chest tighten.

I was about to bend down and steal another kiss when Mrs. Edenbury's door caught my eye. It didn't look quite right. Off center somehow.

Straightening, I took a step toward it. Was that a crack? Before thinking too much about it, I closed the distance and pushed it.

It opened.

Hazel gasped and her head went on a swivel looking up and down the hall.

"Reid!" she hissed.

"What?" I asked innocently. "I just want to make sure she's okay. She left her door unlocked."

Hazel's lips parted and her eyes went wide. "Who even are you right now?" she whispered. "*I* wouldn't even suggest breaking and entering."

I gave her a sheepish shrug, then waved her over with the kind of urgency that said *please don't make me explain this right now.*

"It was open," I whispered. But she was right. Who had I become? Just waltzing into a stranger's apartment like it was nothing, no hesitation, no thought about how bad an idea it could be?

"Hello?" I called into the apartment, keeping up the

façade. "The door was open, and we just wanted to make sure everything is alright."

"Oh, that sounds natural."

I narrowed my eyes at Hazel before taking another step into the apartment, keeping her behind me.

The apartment was a different layout than Hazel's; hers had a small entryway that was walled off. The entrance to the rest of Mrs. Edenbury's apartment was to our right instead. The *smell* of cat hit me first. Cat and perfume.

"Reid, look." Hazel pointed down.

I saw it immediately. The floorboards. They were old, worn, and rich. Not exactly one of a kind, but unlike the floors at Paul's, they definitely reminded me of the picture we'd received of Vermont.

We exchanged a look before I signaled for us to continue.

We crept around the corner, stepping into the living area. After a quick survey of the room, my first surprise was that Hazel's unit was actually the *updated* version of an apartment in this complex; this one was much older. The original wood flooring ended in the entryway, and the rest of this unit was covered in shag carpeting and linoleum tile. Asbestos was one hundred percent lingering in these walls.

"This place kind of gives me the creeps," Hazel whispered, letting the door shut behind her. "I think she's lived here for, like, twenty-five years."

"I believe it," I said taking in the dated light fixtures.

We cautiously stepped further into the apartment. The living room had trinkets everywhere; mostly dolls and figurines. There were even a few life-sized ones sitting on the couch. A gray cat lay sprawled next to one, staring at us but making no move other than to stretch. Another cat slunk into the room, this one black. I crossed my fingers, really hoping that whole *black cat means bad luck* thing was just superstition, and not the universe messing with me.

"Let's hurry and get out of here," Hazel said glancing

around nervously. "I can't believe you went from refusing a stakeout to breaking and entering."

"Just *entering*. There was no breaking involved," I said again.

"Glad you've got your story straight for when we're arrested."

I rolled my eyes and kept scanning the room, not leaving a single corner unchecked. Dropping to my hands and knees, I peered under the couch. Another cat, this one with soft brown fur and huge green eyes, stared back at me like the intruder I was. "Shit, how many cats does this woman have?" I stood up and brushed my pants. Sure enough, cat fur already clung to them.

"I have no idea. I've only been over for tea twice. I think I counted four."

The bedroom door stood open at the end of the hallway. I peeked my head in and looked around. It was mostly more dolls.

"How does anyone live like this?" Hazel asked. "There's stuff everywhere."

I slowly turned to her, eyebrows lost in my hairline. "Um, pot, meet kettle."

She glared at me. "My place is nothing like this."

I huffed out a laugh but didn't bother arguing with her.

We split up and quickly looked through the small apartment. I'd about given up hope when a flash of movement came out of the bathroom. Out sauntered a new cat.

This one was orange and white.

"Vermont," I whisper-yelled. The cat snapped its head up and eyed me in a judgmental way.

"What!" Hazel shrieked, not whispering at all. She came barreling at me from the kitchen. "No way! I can't believe she'd do that. Are you serious? After all the times we had tea together—"

Her voice stopped as soon as she rounded the corner and saw the cat.

"That's not Vermont." Her tone was defeated.

I looked from her to the cat and back to her. "Are you sure?"

She tilted her chin down and blinked slowly. "Yes, I'm sure. You don't think I know what my own cat looks like?"

"I mean, didn't you kind of just get him?"

"He was at Gran's before that, Reid. I'm not an idiot. I can distinguish my grandmother's beloved cat who was sleeping in my apartment for weeks from a random orange cat Mrs. Edenbury probably grabbed off the street. No offense," she added to the cat.

The cat sat back and continued to watch us argue.

All that hope, the rush that had just lit up every nerve in my body, vanished in a blink. My heart crashed. I'd honestly thought we had him. I'd thought this might be over.

"I'm sorry, Hazel. I hoped…" My words trailed off as I stared down at her.

"It's alright." She waved me off. "In a way, I'm happy he's not here. It's nice to know the only person who's shown me kindness in this apartment complex is not actually trying to extort me." She chewed on her lip, but despite her words, I saw no relief in her eyes. "Now, can we please get out of here before we get caught?"

We checked a few more hidden corners—under furniture, behind doors, even inside the kitchen cabinets—before finally admitting defeat. No sign of the cat. With one last glance around, we stepped out of the apartment, making sure to pull the door shut securely behind us.

Shit.

I'd been so sure Mrs. Edenbury had been acting suspicious.

But maybe she had been embarrassed by the state of her apartment and that's why she hadn't wanted Hazel to come inside. Or maybe I'd been reaching all along—seeing something that had never existed.

I avoided meeting Hazel's eyes, afraid of the disappointment I was sure to find there. Silence settled between us. The playfulness from earlier had vanished, replaced by a heavy stillness. Neither of us wanted to talk about how grim the situation was starting to look.

She slung her bursting tote bag over her shoulder, and we headed out. I held open the door to the courtyard for Hazel, but instead of ducking underneath my arm, she dug around in her coat pockets before letting out a soft curse.

"I forgot my car keys on my kitchen table. One sec."

She unlocked her door, and I leaned against the wall of the vestibule, waiting for her to come back. My eye caught the camera pointed at the entry door. I stared longingly at it, thinking about the other one pointed right at the courtyard. If only that footage hadn't been erased. If only she'd come to me a little earlier. This whole thing could've been solved with clear, simple video evidence. Maybe then the police would've taken her seriously.

Now, everything was a mess, we had no help, and time was slipping away.

Then I noticed something.

A small sign just beneath the camera—something the courtyard one didn't have. I squinted, trying to make out the tiny print. I walked over and stood on my tiptoes, scanning the words.

Something…something…contact us…cloud storage.

Cloud storage.

"I got them," Hazel said, slamming her apartment door shut behind her.

I gripped her shoulders and shook.

"What!" she yelped, clearly not expecting that.

"There!" I pointed to the sign under the camera.

"The camera?" she asked, looking at me like I'd lost it. "We've already been over this—"

"Not the camera. *The sign.*" My grin was huge. "I actually think we might be able to figure this out."

TWENTY-SIX

Hazel

To: support@cloudcameras.com
From: Management@courtyardapartments.com
Hello,
A tenant had an issue with theft and has filed a police report.
We need the footage from Thursday, October 24, from
between seven and eight AM. The camera's serial number is
2754689.
Sincerely,
Courtyard Apartments Leasing Office

To: Management@courtyardapartments.com
From: support@cloudcameras.com

A ticket has been opened regarding this request. We store
camera footage in our cloud for sixty days. Please allow up to
seven days to process this request.

This is an automated reply. Please do not respond.

As soon as Reid mentioned the footage might be stored
in the cloud, I'd jumped at the chance to send an email. It had

been his idea to create a fake account posing as the apartment complex's leasing office. With only a week until my winnings were supposed to be deposited, time was running out—and the last thing we wanted was to deal with the real leasing office.

The camera facing the courtyard had a small ID number printed at the bottom. That, paired with the phony email, seemed to be all it took to bypass whatever basic security the ticketing system had in place.

I was jittery with renewed hope. The chance that we might have answers soon had gone from improbable to likely. It was hard not to be too optimistic when this could be the smoking gun we needed. They still had the footage. It wasn't gone. They said they were processing the request. I'd be able to see with my own eyes exactly who took Vermont. I'd have definitive proof. I could take action.

The ordeal had me both on the edge of my seat with impatience, and more content than I'd been in a while.

"Earth to Hazel." Jackson waved a hand in front of my face.

"Sorry?" I blinked, giving him my attention. "Did you say something?"

"I asked when your next client is."

"Oh, I'm done for the day. Just procrastinating leaving with that awful-looking weather outside."

It was a classic late-fall evening—gray and frigid, with the wind swirling around thick snowflakes that refused to stick, melting instead on contact with pavement still warm thanks to the steady stream of passing cars.

The salon had been buzzing all day. We were fully booked, nonstop from open to close. Natalie and Ruby were still with clients up front and Miranda was manning the desk, deep in conversation on the phone. The hours had flown by in the best kind of way. Everyone was getting their hair done for the holidays—family photos, office parties, winter weddings. There was something magical about it all.

"Want to grab a drink?" Jackson asked.

"Maybe tomorrow?" I offered.

Reid had mentioned maybe hanging out tonight to celebrate the potential lead on the footage. We hadn't nailed down a precise plan, but I didn't want to overbook in case he'd been serious. At this point, there was nothing that sounded more appealing than hanging out with Reid. I felt a little pathetic admitting that to myself, but I didn't care. I liked the guy. *A lot.*

That night at his parents' house two days ago was still playing on a loop in my mind. Yesterday, after we got back from my apartment, we'd watched a few reruns of old TV shows before he'd left to meet up with his friend West. Apparently he'd bailed on him last time they had plans and felt guilty about it. I wasn't about to be the kind of girl who made a guy ditch his friends, so I'd smiled and told him to have fun.

I ended up going to Jackson's place just to have something to do, and to push myself to actually build some real friendships. It turned out to be a good time. He fed me cheese and crackers, and we gossiped. Well, mostly *he* gossiped. He spilled all the tea about his friend group and the new guy he was seeing.

I hadn't meant to stay out late, but a text from Reid around midnight (just checking in to make sure I was okay) made me glance at the clock and realize how late it had gotten. By the time I'd made it home, he was already sleeping.

Which meant the added tension of our hook-up still lingered in the air between us. What was going to happen once we were alone again? At night, in his empty house?

I, for one, couldn't wait to find out.

The bell chimed at the front of the salon, but I didn't even bother to look up.

"Reid!" Ruby's excited greeting had me whipping my head toward the entrance.

"Hey sis." He leaned down to give her a hug. He looked adorable, as usual. His glasses were on straight, his hair tucked into a beanie, his black down jacket covering one of his perfectly pressed sweaters.

"What are you doing here? Did you want a haircut? I'm booked solid tonight."

"Nah, I'm good. I'm letting it grow out." He looked toward the back and caught my eye. He winked.

My smile widened.

"I'm here for Hazel."

The words made me melt.

"Oh, so that's why you can't get a drink tonight," Jackson said, crossing his arms and smirking at me.

Practically floating on air, I grabbed my jacket and bag off the hook at the back of the salon.

"What's up?" I asked, stopping just short of him. Were we supposed to hug? Kiss? We hadn't exactly worked out the whole casual-greetings portion of our relationship yet. Especially considering we were in front of his sister.

"Want to grab dinner at the new sushi place that just opened? It's near here, so I figured I'd just drive over."

I'd mentioned being excited about that place last week. Had he really remembered? Of course he'd remembered. He was Reid.

"That's perfect." I was basically beaming at the guy, but it was hard to contain it.

"You two have fun." Ruby shot us both a genuine smile. I was a bit relieved that, at the very least, she didn't seem put off by the idea of Reid and me. "You're coming Friday, right Hazel?"

"Friday?" I looked at Reid.

He rubbed the back of his neck. "It's kind of silly. Instead of dinner this week, we're going out to pick a Christmas tree together. We do it every year."

"That's not silly. That sounds like my dream come true," I said.

He chuckled. "Then you should come. But keep your expectations low."

That wouldn't be necessary. Just being a part of something felt nice. To be included. It had already exceeded all my expectations.

Ruby stuck out her bottom lip. "Please come. I'm sad I missed you at the last dinner."

Happiness bloomed inside me, soft and sudden. "I'll be there."

Reid drove us to the restaurant, with the plan to swing by work and grab my car on the way back. The roads had finally been cleared after the storm. Now gray snow clung to the sides of the street. Some people would argue that winter was the ugliest season in Michigan. I wholeheartedly disagreed. There was something special about it. Almost whimsical. Of course, this feeling was reserved for November and December. Once the holidays were over, winter could hightail it right on out of here as far as I was concerned.

At some point during the drive, Reid had slipped his hand loosely into mine.

Was this a date? Our first?

Sure, most people didn't try to solve a catnapping, move in together, and meet the parents *before* date number one, but I kind of loved how unconventional it all was. Talk about a chaotic meet-cute.

The restaurant was packed. Giant red lamps hung from the ceiling, casting a soft glow around the space.

"I'm kind of surprised you like sushi," I admitted, once we were seated.

"I've never tried it before." He took a sip of his water. Did he look nervous? The idea made me slightly pleased with myself.

"Really?"

"Nope. You'll have to order for me."

I held a hand to my heart. "You trust me?"

That got him to smile wide. "I don't know if there's anyone I trust more than you."

Ugh, my freaking heart.

When the waitress came, I ordered us a few of my favorite rolls.

He mentioned he'd been online with his group before coming over. One of them had looked into the security camera company and found that they had great reviews. Tons of people had posted stories about how they'd been able to recover footage from the cloud they'd thought was lost forever.

It sent my hopes skyrocketing through the roof.

When the rolls arrived, I reached for the soy sauce, splashing some onto the table while pouring into the tiny bowl. Reid carefully pulled out his chopsticks before placing his napkin neatly on his lap. I took my first bite while examining Reid. He picked up a piece of the maki roll, studying it with narrowed eyes.

"This is the part where you put it in your mouth," I said.

He followed my instruction and his eyes widened. "That's actually pretty good."

"Obviously. I picked it."

A sense of satisfaction burrowed its way into my chest as Reid tried each new roll, ranking his favorites. This wasn't his cup of tea, and neither was a thrift store, but he was pushing himself. For me. Or because he wanted to? I wasn't quite sure. Either way, it was disarmingly sweet. I could get used to date nights like these.

Reid might be set in his ways, but he was also warm and soft and loveable.

Loveable?

Shit. Had I really just thought that? I was getting ahead of myself. But he *was* loveable. So sweet, and thoughtful in ways that snuck up on me. It made me ache a little to know that he'd been with someone who couldn't see everything he had to offer. Because he was more than enough.

I hoped I could bring out a good side of him. I hoped he wanted me to.

One way or another, pretty soon, I'd have my answer. This

would be over, and I'd be out of Reid's house. Then we'd have to define whatever we were.

I hoped more than anything he wanted me to be his girlfriend. I *really* wanted to call him my boyfriend.

When the check came, Reid paid without even giving me a chance to reach for it. I hoped it was because he considered this a date as well, and not because my financial situation stressed him out. He barely let me pay for anything when he was around, even forcing me to eat his groceries instead of getting my own.

After dinner, Reid drove me to my car, and we rode back separately to his house. I was grateful for a few moments alone to hype myself up. I put on some playlist called "Main character energy" and took some deep breaths to calm my racing heart.

We'd just been on a date.

We were about to be alone together.

In his house.

After he'd made me orgasm…

The next step was obvious, right? I sure thought so.

When I pulled in, he was waiting for me in the driveway, hands tucked into his jacket pockets, a small smile tugging at his lips. I shut my car door with a satisfying thud and walked over, grinning like an idiot.

Without saying much, we headed inside together. My nerves were eating at me.

"Um, do you want to watch a movie or something?" he asked, eyeing the couch we cozied up on together most nights.

"Oh, sure." Normally, I'd offer to make popcorn or grab snacks or something, but we'd *literally* just eaten. So instead, I flopped onto the couch and waited for him to join me.

He picked whatever movie was ranked number one—no arguments from me—and I sank deeper into the cushions, getting comfortable.

What should I do? Should I lean into him? Look up at him? How do I make sure he knows I want him to kiss me again?

I forced myself to take my eyes off his jawline and back to the TV. Yeah, there was no way in hell I was paying any attention to a single second of this movie. I could barely hear it over the pulse pounding in my ears.

Reid lifted his arm and set it on the back of the couch, just above my shoulders.

That was a good sign. Not a full-on move, but a half-move of sorts.

"Did you read that?" Reid asked, and I realized I'd been staring at the screen without registering anything.

"Um, read what?"

Reid scrunched his eyebrows together and looked down at me. "The year. It's a flashback scene."

"Oh, yeah, no. I didn't see it." I gulped.

He chuckled. "Are you sure you want to watch a movie?"

I blew out a slow breath before shaking my head. "If I'm being honest, all I'm really thinking about doing right now is kissing you."

Reid's smile grew and the relief I felt was instant.

"If I'm being honest, this was just my ploy to get closer to you. All I've been thinking about is kissing you again, too."

"Really?"

He nodded, eyes searching mine.

Then that was it. He dipped his head and our lips met.

His glasses bumped my nose and he pulled back, offering me an apologetic smile. I pulled them off slowly and set them on the table next to us.

"I've never asked. Can you see at all without them?"

"My vision isn't so bad. It's just like everything is in low definition without them."

"No offense, but you really seem like someone who would have bad vision."

He snorted. "What does that even mean?"

"I don't know. Like, you're always at the computer, and—"

"Can I go back to kissing you now?" he interrupted.

I bit my lip to keep from talking and nodded. I couldn't

even remember the last time a guy had me this nervous. It was a good nervous, though.

Reid resumed kissing me. Strong. Confident. When his tongue slipped inside it was all I could do to keep from moaning.

The need from the other night had already returned, but we didn't act on that yet. Reid took his time with me. We made out on the couch for what could have been hours, for all I cared. I could do this forever. We were kind of slowly melting into his couch, so when he finally pulled up for air, he was hovering above me, knee pressed between my legs. I wanted him to stop being so restrained and press his entire body against me.

"Do you…"

"What?" I encouraged, when his words trailed off.

"Do you want to see my room?"

I smiled, my lips deliciously sore. "I've been waiting for you to ask."

He stood up and held out his hand for me, easily lifting me to my feet. He didn't let go of my hand as he led me down the one hallway I hadn't dared to walk down yet.

Reid had never said it was off-limits, but I didn't want to overstep or seem like I was snooping. But I *had* been curious. I'd almost wandered down here the other day while he was out but made myself resist.

"This is the office," he said as we passed an open door on the right.

"Where all the investigative work gets done?" I asked, wiggling my fingers at him.

"It's nothing exciting," he added.

That was an understatement. The walls were white, the desk was wood, the office chair was plush, and that was about it. Absolutely zero personality had been injected into the room. When I looked from the room to Reid, he was scratching the back of his neck, looking self-conscious.

"I think we should make another trip to the thrift store."

He sagged and looked down at me. "I'd like that."

We moved on to the last door. This room was plain too, with everything put away in two dressers. No artwork. But the comforter was plaid, in blues, greens, and oranges.

"Wow, color!" I let go of his hand and flung myself onto the perfectly made bed.

"Regan got that for me," he admitted. "When I went off to college and she was, like, eleven. I've never had the heart to get rid of it."

"I love it."

I realized then that I was on his bed, and he was hovering over me. The want returned like a wave. He looked good, standing above me in his cute little sweater. And the way he constantly squinted without his glasses was adorable.

"So, I'm finally seeing your room," I said.

"Finally," he repeated.

"And now that I'm here? On your bed?"

He shook his head, a soft laugh escaping his lips. "Now that you're here…and on my bed…I'd really like to do something about that."

"I'd really like you to do something about that, too." I propped myself up on my elbows as he took a step closer. He put one knee on one side of me and his hands to my waist. I let out a tiny yelp when he pulled me up further on the bed.

Then he kissed me, and it was perfect again. All my anxiety was erased.

This felt scary-good. I wanted more. I wanted his entire being to consume my entire being. Was that healthy? Probably not. But I felt so safe with him.

His lips moved to my cheek and then down to my neck, where he continued to roam. My nipples hardened as soon as his chest gently brushed my sweater. The layers between us were suffocating. I pulled at the bottom of his sweater, desperate to get a glimpse at what was underneath. He broke away from my neck and helped me pull it off. I was rewarded with my first glimpse of shirtless Reid, lean and muscular and soft at the same time. My breath hitched when his fingers traced the bottom of my own sweater. "Can I?"

I nodded, too eagerly, but I didn't care. Reid's hands gripped the hem and pulled my shirt over my head, leaving me in only my bra. A plain black one, thankfully. Not my cutest piece of lingerie, but it could have been a hell of a lot worse. Wait…what underwear did I have on?

Reid's jaw clenched as he took me in.

"Come back." I grabbed for his biceps and lowered his body to mine. The first contact of his skin on mine made me shiver.

He trailed gentle kisses along my neck, nipping ever so slightly when he got to my collarbone. He shifted us both back on the bed, the movement allowing him to finally press into me. I moaned and arched my hips to get more friction against him.

He sucked in a breath and stopped moving.

"We don't have to rush, or anything—"

"Reid, I will be personally offended if you don't end up inside me tonight," I snapped. Maybe not the classiest thing I could've said, but fuck, I wanted this man. And it wasn't just because it had been a while. I wanted him to have all of me. I craved the closeness.

Reid scanned my face, all serious, before nodding.

Instead of kissing me again, his hand moved to the bra strap on my left shoulder. He pulled it down slowly, exposing me. I arched my back, practically begging to be touched. Then his mouth found mine again, while his fingers slowly traced my breast until they finally found my peaked nipple. I cried out when he tugged it and started playing with it. I'd always had sensitive breasts, but the way he was slowly toying with me was both wonderful and torturous. He hadn't been touching me for nearly long enough when he moved his hand and unhooked my bra with frankly shocking accuracy.

I pulled away for a minute to raise my eyebrows at him, but he just smiled, took off my bra and tossed it aside. When he moved back on top of me and took one of my nipples in his mouth, my eyes rolled into the back of my head. He teased and nipped until I was writhing beneath him. When he moved on to the other, I put my hands in the waistband of his pants, shoving them down.

He helped me get them off before pulling down my leggings.

"You sure?" he asked.

"Please get inside me, like, right now," I breathed.

Reid abandoned me for a minute to grab something out of the bedside table. He tore the package open with his teeth and rolled the condom onto his length.

I smiled. Obviously, he was prepared. Didn't surprise me at all.

He settled back on top of me, and pressed into me. I was already soaking wet by this point, so I eagerly shifted down, desperate to take him.

"You feel incredible," he whispered, slowly moving in me inch by inch.

My anticipation bloomed into outright, feral desire. When he was finally in, I started moving beneath him, impatient for friction. He pumped in and out a few times as I moaned *embarrassingly* loudly. Seriously, I had no control over my vocal responses at that point.

"Sorry," I said after a particularly loud sound of pleasure escaped me.

"What?" he choked out, pausing momentarily. "That's like, insanely hot, Hazel. Please never apologize for that again."

In response, I arched my hips, asking for more. He kissed me and moved inside me a few more times, then to my surprise, he flipped us, so that I was on top. Not usually my preferred position, but the angle alone was hitting me in the *exact* right spot. I gasped and started riding him, savoring the friction of my clit against him and the perfect way he was hitting my g spot.

"Yes, right there," I cried. He grabbed my ass, pressing us somehow even closer together. The pressure was building and building as I rocked.

My movements became more frantic.

My sounds of pleasure became more ragged.

Finally, I started to come undone, my orgasm hitting me with a fierce intensity. As soon as I started coming, Reid let out a loud groan before taking his hand off my butt and moving it behind him to prop himself up. He sat up partway, pressing our torsos together and kissing me deeply as we both came. I stared into his eyes—an all-consuming, overwhelming affection hitting me right in the chest.

He kissed my forehead and I came to the conclusion that he had me—completely.

When it was over and I untangled myself from him, he shot up out of bed. He returned a second later with a washcloth, using it to gently clean me off.

He was so careful with me. Careful with how he looked at me, careful with his touches.

After, he laid back down on the bed, settling in close to me so that our sides touched.

"Hazel, that was…that was amazing."

I blushed. "It was pretty good."

We stayed like that awhile, cuddled into each other. We didn't say much. Part of me wanted to ask what we were, but also, a part of me didn't feel like I needed to. The way he looked at me said a lot.

There wasn't even a mention of me going back to the other room. At one point, he handed me a soft t-shirt and we nestled under the covers.

Eventually, we drifted off to sleep.

TWENTY-SEVEN

Reid

Armchair_Detective: *Did you hear back from the camera company?*
ReidingRainbow: *Not yet, but it's looking promising.*
WhiteKnight31: *I can't believe we missed this at the beginning.*
Armchair_Detective: *I blame the office manager. How could he have not shared this vital information?*
ReidingRainbow: *Either way we should find out by tomorrow.*
WhiteKnight31: *If they actually get back to you on time.*
Armchair_Detective: *Yeah, those big companies are terrible with shit like this.*
ReidingRainbow: *If they don't get back, I'll call.*
Armchair_Detective: *When does the money hit Hazel's account?*
ReidingRainbow: *Next week.*
WhiteKnight31: *You think she'll really give him the money if it comes down to it?*
ReidingRainbow: *If it comes down to it, I do.*

A LOOMING HEADACHE SQUEEZED AT MY TEMPLES. I LIFTED MY glasses to pinch the bridge of my nose. There was no doubt in my mind that Hazel would hand over her winnings if push came to shove. It didn't matter that we had no way of knowing whether the perpetrator would even give Vermont back. He was Gran's, and if I knew one thing about Hazel, it was that she was sentimental. She couldn't get rid of a single thing her grandmother owned; she wasn't about to part with her beloved pet.

It got me *very* anxious thinking about her credit card debt and financial troubles. The number of times I'd thought about asking her to show me her bank account was embarrassing. It was none of my business. We'd just started seeing each other.

It wasn't my job to save her…but I wanted to. I wanted to help. To get her out of this hole. I wanted her to take that money and make good decisions. But I loved the part of her that wouldn't keep it even more. Not if it meant losing something she loved. The part that thought with her heart and not her head.

I could only hope that it wouldn't come to that. I had to keep telling myself that we would get answers. We'd solve this.

"Hello?" A voice called out from the end of the hallway. I pushed back my chair and stood, leaning out just far enough to see Hazel waiting there, all the way at the far end.

"Hello?" I said it back to her like a question.

"I was about to leave for work and wanted to say goodbye."

A grin spread over my face. A goofy, ridiculous one I hadn't been able to control much since Hazel had come around. "Why didn't you come say bye?"

She twirled a piece of hair in her fingers. Damn, she was cute. "I didn't know if I could just waltz into your wing of the house uninvited."

Her use of the word "wing" made me laugh. "Hazel, you've spent every night this week in my bed. You don't need an invitation."

She held up her hands, a smile now on her lips too. "Hey, I don't know what stringent rules you have. I'm trying not to step on your toes."

I stood, taking a few long strides until I was in front of her.

I wrapped my arm around her waist and bent down to kiss her.

"Please, step on my toes. I'd love nothing more."

"Good, because stepping on toes is pretty much my main personality trait."

We kissed again before I let her go, trailing behind her into the entryway where she started to pull on her boots. "I can't wait to get this shift over with so I can spend the rest of the night refreshing that fake email address every five seconds to see if they sent the camera footage."

"You're still coming tonight, right?" I asked.

She paused, staring up at me. I couldn't blame her for forgetting. She had a lot on her mind right now.

I ran a hand along my jaw. "Just that family thing Ruby brought up the other day. It's a silly tradition. You don't have to come if you don't want—"

"Yes! Tonight? I totally forgot that it's already Friday. I wouldn't miss it." She beamed up at me and my heart practically cartwheeled. "Sorry, was that too eager?"

I chuckled. "I like your eagerness." I gave her one last lingering kiss on her forehead before she rushed out the door, running late as usual.

Lateness used to drive me insane. It still did with most people, but not so much with her. Maybe it was because I knew that she wasn't being disrespectful. She had terrible time management skills, and doing daily tasks like having more than a bowl of cereal for breakfast seemed to overwhelm her. Maybe it was because we were still in the early days, but I found everything about her endearing.

And I was so fucking glad she wanted to spend tonight with my family. They were a lot. Suffocating, even. I was well aware. It was something my ex used to bring up often. I hadn't wanted to scare Hazel off, but she'd seemed to genuinely embrace them right off the bat.

I was already mentally calculating where this was headed. I liked relationships. I craved exclusivity and emotional closeness. It had been a while since I'd experienced it, and I knew I wanted it with her.

Everything in my gut told me she was falling for me too.

We still needed to talk, though. Discuss some foundational stuff. I wanted her to be my girlfriend, and I hoped we could establish that sooner rather than later.

Tonight, if possible.

She made me excited about life again. It might be time for her to move back into her apartment, but I didn't love the idea. I liked having her under the same roof as me, knowing she was safe. Knowing her schedule. I liked just popping back from an errand and having her already curled up on the couch.

Hazel made this place feel like home. It never had, before her.

It freaked me out a little, but not enough to back away. At this point, it was full steam ahead. Hopefully she felt the same way.

TWENTY-EIGHT

Hazel

"I still can't believe your family picks out a Christmas tree the week *before* Thanksgiving."

Reid tugged my beanie on so that it fit more snugly around my ears. It was flurrying outside, but barely.

"Mom likes to have the tree up before, so when we have the big dinner it's in the background and the house is all decorated."

"I love that," I said, as we milled about in the parking lot waiting for the rest of his family to arrive.

The Christmas tree lot was thirty minutes away from his house in a more rural area. There was a surprising number of people here for what I deemed to be far too early to buy anything Christmas-related. The entire place was surrounded by thousands of twinkle lights, and trees of all different shapes and sizes were lined up in rows. Apparently, there were different breeds of Christmas trees. I had no idea, but Reid made sure to educate me.

There were also a few stands selling trinkets and ornaments, along with hot chocolate and spiced nuts. The smells teased me.

"Reid?" I asked, batting my eyelashes.

"Yes?"

"Will you buy me a hot chocolate?"

He laughed, shaking his head before throwing an arm around my shoulders and steering me toward the stand. Honestly, I barely even needed a hot drink. I was already glowing just being here with him tonight. He wanted me here. With him. With his family. Luck hadn't been on my side lately, but I felt it right now.

"Did you and your Gran have a tradition around getting a tree?" he asked.

"Nope. This is my first time coming to one of these things." I thought back to all of the Christmases Gran and I had shared together. Cozy evenings spent underneath hand-made crocheted blankets. Buying a ham that was ridiculously big for two people, but we both loved having leftovers for days. Opening our presents for each other on Christmas Eve because we couldn't wait until morning. This would be my first without her, and the weight of that was starting to creep up on me. As if sensing my shift, Reid held me tighter.

"What did you do, then?"

"It probably will not shock you to find out that we had a silver artificial tree, likely from the 1940s, that we put up every year the week before Christmas."

"There's no way that doesn't have lead in it."

"Oh, it most definitely does. The thing is a true antique. It was my great-grandma's before it was ours."

"Do you still have it?" he asked.

"Yep, tucked away in my coat closet. You would be horri-fied to see the inside of that thing. I've kept the worst of my hoarding tendencies from you."

He chuckled. "It's okay, I accept you for who you are."

And my heart exploded.

He hugged me close to his side. "Can we put that tree up together? At your place? I want to see it."

The sentiment made my eyelids heavy with unshed tears.

"Sure," I choked out.

"If there's room, that is."

I laughed and shoved his chest.

He bought our hot chocolates even though I tried to insist on paying. When I pulled out my wallet, he'd given me a look like I should know not to bother.

We resumed our waiting stance near the edge of the parking lot. I checked the time to see that his folks were five minutes behind schedule. We'd been early, only thanks to Reid.

"I'm surprised your family is late when punctual is basically your middle name."

"West, whom you'll finally get to meet, is always late. And my parents are pretty good, but Regan has been slowing them down ever since she moved back in. Ruby and I are the punctual ones, but she probably got a ride with someone else."

"Got it," I said, feeling a slight tremor of nerves, even though I had already met every individual member of his immediate family. I hadn't had the pleasure of meeting West yet. Reid had mentioned him a few times, and I'd even seen him in passing once when he'd been picking up Ruby from the salon for lunch. At the time I'd only registered him as Ruby's friend, and I only remembered him because Jackson and I had talked about how hot he was.

A car pulled up at the same time a pickup entered the lot. Reid's entire family fell out of both vehicles like they'd been in a clown car, all bustling and full of chatter.

"Hazel!" Regan exclaimed as soon as she saw me. Ruby smiled and waved as everyone walked over and embraced me in a frenzy of hugs.

"You look lovely, dear." His mom squeezed my shoulders.

Hanging at the back of the pack was West. He was just as handsome as I remembered him being.

"Hey, I'm Hazel," I said, offering him a mittened hand.

"West." He shot me a charming grin and shook my outstretched hand. "Nice to finally, officially meet you."

"Likewise."

"You're so lucky you left the salon early today," Ruby said as we walked back toward the entrance to the lot as a pack. "Miranda was really in a mood. Told us we all needed to keep more organized schedules, and no more late cancelations."

I balked. "What? Like we have any control over that!"

"I know! It's like she wants us to start charging or something."

Reid launched into a conversation with West about a poker game they were trying to organize. Regan was arguing with her mother, begging her not to take forever to pick out the perfect tree. Mr. Mitchell hung back with a cheery smile on his face, taking in his family dynamic. Even with all the voices talking over each other, everything about the evening was peaceful. I could barely think straight, and still, I loved every second of it. Maybe this was why Reid clung to his routines now. Growing up with siblings and constant family noise probably made him crave the freedom to do exactly what he wanted, when he wanted.

It was unfamiliar, sure, but it felt just like I'd always imagined it would. Stepping into something so different from my usual life helped ease the weight of lingering grief. If I were home right now, bracing for the holidays alone without even Vermont for comfort, I'd probably be drowning in self-pity.

Reid tossed his head back and laughed at something West said. Watching them made me smile. We hadn't talked about it yet, but I hoped there was a semblance of permanence to this current state of ours.

One hour later and a surprising number of arguments about which type of tree to get, the Mitchell family had finally narrowed down their choices to two.

"Just decide!" Regan exclaimed. "I can't walk around this tree park anymore. My feet are going to fall off."

"We still have to take it home and decorate it," Ruby pointed out.

Mrs. Mitchell continued to evaluate the two, going back and forth between the aisles they were in.

"They're both great, honey," Reid's dad said.

"This happens every year," Reid whispered to me, his hot breath on my ear making me shiver.

"It's a big deal, picking a tree. You only get one a year," I said.

Reid covered my mouth with his hand and jerked his gaze to his mom. "Shhh. Don't let her hear you say that. You'll just add flame to her already out-of-control fire."

I giggled and mimed zipping my lips.

Finally, after at least fifteen more minutes of circling the trees and touching the branches, Reid's mom made a decision. The employees came to wrap it up and assist with loading it into the bed of West's truck.

"Alright, everyone, meet back home for decorating and snacks," Mrs. Mitchell announced.

"You got it, Sarge," Ruby said.

I laughed, grinning like an idiot when Reid grabbed my hand and led me back to the car.

"Thanks for inviting me," I said, settling into my seat and pulling on my seatbelt.

"Thanks for coming." He leaned over the center console and kissed me.

I was buzzing with electricity the entire drive to his parents' house. Was this what being happy felt like? Like, truly out of your mind happy? I missed Gran every day, but Reid and his family were filling voids I'd always assumed would be left empty.

Back at their family home, I sat with West on the couch while Reid and the rest of the clan started pulling out bin upon bin of Christmas decorations. It pleased me to find out that they weren't one of those families with the fancy glass ornaments all purchased from the same designer store. No, they had quite the collection. One with each kid's hand-prints. The base of the trunk from every tree they'd ever had, labeled by year of course. A crocheted angel. A fuzzy reindeer. The list went on. Reid's mom was adorable, insisting on showing each one to me and explaining its meaning.

"I still remember my first Christmas here," West whispered to me. "The summaries for each ornament have gotten shorter. I think Ruby gave her a talking-to after it took them nearly three hours to go through everything."

I laughed. "Was that when you moved in here?"

"Yep. Reid has been my best friend since middle school, so I was grateful they let me move in. I miss my parents, but the Mitchells have always been like a second family to me."

I watched as Reid reached all the way to the top of the tree to string rainbow lights, his brow furrowed with a look of concentration.

"Got that whole cat situation figured out?" West asked, before taking a long sip of eggnog.

"Almost." I held up my crossed fingers. "We should know this week."

"Good. I'm glad Reid brought you tonight," he continued, making me instantly flush. Was I about to get the best friend approval? The rest of the family chatted loudly in the background, arguing over the placement of a particular ornament and where the stockings usually hung.

"Not gonna lie, when he first brought you up, I thought there was no way. Reid is so set in his ways, a bit of a buttoned-up guy. As I'm sure you've noticed."

"Definitely," I said, my heart beating faster than before.

"And when he said you were such a mess and didn't have your life together, I was like no way. That's way too much for him to handle."

Too much? A mess?

My body stiffened as I forced the smile not to drop from my face.

I was familiar with those words, but I thought Reid saw me differently. Saw me as more than that. Had I been wrong the whole time? Was I some sort of fixer-upper? A project for him to work on?

"But you two seem to vibe. I'm happy for him." West continued to speak, but I was struggling to focus.

My bubble had officially burst, popped as soon as the careless words left West's mouth. Knowing that Reid had said those things about me to his best friend stung. He must like me, I wasn't doubting that. There was no mistaking the way he acted around me. But did he like me *in spite of* all my flaws? I always thought he didn't see them as harshly as everyone else did.

I clasped my hands together. The whole revelation was making me incredibly self-conscious. Suddenly the rejections from every single person through my entire life rang through my ears. I was always too much, or not enough. A 'hot mess express,' as my so-called high school friends always said. And I *didn't* have my life together. Not in the way Reid did. I was getting blackmailed, for crying out loud, because of my own stupidity. Reid was like an actual adult. He had a home. He wasn't in a mountain of debt. He ate well-rounded meals. I must seem like a child to him. Someone to take care of.

"Are you okay?" West asked. When my vision refocused on him, I could see the concern shining in his eyes.

Shit. My face had faltered, and I probably looked on the brink of tears.

"I'm great," I said, plastering a smile back on.

The decorations were almost up. I just had to make it a little longer before I could lose it.

TWENTY-NINE

Hazel

By the time we pulled back into the driveway of Reid's house, I already had a plan.

I'd texted Jackson on the way, seeing if he wanted to hang out tonight. Thankfully, he was free and told me to come over.

I needed space, and I needed it now.

Reid apparently already thought of me as a mess; I couldn't let him see me break down. I just needed a night to collect myself. Then I could talk to him tomorrow, when I was more put together, without all this raw emotion getting in the way and clouding my judgement.

"Want to watch a Christmas movie, or is it too early?" Reid asked, holding the front door open for me.

"Um, actually Jackson invited me over tonight."

"Jackson," Reid confirmed. "Didn't you two just hang out the other day?"

"We did. And then I blew him off, so I really feel like I should stop by. I think we could become friends if I gave it more of a shot."

A flash of something that looked like disappointment crossed his face, but he nodded. "Of course, you should. I'm glad you're making friends."

"Yep." My mouth went dry. His words were sweet, but they only deepened my sense of being lost and pathetic. Poor little Hazel—couldn't even make a friend. He'd seen me after my night out with those girls from high school. At the time, he'd seemed like my knight in shining armor, but now I saw it differently. I was a liability. Someone who needed checking on. Someone who needed her hand held just to stay upright.

He looked at the time on his phone. "It's almost nine. Are you going to—"

"I'll probably spend the night," I added, rushing back to my room to get an overnight bag together. The tears were stinging, begging to be set free, and I fought like hell to hold them back.

I *knew* I should talk to Reid. And I would. But tomorrow sounded so much better than tonight. I needed to think about this. Collect my thoughts. Lie awake and practice what I'd say to him and rehearse my responses. The last thing I wanted him to see me as was unstable. I couldn't feed into that narrative. I wanted him to see me as more than that. I wanted him to see that I'd already reached my potential. I wasn't someone who needed saving.

"Oh…that'll be fun." Reid leaned against the doorframe, watching me pack. I shot him a smile, hoping I looked mostly normal.

A breath escaped him in a tired-sounding huff. "Listen, I know my family is a lot. I hope tonight wasn't too much too fast."

My chest ached when I met his eyes. "No, it was perfect. I love your family. I'm so happy you included me."

He didn't look convinced, but I didn't have the time to properly reassure him. The gates that held back my flood were about to rupture.

"Okay, I think that's everything I need." I patted my bag.

"Hopefully we get a response tomorrow from the security company," he offered as he trailed behind me, back to the living room.

"Hopefully," I said with forced brightness. "I'm feeling both nauseous and optimistic about it."

His lip turned up. "Yeah, me too."

I slipped my boots back on and grabbed my car keys off the hook by the front of the door. In and out in five minutes flat. That was probably a record for me. Funny how quick I could be when I was motivated. And nothing drove me more right now than the need to hold it together in front of Reid.

"Um, drive safe." He reached out for me before hesitating and dropping his hand.

"I will." I lingered for a second, unsure if I should kiss him, or hug him, or what. Not wanting to add any additional awkwardness to the situation, I stood on my tiptoes and kissed him on the cheek before waving goodbye and getting the hell out of there.

***

"He called you a mess?" Jackson asked, picking the last of the pepperoni off his pizza.

His apartment was surprisingly spacious for a studio. It was one of those sleek, newer buildings in the downtown district, with high, exposed ceilings and polished concrete floors.

I sighed. "West *said* he called me a mess."

"Maybe he misheard."

I raised an eyebrow.

"I mean it *does* sound like something someone would say to describe you."

I groaned, placing my head in my hands. "West is his best friend. If Reid said that to him, he was probably confiding in him why he didn't think we were right together, or something."

"But you said he likes you." He folded his slice of pizza and took a bite.

"I think he does. I mean I know he does…I think." I hated

how much I was second-guessing everything now. The past few days had been borderline magical. I'd been so worried as the deadline for the blackmailer loomed, and I anxiously awaited the camera footage, but Reid was *so* great in knowing exactly how to calm me down. We had movie marathons and went on walks around his neighborhood, bundled in a million layers. He tried teaching me to cook again. He even let me give him a trim in his bathroom.

It felt like we were together. We hadn't made it official yet, but I had been certain that was where it was headed.

Then West had to share. Now every bit of self-doubt I'd ever possessed seemed to be screeching in my ear. I'd only shed a few tears on the way over before putting myself together. Jackson was a new friend, and I didn't want him to see me blubbering constantly.

Gran had raised me to have a thick skin. And for the most part, I did. But the thing about a thick skin was this: once something got through, it didn't just bounce off. It sunk in and stayed there, trapped, pressing against everything else you'd tried to keep buried.

"You don't sound so confident." Jackson bent down and retrieved a glass carafe filled with amber liquid. Setting it on the counter, he grabbed two short tumblers, dropped a few ice cubes into each with a soft clink, then poured the liquid. From the fridge, he pulled out a mixer—something citrusy by the look of it—and topped off the glasses, giving each one a slow swirl before sliding one across the counter.

I winced at the smell.

"What is that?"

"Tequila soda."

"Did you forget the soda?"

He shot me a glare, so I took the beverage, not breathing through my nose as I took a tentative sip. It burned, but I welcomed it. It tasted distinctly like something that would make the churning nerves floating around in my gut subside.

"Bottoms up." Jackson nodded in approval and tipped his own glass back. "Drink that, we're heading out soon."

I nearly choked on my next sip.

"It's almost ten." The horror was clear in my tone.

"Yes, Hazel. A typical time for someone in their twenties to go out on a Friday evening. Plus, it's western night."

I gave him a blank look.

He rolled his eyes. "Line dancing. Cheap drinks. Bull riding."

"And we want to go, because…"

"Because it's fun, Hazel. And your sad, doe eyes look like they need fun right now. And distraction."

I took another big gulp of the drink. Jackson had a point. Plus, there was no way this could be worse than my last night out—the one Reid had to rescue me from. As cheesy as it sounded, western night could be the perfect thing to help me forget about everything running through my mind.

"Fine, let's do it," I said, and Jackson threw up his arms in victory.

He turned up the speaker that had been playing quietly in the background, and we sang along loudly to a throwback early 2000s playlist while we finished our drinks. The alcohol hit me, an unfamiliar warm buzz curling in my chest and making everything a little lighter, less sharp. I didn't fight it.

Half an hour later, Jackson announced that his friends had just arrived at the bar. He ducked into his walk-in closet and threw on an all-black outfit faster than a superhero changed into their costume. I joined him in the bathroom as he ran some gel through his hair. I lifted my eyelids to inspect myself. The tears I'd shed earlier had taken off most of my mascara, but I was just buzzed enough not to care.

Jackson eyed my outfit. An old lumpy sweater and jeans.

"You'll be too hot in that," he said, moving back to his closet and throwing a tight black V-neck t-shirt at me.

I slipped the sweater over my head. "Why do you own

this?" I asked, pulling on the tight shirt whose neckline dipped deep into my cleavage.

He just arched an eyebrow and gave me a smile like I was the most naïve little thing.

Jackson knocked back one more shot of tequila. I declined, considering I was already tipsier than I'd been in ages. I was most definitely a lightweight.

We stumbled out into the freezing night air and into a rideshare car. His place was less than a mile from the bar, but he insisted we ride. "We're not walking in this," he'd said, dramatic as ever.

The driver seemed amused by our antics and cranked up the radio at our request. We threw the windows down despite the cold, badly belting out the lyrics and laughing so hard we could barely breathe.

It was the most fun I'd had in ages. I felt alive. And when Jackson leaned into me to sing a high note, I became sure of something. We'd passed that weird hypothetical line in my head from acquaintance to friend. I'd finally let my guard down, and I had zero regrets.

Maybe I *was* a mess. But messes were fun.

When we spilled out of the car and into the bar, the crowd proved I was the only person in town with an aversion to a late night out. Jackson's two friends, Benny and Tobias, met us inside. They both had huge smiles and hugged me like it wasn't our first time meeting.

Jackson tried to shove another drink down my throat, but I was able to appease him by ordering a mocktail instead. I knew my limits.

Jackson slung an arm around me and Tobias. "We need to dance."

And we did.

Despite my complete lack of coordination, I made an effort, falling into line and doing my best to keep up. Benny was basically a professional. He stuck one hand under my elbow and led me into some semblance of a rhythm. We could have been out there for minutes or hours; I couldn't keep track. My lips hurt from smiling and it was hard to remember the reason I had even gone to Jackson's tonight.

"Water!" I shouted at Jackson, who barely nodded before letting me slip away through the crowd. Once I was on the outskirts, I tracked down one of the large canisters they had against the wall and took a plastic glass. I poured water and chugged it before getting a refill. I caught sight of myself in the mirror. Wild hair. Red-faced. But mostly happy.

My phone vibrated.

> Reid: Hope you're having fun at Jackson's.
> Goodnight!

My chest tightened as I read his words over and over again.

"What's that face for?" Jackson asked, practically limping over to the water station before pouring himself a brimming glass.

I held up my phone to show him the text.

His eyes scanned it, and he pursed his lips. "Aw. That doesn't read like a guy who doesn't like you."

"I know," I said, suddenly met with an overwhelming sensation of missing Reid. If I was at his house right now, I might be curled up next to him in bed. The thought was comforting and tugged at my heart.

"Let's send a selfie," Jackson said, snatching my phone and holding it out. I smiled wide at the camera as he made a kissy face and hovered it next to my cheek. I laughed when I saw it.

"Don't send that, I look gross."

Jackson ignored me, already pressing send. "You look fine."

Reid's response was almost immediate.

> Reid: Oh, you went out?

Jackson and I both hovered over the text, our foreheads nearly pressed together.

"Do you think he's jealous?" Jackson asked.

"Reid? No way." But a little bit of guilt seeped in. Was he bummed that I hadn't invited him? Would he have wanted to come?

I replied.

> Hazel: Yep. Western night. I am apparently the only person who hasn't heard about this.

> Reid: lol West has dragged me there before.

> Reid: Have fun. Get home safe. Let me know if you need me. I'll keep my phone on.

"Awww," Jackson cooed again before I pulled my phone away. "He likes you, Hazel."

I leaned into him. "I hope so."

We danced the rest of the night, and I had one only unfortunate mishap on the mechanical bull that resulted in what would surely be a sore ass tomorrow.

When Jackson and I said goodbye to his friends and piled back into a car, I was almost tempted to head back to Reid's house. But a larger part of me didn't want my night with Jackson to end. When we ordered tacos to be delivered to his place, a quiet ease settled over me, soft and content.

For the first time, I felt like life was going to work out no matter what. I could handle what came next. I was stronger than I gave myself credit for. Gran had raised me right. I could do this. I had to have faith I'd get Vermont back. I wouldn't accept another outcome. I'd fight if I had to.

And as for everything with Reid...I was a catch. I'd tell myself that until I believed the words to be true. Anyone would be lucky to have me in their life.

Back at Jackson's, eating tacos on his kitchen island, my eyes started to droop. Between the evening with Reid's family and the night out with Jackson, I felt full. I didn't want to think about West's comment. I didn't want it to be real. But after giving it some time, and a healing night out, I could handle a mature conversation with Reid. If we were meant to be, we'd get through it. And I had very strong inkling that we would.

"I'm so glad you came over tonight." Jackson smiled at me across the counter. "I was kind of worried you didn't like me."

"Really?" I asked, brows raised.

"Yeah, like, when we both first started, I'd always ask you to hang out and you never wanted to commit to plans."

"I'm sorry. I didn't realize you were serious."

He rolled his eyes. "Of course I was. I want to be friends, Hazel."

"I want to be friends, too." I propped my elbow on the island, resting my chin in my hand.

"Then let me in. I'm nosy and am terrible with secrets, but I'm fun." He put two hands underneath his chin, pretending to frame his face like a prize.

I laughed. "Well, I have a small hill of credit card debt, and apparently don't have my life together, but I'm also fun."

He grinned. "The perfect combo, then."

My phone buzzed on the table. I checked the time. Who the hell was texting me past midnight?

I flipped it over, half-hoping it was Reid. My heart dropped when I saw the new text from an unknown number. I already knew who it was.

> Unknown Number: You're running out of time. I'll be sending the details for the exchange soon.

Dread washed over me when I opened it to see a picture of Vermont. Thankfully, he looked fine, as usual. Curled up on a rug, honestly looking like he didn't have a care in the world. I sighed, slumping against the island.

With my thumb and index finger, I zoomed in on the

picture. There was a couch behind Vermont; some generic leather-looking one. That didn't tell me much.

Then something caught my eye.

I sat straight up and zoomed in further. My eyes practically bugged out of my head.

"Oh my God!" I exclaimed, jumping from the stool.

"What?" Jackson asked, still chewing his last taco.

"Oh my God!" I screamed again. Adrenaline was now coursing through my veins.

"I repeat, *what?*" Jackson asked again.

I looked over at him, eyes wild. "I know who has Vermont."

THIRTY

Reid

My foot bounced aggressively against the floor as I stared at my upturned phone. It was already past nine a.m. and I hadn't heard from Hazel. Had she gotten home alright? Would I look overbearing if I texted her? I followed Jackson on social media and saw that he'd posted a story of them eating late night tacos at his place, so I knew she was fine, but still. I'd like some confirmation from the woman I was falling for.

She'd gone out without me last night and hadn't even texted me to let me know she'd made it home safely. I wasn't her keeper. She could do whatever she wanted. That didn't mean I wasn't confused. I'd been humming with energy and nerves after what I *thought* had been an amazing evening with her and my family. I was planning to ask her to be my girlfriend. I'd been practicing the question the whole car ride home.

Then she'd just bolted and couldn't even look at me.

My family was too much. Too overbearing. *I knew it.* I shouldn't have subjected her to them this early. But she'd seemed like she was having fun, hadn't she?

I raked a hand through my hair, frustrated by the situation. I'd already gone over everything I'd said to Hazel—and everything I'd heard everyone else say to her—trying desperately to figure out what had scared her off. I needed her to talk to me. But I'd give her space. I'd wait until she reached out.

I checked my phone again.

I mean, within reason. If I didn't hear from her soon, I was calling.

"You look strung out."

My heart stopped as I sprang up from my office chair to find West leaning casually against my doorframe.

I clutched my chest. "West? What the fuck, man?"

"I knocked," he said, jerking his finger toward the front of my house.

"There's a doorbell."

"I have a key, why would I bother you?"

I groaned and shook my head. I was definitely changing the locks.

"I brought breakfast sandwiches." He held up a white bag, grease coating the bottom.

"Kitchen," I said, grabbing my laptop off its charging station and following him out into the hallway.

"You working on a Saturday?"

"No. I'm waiting on an email." I propped up the laptop and hit refresh. Still no response from the security company. According to their email signature, their help center was closed on Sundays, so this was our last chance to hear back before next week.

West took the sandwiches out of the bag and lined them up on the table. "I brought one for Hazel, too."

"She isn't here." I didn't bother keeping the frustration out of my tone. West could sniff out one of my bad moods a mile away.

"Is she at the salon?"

"I don't know. She didn't stay here last night." I didn't need to clarify that I was unhappy about that. My voice said it all.

"Everything okay?" West asked carefully.

I shrugged. "I don't know, man. I thought everything was fine, but she bailed on me pretty fast last night. Seemed a little off."

"Oh." West tapped his fingers against the table eyeing me and then dropping his gaze to the island.

I knew my best friend, and I knew a guilty face when I saw one.

"What is it?" I asked.

"Nothing," he said quickly. Too quickly.

"Something is clearly up. It's all over your face." I snatched a sandwich, pulling a piece of paper towel off from the holder by the sink and setting it underneath to catch my crumbs.

"No plate?" West lifted his brows. "Hazel really is getting to you."

"What's wrong?" I repeated, refusing to allow him to change the subject.

He sighed and slung his head back. "It's nothing, seriously. At least I *think* it's nothing."

"Tell me and I'll be the judge of that."

He shook his head, eyeing the floor. "I might have put my foot in my mouth last night and said something stupid to Hazel."

I froze mid-bite before glaring at my best friend. "What did you say?"

He wiped a hand over his eyes. "Oh, man. It was stupid. I didn't mean it as a negative."

I dropped the sandwich, standing up. "West, tell me now."

He took up a defensive stance, holding up his hands in front of his chest. "It really isn't a big deal. But I *might* have mentioned you saying she was a mess and didn't have her life together."

"What!" Now I was raging.

"Like, in an offhand way! I meant it like, you two didn't seem like a match at first, but she was bringing out this fun side of you—I don't know. It's true! She's not who I pictured you with, but I like you two together."

I dragged a hand over my face, my heart going a mile a minute. "Are you fucking serious? You told my girl that I thought she was a mess? How could you possibly think that was a good idea?"

He winced. "I kind of realized it wasn't as soon as I saw her face fall."

"Shit," I breathed, my mind racing. Hazel had to be upset with me. This was the reason she'd run off last night. The worst part was, West wasn't even lying. I had said that about Hazel to downplay things, so that my family would stay out of my business. I hadn't meant it, though. Or I guess I had, but not in the way she was probably thinking.

I *loved* her chaos. I loved her.

Fuck…

Was that seriously what was running through my head right now? It was too soon, way too soon, but once the thought landed, it refused to leave. I'd been pushing it down for a while now, pretending it wasn't real. And now the girl I was in love with was avoiding me.

"Why did you say that to her?" I groaned, slipping back onto the chair.

"I'm sorry. I wasn't thinking." He looked at me sheepishly. "I felt like a dick for saying it, hence the apology sandwiches."

"The apology sandwiches she isn't even here to accept, because she can't even face me right now."

I was pissed at West for saying that to Hazel, but at least now I knew. If that was the reason she took off last night, it wasn't because she thought my family was too much, or because she was second-guessing me. She was hurt. Which gutted me to think about, but at least I could fix this. I could explain, tell her what she meant to me, tell her that without a doubt I wanted her in my life. She'd look past a few stupid words, right? She had to. The Hazel I knew was understanding. Quick to forgive.

But she was also lonely and scared of being abandoned.

Crap, I really needed to talk to her.

I picked up my phone, but before I could text Hazel, the notifications from my group chat distracted me.

Armchair_Detective: *The security company responded!*
WhiteKnight31: *IS IT THE VIDEO!?*
Armchair_Detective: *It's the video! Reid, are you seeing this!? Who is that guy?*
WhiteKnight31: *REID!*

My fingers moved at lightning speed. I closed out of the conversation and pulled up the email. I was standing and pacing the length of my kitchen island now.

"What?" West asked.

"The security company sent over the video from Hazel's courtyard."

I could barely hear myself over my thrumming heart. This was it. I forced my thumb to stay steady as I opened the video.

The quality was surprisingly okay. Not amazing, but completely clear. There was Hazel, standing in the courtyard with her hands on her hips. I could just make out the fuzzy image of Vermont prancing around in the dead fall grass.

Then Hazel leaned over, shook her head, and rushed inside. Vermont remained, lounging in the grass. Not even thirty seconds later, a man exited from one of the units across the building. I held my breath, but he didn't even look down at Vermont as he walked by, heading straight for the front gate.

But instead of the door slamming shut behind him, he held it open.

Someone walked through.

The new person was dressed in a gray sweatshirt, hood up. He looked around, back still to the camera before creeping over to Vermont, leaning down and stretching out his hand.

My heart stopped.

Finally, he looked up, revealing his face to the camera and…

That guy!? Really?

Before my brain completely processed what I saw, I shot Hazel a text.

> Reid: Did you see the video?

> Hazel: I did, but I'm already way ahead of you.

> Reid: Way ahead of me?

> Reid: Hazel?

> Reid: WHAT THE HELL DOES THAT MEAN?

THIRTY-ONE

Hazel

"I can't believe you dragged me into this." Jackson looked up and down the residential street, shaking his head. Remnants of gray snow clung stubbornly to the edges of curbs and the patchy strip of overgrown, dead grass between the sidewalk and the street. Since this was Michigan, potholes also marked every stretch of asphalt.

This street was familiar, even though it had been awhile since I'd been here.

I bundled further into my jacket. My adrenaline hadn't stopped racing. I hadn't slept a wink last night, ever since I put it all together.

"It'll be easy. He has no idea who you are. You're the perfect distraction." I pulled tighter on the straps of the backpack cat carrier we'd picked up at the pet store on the way.

Jackson balled his fists into his coat. "Why can't you just text Reid? He'll have a plan."

I grabbed his arm. "Because we can do this!"

What I didn't say to him was that I *needed* to do this for myself. I was done being the damsel in distress, the one who didn't have her life together. I would get Vermont back and solve all my problems on my own. I'd show Reid and he'd be impressed. Well…probably irritated when I admitted how *exactly* I'd gotten Vermont back, but when he saw that I was fine and it all worked out, he'd be forced to be impressed.

Right?

"I still think you should call him." Jackson eyed the house.

"I need to do this," I said, defiantly. "Reid has been helping me since the day I met him. I need him to see me as more than a charity case."

Jackson frowned. "He already does. You're getting in your head too much!"

The wind whistled as I glanced from the house back to Jackson. A seed of doubt creeped into my mind, but I brushed it away.

"You're not backing out on me, are you?" I asked. This plan hinged on Jackson helping. He looked the part too, dressed in a blue jumpsuit, a thick coat, and a neon orange vest he just happened to have lying around from an old Halloween costume.

He sighed. "No. No. I'm here for your crazy plan. Besides, this will put those improv classes to good use."

I raised an eyebrow at him. "Let's not go overboard on the improv."

He held up a hand. "Hazel, I'm a professional. Now, what the fuck is this guy's name again?"

"Callum."

My blood boiled just saying the name.

That fucking asshole. I should have known. The second I saw my beloved tie-dye sweatshirt in the corner of his video, I had put it together. It was the same sweatshirt Paul had lent him, the one he'd said he had *no clue* what happened to.

I'd never liked Callum all that much, but I couldn't believe he'd stoop so low. We were friends. I mean, kind of. As much as anyone could be friends with their boyfriend-at-the-time's slightly misogynistic best friend. I always thought he was a little dense, and way too eager to say "yes" to whatever Paul wanted. But we'd hung out for *years*. I'd even stayed with Paul in this very house when we'd first moved out here, for crying out loud. Granted, the house was gross, and I'd made Paul find us an apartment almost immediately, but *still*.

Reid and I had been so preoccupied with the idea that Paul could have done this, I hadn't even considered Callum. To be fair, even if we had considered him as a suspect, I would have assumed there'd be no way in hell he could pull off something like this.

Reid must have been right. It had been a crime of opportunity. For whatever reason, Callum had been at my apartment that day. Probably to ask for money, knowing him. I'd redownloaded my apps to scroll back through my messages from weeks ago, and he had replied to my lottery win story with a jokey meme about begging for money. I'd responded with a 'lol' and thought that was it. But it clearly wasn't. He'd come to my apartment, and when he saw me leave Vermont alone, he must have acted on impulse.

The fucker.

I'd probably never get a true explanation, because I had absolutely zero intention of confronting him.

"How much time do you think you can buy me?" I asked Jackson while we stood at the edge of the property line, on the sidewalk.

Jackson frowned and looked at the white house with its peeling siding. "I don't know. Maybe, like, five minutes? My limited electrical knowledge won't last me long."

"That should be all I need," I said.

The plan was simple.

Jackson would knock on the door and pretend to be from the city. He'd show Callum a line that needed work at the edge of his property, on the side of the house, just far enough away from the front door to break his line of sight. He'd force Callum to fill out a fake survey we'd printed off and I'd be able to slip in, find Vermont, and exit out the back door.

In. Out. It would only take a few minutes.

"You ready?" I asked, stepping behind the tree so I could

keep an eye on the door and spring into action as soon as Callum took the bait.

"Are *you* ready?" Jackson asked. "This is insane."

"Let's just get it over with before I change my mind."

Jackson gawked at me. "Seriously? No. you should think this through."

"Go," I hissed, waving him away as I huddled behind the tree. He staggered out and pulled the baseball cap he wore tighter over his head.

If last night hadn't cemented the friendship, this surely would. Or he'd think I was a nut after this and never speak to me again. But if I knew one thing about Jackson, it was that he lived for the drama. The way he sauntered up to Callum's front steps told me he was immediately falling into character. I would have laughed had I not been so on edge.

He knocked and I stopped breathing.

I counted.

One.

Two.

Callum opened the door, rubbing an eye and looking sleepy. Good. I hoped we'd woken him up, the asshole. He didn't deserve to be well-rested.

I could hear the bass of their voices but not the actual words. Jackson pointed to the side of the house and Callum shook his head with irritation. His scrawny, stupid, little head.

I held my breath when he dipped back inside, but then almost let out a squeal when he reemerged wearing boots and tugging on a jacket. He followed Jackson, closing the front door behind him.

I left the cover of the tree, creeping toward the entrance. As soon as Jackson and Callum disappeared completely around the side of the house, I took off. I slowed when I got to his stairs, peeking to make sure they hadn't re-emerged, but I could still hear them talking.

"This is the line we need to work on. Could be without power for a few days."

"A few days? That's ridiculous, man. Why didn't I get a letter or something about this?"

I crept up the steps and placed my hand on the doorknob. I held my breath as I slowly turned it and slipped inside, letting the door shut lightly behind me.

The house was just as dingy as I remembered it—balled-up clothes and cans everywhere, fruit flies buzzing around the kitchen, the faint smell of musty body odor covered up by an aggressive amount of cologne.

I had to be quick.

I ducked and peered into the kitchen on the left side of the house, not wanting to risk being seen through the window that led to the side yard where Jackson and Callum were currently. No sign of Vermont, but I did notice a bowl of water on the ground.

He was here. Somewhere.

"Vermont," I whispered, before making a cooing sound.

I stepped into the living room, snapping my head from side to side. The couch from the photo caught my eye immediately. No sign of Vermont, but there was my sweatshirt, draped over the armrest like it was his.

My anger flared as I yanked it off the couch. Shrugging one backpack strap off my shoulder, I stuffed the hoodie inside, grimacing at the smell. Hopefully if I washed it a dozen times, that would eventually fade.

I kept moving. A short hallway branched off the living room, leading to the bathroom and his bedroom.

The bathroom door was open. Inside, the only sign of life was a makeshift litter box shoved into the corner.

I side-stepped across the hall, pushing Callum's bedroom door open. My eyes barely scanned the room before they landed on him, and my heart flew into my throat.

"Vermont!" I whisper-shrieked. His fur was slightly matted, his limbs lazily stretched in every direction, soaking in the rays of morning sun filtering through the blinds. When he spotted me in the doorway, his head lifted slowly, ears twitching as if deciding whether I was worth the effort.

Tears brimmed the corners of my eyes. I fell to my knees and he stretched, letting out a small meow as he got up to nuzzle my hand.

"You scared the shit out of me. And here you are just lounging about," I said through a laugh.

He blinked at me innocently, a purr vibrating his entire body. I stroked his chin before I shrugged off the cat carrier backpack and set it down. I took out one of the treats I'd bought, trying to bribe him not to make a fuss. Thankfully, Vermont, the even-tempered cat he was, let me pick him up and set him inside without a struggle. I wrapped him in the sweatshirt, giving him a makeshift bed of sorts before I zipped it closed. He got settled, pressing his face against the mesh siding.

Got him, Gran.

I had to keep it together, and then I could happy-sob on the way home.

I stood, slinging the bag over my shoulder. I took two steps toward the half-open bedroom door, preparing to slip out and down the hallway to the back door and escape out the yard.

That was the exact moment the sound of a slamming door and footsteps halted me in my tracks.

THIRTY-TWO

Reid

"Slow down!" West called from half a block behind me.

My steps hit the pavement with determination. I was jogging at this point. I hadn't wanted to park right in front of Callum's house in case I was totally off base, and Hazel hadn't come here to confront him without me.

But my gut told me she was here. I'd tried calling her close to five hundred times after that vague text she'd sent, but her phone had been switched off. I was full-on panicking at this point.

Thankfully, Callum was not private when it came to the internet. I was able to figure out his last name from his social media, and a quick white pages search sent me straight to his current address.

West had driven us. I was shaking too hard, and he said if I got behind the wheel, we'd end up in a ditch or something.

I really hoped Hazel wasn't here, but deep down I knew that she was.

Damnit. Why hadn't she texted me?

I slowed down when I reached the end of his block, looking for any signs of Hazel. When I didn't see her or her car, relief trickled through me.

"Reid?" I jerked my gaze toward the man addressing me. He looked like he worked construction or something, wearing a neon vest and bulky boots. I didn't recognize him. West finally caught up with me, folding over to catch his breath.

"Sorry, who—" but before I could finish my question, the man tore off his beanie and recognition hit.

Jackson.

Shit. If he was here, then that meant…

My gaze whipped up and down the block. "Where's Hazel?"

His face contorted into one of discomfort. Dread racked through me.

"Uh, well. You see…."

"What?" I demanded.

Jackson looked back down the street, not meeting my eyes. "She may or may not be currently stuck inside that house with the man who stole her cat."

"What!?" I barked. West grabbed my arm, which was the only way I realized I had launched myself in the direction of the front steps.

"For how long?" I demanded.

"Not that long," he added hurriedly. "We had this plan. I was going to distract him, and Hazel would sneak in and out with Vermont. But he had the attention span of a fly. I could only keep him outside for, like, two minutes before he blew me off. And Hazel didn't have a chance to leave. This was only, like, five minutes ago, though. I was debating knocking again to give her a shot to get out."

I nodded, trying to process the information in somewhat of a calm manner to come up with a plan. But at this point, I was half a second away from knocking on the door myself and barging inside. I didn't give a fuck if Callum tried to stop me.

"Alright, chill, Mr. Action-hero," West said, eyeing me up and down. He could tell exactly what was going through my mind.

"What do we do?" Jackson asked, looking to both of us. "I tried texting her, but I think she left her phone in her car."

"We need to do something now," I said, eyes fixed on the house, as the chaos in my mind finally began to settle into something resembling a coherent thought. "Okay, so there was no scream or scuffle, right?"

Jackson nodded.

"Good." I let out a breath. "So Callum hasn't discovered she's in there yet. But she hasn't come out, which means she might be stuck."

"Shit," West muttered.

"Here's what we're going to do," I continued, Jackson hanging on my every word. "You knock on the door again, make up some bullshit excuse. Say you need his email, I don't care. Just get him to answer. I'll go around back and see if I can see into a window, or something."

"What can I do?" West asked.

I glared at him, still not forgetting that he was likely the reason Hazel hadn't wanted to talk to me in the first place. "You've done enough."

He threw his hands up. "I'm sorry, okay? How many times can I say it?"

Jackson pursed his lips. "Oh, so you're the friend with the big mouth?"

We both shot West a dirty look.

West nodded toward the end of the block. "I'm going to wait by the car. Holler if you need me."

I clenched and unclenched my fists, trying to get the energy into one spot. Hazel was inside, with someone unhinged enough to hold her cat for ransom. I didn't want to cause a scene or start a fight, but if I didn't get her out of there in the next few minutes, I was barging in, subtleties be damned.

What could he do? Call the cops? "Yes officer, these two broke in to take a cat that I stole and have been using as leverage to extort a lot of money."

"Okay, you go," I said to Jackson, pointing at the front door as I was already slinking around to the side of the house. I crouched in the corner by the bush and waited for him to approach the front door.

I looked in the first window I came to and saw Callum there, alone, flipping through the channels on his TV. I ducked below the window. Then I heard a knock. I peeked in the window again and Callum rolled his eyes before throwing the remote at the couch and heading for the front door. I sprinted.

I passed one window on the way, but it faced into a hallway. I jumped over a short chain link fence into his yard, with agility that would have shocked me if I wasn't so high on adrenaline. The yard was unkempt, with a shed that was practically falling over in the corner, and overgrown dead weeds wherever you looked. One sad lawn chair with a broken arm sat among them.

There was a door leading to the yard, and a window on either side. Movement caught my eye in one and I moved toward it. It was high up, but still chest level for me. When I peered through, Hazel was looking back at me, her eyes wide.

"What are you doing here?" she mouthed.

"Open this." I tapped at the window.

"It's stuck," she mouthed, pulling it up to show me. The window frame was covered in layers of caked-on grime and paint.

"Keep pulling," I said, this time pressing my own hands to the glass and pushing up with as much force as I could muster from this angle. A sharp noise cracked out, and the window jerked upward an inch.

I put my hand underneath and pulled up even harder. It continued to move up in the track, struggling and resisting with each push.

"Go. Go. Go." Hazel looked back. "I can hear him."

A vein in my neck bulged as I pushed open the window just enough for Hazel to be able to squeeze through.

"Give me your backpack," I said.

She handed it through. When I took it, I realized it wasn't a backpack at all. Vermont's face pressed against the mesh side.

"You got him!" I said, unable to contain my excitement.

Hazel put one leg out the window and I reached up to help her.

"What the fuck?" A man's voice roared and Hazel was jerked backward, her leg hitting the window frame in the process.

All I saw was red.

Callum stood behind Hazel, gripping the side of her shirt.

"Let her fucking go," I seethed.

He narrowed his beady eyes. "Give me the money and I will."

"Get off me, asshole!" Hazel squirmed, and my rage took over. Without thinking, I set Vermont on the ground. I put both my hands on the windowsill and hoisted myself up and through the window, doing a kind of duck and tuck roll-to-stand that felt pretty cool, but probably looked ridiculous.

"Back up," Callum said, glaring at me.

I shoved his chest without a second thought. "We're leaving, and we're taking the cat. And you're going to leave Hazel alone, got it?"

"No, I don't got it," he said, trying his best to look menacing despite the ridiculous cropped muscle tee and flannel pajama bottoms he wore.

Hazel bit down on the hand holding her sweater and he yelped, letting go.

"You bitch!"

"What's wrong with you?" she shouted. "I can't believe you'd do this to me. You know how broke I've always been."

"I'm broke too!" he yelled, glaring at her. "And I can't afford this fucking house by myself." He lifted his hands up.

"That's not my problem!"

"When Paul told me he was moving to this side of the state, I wanted him to take the second bedroom. Then *you* decided you two should move in together, and then all of a sudden I had a whole mortgage to pay without him."

I glanced at Hazel to see her reaction, and her mouth fell open.

"Are you fucking serious, Callum? Paul literally moved out here with me. We were *always* planning to live together. Get other roommates, you freak! I'm sure it's not that hard, especially with how nice you keep the place." I winced, wishing she could refrain from the sarcastic digs while Callum was so red-faced and angry.

He took a step toward her, but I placed myself between them. I was not going to allow him to touch her again.

The room was small, and Callum and I were completely up in each other's faces. I'd never been in a fight before, and I didn't want to start today, but it was quickly becoming clear I had no other option.

"We're leaving," I said firmly.

Callum scowled, his jagged front tooth sticking out. "The fuck you are."

"Hazel, go," I said.

"I'm not leaving you."

"I got this."

I did not have this. I didn't know what the hell I was doing, but I knew that I needed her out of here.

Before I could process what was happening, Callum reached back, wound up, and socked me right in the eye.

I cursed, clutching my face. My glasses sat crooked on my nose, one lens fractured with a jagged crack.

Without thinking, I lunged forward and punched him straight in the gut.

He made a retching sound and doubled over. I had never hit someone before in my life. I shook my hand out, in shock. I flexed my fingers a few times to make sure I hadn't done any real damage.

Hazel sprang up behind me. I tried to pull her back, but

she was too fast. She kicked him right between the legs with more force than I'd have thought her capable of.

Ouch.

"Fuuuckk," he cried out, grasping himself, eyes squeezed shut.

I wasn't about to wait around for him to right himself.

"Let's go," I hurried Hazel out the window. I steadied her as she slipped through, her feet landing softly on the patch of grass below. She shouldered the bag with Vermont, and I swung one leg out the window before ducking and squeezing the rest of the way out.

I glanced back to see Callum limping toward the window, his face basically maroon. My left eye blurred and I swiped at it before realizing I was bleeding a little.

Callum kept shouting obscenities after us, but we were already gone. I gave Hazel a boost over the fence, then scrambled after her, and together we tore down the sidewalk, hearts pounding and feet slapping the pavement.

"Run," Hazel yelled at Jackson as we passed him.

We sprinted down the street, and the next one, not stopping until Callum's screams had completely faded away.

THIRTY-THREE

Hazel

My chest heaved, every ragged breath visible in the cold air. The street was empty behind me. A soft meow drifted from my backpack, reminding me that while the events that had just transpired were absolutely horrible, at least it was over.

Any positive thoughts I had abruptly shattered as soon as I looked at Reid. His broken glasses sat lopsided on his face, and a cut marked the skin beneath his left eye.

"Your eye," I choked out, still sucking in breath after breath.

Footsteps pounded the concrete behind us as Jackson and West finally caught up. I remained rooted in place, staring at Reid.

Jackson grabbed me by the shoulders and shook me lightly. "Holy shit, Hazel. Did you get him?"

I nodded, unwilling to take my eyes off Reid. He was still bent over and hadn't yet met my gaze.

"Who was that asshole?" West asked.

"My ex's best friend." Damn, I couldn't believe I hadn't even thought of Callum. He had seemed so harmless. Obnoxious, sure, but harmless nonetheless. He'd always been a little annoyed any time Paul chose to hang out with me instead of him, but the two of us had broken up months ago. How could I possibly have known he'd do something this unhinged? We hadn't even spoken since the breakup, aside from the occasional shared memes on social media. Turned out he was secretly psychotic. I wondered if Paul knew. I hoped he didn't.

"Good thing he spends all his time lifting and can't do cardio for shit," Jackson said through a breathless laugh. "He only chased us for, like, half a block before giving up."

"Probably thought better of it when he considered the numbers," West said.

Reid was stewing. There was no other word for it. He finally caught his breath, drawing in one last ragged inhale. He looked lost. In disbelief. Then his eyes found mine and his expression hardened.

"What the hell, Hazel?" he barked.

"Yikes. You look rough." West squinted, taking in his friend's face.

Reid glared at him. "Not now."

This was a nightmare. A complete and total nightmare.

Jackson let out a low whistle as he looked between Reid and me. He turned to West. "I think that might be our cue to get the hell out of here."

Part of me didn't want to be left alone with Reid. I had a pretty good feeling I was about to be heavily reprimanded.

"What were you thinking?" he demanded, taking a step toward me.

West eyed Reid and then bumped Jackson in the ribs with his elbow. "I'll drive," he said.

Jackson shot me a thumbs up that honestly would have made me laugh had Reid not been staring at me so intensely right now.

They both backed away and I watched as they turned the corner. When I met Reid's eyes again, it was clear he hadn't even spared them a parting glance.

"I'm sorry," I started to apologize, but Reid shook his head causing me to snap my mouth shut.

"I can't believe you'd come here without telling me." He shook his head. I couldn't tell if he was more disappointed or angry. Or a solid mix of the two.

His eyes pierced me. Yep. *Definitely* a mix of the two.

"I thought I could do this by myself," I offered, too emotionally exhausted to defend myself. Any adrenaline had faded away.

"What? Why?" His eyebrows drew together, a fraction of the harsh look melting away. "You didn't *need* to do this by yourself. I would have been here in an instant if you called."

I knew that. Even if I tried to drag him into some hare-brained idea he was completely opposed to, he still would have come if I asked. What did that say about me?

"Looks like I needed your help anyway," I muttered, completely deflated at this point.

Reid had gotten punched in the face. Because of me. There was no way to come back from this. I was a freaking inarguable monstrosity of a mess. It didn't matter that this whole ordeal was over. I'd royally screwed up. I wasn't *right* for him. There was no way this hadn't woken him up from whatever spell I'd managed to cast over him the past few weeks. He must want me out of his life for good now.

Any moments of closeness between us felt like distant memories.

"What are you talking about?" he asked. He looked tired. So tired.

"I just wanted to solve my own problem for once," I said.

He dragged a hand over his chin and adjusted his glasses, though they were barely hanging on. He scanned my face, and a million thoughts were clearly spinning through his mind. I was curious which one he'd settle on first. He took a step toward me, and I retreated instinctively. He frowned.

"Do you know how scared I was when you sent that vague text?" he asked, obviously being careful with his tone. "I know you, and I knew you were doing something stupid. Irresponsible."

I looked away from him, keeping my eyes trained firmly on the ground. "That's me," I admitted, all my fight gone.

Reid started pacing in front of me, waving his hands in the air. "I nearly had a heart attack when West drove us over here. And then Jackson telling me you were inside? How could you do that?"

I kept quiet, letting him seethe. I deserved it. It *was* a reckless plan. Classic Hazel.

"My car is down that street," I finally said, pointing. "I can drive you home. We should probably get your cut cleaned up."

He reached up and swiped at the small gash, smearing some blood onto his fingers. He brought his hand in front of his face, looking surprised. As if he'd forgotten he'd just been hit in the face because of me.

Without waiting to be berated further, I brushed by him, walking toward my car. Reid followed me wordlessly. A tension hung over us. It felt a lot like I was headed to my own execution.

The soft meow that came from my backpack was my only comfort.

Once at my car, I opened the back door, setting Vermont carefully in the back seat.

Reid slid into the passenger side, remaining silent.

I wanted to beg him to talk to me, but then figured nothing good could come from that, so I turned the radio on instead.

The drive went by in a blur. You know those moments when you were conscious you were driving, but couldn't actually remember it? Like a phantom took over and was operating for you for a bit? That's what the drive home was like. Could've been hours, for how aware I was. The entire time, I was mostly focused on holding back tears.

Funny, I should have been on cloud nine. I had Vermont back. I would get my winnings in the next few days, and I'd be able to set myself up for a better financial future. But relief and happiness remained completely out of reach.

And it was all due to the tragic nature of the situation seated directly next to me.

Reid was pissed. And I figured he was done with me. That cast a shadow over everything. I'd hoped to get Vermont back and show him I'd solved my own problem. Instead, I'd roped him into the rescue and gotten him beat up. I was a train-wreck. He'd be lucky to jump out now before I caused him any real damage.

"I can't believe you're so irresponsible," he whispered, staring straight ahead.

Yep, there it was.

"I'm sorry," I said, my voice small. All I could do was apologize and get out of his hair as quickly as possible.

"Anything could have happened to you."

"I know."

He sighed and shook his head. "What a dick. I knew that guy looked like bad news."

"He sucks," I agreed, eyes on the road.

Silence fell over us again as I drove us the rest of the way. I gulped down the lump in my throat.

When I pulled into the driveway, the crushing sense of finality washed over me. Reid unbuckled and turned to look at me, but I was already out of the car with Vermont.

I pulled off the spare key he'd given me, unwinding it from my keychain. I unlocked the front door for likely the last time, and walked inside, setting the key on the shelf in the entry. Reid was at my back.

"What are you doing?"

I pulled my boots off and set Vermont down. I didn't want to take him out of the carrier in Reid's house. I didn't want to make a mess.

"I can get my stuff together pretty quickly." I moved into the kitchen without waiting for him to respond. If I stopped to think too hard about this, I'd cry, and I didn't want to cry in front of Reid. Not now.

Before heading back to my room, I stopped at the sink and wet a paper towel. I turned to Reid. "For your cut."

He took it from me and pressed it against the dried blood. "What are you talking about? You can't leave right now. Callum knows where you live. I'm not letting that guy get near you."

I shrugged. "I doubt he'll come after me. I got him pretty good in the balls. With any luck, maybe I did permanent damage."

His lip curved up at that, but it fell when he took in my downcast face.

"Can you slow down for a second and talk to me?" he asked, his tone softer than it had been in the car.

I sighed. "I don't really want to talk about how careless and reckless I am right now, if that's okay. I'm tired."

He blew out a breath and shook his head before narrowing his eyes. "I'm sorry for going all scolding mode on you, but I was just scared. *You* scared me. Something way worse could have happened. You could have gotten hurt."

My heart lifted a little at his words, but I could still barely look at him for fear of what I'd find there.

"I get it. You're upset. I'll just get out of here." I tried to turn away from him again but he grabbed my arm, holding on gently.

"You're right. I *am* upset. I'm allowed to be upset with you, Hazel. Especially when you do stupid shit. But that doesn't mean I'm going anywhere, or that I want *you* to go anywhere."

I blinked up at him, finally meeting his pleading eyes.

"Please, just talk to me," he said.

"About what?" I asked, still struggling to believe him.

His eyes scanned mine before he let out a ragged sigh. "Look, I think I know why you went alone today. West said something to you last night that upset you—"

"It's fine," I said quickly.

"It's *not* fine. It's the opposite of fine."

I shrugged haplessly, letting my arm fall away from his loose grip. "He didn't say anything I didn't already know. It's true. I'm a mess. I don't have my life together."

"Hazel—"

"No, it's okay. Really. I get it." I took a step back, but he mirrored my movements, not letting me get too far from him. "I just thought…I thought you saw me differently."

"I do!"

"I thought my flaws weren't as magnified when you were looking at me."

He shook his head. "I don't even see flaws, Hazel. I just see *you*."

That was it. I couldn't hold them back anymore. Tears were officially flowing now.

Reid's face softened. "I'm sorry West said that to you. Especially when the only thoughts that have been running through my head lately have been about how incredible you are."

"What?" I choked out, pointing at his destroyed glasses. "*Incredible*? You're delusional! Look what I got you into today."

He tilted his head. "Well, today wasn't ideal," he admitted. "But you love harder than you think, sometimes, and I wouldn't change a thing about you. Other than maybe insist you come to me first before acting on any potentially dangerous impulses in the future."

I shook my head and tried to move away but he held onto me, grounding me in place.

"I *like* your brand of mess. I've never felt so accepted by anyone until you, and I'm sorry if I made you feel like I didn't accept you, for even a second."

I stared up at him, my tears stopped dead in their tracks. His words weren't quite computing. "I—*I* accept *you*?" I asked, having a hard time believing that I'd had any positive influence over Reid's life whatsoever.

His gaze bored into mine. "You do. You let me be myself,

but you still challenge me to not be so freaking stubborn and stuck in my ways. I'm happier when you're around. I worry about you, sure, but that's only because I care. *So* much."

His words wrapped around me like a security blanket. They were exactly what I wanted to hear. But he was too good for me. He always had been. "You'd be way better off without me, Reid. Trust me."

"Well, I don't want to be without you!" He rubbed his hands up and down my arms. "You're so…alive. So unapologetically yourself. I don't even care that you're always running late. I think it's cute that you can't multitask, because you constantly have a million thoughts running through your head. I love that you think cooking dinner together is fun and that you always beg me to try new things, even when I fight you on it. You don't think online sleuthing is the dumbest hobby ever to exist. And for whatever reason, you actually *like* spending time with my overbearing family. I can't get enough of you. And I sure as hell am *not* better off without you."

My face crumpled for a different reason entirely. He breathed, stepping even closer into my orbit, and I had to crane my neck to look up at him.

"You said once that stability wouldn't be so bad. And I can see why you'd think that. You've had to be flexible, to accept what you were given and make the best of it. You're *so* strong. And I want nothing more than to be your stability. I want you to be able to lean on me. Whether it's rescuing your cat or just crying on my shoulder because you had a hard day. I want to be here for you, not because you need me, but because you want me."

I couldn't take it anymore. I wrapped my arms around his waist and fell against his chest, squeezing him like my life depended on it.

He choked out a relieved laugh and pulled me to him, holding on tight.

"I've loved every minute I've spent with you," I said into his chest. "You make me feel so safe, it's almost scary. Because what if I need you and then you're gone?" I pulled away slightly to look up at him.

"I'm not going anywhere," he said, and for some reason, I believed him more than anyone who'd ever said it before.

"Chaotic things will probably keep happening to me," I pointed out.

"I don't care." He tucked a piece of hair behind my ear.

"You say that now, but—"

"I love you, Hazel."

I blinked and stared up at him. I didn't see anything but earnestness in his eyes.

"W-what?" I sputtered. How could he? I was utterly unlovable. There was no way someone as amazing as Reid could possibly love me—

"I'm in love with you," he repeated, cupping my cheek. "I didn't want to say it in case it was too soon, and I scared you off, but you deserve to know. You think you're hard to love, but you're not. Falling for you has been the easiest thing I've ever done. In fact, it was impossible to stop."

He leaned down and kissed me, my wet tears transferring onto his cheeks. When he pulled away, I blinked back at him, still in disbelief.

"Are you going to say anything or..." his words trailed off, and I realized he was actually nervous. I wanted to laugh. As if I had any choice but to love him back.

My brain momentarily forgot how to send signals to my mouth to speak.

Reid's eyebrows lifted as he traced a slow circle against my cheek with his thumb. The picture of patience. Always. A rock. My rock.

"I love you too," I finally got out. "Of course I do. You're amazing, Reid. You helped me when you didn't have to, just because that's the kind of person you are—good to everyone. *I accepted you?* You accepted me! I've never felt more secure than when I'm with you."

He let out a relieved laugh before leaning down and stealing another kiss.

I should never have doubted him. I was so used to no one staying, of having people pass through my life without a second glance. But Reid saw me. Really saw me.

Vermont let out a demanding meow from the front hallway.

Reid pulled away, a huge grin still on his face. "Should we let him explore? I'd like to officially meet the little guy, after all this build up."

I smiled back at him. "Hopefully he lives up to the hype."

"Maybe we should go out and get a litter box and some things for the house," he said, wiping the last of my tears from my cheeks with his thumbs.

My heart nearly burst. I wasn't about to move in here for real, but I didn't want to bring up going back to my apartment. Not yet. I just wanted to cozy up with Reid and Vermont on the couch and savor this feeling—the overwhelming peace that came with finally no longer feeling alone.

"Maybe some new glasses, too."

"Oh." He laughed and took off his mangled pair. "Don't worry, I have backups."

"Of course you do. Always prepared." I kept beaming up at him, and he mirrored it right back.

Reid carefully unzipped the backpack and let Vermont sniff his hand. Vermont stepped out of the carrier like he owned the place, rubbing against Reid. Reid shot me a smile. My heart was so whole it might burst.

There was no way to know for sure if Reid was in this for the long haul. It didn't make sense to assume he would be, not after such a short time.

But deep down, I knew.

He wasn't going anywhere. And neither was I.

THIRTY-FOUR

Hazel – One Month Later

I COULDN'T BREATHE. IT WAS LIKE SOMEONE HAD PLACED something heavy over my mouth, waiting for me to suffocate.

Jerking awake, I lurched my head back with a gasp, only to find Vermont huddled right up by my face on my pillow. He let out a demanding "Meow."

My bedside clock told me it was just before nine. I should be grateful he'd let me sleep in for once. Typically, he was a lot more aggressive with his demands for breakfast earlier in the morning. I practically had to set up formal negotiations with him to let me sleep in at least until the sun rose.

I rubbed underneath his chin before throwing the comforter off me. My tie-dye sweatshirt lay abandoned on the floor. I nabbed it and pulled it on.

The cans of wet food were all stacked on the windowsill. Reid had begged me to find a cabinet—any cabinet—but my kitchen was small and already bursting at the seams.

I took one down, opened it with a can opener, and set it down next to the water bowl on the floor. Vermont wasted no time trotting over to it and wolfing it down.

I threw on a pot of coffee and pulled my blinds open. Fresh snow blanketed the street outside, covering each car still parked on the street. I caught sight of mine, relieved I didn't have to drive anywhere today. It looked like we'd be getting a white Christmas tomorrow after all. Gran would have loved it.

I yawned and stretched, waiting for the ancient machine to finish brewing my coffee. Jackson had dragged me to a Christmas pop-up bar last night. He'd drank one too many 'Dirty Rudolph's and I'd had to drive him home. We were out entirely too late, but I had been having so much fun I hadn't even cared. Plus, the salon was closed until the 27th. I might as well take advantage of my time off. I couldn't wait to spend the next few days cozied up, eating good food, and spending time with my favorite people.

A knock sounded through the apartment.

I raced to answer it, my socks sliding on the floor right before I reached the door to swing it open. Reid stood there holding a large bag, smiling in the new glasses I'd bought for him, and a beanie tugged down over his ears.

"Merry Christmas Eve," he said.

"I thought you were coming over later." I threw my arms around him and held on tight, breathing him in like I always did.

"Couldn't wait." He kissed the top of my head. "Plus, I had to make sure you were still alive after Jackson drunk called me from your phone last night, begging me to order you two a pizza."

I rolled my eyes. "*I* was fine. He, on the other hand, is likely regretting his decisions right now, since he has to drive two hours to his family's house later this morning."

Reid walked past me and set the bag underneath the silver Christmas tree that he'd helped me put up weeks ago. He'd tried to insist that we wear N95 masks while doing it.

Seeing him carefully arrange the bag of gifts underneath the tree hit me in a soft, unexpected way. I'd been so scared for my first Christmas without Gran—worried the loneliness and memories would consume me. But having Reid Mitchell as a boyfriend meant I'd never be lonely again.

For someone who claimed to appreciate his alone time, he always seemed to want me around. And I mean *always*. Some nights, when I was too tired from a long shift to pack up Vermont and head to his place, I'd tell him not to come over because I was just going to crash. He never listened. He'd come anyway, just to sleep on my "too soft" bed and hold me. Ugh, I loved that man. I had a hard time remembering ever feeling as important as when he set his gaze on me. He'd made a place for me in his life, and I never had to question, even for a second, if I fit there.

"Vermont," he cooed, holding up a toy mouse. Vermont pranced into the room, immediately greeting Reid with a friendly headbutt to the leg. Reid scratched his back and set down the toy that was surely filled with catnip. "Gotta make sure I'm still his favorite."

Reid *was* my cat's favorite. And it was annoying. It was like he didn't even know, or appreciate, everything I'd gone through to get him back. I could call the stinker ungrateful all I wanted, but nothing gave me more joy than watching those two cuddled up on the couch together.

"You spoil him," I said with a laugh.

"I brought donuts for you, too," he said, holding out a small brown bag.

"Yay!" I took the bag from him and brought it to the kitchen, arranging the donuts on a plate before pouring us coffee, splashing some peppermint creamer into both mugs.

Life had been good the past month. Like blissfully, amazingly, stupidly good.

After the whole ordeal with Callum went down, I'd thought we were in the clear. Despite Reid begging me not to, the first thing I'd done was call Paul to rip him a new one. It was his best friend, after all. I had to know if he knew. But he was actually, genuinely shocked. Angry, even. He'd called Callum a creepy bastard, told me he was sorry, and said that Callum would absolutely not be bothering me again. I was ninety-nine percent sure Paul had gone over and beaten the crap out of him. Probably did a lot more damage than Reid and I had.

Even though Paul was an ex for a reason, I was still a little bit happy that he'd stood up for me like that. And I was grateful the person who'd been threatening me all that time hadn't been someone I'd been so close to. It offered a grain of comfort.

Reid wasn't as willing as I was to let Paul handle everything. He'd insisted we go to the police with every piece of evidence we had—the cameras, the messages, the letters. It helped that Callum had left me two threatening voicemails right after we'd rescued Vermont. With all that evidence, I was able to file for a restraining order. Although I really didn't think it was necessary, Reid said the added layer of security helped him sleep better at night.

I watched dreamily as Reid carefully arranged the presents he'd brought for me under the tree.

"What's that one?" I asked, when he set a bright red card on top.

"Oh, just something small." His cheeks turned pink.

"What is it?" I demanded, reaching for it.

"Just something small, it's not your real present," he added hurriedly. He was so cute when he was flustered.

"If it's not real, can I open it now?"

"Umm…"

When his voice trailed off, I took that as my permission to tear the card open. My eyebrows shot up as I scanned the words, before a laugh burst out of me. "A gift card to a car wash?"

He shrugged. "Like I said, it's not your main present."

"You're ridiculous," I said, still laughing before wrapping my arms around him and planting a kiss on his cheek.

He chuckled. "Can't blame a guy for trying. You'll like the other ones more, I promise."

I clapped my hands in excitement. "Can we open them tonight?"

"Of course." He kissed my nose and my chest swelled. Even though his family was a presents-on-Christmas-morning one, he wanted to open our gifts together the night before, because that's what Gran and I had always done. Then, first thing tomorrow morning, we'd head over to his family's Christmas. I couldn't be more excited to spend another holiday with them.

Thanksgiving had been a dream—plates and plates of amazing dishes, Ruby and Regan taking me under their wing like I'd always belonged, laughing as his dad and West tried to walk me through the rules of football while the Lions played in the background. Reid's mom had hugged me every chance she got, making sure I was comfortable and okay. It had been perfect.

And tomorrow would be amazing too, full of new memories to cherish. I couldn't remember the last time I'd been this excited for Christmas. Maybe it was because I had money to spend on presents, for once.

A few days after we got Vermont back, the lottery winnings were deposited into my account. I nearly fainted when I saw the number. I had never seen my statement so far into the green before. Reid was practically chomping at the bit to take a look at my financials and help me get everything sorted, but to his credit, he played it cool, acted like it wasn't killing him not to help me.

I had every intention of paying off my debts—and I did—but first, I'd taken Reid to a nice restaurant to thank him for everything. He *still* tried to pay. I had to corner the waiter by the bar before they brought the check to the table.

And when I told Reid I wanted to go out to a casino one night to honor Gran, I thought he was going to have a heart attack. But we went, along with West, his sisters, and Jackson. Reid even won seventy-five dollars on a slot machine. It was a sight watching him go from not wanting to be there at all, to jumping up and down with pure joy as the lights lit up around him. I died laughing.

Gran would have loved him.

Now, all of my ducks were in a row. I was more financially free than I'd ever been. Sure, I still had to work every day, but I was no longer living paycheck to paycheck. I had savings. I could splurge occasionally on something nice for myself.

And a few nice things for Reid, too. I was so excited for him to open the presents I'd carefully picked out for him. But mostly, I was just excited to be with him today, tucked under his arm.

"What should we watch first?" he asked, plopping onto the couch. Vermont followed, curling up on the back of the cushion. "I'm thinking all-day movie marathon."

"The Grinch. It was always our favorite."

"The Grinch it is," he said, picking up the remote.

I set the donuts and coffee in front of us and curled into his side.

"This is perfect," I whispered.

"It'll be even better when we're already in the same place," he said, kissing the top of my head.

I pinched his side. Reid had been joking about me moving in with him again ever since I'd got Vermont back. When I insisted it was too soon, he'd said I could still stay in the guest room. I told him that would be ridiculous, and he'd backed off. What he hadn't backed off from was the security at my current apartment. He'd even installed a new video doorbell at my door. I think even with the restraining order, he wasn't in love with the idea of me being here. But I was hardly alone. Reid and I spent one, maybe two nights apart per week. I was sure we'd figure out the whole moving-in thing eventually, but I wasn't in any hurry.

His lips pressed against the top of my head as the opening credits to the movie played.

"How are you holding up today?" he asked.

"Better now that you're here." I squeezed around his middle.

Everything was always better when he was around. Every

day I spent with Reid, I grew more and more confident that this was it for me.

He felt like more than my boyfriend, or even the love of my life. He felt like family. He felt like home.

He felt like forever.

Epilogue

REID - SIX MONTHS LATER

Armchair_Detective: *Cat tax, please.*

ReidingRainbow: *(ATT: picture of orange cat curled up on couch)*

WhiteKnight31: *Stop distracting yourself and finish the blog post, Eddie.*

Armchair_Detective: *It's basically done. And shouldn't you be looking at hotels for next month?*

ReidingRainbow: *Already booked a refundable one. Figured you guys could just send me the money.*

WhiteKnight31: *Of course you did. Leave it to Reid to figure out the logistics.*

Armchair_Detective: *I still can't believe it took you getting a girlfriend for us all to finally get together.*

WhiteKnight31: *Yeah, tell Hazel thanks again for the tickets. This Cold Case Convention is going to be a blast.*

ReidingRainbow: *I'll let her know.*

Armchair_Detective: *Maybe we can finally start up that podcast we talked about.*

WhiteKnight31: *You mean the podcast you talked about.*

ReidingRainbow: *Got to run. The moving truck will be here any minute.*

_Armchair_Detective_: _Fine, but I'm not dropping this podcast discussion._

"YOU'RE SURE?" HAZEL QUESTIONED ME, HER EYES narrowed. Vermont was on the counter pressing his head against her hand, demanding pets again.

When she'd first started bringing him over all the time, I'd tried for maybe five seconds to enforce a no-cats-in-the-kitchen rule, but it was pointless. Vermont had a mind of his own, and it was a challenge to keep nudging him away. I found it easier just to constantly disinfect instead.

"I like it there," I said.

She glanced from me to her giant grandfather clock, now standing in the entry hallway right before you hit the living room. It was a deep, massive piece, but with the high ceilings in this house, it fit a lot better than in her cramped apartment.

"You sure? Because we can move it."

"We actually physically can't move it," I pointed out. "I'm not sure how you got it in your apartment in the first place."

"A really nice delivery man."

I chuckled. "Well, it's perfect there."

She huffed and crossed her arms as if she thought I was being difficult for being too agreeable. "We can ask West to come back and help us."

"Seriously, I like it there."

"I don't believe you."

"I like your stuff," I said, for what felt like the millionth time. When I'd asked her to move in with me, it hadn't been conditional. I wanted her, mess and all. Since we'd gotten together, my house had felt even emptier. Even with the occasional knickknacks she'd bring by, it was a huge space to fill up.

Not anymore, though. After this morning's move, our house was exploding with all of Hazel's things.

Our house.

I liked the sound of that.

The moving truck had left hours ago and now we were sorting through boxes, combining her stuff with mine.

Nothing had ever felt so right.

I *had* drawn the line at her two coffee tables, though. One could only be pushed so far.

I'd been trying to get her to move in for months. Honestly, I'd never wanted her to leave in the first place. But even after we made it official, she'd insisted on finishing out the lease at her old apartment.

Which I understood. We were brand new. It gave us a chance to date for real and get to know each other without the pressure she'd been under when we first met. But getting to know a healed version of Hazel had only made me fall for her that much harder.

She'd quickly become a staple at our weekly family dinners; my parents were now more excited to see her than to see me. She fit right in with Ruby and Regan, and they'd added her to a group chat without me almost immediately. And Hazel was completely pumped about the annual trip to Florida we took every Labor Day. She'd been thrilled when she found out she was invited—as if I'd ever consider going without her.

Vermont was like an adopted son to me now. Hazel would never admit it, but he took to me even more than her. Anytime they were at the house over the past six months, he could be found curled up on the back of my office chair, or splayed across my laptop keyboard, demanding attention.

She'd told me that Gran would have been obsessed with me, which had made my heart clench. I wished I'd had the chance to meet the incredible woman who raised the woman I was so completely in love with.

When it finally came time for us to move in together, she'd asked me what she could bring and what she couldn't. I told her to bring it all. There was still hesitation in her eyes, a fear I wasn't telling the truth, that I'd regret letting her clutter my life. But I'd meant every word. My life had been monochromatic. She brought color and liveliness into it.

Hazel's bottom lip jutted out as she surveyed the explosion of boxes and antiques strewn about the living room, and the mug collection currently taking up over half of the kitchen island.

"Baby, I'm so happy you're moving in right now, we could go out and buy anything you wanted." I grabbed her hand. "What about a clock for each room? A disco ball?"

"Don't be tacky." She rolled her eyes with a laugh. "And living together will hardly be any different than the past few months. I basically live here now."

I disagreed completely. Basically living together and *actually* living together were two different things entirely. While she did spend most nights here, I hated when I'd get a text from her saying she was staying home tonight. *I* wanted to be home.

She had injected joy into my life in every possible way. In the way she'd grown so close with my family. In the way she'd pull up a chair and quietly linger behind me while I talked with my sleuthing group about whatever cold case we were digging into. In the way she kept experimenting in the kitchen, even without having the slightest natural talent for cooking. In the way she insisted on stopping at thrift stores every weekend just to find some little thing to take home. And in the way she still went out and bought a lottery ticket every time she had a hard day—and somehow got me into the habit, too.

God, I loved her.

I wrapped her in my arms. Holding her close, I ducked my head and kissed her.

"What was that for?" she asked, smiling.

"I'm just so happy you're here."

"I'm already *always* here," she said.

"I know. But this feels permanent. Official."

"It does," she agreed with a grin, before snaking her arms around me and holding on tight.

She did that a lot—hugged me like she was worried I might evaporate at any moment. She could do it all she wanted.

I was hers for good.

The End

Thank you

Thank you for reading Always the Boyfriend! I hope you love Hazel and Reid as much as I do. As an indie author, support from readers like you means everything! If you enjoyed this book, please take a few moments to leave a review.

Keep reading for a sneak peek of…

A forced proximity romance about a shy writer, a bad boy actor, and the reality dating show they're both stuck on…
Available now on Amazon

The Reality of It All

"Calla, you almost ready?"

I tore my gaze away from my reflection to find Brady hovering in the door of my suite.

"Um, can I have a few more minutes?"

"Of course." He flashed a reassuring smile that did little to settle the queasy feeling in my stomach. "I'll knock again in five, but then we really have to go." His tan hair flopped forward as he raised a walkie-talkie to his mouth. "Number two needs five more minutes. I repeat. Number two needs five more minutes."

The way he so effortlessly reduced me to a number made me wince. Brady seemed nice for someone who worked in reality television, but then again, I was completely oblivious to this world. Anyone who knew me would never have said I was the kind of person to do this sort of thing. They'd all have insisted that quiet, shy Calla did not have the right personality for TV.

I looked back at myself in the mirror, taking in my bright blue eyes, now lined with soft brown liner. Rosy blush dotted both of my cheeks, and my raven hair was styled in a long braid. The hair and makeup team had begged me to wear my hair down in loose, long waves, but I'd insisted on wearing it pulled back. The makeup already felt like a lot. This was a writing competition, after all; it wasn't like I was going on *The Bachelor*.

Smoothing one of my eyebrows, I continued to inspect myself. I had never felt self-conscious before now, but I had also never experienced the stress of considering what the general public might think of me. People were harsh and cruel, and I feared I would be no match for their scrutiny. Sure, I was pretty, but not in the way that caused people to stop and stare. Everything about me was intentionally under-stated, just how I liked it.

This was a writing competition, I reminded myself again. For authors. How many people would even watch? And if anyone did, surely they'd care more about my talent than the way I looked.

Calla Scott, budding novelist from Chicago, arriving for her chance to compete on The Next Great American Classic.

The whole idea was unfathomable. When my sister, Piper, had applied for me, I'd told her she was being utterly ridiculous. Then, when the call came announcing that I'd been selected, apprehension had smacked me in the face.

Of course, I'd declined. I had already sold my first novel two years before. Sure, there had been a bit of a publishing delay, and now I had terrible writer's block, but I'd still sold it. I hadn't written anything new since the accident, but I found it hard to fathom that a show could help with that.

But Piper had begged me, with tears in her eyes. She'd said I was fading into nothing right in front of her. I believe her exact words had been something along the lines of, *your numbness is sucking the life out of me.*

So, because I loved my sister, and not because I thought this experience would have some profound effect on me, I'd agreed.

Another knock.

"Calla. It's time."

Standing from the vanity, I tugged on the hem of my most comfortable sweater, ensuring it lay smooth. It was my favorite and made me feel like a writer whenever I put it on, which is why I'd found it so strange earlier when the producer had begged me to change. What said 'writer' more than a cable-knit sweater? It was even weirder when they'd strongly suggested I wear a dress. Why would I wear a fancy gown to pitch book ideas? Surely the other contestants would be wearing similar things.

"Let's do this," I said, with more confidence than I felt.

"That's the spirit."

Brady ushered me through the door of my room, and I found myself face to face with a mounted deer head. It stared right into my soul before I tore my eyes away and continued down the hall. The whole thing was being filmed at a remote lodge in Montana. It seemed a bit random, but when I'd asked, Brady had mentioned something about a state tax credit and budget restrictions.

"Don't get overwhelmed, but you'll be meeting a lot of people when we first get down there. We've split everyone into two groups. You'll meet one set first, and then we'll bring the others in."

I practically had to jog to keep up with his hurried pace.

"I'll put you in one of the side rooms we use for interviews and knock when it's time for your big entrance.

"The sound guy will come in and get you all mic'd up. Remember, any time you're in the lodge, there will be hidden cameras recording you. It's vitally important that you don't remove your mic during filming, and you stay in the designated rooms. You remember which ones those are, right?"

He'd provided me with a map yesterday that labeled all of the areas of the lodge that we'd have access to. I thought back to that, recalling most of the information. My head spun trying to process it all. I was surprised to learn they'd be filming us even during our downtime. Wouldn't people just be tuning in for the competition aspect? Maybe they thought there would be drama among the contestants. They certainly wouldn't be getting that from me. Confrontation gave me hives.

Brady stopped abruptly at a wooden door in the middle of the hallway. I recognized it instantly as the room where we'd filmed my introduction interview. They had peppered me with question after question about my "sob story," as the producers had so eloquently called it. I had tried to limit the information I'd shared with them as much as possible. The last thing I wanted was for people to root for me because they felt sorry for me.

"Okay, here we are." He ushered me inside. "Our sound guy will be here in a moment, then someone will come get you when we're ready."

I nodded.

Brady sighed. "You know you'll actually have to speak once you get out there, right?"

"Of course," I said hollowly. Piper had made me promise to make an effort, but my heart wasn't in this at all. I suddenly felt desperate to be back home in the comfort of my small apartment.

"Good luck." Brady squeezed my arm and closed the door, sealing me inside the windowless room; one which had most likely been a closet before they decided to film in here.

Tears welled up at the corners of my eyes and an over-whelming sense of feeling out of place washed over me. In the past two years since the accident, this was the farthest I'd ventured from home. I already missed my mother, whom I spoke to almost daily. And I missed Piper, who, despite being single and having better things to do, always dropped in to check on me every Friday. She knew weekends hit me the hardest.

I was still afraid that coming here had been a mistake, but I pulled my shoulders back and drew in a deep breath.

I'd promised Piper I would give this a fair shot.

Plus, I couldn't hide forever.

Twenty minutes later, a microphone hung around my neck, connected to a wire around my waist. I'd been given very strict instructions not to remove the mic under any circumstances; the sound guy had basically put the fear of God in me.

The door opened, revealing Shay.

Shay was the other producer—or handler, as they called themselves. She and Brady oversaw the contestants. They ensured we were in the right place at the right time, and had conducted our original interviews. Shay was maybe forty, with a cropped hairstyle and a stern look about her. While Brady at least pretended to be empathetic and kind, Shay's eyes held no warmth.

When I arrived from the airport two days ago, she had immediately taken me to be interviewed. I had begged for a shower and a nap and she had begrudgingly agreed, complaining the entire time that we'd be behind schedule. After that, I was definitely on her bad side.

"Let's go." She waved me out of the room.

I followed, not wanting to give her any more reasons to dislike me.

She pointed down the hall. "Follow this to the main lounge. The other contestants will trickle in slowly. Introduce yourself as they come. The host will join you all shortly. Whatever you do, do not leave the lounge until instructed to do so."

I nodded, even though she wasn't looking at me.

"Got it?" she barked.

"Got it," I squeaked.

"Don't forget your voice. This is a TV show."

"I won't," I insisted.

Following her direction, I took tentative steps toward the space where the hallway opened up into a room. Beyond the arch were high, vaulted ceilings. Cameras were likely embedded in every wooden beam. Brady had told me to pretend they didn't exist.

The hallway shrank before me. Five more steps and I'd be there. No turning back now.

Four.

Three.

Two.

One.

The room was a grand, open space, with several couches and chairs arranged around a massive stone fireplace. Walls of large windows on both sides of the room let in the afternoon sunlight. Before I could take in anything more, someone let out a loud squeal. A short blonde I hadn't noticed at first came ambling toward me.

"Hi, I'm Trace. It's so nice to meet you."

She opened her arms and heat pricked the back of my neck. I was decidedly not a hugger. But I had already anticipated this would happen today, so I braced myself and returned the quick hug.

"I'm Calla. It's nice to meet you."

"Where are you from?" she asked, still hovering close to me.

"Chicago. What about you?"

"Nashville."

My shoulders sagged with relief as I took in the genuine warmth in her expression. At least not everyone on this show would be cutthroat.

Trace looked like sunshine would, if it were a person. She wore a short pink dress, cowboy boots, and a hat. She was adorable, but also not what I was expecting from an author. Then I felt like a jerk for making any type of assumption simply based on what she was wearing.

"Cute dress," I said. "That color is great on you."

"Thank you. I spent hours picking it out." She beamed at me. "I love your sweater. It's so cozy."

"Thanks." I blushed and played with the hole in my right sleeve. Maybe I should have dressed up more for this after all.

"This is a little nerve-wracking, right?" she said in her subtle Southern drawl.

"I'm so glad you said that." I was only five feet six inches, but I had at least four inches on Trace.

"I was a bundle of nerves last night. Could hardly sleep."

"Me either," I admitted. "Every time I rolled over to check the time, only fifteen minutes had passed."

"It was the absolute worst, and they took my phone so I couldn't even distract myself," she said, before asking me more about Chicago and my flight in.

I answered her questions, grateful to find such a friendly ally so early on. Maybe Piper was right and this experience would be good for me.

"And this lodge is stunning," Trace continued. "I can't believe we get to stay here."

"The views are breathtaking," I said, staring out the enormous floor-to-ceiling windows. Rolling plains stretched out away from us until they dissolved into mountains in the distance. I had never been this far west before, and I doubted I'd ever get sick of staring at that view.

"I wonder where we'll all be recording," Trace said, peering down the hall.

"Recording?" Confusion knit my brow. "Like cameras? I'm pretty sure they're all hidden."

"No silly. *Recording equipment.*"

Her emphasis did not help my comprehension.

"Like laptops and notebooks? I'm sure they'll provide us something to write with."

"What do you—"

She stopped talking as we both turned our heads to see a stunning, tall, tanned woman saunter into the room. She wore a black dress with cutouts that instantly made me feel all kinds of inferior. Apparently, I was the dowdiest writer they could find in the continental US.

Trace raced over to hug the new arrival while I hung back and waved, hoping to excuse myself from the obligatory interaction.

"I'm Sofia." She grabbed my shoulders before giving me two air kisses on either cheek.

"Calla," I said.

"This place is adorable." Sofia waved her arms and walked around the room as if already starring in her own personal fashion show.

"Where are you from?" Trace asked.

"I'm in Miami right now."

"Oh, it's beautiful there!" Trace exclaimed.

"It is," Sofia said, turning her face and pursing her lips, almost as if to give the hidden cameras her best angles. She didn't bother asking us any questions. Trace snuck a smile at me and winked.

"So, what do all y'all do for work?" Trace asked.

"I'm a full-time model," Sofia said with a bored tone.

"Wow," Trace gushed. "That's awesome. I'm just a wait-ress. . . Well, you know, at least until I make it big. What about you, Calla?"

I did not want to admit the reality—that I'd been living off the modest advance for my first novel, but had recently depleted it, plunging myself into a mild financial crisis.

"Um, I'm between things right now," I said.

Trace nudged me. "I get it. All of us hanging in the balance until we become superstars."

"Wait, what?" The word superstar felt like an odd choice to describe a successful author.

My question hung in the air unanswered as another new arrival walked into the lounge.

A girl dressed in a flowing, all-white two-piece set waltzed in, her long black hair in braids that hung almost to her waist.

"Hey everyone," she called out. "I'm Rachel," she greeted us, and in return, we all introduced ourselves.

I was beyond grateful she offered us each an outstretched hand instead of trying to pull us in for hugs.

"You're stunning," Trace said. I couldn't help but notice Sofia eyeing Rachel up and down, sussing out the competition.

Brady stood in the entrance to the hallway. "Ladies, you're doing great. If you could just migrate over to the couch by the fireplace and continue chatting for a few minutes, the host will be in shortly."

"Thanks, Brady!" Trace called.

"Calla, right?" Rachel asked, as we all followed Brady's instructions and made ourselves comfortable by the fire.

I nodded before remembering I needed to speak more. "Right."

"You seem nervous," she observed.

"Do I?"

"You're balling up your fists so tight in your sweater, I'm worried you might rip it," she pointed out.

I immediately released my hands. "I guess I am a little nervous. And right now, I'm wishing I hadn't worn this stupid sweater."

Rachel shrugged. "I was thinking how jealous I was of your outfit. You look comfortable."

I stifled a groan. "You are not jealous. I look like I'm headed to the grocery store. Meanwhile, you literally look flawless." I gestured at her.

"Thanks." She tugged at the white fabric. "I wasn't sure what to wear. They gave us no indication of what the first day would entail."

"I know. I tried to get something out of Brady, but he gave me nothing," I said as we all leaned forward in our seats. "They tried to get me to change into a dress. Like, for what?"

"Same!" Rachel exclaimed. "I didn't want to, just in case

there was some kind of surprise competition. I need to move." She gave Sofia's skintight dress a once-over.

Sofia giggled. "Move? All I cared about was looking as hot as possible."

Rachel shot me a look with raised eyebrows, and I tilted my head. What kind of writing competition would involve that much movement? I looked over at Trace, who now also appeared perplexed.

"What's all y'all's favorite genre?" she asked after a moment of silence.

"Probably romance or fantasy?" I responded quickly.

She gave me a funny look. "I meant music, silly."

"Oh." It was a strange question, but I suppose it was nice to get to know these women. We'd be spending the next few weeks together, after all. "I guess I listen to mostly folk, indie-type music."

"R&B for sure," Rachel said.

"Pop," Sofia said. "I'll listen to anything that's Top Forty."

"How fun. We're all different." Trace clapped her hands in excitement. "I only sing country."

"Wow, you sing?" I turned toward her. "I'm totally tone-deaf. I'd love to hear you sometime."

Trace's mouth dropped open and she whipped her head around, looking at us all. "What do you mean you're tone-deaf?"

"Same here," Rachel agreed. "Can't carry a tune to save my life."

"I'm not that bad. I can act a little, too," Sofia said.

Trace looked between us all "Are you. . . are you not all here to sing? I'm so confused."

"Sing?" Rachel balked. "I'm a dancer."

I snorted. "I can't do either." Puzzle pieces flew through my mind, but I couldn't connect them. "Uh, I'm a writer."

"Then why are you on a singing competition?" Trace asked, bewildered.

"I'm not," I said, panic rising in my chest. *What the hell was going on?* "I'm here for a writing competition."

Rachel snorted. "I don't know what you're all talking about, but I'm here to dance."

We all looked at each other, wild-eyed, before turning to Sofia.

She gave a dismissive flick of her wrist. "What? I'm just here to get famous."

Ice ran down my spine. Something was seriously wrong.

Keep Reading! *The Reality of It All* is out now.

Also by Allison Speka

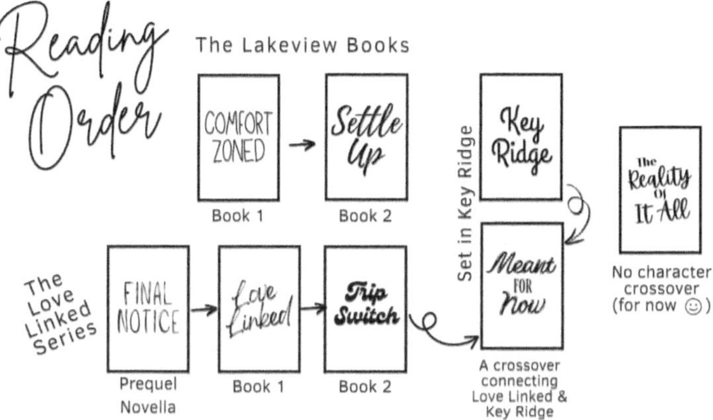

Comfort Zoned - A romance about finding yourself and stepping out of your comfort zone.

Settle Up - An aspiring rockstar romance.

Key Ridge - A haters-to-lovers, small-town, snowboarding romance.

Final Notice - An assistant harboring feelings for her playboy boss.

Love Linked - A forbidden workplace, millionaire boss romance.

Trip Switch - A hopeless romantic, a grumpy tattoo artist, and a dream vacation gone wrong.

Meant for Now - A reverse grumpy sunshine, small town, "just a fling" romance.

The Reality of It All - A reality dating show with a twist…every contestant has been tricked into being there.

About the Author

Allison Speka aims to bring a refreshing blend of passion and authenticity to her writing. A self-proclaimed romance aficionado, Allison has been lost in the pages of love stories since she discovered the genre. She met her partner in Chicago before they both picked up and moved to Colorado six years ago.

Follow her journey!
    TikTok: @AllisonSpeka
    Instagram: @AllisonSpeka

Thank you for reading